PRAISE FOR *Refuge*

"[Nayeri's] exploration of the exile's predicament is tender and urgent."

—*The New Yorker*

"Rich and colorful, bolts of words prettily unfurling . . . [*Refuge*] has the kind of immediacy commonly associated with memoir, which lends it heft, intimacy, atmosphere."

—*The New York Times*

"The novel embraces a number of settings with humor and authority, capturing time and place through the lens of believably awkward and tender family interactions. . . . Heartrending."

—*The New York Times Book Review*

"Crystalline, vivid, moving, and without pretensions, Nayeri's writing is fluid and spare. . . . *Refuge* is a timely novel, about a theme that touches and moves so many, no matter where you are from."

—*Los Angeles Review of Books*

"The strains and indignities that come with remaking a life give Niloo's story poignancy and relevance."

—*The New York Times* (Editor's Choice)

"[An] urgent, resonating contemporary story, highlighting today's scattered, displaced, lost, all-forced-to-be refugees in search of the titular refuge . . . Nayeri carefully illuminates the plight of the ever-searching, never-belonging global wanderer."

—*The Christian Science Monitor*

"There is so much beauty and pain expressed in her prose. . . . It's stunning."

—BuzzFeed

"The immigrant experience is at the heart of Dina Nayeri's powerful novel of a family split by circumstances."

—Minneapolis *Star Tribune*

"A lush, brimming novel of exile."

—*Newsday*

"Topical and urgent."

—*W* magazine

"A nuanced look at what it means to seek refuge; novels don't get more timely than this."

—*The Millions*

"A searing and moving meditation on the migrant experience . . . Nayeri charts the desperate journeys and the hopes and fates of other refugees of different nationalities seeking sanctuary in Europe. A timely read and a compelling one."

—Malcolm Forbes, *The National*

"A beautiful and poignant portrait of the many different experiences of the displaced. A timely and necessary work . . . A vital read for anyone trying to understand what it means to lose and look for home."

—*Bustle*

"Niloo's story, and her complex relationship with her father, expose a narrative of immigration that is necessary and nuanced."

—Read It Forward

"A poignant reflection on the plight of refugees . . . Nayeri uses gentle humor and evocative prose to illuminate the power of familial bonds and to bestow individuality on those anonymous people caught between love of country and need for refuge. A beautiful addition to the burgeoning literature of exile." —*Library Journal* (starred review)

"Richly imagined and frequently moving . . . [Manages] various threads—the personal, the political, the cultural, the generational—deftly, and the result is poignant, wise, and often funny . . . A vital, timely novel about what it means to seek refuge."

—*Kirkus Reviews*

"Set against landscapes of political unrest, Nayeri's novel of a daughter and father seeking to reconcile their long-distance perceptions of family offers a captivating, multilayered exploration of lives caught between worlds." —*Booklist*

"A heart-splicing portrayal of the current refugee crisis . . . These are people who, seeking asylum, arrive in countries that aren't their own but must be made inhabitable, if not home." —*The Riveter*

"A nuanced and remarkably textured narrative about a world few of us experience."

—*BookPage*

"Nayeri's prose sings while moving nimbly with equal parts seriousness and humor."

—*Publishers Weekly*

"Beautifully elegiac, *Refuge* brings into focus the entire experience of emigration. . . . Nayeri is brilliant on parental imperfections and the negotiations children make with their families, and she offers a remarkably textured portrayal of drug addiction and of everyday Iran that defies news-media stereotypes."

—Matthew Thomas, *New York Times*–bestselling author of *We Are Not Ourselves*

"Dina Nayeri's prose has something all too rare in books these days: a wild, beating heart. Read this book to feel your own heart expand."

—Boris Fishman, author of *A Replacement Life*

"For anyone who has wondered about the distance between contemporary American and Iranian lives and thought, this book is essential reading. If any book can close that distance, this one can." —Charles Baxter, author of *The Feast of Love*

"Deeply felt . . . I was completely taken up by this book—invigorated by the intelligence, and inspired by the sensual descriptions of Iranian food and Amsterdam life. I'll keep this one in my bookshelf of favorites."

—Alice Elliott Dark, author of *Naked to the Waist*,
Think of England, and *In the Gloaming*

REFUGE

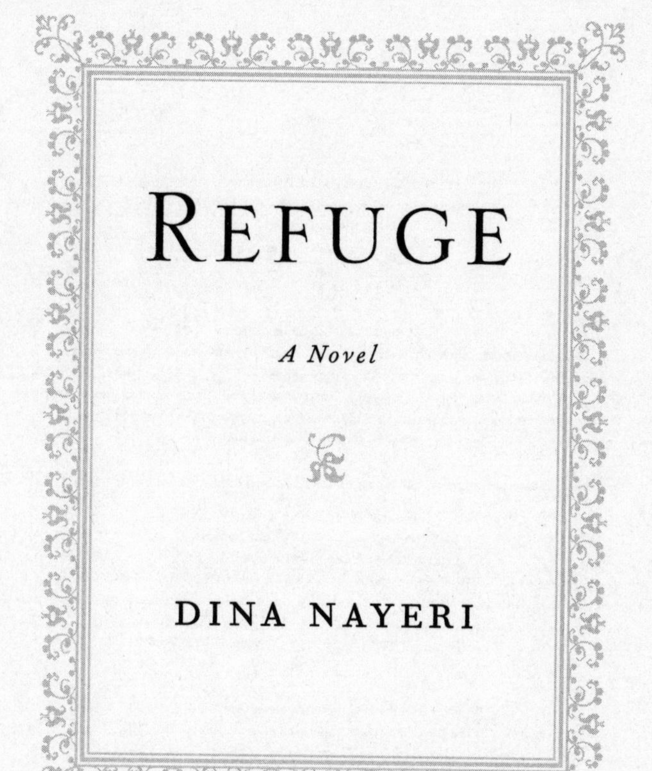

REFUGE

A Novel

DINA NAYERI

RIVERHEAD BOOKS
New York

RIVERHEAD BOOKS
An imprint of Penguin Random House LLC
375 Hudson Street
New York, New York 10014

The Library of Congress has catalogued the Riverhead hardcover edition as follows:

Names: Nayeri, Dina, author.
Title: Refuge : a novel / by Dina Nayeri.
Description: New York : Riverhead Books, 2017.
Identifiers: LCCN 2016039407 | ISBN 9781594487057 | ISBN 9780399576409 (ebook)
Subjects: LCSH: Fathers and daughters—Fiction. | Culture conflict—Fiction. | Domestic fiction.
Classification: LCC PS3622.I457 R44 2017 | DDC 813/.6—dc23
LC record available at https://lccn.loc.gov/2016039407
p. cm.

First Riverhead hardcover edition: July 2017
First Riverhead trade paperback edition: July 2018
Riverhead trade paperback ISBN: 9780399573255

Printed in the United States of America
1 3 5 7 9 10 8 6 4 2

Book design by Gretchen Achilles

For Sam and Elena, who appeared one day

and brought all the joy. And for my insatiable Persian family,

a scattered village of poets and pleasure-seekers.

I am always going home, always to my father's house.

—NOVALIS

The way appears.

—JALAL AD-DIN RUMI

No way, you will not make the Netherlands home.

—GEERT WILDERS, message to refugees, 2015

Refuge

Dr. Hamidi's Difficult Divorce

JUNE 2009

Isfahan, Iran

In order to finalize his own ugly business, as if the universe were demanding one last slice of flesh, Bahman was compelled to watch thirteen consecutive divorces, a full docket. By the sixth one, he stared baffled at his young lawyer—who was also slowly succumbing to the malaise of it, uneasy shoulders sinking, loose lips draped over half his cigarette—and mouthed, "This is absurd."

"Forgive me, Agha Doctor, what do you mean?" The attorney raised both eyebrows as if Bahman should have expected this farce, as if an ordinary man should be accustomed to watching pale husbands slump and flinch, pretty wives crumble thirteen times just to complete his own errand. There is always an instant, isn't there, when youth fails? And who wants to see it?

They sat in plastic chairs just outside the cleric's office, watching through the crack in the door, which had been left ajar, it seemed, expressly for that purpose. His young lawyer kept wiping his hands on his cheap gray trousers and sipping hot tea. Sometimes the boy would get up to refill the two fingers of liquid in his tulip glass from the rusted samovar atop a long table in the corner where two secretaries in black chadors were engaged in some joyless business. Why had he hired the fidgety lawyer? After all, despite Bahman's secular education and volumes of subversive poetry, his children's indulgent American degrees and his fugitive first wife, he was still the male in an Iranian divorce: a secure position. Things would go easily for him here. Though, yes, he was planning to tell some lies, and, more important, when is a third divorce ever easy?

Yesterday, drinking at home from his own samovar, Bahman had reflected on today's errand with anticipation. It had been coming for a long time. He considered how the next chapter of his life might read. Perhaps he would buy a new couch and lose weight. Maybe get a new crown on his molar and take a plane trip somewhere warm, somewhere without visa hassles: Cyprus, or Dubai, or Istanbul. He might even arrange to see his children.

On that last morning before his court date, Sanaz didn't yell or throw anything. Instead, he heard her weeping in the guest bedroom and knocked on the half-open door. He stood there, shuffling in the doorway in his royal blue pajamas. And when she looked at him with wrecked eyes, covered in all that garish makeup, her chipped toenails three shades of red and filed far too straight, he worked up the courage to say, "Why are you sad, *azizam*?" Then, gathering himself, he whispered, "Don't you know how young you are? Same age and already Niloo—"

"*Aaakh*, dirt on my head . . . always Niloo, Niloo!" She spat mucus and tears. "You are a weak man without reputation or rank or anything and your bastard daughter is nothing to me." He wanted to point out that Niloo was the furthest thing from a bastard. Of his three wives, the first had been the most educated and charming. Pari was the love of his youth, and her talents had passed on to their children. He had a photo of him and Pari at a picnic in Ardestoon, her head on his shoulder, his hand on her cheek as if it was any ordinary privilege. Do young men realize what they take for granted? In the photo he seems oblivious to the cheek he is touching. Was Pari loved enough before she ran away to America?

He was ashamed of having blurted Niloo's name so gracelessly, in such a discussion. It was an ungainly moment and he fled the scene. He had not spoken of their embarrassing age difference in three years—three years of lost friendships, of angry relatives, of humiliation, isolation, and money hemorrhaging as if from a wet paper bag. Releasing the words like that, alone in a doorway in blue pajamas, felt like the skin of his heart peeling away. For half a day, he loitered in a tea shop near the Thirty-Three Arches waiting for that overexposed, raw flesh feeling to subside.

Between two routine cavity fillings, he walked by the courthouse to prepare himself for the next day. Rows of men with typewriters sat outside, hawking their services for a few hundred *tomans* a page—petitions and eloquent appeals and supplications in impressive legalese. Rows and rows of peddler-poets, would-be scholars, novelists, historians, and songwriters selling fluency to those whose words had run out. Farther out in the fringes, lingering greasily near both the male and female entrances to the courthouse, idling away the hours smoking cigarettes and casting furtive glances at petitioners, were the witnesses for hire, extra pairs of eyes to reclaim those moments lost to inopportune privacy.

Bahman watched a woman rush out of the courthouse, speak to one for ten minutes as she clutched her black coverings to her mouth, and guide him to the men's entrance. *How long have the courts been so willfully blind?* He wandered back to his office.

Today, on entering the courthouse through that same door, he had been inspected for weapons by three *pasdars*. His mobile phone was taken away and his late father's green handkerchief was eyed with great suspicion, since it resembled the wristbands of Green Movement protesters. Luckily, his modest suit and the counting beads worrying away in his fingers (signs of a resigned, aged sort of life . . . *pickled, fallen into place*, as they say in the village) saved him and the guards waved him through, returning to their bags of pistachios and sunflowers, cracking and chewing and spitting as they talked. They were young men, none over thirty. Probably they were sick of frisking the old men who passed through these doors to divorce their sisters or mothers or former lovers. The thought saddened Bahman, and before he went in, he said to the youngest *pasdar*, "Ghotbi will be good, I think." He glanced around as he considered what more he could say about the new Iranian national soccer coach. "World Cup for sure."

The young *pasdar* eyed him strangely for a second. Then he grinned. "For sure, Agha Doctor." He held out his bag of pistachios and patted Bahman on the back, a rude gesture considering Bahman's age, and yet this is what he had wanted, to be young like the boy. Bahman took one and nodded thanks. The boy said, "If life was simple, I'd go to South Africa and watch all the games from the front."

Now, squirming under the harsh light of the courthouse waiting room, he heard a couple explaining their situation to the judge. Though inclined to resist this circus, which felt much like watching twenty strangers on the toilet, he strained to listen. He might as well let go of his private distaste now that he was stuck. From the moment he stepped into this muggy clerical office and breathed its overused air, he'd been caught in a wonderland crafted by Rumi or Hafez or some other cruel wit.

"I grant her divorce," the young man said, "let her have it." This caught Bahman's attention because what Iranian man would agree to a divorce he didn't initiate? It's a matter of pride. If the wife requests it, only madness and impotence are legal reasons. If this is a case of mutual abandonment, the man should request it for both of them, since he needs to show no cause and it's a smaller headache for everyone. Is this boy admitting to insanity? Impotence? Maybe he wants to rub yogurt on the marriage gift, to negotiate away the sum to which every divorced woman is entitled. Maybe his family made a lazy deal for him—sometimes young men in love agree to hefty marriage gifts at the time of the *aghd*, thinking they will never divorce, or that if they do, they will be too heartbroken to care.

"Why are you seeking divorce so soon?" the judge asked the young woman. "So little time living together," he said, and flipped some pages. Bahman sat forward in his chair, staring openly into the room, because at least the universe was offering him the pleasure of a decent story—in divorce court, everyone lies.

The young wife looked more weathered than her husband, her grief-pale skin shiny in spots while he seemed to have spent time outdoors. A voice behind the door, a mother or sister perhaps, was weeping. Maybe the girl couldn't have children. Maybe he was a philanderer. Maybe *she* was a philanderer—women did that too, of course, and why not? A life of pleasure is at least lived. Maybe he had lost all their money gambling, or couldn't perform in the bedroom. Or she had promised to care for an ailing parent who had sucked the life out of her. The judge continued his inspection of the pair—how could so young a couple have bungled it so quickly?

The wife, hardly more than a teenager, tucked in the edges of her headscarf, her expression full of guilt and failure. She was younger than his daughter Niloo, and Bahman wished he could speak to this girl, to say, *I don't know you, but listen: you couldn't have done anything to fix things*. She rubbed the side of her neck again and again, the same gesture that comforted Pari, his first wife, when she was nervous or angry or confused. Bahman watched the girl, and soon everything faded but the rhythm of her fingers. In their worst moments, Pari had clutched her own throat with both hands, rubbing and clawing as if to remove an iron collar.

"A strange punishment, having to watch this," Bahman muttered, meaning to compare the situation to the forced mass witness, in certain backward countries, of executions and beatings. And yet, wasn't he living in one of those same countries, the ones involved in every human ugliness and ruin? Didn't rural mullahs reign free far from the eyes of scholars and doctors? But who could say such things aloud? Much less so in a court of law, in these troubled times. Even here in Isfahan, a big city, scholars and doctors kept their eyes closed. On and on, the world slumbered.

He considered it and thought this notion poetic and true enough to say aloud. "The world slumbers, my friend." He glanced at his lawyer.

The boy stared. "You will get the best service," he said. "The best. All will be well, Doctor." He scratched at a strange bald patch on his chin. Bahman wiped the tea out of his own thick but tidy mustache. Each morning he trimmed it straight with a ruler held above his lips.

That morning, in the sterile gray brick hotel that had housed him for a single night, uninviting down to its last metal beam, he woke with a distended stomach. He had long given up meat, grains, sugar, and dairy. He ate stingily, slept militantly, and consumed enough water to run a small mill. And yet, somehow, every third morning, he woke with a stomach that looked three months' pregnant. No pain, no nausea. Just a tight drum that said, *Hello, old friend. Let's take a holiday. Remember all the work we did, back when we played soccer all afternoon and ate sultan-kabobs and made love for two hours without the smallest complaint? No more of that; it's twilight.*

Now he was afraid of falling asleep before his young wife for fear of his unruly stomach. It seemed strange for fifty-five. Despite a lifetime of study, poetry, food, and invigorating old-world living, Bahman was losing. His father's muddled village genes began to prevail, afflicting him with wild, unpredictable physical changes. The hair follicles in the back of his head were the latest to succumb, abandoning their places to a swirl of unseemly baldness.

Bahman shifted in the hard curve of the plastic chair (*like sitting in a salad bowl*, he thought) and leaned in to peer past the judge's door. His beads dangled on his knee as he counted to thirty-three, then started at one again. The air carried the smell of cheap cleaning solutions and of unwashed men. The naked bulbs overhead shone too brightly, making the squeaky linoleum floor seem institutional and depressing. Everywhere ran the hurried black streaks of people's shoes. The young wife facing the judge rushed to speak. "Too soon or not, we've agreed. By mutual consent." How many people were crammed in the cleric's office?

"No, not mutual," said her husband. "That is not what I said. I never left. I stayed and worked my fingers raw and I suffered every degradation to please her. Now that she requests it, I grant the divorce. It's a different thing, *agha*."

It is indeed different to have your hand forced. Bahman didn't want to end things, of course, but what do you do when the woman is no longer the same? Sanaz, the girl who had brought him back to life, had turned thirty, dyed her hair a garish medley of blonde and black, and, for all practical purposes, lost her mind. He would have been fine if she had grown demanding and firm, running the household with unkind hands as some women do, or if she had shown signs of aging so that, when they both smiled, their worn cheeks and lined eyes might begin to match. He would have welcomed odd hobbies or a desire to go to underground parties. He would have loved it if she grew fat and happy. And to be perfectly honest, he would have looked the other way if suddenly, as happens often in marriages like his, a male "cousin" her own age started coming around sometimes, taking her to family functions. But instead of lovers, she had taken to rants and rages, her silences sometimes lasting days, then broken by screaming fits in which she threw his toothbrushes into the *aftabeh*, the washbasin beside the toilet, or ripped the pages out of all his poetry books or called him vile names, accusing him of impotence and stinginess and cruelty.

A few weeks ago, she hurled threats of divorce, and though he had never considered it himself, it seemed a very sensible thing. That night in bed, he turned it over in his mind and it calmed his stomach so that it unclenched for an hour or two.

The Sanaz he knew was gone, and there was nothing to be done about it. He wouldn't try to change her. She had promised to vacate the house without trouble if he stayed one night in a hotel so that her sister and brother-in-law, an Agha Soleimani, could collect her personal things. She was showing kindness, and he imagined that she preferred not to wreck their memories, all his aging photos of Nain, Tehran, and Ardestoon with his son and daughter, children from another lifetime, when they were young and relied on him for every small joy. And the photos of the four visits with them since; of course, she wouldn't touch those, or the sketches or the poems. And, when this was over, he would still have the throws and *ghilim* rugs that his mother had woven. Life would remain intact. Blessings abounded.

Sometimes he examined his old furniture, pieces he had bought in the eighties or nineties, chipped armoires, fading rugs, and couches that smelled of decades of cigarettes, and he thought: *Everything in life feels like this couch.* The past was like a crisp, airy sitting room awash in warm hues, and the present is that same room shut up for twenty years in its own dust and decay then thrust into harsh daylight. Niloo and Kian, his first set of children, the children of his youth, flung at a tender age to America and Europe, were forever encased in soft candlelight.

"But do you *want* to divorce?" asked the judge, and through the crack in the door, Bahman saw him draw two blue file folders close to his face, never looking up.

"I don't want a divorce; I want that in the record. I am amenable, that's all."

"*Ei vai*, mister, it comes to the same thing," the judge sighed, and mumbled something to his secretary, a severe woman of about sixty who was leaning over the judge's desk and may or may not have been shaking her head. Bahman couldn't see her figure; her heavy chador obscured every subtle movement. Her neck was gone, its turns and tensions lost. The cleric turned back to the husband. "Do you want to keep the marriage gift? Is that your issue? You still owe what was promised."

How young they were, this troubled couple . . . but, yes, the boy ought to pay. Bahman was prepared to pay, as any man should. He had made mistakes, been selfish and hedonistic and afraid, and now, slowly waking up to these things, dreaming of newness and rigor, of study and frugality and discipline (a small taste of Niloo's ways), he felt that paying Sanaz was a necessary and just step.

"No, Your Honor," said the boy. "I only want the official court record to show the truth that I'm only going along. To hell with the money. I'll pay it when it comes to me, Allah willing."

Oh, but Bahman too had said "when it comes to me" to poor Pari . . . and he had never come through in any meaningful way. *How is Pari?* he wondered.

The court secretary muttered at the young husband's cursing. "*Khanom,*" the judge said, turning to the young wife. "Your husband seems to be suffering here . . . look, he's barely making sense. Why don't you go with him? See if you can't live with him for a few months. Maybe he can make you happy if you try."

At that, Bahman chuckled into his fist. He wished he could call his daughter to share the joke. Since she had left Iran as a child, he had seen Niloo four times, in four short visits throughout her adolescence and adulthood. Somewhere in there, in the years between Niloo the eight-year-old Isfahani girl and Niloo the thirty-year-old American or European or whatever she now was, they had come close to sharing two or three jokes about love and sex. Though it was uncomfortable to interact with her as a foreign adult, she had his sense of humor. She would laugh at this, he was certain. Niloo had studied at Yale, a name he didn't know until she said it one day when she was eighteen, swearing that it was as good as that *other* one, the one Iranians recognize for mass-producing famous doctors and senators and things. Bahman believed her, even before he looked up "Yale" on the Internet in the grimy offices of his friend the agricultural supply salesman. After that he made sure to say around town, "I sent one daughter to Yale. I'll send the other."

During the American election, he had called Niloo in the middle of the night. "Niloo *joon*," he said, "I've had a prophetic dream about the man you should choose for your president. It's a riddle: Obama is better pronounced *oo-ba-ma*. And in Farsi this means *he is with us*. John McCain is pronounced *joon-mikkane*, which, as you know, means *he works hard*. But who cares if someone works hard if he is not with you? This is what I'm thinking." He knew he sounded stoned. She probably smelled the hashish and opium through the telephone, or sensed it by whatever magic instinct was granted to families of hedonists. She gave a small laugh and said that, yes, she would vote for the one who is *with us*. "We're having an election soon too," he said weakly. "Mousavi. That's our man here." She said, yes, she knew that too.

On hanging up, he had been embarrassed. His daughter thought him a clown, not a wordsmith or a poet, but an aging addict.

Niloo had married a weighty European man—not weighty in physique, as the man was very tall and thin; but weighty, as they say, in all other matters. From what Bahman could tell, Niloo had grown into a serious woman. Ever since her mother took her out of Iran, she worked or studied constantly, never taking time to feast or to delight or to lose herself, though she had been a happy child with a wild, musical laugh, a dangerous sweet tooth, dancing feet, and lots of clever schemes. Now she toiled and toiled, trying to prove something. Maybe his weighty son-in-law with the unpronounceable name needed an unsmiling wife for his friends, a wife who could quote Shakespeare and Molière alongside the great Rumi.

He had met the boy once in Istanbul, years after the wedding, which had been a secret affair with no photos. He hoped the boy made Niloo happy. The idea calmed his heart since he had spent decades shrinking under the darkest worries: *What if I sent my children to America only to see them suffer?* But the boy loved Niloo from the depths of his belly, a love that bent and broke him as Bahman too was bent and broken. A love he had thought Sanaz felt for him. But you can't make someone love you, as they say, and shouldn't try, unless you're twenty and have a muscular heart, a heart itching to be broken in. Sometimes, in calmer years, failing isn't such a curse.

The young wife was shouting now, her voice shaking, fists balled like six-year-old Niloo caught up in the first pangs of conviction, ready to battle away the hours and the days. "No, that is not possible," she said to the cleric. She grabbed her husband's arm, whispering, urging him to remember their private talks. "We agreed. He can call it what he wants. It's all decided. We've sat up all night with uncles and both fathers and everyone. We're here and we've agreed."

"Yes, *khanom*," said the judge. "But nothing is agreed until the court too has agreed. The man here doesn't seem to want it. What's the trouble in the marriage?"

The girl hesitated, battling with herself. Clearly, there was something shameful she didn't want to make public. "He's never there," she shouted, her hands flailing over the judge's papers as she pushed against his desk to steady herself. "He's an addict. We don't get along. We can't have children. What does the reason matter? We've agreed. And he has agreed to pay."

"I'm not an addict," shot the husband. "What are you talking about? No, Your Honor, I don't drink anything. I don't smoke anything. I eat nothing but bread and cheese and dry herbs. She has taken everything from me, so she can have this too. But I want the court to have the correct story because I will not leave this world with lies on my lips. I swear to Hassan and Hossein and every imam—"

The wretched husband was raising his voice, losing control of himself. "Yes, yes, calm down," said the judge. "Who's talking about leaving this world, *agha*?"

"I'm done with this life, and I swear, I just want to leave my house in order."

At this, a fury of voices broke out inside the chambers. It seemed at least three relatives were standing behind the door, obscured till now. The girl moaned and flung herself into an older woman's arms. "He will kill me with this drama."

Bahman turned to his attorney and said, "Could you not have gotten the time correct at least?" This spectacle was making him nervous for his own turn, the tales he too was preparing to weave. "Can we pay someone?"

"*Agha*, it's not an exact thing," said the attorney, massaging his knees. "Do you do your root canals at the very hour you say? And, anyhow, there's tea just there."

"That boy is an addict," said Bahman. "Ranting about killing himself. Making foolish requests about who petitioned whom for what." Statistically almost every other working-class twentysomething man in Iran was an addict—and just listening to his accent, it was clear he had never stepped into university.

"What boy?" said the attorney, downing the cold remnants in his cup.

"My friend, wake up," said Bahman, tapping the lawyer's chin with his counting beads as you would a child. "Listen to what is going on there!"

"I'll get us some chai," said the attorney, and got up to refill his own cup and to fetch one for Bahman. He let out exhausted grumbles as he hauled himself up.

By the time the relatives in the chambers calmed the man and his wife, the judge seemed to have lost his patience. He ordered that they live together for a month and not come back a day before the end of the sentence. "I can't! Please, *agha*," the woman begged the judge, her hands trembling on his desk so he could see. "You don't know how it is. Please, for the love of the prophet."

The judge shook his head. "You don't have to share his bedroom. Go on now."

But the woman wouldn't leave. Before the words had traveled past the judge's gray lips, she had thrown herself onto his desk, causing such commotion that the judge sprang up and the court secretary rushed to remove her. Her mother (or aunt or whoever) took her by the waist and was trying to calm her when the girl looked tearfully up and began to whisper prayers.

Bahman too was on his feet. Without his permission his weary shoes had taken him to the threshold of the chambers and his hand was on the edge of the door. His lawyer called him back as he peered in. This wretched girl was Niloo's age. Look at the desperation in her eyes—a trapped bird. Had Niloo ever, in her young life, felt caged by circumstance? Had he, with his fatherly hopes for her and her brother, sent them off to a foreign land to struggle and pray to deaf gods? Did she belong to a place, to a people? Was she satisfied down to the soft of her bones?

The judge decided that the young wife would spend two days in jail, so that she might learn to behave herself in a courtroom. Bahman wanted to burst in, for once in his life to thunder at the senselessness of the world. This judge was his age, his peer. *Have some patience, brother*, he wanted to say; *she's a weak thing and she's at your mercy*. But something about those words seemed presumptuous and offensive to the girl, and who wants to draw such attention to themselves? He would send the family some money, if he could find their name. Maybe this unhappy wife could run away in the night. Maybe she had a lover she hoped to marry, the reason for her desperation. *Of course*. Bahman hoped the girl had a lover who would protect her—why else would one fling one's body onto the desk of some old mullah?

He returned to his seat, smiling at the thought. He patted his lawyer's hand, accepted the cup of tea and sugar cube that were offered, and said, "Please get me that young woman's name and address," and when the boy opened his mouth, Bahman clutched his beads and said, "No, friend. Enough objections from you."

Me and Baba and Ardestoon

I've seen my father four times in the last twenty-two years. I left him and Isfahan in 1987, under a scratchy blanket in the back of a brown Jeep when I was eight and Baba was thirty-three. Now I'm thirty. At the start of each brief visit, in Oklahoma or London or Madrid or Istanbul, the man who greets me is different from the last, and so much older. It's an icy palm to the breast, a jolt of the universe that I knew to expect after the second and third times. He will have changed, I remind myself as I scan airport terminals and approach restaurant tables with a lone man waiting. But the trips are short, and later I always change him back, overriding the signs of aging, the cane, the white hair, the extra skin that hides the flash of mischief in his eyes. My Baba will always be thirty-three—a hard thirty-three, like Jesus or the number of green prayer beads that he counts with both hands despite his devotion to hedonism and his own personal divinity.

Sometimes, when drunk, Baba says things like, "I am God! What is God besides science and poetry?" Then he recites twenty minutes of perfect Hafez.

When I was three, I'd fling my arms up and shout, "I'm God too!" and he'd lift me up to the sky, my baby-fine russet hair falling on his face, indistinguishable from his own. Every evening, I waited for him on our front stoop and when I spotted him walking down the road I ran over and said hello to his hidden pastries first. "Hello, *zoolbia*! Hello, *baghlava*!" I said to his bulging jacket. "*Sour cherries? Ice cream?* Are you in there?" He pretended to be offended. "What about your Baba?" he'd say.

Baba used to ask me to walk on his back. My toes digging into his flesh, I felt his muscles shift and loosen, like tectonic plates. He was the ground. Now those plates have drifted far away and the ground has vanished. I can't shake this image of him. Baba, ageless at thirty-three, forever reveling and devoted to himself, my toy spatula dripping chocolate ice cream on his soft, massive back as he hummed. Baba and I used to read *The Little Prince* together and eat sour plums. I had two editions of that book because Maman wanted me to learn English, but Baba and I read from the Farsi one—he would never ruin a good story with lessons, or taint any pleasure with added practicality. Sometimes, when the Islamic Republic didn't intercept cartoon hour (a single hour of children's programming for the entire week), we watched the animated version. Every Tuesday we watched the girl in the rose bloom while he salted cucumbers for me and checked my teeth. Strangely, for a dentist, his pockets were always full of candy. On our last visit, a year ago in Istanbul, I noticed two of his back teeth missing and I cried for most of the afternoon.

As a kid, I got the majority of Baba's attention, even though my younger brother, Kian, was a clone of him: chubby with a huge personality and scornful charm that made people crave his affection. Gradually, he grew into a brooding, solemn child, which made him even cuter. At two he started memorizing the songs of the Iranian Revolution. "A caged bird," he crooned, all doleful and lispy and chunky-fisted, "is heartsick of walls."

"Shit, Pari *joon*," Baba said to Maman, "are you making him a revolutionary?"

"I sing him songs about geese and rabbits." She was twenty-eight and vigilant.

"Then how did he learn this garbage?"

"I don't know . . . how did Niloo learn all those dirty songs?" she said, knowing very well that I learned them on trips to Baba's village. "Let's worry about the one growing up with zero impulse control, not the one with a heart for the people." I'm sure Baba scoffed in defense of me then, or maybe just in protest of impulse control.

It seemed that Kian had learned to turn on the radio by himself and had developed strong feelings for the droning, melodic propaganda music sanctioned by the mullahs. Baba just shook his head and looked the other way. A few months later, Kian got the mumps on top of all his fat and officially became the most desirable child on the block, since in Iran juvenile attractiveness is measured by sheer volume of flesh. So, he got his attention from other places, and was fine without Baba's.

Like many young men in Iran, Baba went from the highs and stupors of being in love to the highs and stupors of opium. He became an addict and would sneak away at night. Sometimes he lost his temper in awful ways. These instances were rare and, I later learned, correlated with opium rages from which I was mostly shielded—but I saw things, a blurry Maman out by the swimming pool, the whip of a garden hose, a shriek. Afterward, he would try to atone by picking baskets of fruit for her from faraway gardens, or buying her beautiful clothes, or writing poetry that he hid around the house. He raised angry hands at his brothers too. Not often, though. It's hard to imagine it, those same fleshy, nimble hands that could make the worst toothache go away with a flick of the wrist and a press of the gauze; those same brothers he employed as technicians in his dental office just because they needed employing, though neither had any training beyond farming.

Baba, a giant with his thick red mustache and full laugh, green counting beads in one hand, his other hand full of pistachios or sour cherries, was a fixture you could see coming from far down the street. He was always chomping on something. He smoked and drank and ate sumptuously and memorized entire books of old poetry. His body was huge, and covered in red hair from head to toe.

Every Friday he piled his family into the car and we were dragged to Ardestoon village as if by hidden magnets in Baba's shoes. As we approached the village, everyone's accents slowly changed. Chubby Kian kept on chanting revolution songs and love songs and songs of martyrdom and death ("The air of the cage is the death of the soul!"). Our voices lost their city refinement and we began to talk with lilts and drawls and idioms, tongues smacking, voices rising.

Ardestoon, my father's childhood home, is an ancient village of unpaved roads dotted with crushed mulberries, handcrafted outdoor rugs swept with brooms, rows of pickle jars the size of children lining every house. It has two rivers, two gardens, an orchard connected to a natural pool with ducks, a mosque, a medium-sized mountain, and a famous two-story aqueduct, an eight-hundred-year-old structure that the people of the village don't even realize they should be proud of, because they are too busy living uncomplicated lives that Baba calls "overflowing and poetic." "Life in Ardestoon," he says, "is a shank of lamb so bursting with marrow, you can suck until your cheeks are full and there's still more to pry with a pinky or to shake out fist over fist. Niloo *joon*, never be the one who looks around worrying if her face is greasy."

When I was two, my front teeth broke in an accident and Baba performed the surgery himself. His brothers chased me around the dental chair, Uncle Hossein forcing me into it. Behind his back, Baba held a giant needle that haunted my nightmares for months. After that, the only way I'd let Baba touch me was if I was lost in the games or the books we shared. And each time, after a few minutes, I would remember to guard myself again. I trembled when Baba tried to stroke my cheek or kiss my face or hold my hand. I thought, *If I stick my hand inside his big, muscular one, he will have me trapped. I won't be strong enough to pull away. And then what if he takes more of my teeth? Or my fingers or toes?*

And yet, I was becoming like him. It was Maman's greatest fear for me. Sometimes she says, in stunned whispers, "Those are your Baba's excuses. Oh, Niloo, that's your Baba's frenzy. Watch yourself, you have that blood."

Uncle Ali, Baba's youngest brother, was thirteen when I was born and used to watch over me when my parents disappeared on trips, Maman to do volunteer medical work in poor communities, Baba to smoke huge quantities of opium with his friends, read poetry, and find bliss and torment together.

Uncle Ali and I had a good time, though. One day, he told me how to entice my playschool love, Ali Mansoori, who was a year older and therefore untouchable. "Next time, little *khanom*, don't follow him all around the kindergarten tempting him to tell you to go away. Next time, walk past him and flip your pretty hair and say, 'Excuse me, boy. I'm trying to pass.'" Uncle Ali always called me *little miss* or *Miss Niloo*. He put me on the seat of his motorcycle and started doing a very convincing Tehrani street girl impression, sauntering past with hips swaying, eyes batting. I drank up the attention, howling at his antics. "Another thing," he said. "Do you always call this kid by his full name? What's this 'Ali-Mansoori, AliMansoori' business? No, Niloo *khanom*. Better to get his name wrong altogether. Next time call him Javad or Kamal or something, a *dehati* worker name, so he knows he's below you."

"But he's not below me," I said. "He goes to my school." Baba had told me that no one is below anyone else if they have the same education.

"Never say that, though. Treat him like he's a fat fly in your cherry rice. Understood?"

"Understood," I said and grabbed his ears in both fists and kissed him on the nose. The next day, I followed Ali Mansoori around as usual, gave him my lunch, and watched him eat it with a big goofy grin on my face.

You can't fight instinct. You can't teach genuine restraint. I got my instincts from a man whose supply of restraint was as limited and unpredictable as the supply of black market music tapes or the last stash of sour cherries in the freezer.

When, later that afternoon, my teacher called Baba's office and told him that I had not eaten, she was vague on the details, probably afraid that he would chastise her for letting another kid eat my lunch. An hour later, a waiter from the local fancy kabob place that served diplomats and doctors and my father walked into the kindergarten, still wearing his white button-up shirt and his black bow tie, and delivered a full lamb shank dinner for me. He made a show of laying it out on my low desk and pouring the yogurt drink and arranging the bread in a basket as the teacher protested, her deep discomfort showing in the way she held herself around the middle. And yet, she couldn't argue. She was the one who had called the eccentric Dr. Hamidi. "For the little Khanom Hamidi," said the waiter, bowing.

The other kids watched this spectacle, the weird adult feast, while chomping on apple slices and fruit leathers. It seemed there was no predicting or changing Baba's large ways; he was rash, oblivious to other people's reactions. Already, I felt the divide between us and everyone else, even Uncle Ali: Baba and I had bad instincts. We had our secret other world of spatula ice creams, hunting foreign candy, birthday pranks on neighbors, and disappearing in the Ardestoon orchards to pick mulberries and raw almond buds while the others sat around hookahs and wondered where we were. They said, "Niloo and the doctor are off slaying djinns."

The last thing Maman wanted was to leave Iran—Baba's village had saved her. She came from a somber, determined family in Tehran. Her father, a small-town mayor, wore suits and had his head permanently buried in matters that seemed criminal to interrupt. Not like Baba, who was constantly begging for interruption, always a foot tapping, mustache twitching, a furtive hand in a pocket digging for pistachios. At twenty, Maman was happy to leave Tehran and become a part of the warm village full of roving chickens and untamed rabbits and pheasants, where her mother-in-law kissed her every morning, and made delicious stews with cilantro from the garden, and whispered all of Baba's hiding spots.

Soon she grew from the serious daughter of a serious man into someone who could stop and take a breath, a woman who loved planting herbs, mending wounds, and otherwise working with her hands. But in less than a decade, her medical career and Christian faith had made her a target. In the winter and spring of 1987, the moral police began stalking her office. Twice at red lights, they climbed into her car and took her for questioning. All of this she hid from us, thinking it would go away.

For months she lived in fear, until finally, she had no choice but to tell Baba. In the time that followed, I heard a lot of fighting at night, muffled voices raised in fear and anger and sadness. In late spring when I was eight and the orchards were in full bloom, Baba took me aside and said that I should make a list of everything I love best about Ardestoon. We would check them all off one by one.

Elated, I made a list of seventeen things: Hearing my grandfather tell a story by a fire. Doing riddles while we pick mulberries. Playing nighttime hide-and-seek in the garden. Adopting my second baby chicken. Cooking bread in the *tanoor.* Eating sour green plums with salt by the river. Climbing the mountain. Making a cooking hole like the nomads in the desert and actually cooking a pot of real rice. Swimming in the duck pond. Going for a walk with walking sticks, just me and Baba, no Kian. That we then did all those things, as if checking them off a list, didn't strike me as suspicious. My parents didn't tell anyone in the village, not even Baba's mother, that we were leaving. Maman said her goodbyes silently, to herself, and, like Baba, tried to create good final memories. No one but the two of them knew this was goodbye.

Later in the visit, I saw Maman crying in the kitchen. When I approached her, she gave me one of my grandmother's shawls. It smelled like her sweaty henna hair, and sweet mix of fenugreek and spray roses. "Hide this in your bag."

I took the shawl and went. I found Baba drinking tea in the sitting room. I hesitated before crawling onto his lap, but he coaxed a finger into my mouth, prodding it open. "Can I just take one small look?" he said. I jumped up, ready to run away. "Come back. No checking teeth.

I'll tell you a story." I sat on the carpet beside him, crossing my ankles as he had done, leaving an inch between our knees.

"What's happening?" I asked. "Next week are we coming back to Ardestoon?"

He was silent for a while, then, in a rare moment of honesty, said, "You and Kian get to go on a big trip with your mother. And, later, we'll all come back here."

"You're not coming on the trip?" I asked, panicking.

"No," he said. "Someone has to stay and take care of the house." He hesitated. "Later, I'll join you," he said, and that may or may not have been a purposeful lie. At the time, I believed it and it was crucial. He sucked some tea out of his mustache.

"So we'll be on the trip together," I said. It seemed like an exciting idea.

"I'll visit, yes," he said. I must have looked stricken, and I remember the uncertainty in his voice pushing me toward a meltdown. But quickly Baba corrected himself. "I didn't mean visit. Yes, I'll join you. Go play now, *azizam*. Baba is tired."

Before I was at the door, he called me back. "Niloo *joon*, take care of these for me," he said, and gave me two photos he had removed from his waiting room. Baba had dozens of framed photos in mismatched settings covering an entire wall in his office. The images were old and new, natural, black-and-white, sepia, some tattered and fraying or burned at the edges. The biggest photo overlooking the waiting area showed me in a nurse's hat, baby-red hair blazing, a silencing finger to my lips.

"When I was a boy, every time the urge to sprout wings came on, my photos made me happy." He sipped his tea and wiped his face, trying to hide his sadness. "When you're older, you'll grow big beautiful wings. You'll know many sophisticated people, and you'll do things and see things. But every time you see your Baba, I'll bring you a picture and a story from here, so you don't fly off into oblivion."

He straightened the photos in my hand, the Farsi Kodak stamp long faded off the stained yellowish paper. The first was an old black-and-white of a man at the head of a line of men, all in black suits. The man was holding a cane and bowing slightly to a foreigner in a gray tunic and white hat shaped like a capsized boat. The foreigner was extending his hand importantly. Baba pointed out some scribbled marks on the back, written in light pencil. "Three great men have visited Ardestoon in the last hundred years," he said. Baba's stories always begin with lists. *Seven accidents that happened on our honeymoon. Five signs that I was going to fall in love with your mother. Twelve natural disasters that led to the birth of your grandfather.* "This is your great-great-uncle with Nehru, the first prime minister of India, the second great man who visited. It was a very important moment for Ardestoon." One of the gas burners died out and Baba reached for his matches. "This other photo is your great-grandfather Hamidi surrounded by your relations. Keep them for later."

I tapped the photos against my leg to make a neat stack. Baba took the more frayed one from me and filed the edges with his fingernail. He put it back in a way that made me understand these photos were very special.

"Have you brushed your teeth?" he asked, reminding me of my ever-growing list of fears. I ran off before he could try to steal another look inside my mouth.

I never visited his office again. Two nights later, Uncle Ali came for us in a brown Jeep. He parked behind the house, in a walled alley too narrow for driving. He wedged the car in somehow and signaled for us to run out. We squeezed past the high wall of spray roses and honeysuckles, the backs of our shirts stained yellow, and piled in the backseat, hiding our one suitcase with us under a scratchy blanket.

Though it was a detour from the airport, Uncle Ali drove us past Baba's office. I spotted his shadow in the window, and thinking we were just going away for a short vacation, I waved happily at him. He waved too, or rather, just raised a hand to the glass. He must have worried about who would be watching, and in any case, Ali didn't stop the Jeep. He paused only briefly and told us to wave goodbye to our Baba. His voice was different, rougher, not so young, and he didn't look at me or at Maman.

The next time I saw Baba, I was fourteen years old.

The mystic Al-Ghazali said that the inhabitants of heaven remain forever thirty-three. It reminds me of Iran, stuck in 1976 in the imagination of every exile. Iranians often say that when they visit Tehran or Shiraz or Isfahan, they find even the smallest changes confusing and painful—a beloved corner shop gone to dust, the smell of bread that once filled a street, a rose garden neglected. In their memories, they always change it back. Iran is like an aging parent, they say.

My Baba at thirty-three was Iran from a time. And now . . . his decline and Iran's are the same for me. On the rare occasions when he phones, he complains that I never visit: *Come and see your grandmother, Niloo* joon. But I ask him to meet me in other cities in foreign countries, wherever he can get a visa. We have had four visits.

What I don't tell him is that I don't want to see him. My real Baba is a thirty-three-year-old storybook hero: untouchable, unquenchable, a star. When we meet, a weight drags down my shoulders, like the time a shelf broke and a row of books crashed into my arms. My fingers tremble and my mouth fills with sour. All I see are more details erased from my original Baba, replaced with slackening cheeks and rotting teeth. And then I'm a different Niloo, not a sensible academic who toils and believes that she's made herself over into something great, but a kid who just saw her father age twenty years in a second. That other Niloo, the one with the plaque on her door, would never admit these things. She'd never say: I don't want to see Baba because I'm afraid of decaying too.

The Other Dr. Hamidi

AUGUST 2009

Amsterdam, Netherlands

Niloo realizes her mistake the instant the latch clicks shut behind her, the front door pressing against her stiff back as she kicks off her loafers, her toes touching cold hardwood—she should have been home an hour ago. Guillaume is crashing about the kitchen island, piling pots onto the counter. Now and then he runs a hand through his hair, cut shaggy and long like that of many Frenchmen his age. A tube of tomato paste bleeds on a chopping board beside a bunch of crushed garlic bulbs. Her basil plant has been stripped. At the edge of the island, beside an enormous vase stuffed with budding cotton branches, sits Gui's tablet, unobtrusive at first, then alive with instructions blaring out in her mother's accented English.

Maman Pari has helped Guillaume cook via video chat a handful of times over the years—cooking is his one skill that doesn't improve under pressure—and now her hairs, dyed toffee brown, are kissing the lens, her big dramatic eyes filling the screen. "Gay, you are listen?" she says. "Is burn, the sauce. Turn off! Off!"

Gui rushes to the back burner. When he sees Niloo, he stops amid the chaos just to glare. "I'm so sorry," she says, wriggling out of her backpack and wiping the rainwater off it with the hem of her T-shirt. "I can be ready in ten minutes."

Gui's law school mentor, a Dutch professor named Dr. Heldring, is eating with them tonight. He is the person who first suggested Amsterdam to Guillaume, then made the calls and the recommendations that led to his current job.

Remembering their plans, she feels robbed of the evening. She had looked forward to sorting through a mountain of printouts tonight—articles and data and copies of chapters from textbooks. On Mondays, Tuesdays, and Thursdays, Niloo teaches anthropology classes at the University of Amsterdam—a first-year lecture and a seminar in dental anthropology (her favorite course, which she designed, on how archaeologists study buried teeth and jaws). On Fridays, like today, she has a full day for research—Niloo's research interests cluster around all that can be known just from the evolution of our teeth and jaws. She spends Fridays alone in her windowless office, often staying late to organize materials and clean out her inbox.

Maman scolds from beside the vase of cotton buds. "Gay is wait all day for you. Niloofar? Niloofar, get into screen right now." Craning her neck as if she can see farther into their kitchen, Maman mourns the lamb. "We make roast but is burn now—" Niloo says goodbye to her mother and switches off the tablet. She turns to Gui, but he refuses to speak. Instead, he starts dialing Pari on his mobile.

Niloo heads for the bedroom, peeling off her T-shirt, a ragged thing with a flaking Yale logo that she wears with old jeans on research days. If she cuts corners on hair and makeup, she'll be able to scrape together fifteen or twenty minutes of cathartic sorting—enough to wrap up a few things so she doesn't spend the entire dinner suffering that awful incomplete feeling. Before getting in the shower, she sits on the closet floor in her bra and jeans, pulls three folders out of her backpack, and begins to rifle through the papers, making piles to toss, to review, to file away. She wonders if Gui expects her to dress up—she's uncomfortable wasting nice clothes on ordinary days.

Working through her to-do pile on the closet floor, she doesn't notice the thirty minutes pass until Guillaume is standing over her, looking bewildered and furious. "What the fuck, Niloo? Heldring will be here in ten minutes!"

Usually Guillaume indulges her eccentricities—the absentmindedness, the possessiveness, the Perimeter. "Niloo Face, you're kind of mental," he used to tease, years ago. The day they met outside Old Campus, she had scribbled *Niloofar* and her phone number sloppily on half a page of lecture notes, then asked for it back so she could fix it ("It looks like Niloo*face*") and because she realized she needed the notes. If this guy wanted her number so badly, he should use *his* notes.

But now he's livid, his face flushing, and she jumps up, scattering the pages on her lap. "I'll be ready in ten," she says, a stray breath catching in her throat. The doorbell rings. "Where's my green blouse?" She kicks some laundry on the floor.

"The faded one?" says Gui, heading to the door. "Niloo, please make an effort. I'll make him a cocktail, but you be out there in twenty minutes dressed for a nice dinner. I swear, I'd never do this shit to you."

Sometimes when she's distracted, Gui rummages through her

clothes, tossing the old and familiar, worn-out things. She rarely mentions it, because clothes don't matter and, besides, he bought most of them for her. Still, it feels like a violation.

Minutes later, she emerges from the bedroom, her wet hair pinned. Guillaume busies himself with a bowl of olives and cornichons, glancing only once at her sky blue cotton skirt and clean white T-shirt. She greets Dr. Heldring, a smiley, beady-eyed man with white curls. He pats her cheeks, his breath reeking of gin. "How lovely you are, dear Neely."

They uncork the first bottle and fall into comfortable chatter. The roast lamb is charred. Niloo salvages a hefty nugget from the center of it with a sharp knife. They eat it at their wooden table overlooking a small canal, smothering it with Gui's buttery mashed potatoes and drowning it in a heavy Cabernet. "This is just terrific lamb," Dr. Heldring croons to himself. "Wonderful lamb."

"Niloo's mother's recipe," says Gui, barely glancing at her. Neither of them eats very much. When he's upset, Gui says irrelevant things. "Maman Pari is the best," he says, refilling his mentor's glass. "Every time she opens her mouth, some fantastic mangled thing comes out."

This angers Niloo but it's too late to change the subject. "Ah yes, I remember," says the old man. "You came from Tehran as a girl, didn't you?"

"Isfahan," she says, wiping a clump of potato from her shirt with her napkin.

"Niloo has a third passport now," says Gui, a hint of pride in his voice. "I finally added her to my *livret de famille*."

"Congratulations, dear," says Dr. Heldring. "What a worldly woman you are. And where is your father? Back home?"

Briefly she's confused by the word *home*. "Yes, he's in Isfahan. A dentist."

Her father, at every age, laughs like a feral child, the kind you find toddling on Isfahan streets, roaming, no social education. He is all silliness and pleasure-seeking. Though she's inherited his unseemly laugh, Niloo takes care to hide it, in case her colleagues should take her less seriously.

Niloo's choices, since Iran, have always been deliberate. Case study: the day she decided on Gui. In her third year at Yale, she needed a boyfriend, so she began to accept dates. Twelve in fourteen nights. Men liked her, she soon realized, for all the wrong reasons. It seemed that her attempts to appear serious about the project, to be more like them, these American men with goals, were considered cute. "Can I bite your cheek?" one said. Another stuck his pinky in her dimple, a startling gesture. Didn't these boys sense the gravity of the process? They spent months preparing for job interviews and polishing resumes; surely finding the right partner was equally important. She glared when they teased her, pleating her eyebrows tighter.

When, on the third night (tacos with an unwashed film buff), she realized that she was forgetting details, she created a chart of the boys and scored them on a range of essential qualities: looks, manners, intelligence, drive, size of family (does he have dozens of aunts and uncles waiting for him somewhere, wanting to meet his friends and lovers over rowdy family meals?). Gui scored three standard deviations above the mean and so she threw away the list of others and became his girlfriend. They ate dinners together and took turns sleeping in each other's dorm rooms, but they both had research papers to write and post-graduation plans to make. What they found in each other was balance: Gui sat with her for hours while she worked. He gave her long hugs without forcing her to ask. His youth displayed itself in his warmth and indiscriminating kindness and he seemed unaware that he needed her protection. At the same time, his sheltered upbringing in New York and Provence promised respite from her own story, her ripped-up roots. She learned that Gui's parents still lived in the house where his father was born. And they traveled to the same French village every summer.

Now, after years, she has collected many more details to love. The best thing about Gui is the oblivious way he dances. Big grin, two fists in front of his chest, like a happy teenager, head rolling, eyebrows summoning. Or, when the rhythm eludes him, like an old man trying not to lose his balance while slowly grinding an insect or a cigarette butt under each foot. He doesn't care—shame is not a concept he knows. This, to Niloo, the architect of at least a dozen new kinds of shame, is superhuman.

Early in their first attempt at cohabitation, when they had just graduated from Yale and moved to New York, they cooked chicken thighs together. Gui reached for the bottle of green herbs. "Can you please not *Provençal* everything?" she said.

"It's just a bit of tarragon," he said as he brought the bottle to his nose. "That's like saying you *Persian* something just because you add turmeric."

"Exactly," she said, happy that he understood this detail from her history.

"Exactly," he hummed, and kissed her cheek, as if he had won the point. He added more bitter green herbs.

And that's how they understood each other, in conflicting conclusions drawn from thousands of tiny details that they observed together, all those French and Farsi things, Persian and Provençal things, for the next decade. They built their hybrid world in harmonious hues, bunches of dried lavender in antique copper tumblers tastefully balanced beside the blue Isfahani ostrich egg painted with scenes from the *Shahnameh*, a long-ago gift from Bahman. What they share is America, the television characters and the jokes and the lunch meats their mothers put in their lunchboxes (Gui's as a cultural novelty, Niloo's as a financial necessity).

At the mention of Baba, Gui's tone grows soft and resigned, as if confiding a family secret. "Niloo's father has had trouble getting visas. We saw him in Istanbul last year. He's a good man." Dr. Heldring nods in sympathy and this too angers Niloo.

"You know," says Gui, reaching for Niloo's hand across the table. He gives her a playful look, like he's about to have his revenge for earlier. "In college, I had no idea Niloo had gone through this whole fantastic refugee saga; I thought she was just into vintage clothes and really liked the dining hall mini muffins." Niloo laughs. She enjoys it when Gui mocks her outright; it makes her seem strong, unlike the way she feels when he's all sad eyes and folded hands, conjuring images of fathers knocking at border gates for the benefit of some stranger.

As the evening drifts on, they talk of life in Amsterdam, their work, and the apartment in the Pijp that they've recently bought and are now renovating. "It's a wreck," says Gui. "The contractors keep extending the finish date."

"I tried to tell you. Their estimates don't correlate with the plans. I did the math," says Niloo. She's misplaced hours at the office studying the renovation plans, making small edits, imagining the curtains, the tiles, the wood floors. Sometimes she loses an entire day sitting at her computer with red eyes and slumped shoulders.

"Okay, Rain Man." He throws up both hands and turns to Heldring. "My wife is so intense. It's part of her charm." He reclaims Niloo's hand as he speaks.

"Intense women are the best kind," says the professor, enjoying their chaos.

"I'm just trying to prevent waste," she says. She chews her other thumbnail.

"She doesn't like waste," Gui drones. He glances at her watch, a Seiko she wears every day, though he bought her one from Hermès. He drains his glass, his cheeks flushing. Dr. Heldring clears his throat, eager for more. Gui doesn't mind—the old man is like a father to him. "Heldring," he says, "did I ever tell you that the first time Niloo spent the night, she wore polyester pajamas so shiny they lit the whole room lime green? I was barely twenty. I didn't know what women wore to bed, but it was like she landed on earth five minutes before, saw Yale on a T-shirt, and said why the hell not. I thought, I love this girl."

Heldring beams at the couple. "Well, and look at you now." He raises his glass. "Four years married, a decade of adventures, an apartment, and a *livret de famille*."

"Hear! Hear!" Guillaume beams and clinks his professor's glass.

And here is something they have in common: licenses and certificates and official ties; they hold weight. She recalls that on the day she got her French passport, Guillaume watched her place it inside the Perimeter—a space forbidden to him. He pretended to be too busy to notice, his gaze focused elsewhere as he loosened his necktie. But he couldn't veil the pride in his eyes as he watched that little red booklet disappear into a file folder she had marked *Important*.

Gui has never asked her for an explanation. He accepts whatever borders she draws, making sense of them in his own quiet way, without much discussion. He doesn't ask, for example, why she hates his hunting jacket. At Yale, it took Niloo two winters to believe that hunting jackets are attire intended for the rich, not the homeless. She had seen only one other before her classmates began appearing all over New Haven in them during that freshman November. On her first night in America, after two years as refugees, Niloo, age ten, her mother, and her brother, Kian, had slept at Jesus House, a homeless shelter behind a busy bus stop in the concrete belly of Oklahoma City. It had lasted only one night, a logistical oversight by their sponsor family. If you asked her now, she would say it was a week, because how can the senses retain so much from a single night twenty years ago? The thirst for sleep and the shared bed with sheets that crawled and bit. Her mother's warm breath on her neck. Her brother's icy legs wrapped around hers for comfort. Her backpack, the lifetime of treasures she wanted to keep close, blistering her shoulder blades all night long like new wings taking root. The mad-eyed woman watching them from a corner, urine stench wafting from her bed now and then, and the lonely shouts that rose with the sun from the corners of the empty street. Then, early morning hunger pangs and glazed donuts from the neighboring church, the homeless man in the heavy olive jacket that swallowed his skeletal frame, pumping the last of the instant coffee from the dispenser.

It was a single sleep, a hiccup, that came and went between two good lives: the years of idling among mulberry trees in her own village, sitting barefoot with Baba on the cool stone floor of his childhood home, of sated calm, followed by the years of academic rise and financial gain, American prosperity. If one were to write Niloo's story, one shouldn't dwell on that black interlude night. Except that it returns every time she wastes an hour, a dollar, an opportunity. It returns when life offers a break from the striving. The very fact of that night (and the two wandering years that led to it) warns her that she can never be too vigilant.

Years later, after graduation, on their first night living together in New York, Gui discovered and named the Perimeter. They had finished moving their boxes and were giddy with the realness of their shared space, a first for them both. Their boxes were scattered everywhere, some open, leaking contents, others still taped shut. Every room was a jumble of items, clothes and shampoo bottles and colanders and coffee cups and photo albums all strewn together on a bath mat in the living room, kitchen floor carpeted with books and plates, the couch that came with their apartment draped in winter coats.

And, in one corner of their bedroom, apart from the clutter, Niloo had arranged a neat little rectangle of items—two long umbrellas and two walls forming a border around Niloo's backpack; her mother-of-pearl jewelry box; a small folder containing her passport, naturalization papers, and diplomas; and a box of sentimental books, her father's photos, some rocks and trinkets from Iran.

Gui stripped off his shirt and tossed it away. He sighed contentedly and dove onto the mattress on the floor. "We're here, Niloo Face! Come and spoon me."

But Niloo had stiffened, was staring at his discarded shirt. "Can you move your shirt from that corner, please?" she asked.

"Hmm?" he murmured into his pillow. He was drifting off, his words muffled. "Okay, I'll be the outer spoon again. You're such a slave to archaic gender roles."

"No, seriously," she said, eyes trained on the offending shirt. "That's my corner. Move your shirt." She tapped Gui on the shoulder. "Move your shirt, Gui!"

Yes, she could have moved it herself. But they lived together now and she needed Gui to understand: Niloo could adjust to any living condition. She had shared a tiny Oklahoma bedroom with her brother, a verminous homeless shelter bed with her mother, an Ardestooni mountain house with twenty cousins. She could shower or not shower, eat or not eat. She could get as excited about seared scallops on a glistening seaside terrace as a two-dollar pizza slice in a moldy dive. But all that adjusting depended on one thing: in every new place she had a corner, just a corner, that was hers only. She couldn't compromise that corner.

Finally, Niloo jumped up from the mattress, picked up Gui's sweaty shirt, and hurled it back at him. "Not on my stuff," she said.

He woke, startled. "What the fuck," he said, tossing the shirt aside. "What stuff? There's stuff everywhere!" He had a disappointed look. It lasted only a second.

"No," she said, trying to regulate her breathing, "I mean *this* stuff." She lifted the backpack, pointed to the umbrellas. "See?" *Please see*, she begged silently. *I don't need much. You can change up and move around and take away everything else.*

And then he had come through for her, this man she had chosen to love for exactly this reason: he could understand much more than his experience should allow. "Oh, Chicken, did you make yourself a little perimeter with the umbrellas?" he said, a slow smile warming his face. "You know, you're kind of a special case." Though he meant it kindly, he placed the emphasis on *case*, not on *special,* and she knew that this time it wasn't an admiring nod to her uniqueness. "Come, you crazy." And he opened his arms and she dove into them and it was over. Though, she wanted to ask, since when is *crazy* a term of endearment? Later she argued that everyone should prepare the items they'd rescue in a fire or flood. But by the time he changed her name in his contacts to "Crazy Chicken," it was too late to say more.

After that, he spoke of the Perimeter with a kind of everyday reverence, acknowledging it, respecting it, like a home medical device or a movable temple that lived in a corner of their every home, every hotel room, even his parents' guest room in Provence. "I'll put the suitcases here," he would say casually. "Let's do the Perimeter with the side table and that chair." He spoke of it as if it were *their* thing, not only hers, and the constancy of this effort made her want to give him what he wanted most: to be included. Once or twice she didn't speak when he left his keys or wallet inside the Perimeter, but they both felt her discomfort, and he removed the items without further discussion. Once, in an Amsterdam hotel room on their first scouting trip, when they were sizing up the city, he set up the Perimeter using shoe trees from the closet, and she took his hand and pulled him into the rectangle of her precious things. Then she stepped outside of it and looked on. "Now it's done," she said. "You'll have to sleep standing up, though." He was happy for a week.

Before their move to Amsterdam, at a sunny Gramercy restaurant with napkin rings made of red rowan berries, Guillaume finally met Maman. Niloo squirmed, trying to unthink the treacherous thought that her mother might embarrass her. For as long as she remembered, Niloo had worshipped her mother, but after Yale and graduate school and decades among savvy nomadic second-generation peers (not friends—of those, Niloo has almost none), she understood that the scent of home would never fade from her parents as it had faded from her.

Gui asked Maman about the Hamidis and she told him stories from Iran: how Bahman ranted for months when she became involved with an underground church, but drove to Tehran and back in one long stretch just to stand in a doorway and watch his wife, clad in white, gripping an Armenian man's hands as he dipped her in a plastic tub decorated with cartoon fishes; the time Niloo and Kian didn't speak for two weeks, but Kian saved all his rocks and sticks and old photographs for her because she liked to dig in the ground and in basements and attics for treasures. "In our family," Maman explained, in her pretty broken

English, as she brandished the soup spoon she was using to cut her beets and scoop her goat cheese, "they are appreciate behind your back. But they resist to appreciate in front of you."

Gui chuckled and nodded and took a bite of his bloody cheeseburger.

"Maman, stop," Niloo whispered through her teeth, alarmed at so much sharing, an act that looks very much like begging. Then she chided Maman in clipped Farsi for using her spoon to eat salad. Her mother told her in Farsi to kindly mind her own plate. And Niloo told her that, by the way, Gui is an atheist. She wasn't sure why she said that. It was just a cruel instinct, an itch that required a long witchy nail.

Maman flushed. Gui listened to their quarrelsome Farsi. He cleared the back of his mouth with his tongue, swallowed hard, then shot her that look again—it lasted only a second, but Gui made it count. They moved on to explaining to Maman why they didn't want a wedding. Later, watching the waiter remove Gui's half-eaten burger, Maman talked pointedly of Ardestoon, of the baskets of greens at every doorstep and the wreaths of garlic in every kitchen, the inspiring lack of waste. "Is never too much or too little," she said. She glanced after the waiter and smiled.

That night in bed, Guillaume mentioned her mother's remark about the Hamidis' veiled affection for each other. But Niloo wanted no part of it, because wasn't it a common trait among families to put on many faces for one another? Certainly, it was nothing to gawk at. "I'm exhausted," Niloo said and went to sleep.

"I don't like that you're cruel to your mother," she heard him mutter as she drifted off. If she'd had the energy, she would've explained that what sounds in Farsi like bickering is only comfortable banter, that her mother had no greater defender than Niloo, and how dare he presume to know her relationship with her parents. For all his fascination, had he even listened to the point Maman was making? But Niloo didn't say any of that because it's important not to care what men think. She saw him sizing up her family as he ate his embarrassingly overpriced burger, thinking they were so Iranian, so provincial. She wished she could show Gui their houses in Isfahan and Ardestoon, their fruit orchards and vast lands. But Gui had met her when she was a financial aid kid. Once, in their first month, she dumped him because he threw away a pocketful of loose change. Despite their similar stations at birth, Gui had grown up richly sheltered and she had been a poor refugee. And so Niloo had only one hand to play, over and over, against all of Gui's silent judgments: that he cared openly and loudly, loved *her* openly and loudly (saw no reason not to trust and trust), as reckless with his heart as he was with his pocket change; and that, despite all their hours of fun together, it was likely that Niloo didn't have quite as large a store of love and need to spend on him as he had for her.

Or maybe that was a dishonest thought. Her mother, in her adoration of Gui, would claim that it was just an empty thing Niloo liked to say to his face, a very Hamidi trick, to save face, while "appreciating" behind his back. In truth she had never tried to live without Gui. And that's the only way you know for real, isn't it?

Over years, Gui and Maman grew close, whispering and hatching plots. She taught him how to bake rice with saffron yogurt. She poured the bright yellow liquid from a big bowl, wiped the residue with two fingers, and said, as if it were part of the instruction, "In old times, there were no spatulas, only fingers." Delighted, Gui spent the rest of the lesson chasing after her, wiping and tidying as she tossed onion skins and dropped puddles of goop and lectured about wasting ingredients.

She said, "Gay, why you water potted plants? Put ice cube." And Gui obeyed.

She said, "Gay, wash all meat there . . . except than fish. Fish retains water." Niloo caught Gui playing a game where he tried to make her say "except than" again and again. ("Should I pepper *all* the dishes . . . ?" "Should I whisk *all* the sauces . . . ?) When she responded as expected ("Except than raisin rice!"), he strained not to laugh, but Maman's sidelong glances assured Niloo that she was just playing along.

After Maman left, Gui texted her to say that they missed her and that they loved the food she had left in the freezer. Maman replied: *Me too, Gay joon. I have my own blue time that I have after each leave*. For an hour Niloo nursed an ache in her chest, guilt and sadness for her mother, for her parents, who had slowly become foreigners to her, the music of their talks no longer natural to her ears. She remembered that during visits, Kian wrote down funny things Baba said. So she took out a notebook and wrote, *My own blue time after each leave.*

It's still light when Dr. Heldring says goodnight—summers in Holland mean endless, hazy dusks, hours of bashful night. Gui listens to Charles Aznavour and Yves Montand as they clean the kitchen. She thinks of the evening's conversation. A hot shame washes over her—why did Gui bring up all those things? She wonders why they never listen to Iranian music, why she has never bothered to acquire any (maybe she should start), though a few fading tunes linger in her memory. She thinks of Baba, his music, photos, poetry. Gui suggests they go to Marqt to restock—neither ate much, though their guest politely devoured his lamb. "The old man has no taste buds left," he says. "I don't know why I worried so much about the cooking."

An hour later, they stand at the self-serve checkout, bagging their easy-peel oranges, beet salad, muesli, and avocados. Gui is gnawing on the Old Amsterdam; she grabs it from him and scans it, trying not to smile at the wounded pout and empty hand cupped near his mouth. She gives it back, swipes her credit card, and waits, counting tomorrow's tasks on her fingers. "I'm turning you in for stealing that cheese," she mutters, and swipes again when the machine flashes an error message. *Declined*, the screen reads in an accusatory Dutch font. *Please wait for assistance.*

"Try mine," says Gui, tossing the remaining cheese into Niloo's canvas tote.

They share an account, a fat one, so she should give no thought to this. But something about the clerk approaching, her brisk gait and sleepy eyes, scratches at the wall of her chest. She thinks of dinner, the talk of visas and Baba, of her French passport. Then the dull green letters on the screen, that hateful word, *declined*. "I'm calling the bank," she says, dialing the numbers on the back of the card.

"Chicken, please," Gui whines, reaching for his wallet. "Let's go."

Niloo bats his hand away each time he tries to get past her with his card. She continues to swipe, only half aware that she is angering the line of customers, but something prevents her from letting them get away with this accusation. Her card is fine. It should work. Someone should apologize and make amends. They should see that she's a high-functioning, honorable member of society.

The bank rep on the phone tells her that the charges are going through, but not sticking. "Don't worry, madam," she says, her Amsterdam accent chopped and singsong and questioning all at once. "There is no fraud on your card. Perhaps just pay cash today and try the card again elsewhere."

"No!" Niloo's voice rises. She glimpses herself through Gui's eyes, of course, but she looks away. She longs for her own card to go through, for the screen to say, *PIN OK*, as it has hundreds of times before, as it does for every ordinary person.

"This card has been declined," says the clerk after a cursory swipe of her key card. She's chewing the inside of her cheek. "Maybe try another?"

"Yes," says Gui, holding out his. "Great idea!"

Niloo snatches and pockets it. "I want to find out what's wrong." She speaks half into her phone, half at the sales clerk, struggling not to turn and glance at the line of furious customers. "Van Lanschot says it's not them. It's your machine."

The clerk rolls her black-lined eyes and takes a loud breath. Niloo keeps her eyes fixed on a spot on the wall as a manager is called, as he approaches, a smiling rosy man with legs like stilts in cheap red jeans. She stares into that wall, taking comfort in his Friesland accent, his crooked teeth, his milk-guzzling Dutch height. He exchanges a glance with the clerk, checks the machine, and chuckles, relieved. "Ahhh, yes, try again now."

The card fails again, this time because she has swiped too often and has, in fact, triggered the fraud system at Van Lanschot. Gui pleads for her to let it go.

When her mother's debit card failed at that Food for Less in Oklahoma, her account was overdrawn by two dollars. She watched Maman wander the aisles, demurely replacing a box of Cheerios, a loaf of wheat bread, until she had only what she could pay for in cash—Niloo chipped in two dollars, and Kian parted with a dime and three quarters he had saved. Maman didn't mind ("At home, remind me to deposit my paycheck and pay you back," she said in Farsi, her tone cheery)—she moved on.

The crimson-legged manager raises both hands in defeat. "*Mevrouw*, why not listen to the gentleman?" Then he looks at the declined receipt, weighing their twenty euros of food against some unknown metric, and says in mellow tones, "Thinking again, so often we see you here. Better you have it on us." A gesture so un-Dutch that Niloo would suspect it even if she weren't in the middle of a hysterical episode. Such an offer is Iranian—does he detect her roots? If so, he would also know that she can't accept.

Guillaume beams. "Great!" he says, feeling no shame, no need even to say thank you. "Let's go eat something unburned."

But what Niloo feels is animal panic, the sensation of a world spitting her into another tier, one she has occupied before and that awaits her, that has missed her and knows she will be back. She says, "No, absolutely not. I'll go to the ATM," and walks away before anyone can contradict her.

At home, Gui loses every ounce of his shit the second the door is closed. She tries to explain about charity, about how she has vowed never to accept it in her adulthood. "Fuck all your weird shame," he says. "I don't deserve so much pathological bullshit." He storms off toward their bedroom with the beet salad, probably hoping the relocation of her favorite dish will force Niloo to come and apologize. How little he knows about the workings of the Iranian stomach.

Niloo and Gui don't speak again until morning. Over breakfast, they reach another unsatisfying truce. Trying to sift the misery out of her voice, she offers a solution. "What if we make a new set of rules and stick to it this time?"

He sighs. "Good idea, Niloo Face." He drops his spoon into his bowl, slips into his suit jacket. "You write the first draft." He kisses her nose goodbye, another weary amends, and rushes to the door, taking along a piece of seven-grain bread tearing around a mash of avocado and a hunk of melted Old Amsterdam.

"We're too old for Niloo Face," she mutters and immediately regrets it. Why can't she just leave things alone? But she gets these itches. It's an illness.

"Don't worry. I got this," she says to the shutting door. Alone, she scratches her calf with a big toe then does the other calf. She putters around the kitchen making mental lists while her tea brews, then sits at the small oval end of the wooden dining table. She will handle this. She's handled things since her first days in Oklahoma, when she was no longer Niloo, but "that Middle Eastern kid," and her teachers noticed a tic in her neck. When she heard them discussing trauma and therapy and special classes, she rid herself of the tic through sheer will—she vowed to sit still and suffer and not move her neck, not even once, not as long as the American teachers watched. After three months of discipline, the tic was gone.

But Gui doesn't need that kind of control. When something goes wrong, someone fixes it and apologizes for the inconvenience. His opinion matters, even to strangers. Early in their courtship, Niloo adopted a habit of asking Gui after every party or meal, "Did I behave well?" She stopped as soon as her brain turned twenty-three.

She goes to the bedroom, to the corner of the walk-in closet, and sits in the Perimeter. She flips through the file folder with her passport and naturalization certificates, her marriage license, her Yale degree, the deed to the new apartment in the Pijp, and the construction contracts. She counts them again: nine documents that entitle her to her life. She gathers her backpack to her chest and hugs it tight, takes a breath until her lungs ache, holds it for a beat and forces it out. When she opens her eyes, the atmosphere is no longer weighing down on her arms and chest. She recalls the day she made up this trick; she was ten and trying to vanquish the tic alone—no one, she promised, would see her that weak again. The memory is a relief, a testament to an inborn ability to govern her fate, to the iron will of child Niloo.

But before that, in Ardestoon, she had another trick. At night she hid under a musty woolen blanket and she returned to the day's events, to an earlier, separate Niloo—*This is how it happened*, she'd say, analyzing lost books or skinned arms. She didn't change any outcomes. She only watched, like a home video, and the more she looked the more it seemed that *she* was deciding what came next. In time, events became memories that became stories that she's conjured in every bed since. And, though the habit is unbefitting a scientist, this is how she visits her cousins, her grandmother. She visits Baba, whom, in life, she has avoided; they drink good tea and talk all night, solving the riddles of family, understanding each other instinctively. In her memories, she is willing to know things that in life would make her turn away.

She kicks the closet door, shutting herself in, opens her laptop, and begins to write new rules for her young marriage. Halfway through, she pauses, lies back on the carpet, and thinks instead of Baba and of home and of that last mulberry hunt in Ardestoon.

The Village Crumbles

JUNE 2009

Isfahan, Iran

The next case was a cement block to the ribs, a sorrowful situation from which Bahman tried twice to avert his gaze: a mother desperate to keep her child. She kept saying, "Your Honor, she needs me. Your Honor, we're in the middle of a long story, a little each night. Please just delay for a week." The child cried openly, no one bothering to protect her future psyche from the memory of this day. The judge sent them away, ordering over the mother's wails that the stolen child be returned. "A child belongs to her father," he said. "You have no right taking her like this."

Over an hour or two, Bahman worked his way through three glasses of tea and six more divorces.

The eighth: a sterile woman of only twenty, unsure how she became sterile or even that she was sterile at all, except for the testimony of a previous husband who claimed that it was so. According to documents only recently uncovered by the unhappy new husband, this other man attempted to impregnate her "every morning for a year!" The man looked disgusted as he read this to the judge. "I didn't even know she was married before!" he yelled.

"She's not sterile," Bahman mumbled to himself (and maybe to his tired lawyer), his interest rising with every drop of angry sweat the husband wiped from his brow. From the flash in the woman's eye, Bahman suspected secret stashes of birth control, homemade lady condoms and vinegar, and maybe even proper hormones. "Good for you, child," he whispered over his counting beads.

The ninth was simple: a man who had taken a second wife without consent. He was chastised and consent pried from his first wife's clenched fist.

The tenth: the teenage children of two families that had wanted to cement their bonds through marriage. The young couple hated each other too much to consummate, and they had dragged their parents here to secure a divorce for them.

"Too soon," said the judge. "Someone must teach them the ins and outs of it."

"It's not a matter of teaching, Your Honor," said one of the fathers, hinting with his lecherous eyes that his son had much experience. "He refuses to touch her! What about our family? Our line? Mistakes were made by us all."

The eleventh was a charade: a couple in love who were each making a spectacle in family court to get the other to admit fault. The judge saw them stare at each other for too long, gave them a lecture, kicked them out, and marked their files.

Bahman got up during the twelfth to stretch his back. Once it had been strong enough to carry his children. Now he bent side to side, then bent forward at the waist, letting his arms hang, before realizing he looked foolish. This wasn't his peaceful dental office with its blue walls and soothing fountain, its tranquil old-world music lulling his patients away from fears of pain and toothlessness. He was about to turn to the restroom when the court secretary called in an old man two chairs away. He hobbled past Bahman into the chambers, and something in his sad gait made Bahman want to watch and witness whatever was about to happen.

When the judge asked his purpose in the court, the man trembled and shuffled from foot to foot, his gaze always on the edge of the judge's desk. It seemed he had never been in a courtroom. He wore a skullcap and loose gray trousers, the kind village men and Tehrani gardeners wore; they reminded Bahman of his favorite blue pajamas. The man's deeply grooved face was covered in white stubble.

Bahman moved toward the door. He lit a cigarette and watched the man's fingers shake. "Please, Hajj Agha," said the judge. "Tell me how I can help. Don't worry about the assistants and documents and things."

Bahman scoffed. This was a lot of exaggerated politeness for a mullah. The old man cleared his throat and pulled a thin sheet of paper from his pocket. From the sound of it, the soft weathered rustling, it seemed that he had folded and unfolded this paper ten thousand and one times. Without answering the judge, the old man began to read. "I request the honor of your interference in a situation that has been a scab on my heart . . ." His wiry voice broke twice.

The judge stopped him. "Grandfather," he said, his brow pained. Maybe, thought Bahman, this mullah wasn't a soulless reptile like all the others. Yes, he had sent several women back to their unhappy marriages, and he had taken a child from her mother, and upheld only about half the marriage gifts today, but he didn't write all those vile laws, did he? The judge continued, "Let us talk, you and I. Do you want Khanom Jamshiri here to get you a cup of chai? *Khanom*, if you don't mind . . ."

The secretary clutched her black chador and shuffled out to the samovar. As she passed by, Bahman called after her, "It's cold and sludgy, *khanom*."

She shot him a look. The old man collected himself and said, in a near whisper, "It's very difficult. Very difficult. I wrote it all down."

"Just state the trouble," said the cleric. "I can see you're a wise, literate man."

The man straightened. "I learned to read so I could search for her."

"Start at the beginning, *agha*," said the weary judge, adjusting his robes. "Ahh, here is Khanom Jamshiri with the tea. Thank you, sister."

The judge sipped from the cup that the court secretary placed in his hands, but the old man didn't touch his. He took it with a little bow and placed it carefully on the edge of the judge's desk. He shuffled again in his *shalwar*, adjusting the waist as he spoke. Then he said, "Sir, I need a divorce. My Marzieh seems to be finished with me . . . and I think it's only right that I set her free now."

"Where is the lady?" asked the judge. "May I ask how old she is?"

The man cleared his throat again, straightened his cap, and kept his eyes on the edge of the judge's desk as he spoke. "She is in her fifties. We're not sure of the details, Mullah Agha." Both the judge and Bahman chuckled at *Mullah Agha*, a strange double title that flogged itself from both sides. "It always seemed like twenty years' difference, give or take. I bought her a cake every year in late summer."

"*Akh*, for Rumi's sake," said Bahman to his lawyer. The lawyer nodded and checked his watch while Bahman said a quick word to four other dead poets on behalf of the withered husband. The man had begun speaking again.

"We had our time," he said. "She's too young to be burdened by an old man."

"Don't despair, grandfather," said the judge. "Maybe we can convince her to come back. Where might she have gone?"

"I don't know," said the man. "Her family is all dead or scattered. We only had each other from the start. But now I think, maybe she found another man."

"Are you certain of this? If so, she can be made to answer for her actions."

"No, no, no, Agha Judge, I must be mistaken," said the old man, his color fleeing, his voice and fingers shaking in some kind of bizarre fearful unison. "No, she's a good woman. I just think . . . I hope she has someone to watch over her."

The judge asked to see the paper in the man's hand. He looked through his files, and massaged his temple with two fingers. He mumbled some suggestions for how to bring her back. "A kind man like you should have someone to care for him." Finally, as an afterthought, he asked, "When did the lady leave? Did she leave any kind of message? Maybe in a letter or on the telephone?"

The man counted on his fingers, then he said, his eyes all earnestness and concern, "It will be sixteen years ago this month that I saw her. We had breakfast."

"*Eiii baba*," moaned the judge, his color draining. Khanom Jamshiri too sighed and muttered some similar thing. They exchanged a glance and went silent.

"We're not the sort for ceremony," the old man continued. "I haven't heard her voice since she left. But now I can read, so I gathered some leftover documents and went to three villages around Isfahan showing her name. I told the story."

The judge motioned for Khanom Jamshiri to approach him. He whispered something in her ear. Bahman didn't need to hear it. Khanom Jamshiri hurried away down the hall, to another office. Bahman watched her disappear behind a door past the long corridor, and he knew she was checking death records.

When she returned, she whispered to the judge, her face stark white against his pockmarked brown skin. He massaged his temple again, as he read a single sheet of paper that the secretary had given him. Bahman had no doubt the woman in question was long dead. Maybe at some point, her husband had known this and old age was offering him a convenient lapse in memory. The judge looked up, ready to give the man the news in the records. But then, the old man lifted his gaze from the edge of the desk. A soft smile smoothed the lines on his face. He said, "What I want, *agha*, is for my dear Marzieh to move forward, to live out her young life happy and well-fed, in a big, big room full of family. We had our love. No sense to be missing each other all this time, haunting each other's nights this way. It's not healthy."

The judge looked at the paper again, then he said, his every word coated with a kind of exhaustion that takes decades to set in, "Grandfather, I grant you your divorce. You can keep the marriage gift. She is absolved of all wrongdoing. Go."

"Oh." The man beamed. He seemed surprised down to his yellowing toenails. "I was expecting a long, hard thing, lots of papers." From his pocket he retrieved a bag of unskinned pistachios; the best kind, right off the tree.

The judge didn't object to the gift. He got up from behind his desk and shook the man's hand with both of his. He touched his face as he would his own father's and said the pistachios made his day bright. Then the man left and Bahman was called in.

"*Agha*, let me warn you," the judge groaned before even glancing at Bahman. "This day is almost done for me." He looked up with the desperate, bloodshot eyes of a man who has just crumbled a dozen villages.

Bahman introduced himself, extending his hand to the judge. His lawyer stood behind him, clasping his wrist in front of his groin. Suddenly the boy seemed more than useless; his presence made Bahman look as unsure of himself as the old man, except he inspired no sympathy with his paid attorney and his suit.

"I've come for a divorce, Your Honor," he said. "I won't give reasons, since you're very busy and I have the right to divorce. I've prepared the papers, am ready to pay the full marriage gift, in gold coins as originally agreed, and I have no wish to speak ill of my wife." The lawyer laid several typed petitions on the judge's desk.

The judge chuckled, fanned the papers on his desk, and smiled at Bahman. "Doctor Hamidi, you make my work easier. I'm sad to see you here with this riffraff." He said this as if they were old friends, a customary nod among educated sorts who run into each other in inhospitable places—though, to be fair, Bahman was the only one with an unbiased education in the sciences, humanities, and all that.

Bahman nodded. "Yes, I was listening outside. It's very sad."

"As is the world," said the judge. He was quiet for a moment, his fingernail digging into one of the unskinned pistachios. Bahman too played with his green counting beads, turning them over his knuckles as he waited for the judge to speak. He reminded himself to wash them tonight, after this errand was done; a film of hand grease was covering each orb. "Humor me with the story," said the cleric.

Bahman nodded again, aware of his docility. "Medically speaking," he said (he tossed this phrase around to amuse himself since his credentials extended no further than teeth and gums), "she has a borderline personality that's manifesting in a kind of hysteria. She will be happier with her family. She is already collecting her things. We have no children. She's young, and that's something she has that I don't."

It seemed to Bahman that the judge would sign some papers and send him off with the same quickness and warmth with which he had treated the old man's case. Putting aside his turban and graying robes, his unsophisticated beard, one might admit that this man's eyes showed caring and weariness, the same weariness Bahman had felt for some time. Maybe the cleric didn't believe in these laws he was forced to protect. Certainly he had seen enough to acquire a different sort of wisdom than the politicians and the revolutionaries possessed, all those fiery, villainous prophets who saw the world as a single droning mass to gorge on their burdensome dogmas. Clerics and politicians, as everyone knows, have no appreciation for the individual and no ear for stories; they are blind to everything that happens in the quiet hours when nothing is happening. That is what makes them dangerous.

The cleric smiled. "My friend . . . this day and age, these people . . ." He shook his head as he folded down the tops of some of the pages in Bahman's file.

"It's one long madness," said Bahman, feeling like a recording of himself. For years he had offered up such cynical commentary on the world and yet hadn't he, along with everyone else, just stood by and watched? Hadn't he sat still, smoking from his *manghal*, while his children were taken away? While his dreams were kneaded down into a smaller and smaller ball, until they fit in the palm of a hand?

From the end of the corridor, something clattered, and a shrill confusion of voices spat out warnings and explanations and obscenities, all blended together like the mismatched strands of woolen yarn that his mother rolled together into mottled balls. Khanom Jamshiri ambled out of her chair, and, to be fair, why would she move any faster? The corridor was always a sweaty, loud mess of turmoil and high drama.

At this moment, the judge must have stumbled onto a page about Bahman's previous marriages. "You have children," he said.

"Yes," said Bahman, keeping it vague, leaving out any dangerous words like *America* or *Holland*. "Two of them are studying abroad. Their mother took them from me in secret, and now she's out of our reach. The other is the adopted daughter of my second wife. I have no biological claim on her. I give money, of course."

"How old is that child?" asked the judge.

"She's young. Eight now," said Bahman, unable to hide his annoyance. "She was with us from three to four. Then we divorced, I remarried, and so on. None of that is related to this marriage . . . We have no disagreements. I will pay the gift."

Though Sanaz's family had contracted a handsome sum for her, it was true that the marriage gift wasn't enough to sustain her forever. And his savings and investments probably were, so it was in her interest to stay married. In that case, she should have treated him more kindly. What he really wanted was to save his fortune and use it to entice his children back to Iran, where he had his beloved village and his practice and his opium. He couldn't leave these things, but would they come, if he had a vacation home on the Caspian Sea? Or a tea farm by the mountains?

"The two who are 'studying' . . . aren't they more than thirty years old?"

Bahman didn't answer. The clatter outside grew to an untenable volume and moved closer, Khanom Jamshiri's voice becoming one with the approaching throng.

"What is going on out there?" asked the cleric. Bahman's lawyer, who had yet to do anything but nod and hand over papers, stuck his head outside.

"I'm confused about this other daughter," said the judge, returning to Bahman's documents. "Who is she? What did you want with her?"

The story was an embarrassment, because he had to confess this thing that many husbands have to confess—when you marry younger women, often someone else comes along and excites them. This can happen to anyone, irrespective of generation or politics. It happens because the world is a sweaty cave crowded with bodies clamoring and fighting to capture every good thing for themselves. Young men are the hungriest, the most brutish and unashamed before their chosen deities. And who was Bahman's god? Science? Family? Love? The old poets, it would be fair to say, were Bahman's prayer stone, the recipients of his regret, in those private moments when he was compelled to bend and drop his gaze, to kneel and kiss the ground. He cringed at the fact that once, at twenty, when he had long hair stained by the Ardestoon sun, when he wore bell-bottoms to class and carried a soccer ball everywhere, he too had enticed an unhappy woman from her husband's cold bed.

Of course, he wasn't going to tell the judge the real story, the simple dull one where everyone sins. It's best to blame the infidelities and missteps and dark impulses, especially the ones that result in children, to people who are safely dead.

"My second wife, Fatimeh, had a sister who died of stomach cancer," he said, and this part was true. The woman did die, husbandless, childless—her gift to her family was the clean slate she left for them to befoul.

After a lifetime in Ardestoon, Bahman knew that the art of lying in divorce court, and in fact, of all yarn weaving, is to be confusing but precise. Pile on the irrelevant details, make them circular and long, but be sure to include dates and places and anything that might rouse the listener's curiosity. Thus prevent the listener from asking questions. So, Bahman wove a story as dramatic and mouthwatering, as full of mud and clutter, as the kind he used to tell Niloo at bedtime decades ago. The kind he had heard thirteen times today in this courtroom:

The cancer killed Fatimeh's poor sister fast, sparing her two-year-old daughter any memories. For a grim, hungry year, the girl lived with her wayward poet father, a handsome man with excellent white teeth who made his living as a roving office clerk, occasional setar *player, extra security at underground parties, driver, and maybe even a witness for hire. One day, this cad left the girl, Shirin, sitting by the gate of a mosque with her birth certificate and a note pinned to her jacket. She obeyed her baba, not daring to unpin it or to move from the gate for three hours.*

All that sad jacket business made Bahman proud—he had a touch of the storyteller in him, after all. And Shirin was indeed a sweet, simple child who followed every instruction if it was clear and didn't deprive her of her next meal.

So . . . then the white-toothed devil disappeared into the ether like a character in a bad American film. (Bahman repeated this detail for the judge, emphasizing its awfulness, adding, "not that I've watched any.") *The man's mobile was disconnected, his small house cleaned out. As far as Bahman knew, he just left the girl in the street outside the mosque, crying after him. Who knows what would have happened if a kind cleric hadn't stumbled upon her, rolled up his sleeves, and called every agency and courthouse until he found Bahman? Oh, and this wayward poet; the girl's real father? He was dead too, of course, and unable to testify to anything.*

"*Agha*, you won't believe the difficulties that were suffered," Bahman droned.

The girl's birth certificates turned out to be fakes, leaving no record of her. Her mother was unmarried and so she had lied to hospitals and to bureaus and everyone about her name, her daughter's name.

On and on Bahman went, omitting no detail. The truth was this:

The white-toothed villain was indeed little Shirin's biological father. He worked for Bahman as a temporary hygienist once. But it was Bahman's second wife, Fatimeh, not her sister, who was the object of his lust and mother of his child. Bahman married her anyway, promising to love her and the child. He harbored such guilt over Pari's fate, all alone abroad, and now Fatimeh needed him to care for her. Better to repay the universe. At night lying awake, he thought: here is a second family, a second chubby daughter, a second chance at fatherhood and youth and the love of a little creature with clapping hands and laughing eyes. But could he do it? Could a godless addict to opium and verse ever be a good father? He had failed once.

He paid to change the papers to establish that Shirin was not born to his new wife but adopted by her. The people in her village forgot so fast that he lost a kilo of faith in his community's judgment and good sense and gained it all back for its capacity to love, all in one quick month.

Did the judge believe him? From the beginning, the sadness in the cleric's voice had shamed Bahman. In his thoughts he had judged this man a thousand times today. And, in the privacy of his sitting room, all Bahman did was complain about the state of the world, about its irrational nature, the fools who run it. Maybe he would make a few changes after the divorce, however small. One should take steps toward one's own happiness whenever possible.

The judge was just starting up again about the soul-killing nature of divorce, when the door slammed open and a confusion of bodies burst in, shouting at one another and at Khanom Jamshiri, who had gathered the ends of her chador in her hands as if she expected someone to trip over them.

Among them were Bahman's wife, Sanaz, her sister and brother-in-law, Agha Soleimani, and three strange men in faded ill-fitting suits and work shoes caked with mud and concrete. Others seemed to have followed them in, a few security guards and another assistant, a man in a village cap. One of the men glared at him through a wooly beard with sandy patches that struck Bahman as familiar. "What is the meaning of this?" he whispered to Sanaz, whose cheeks were red from weeping and her eyes swollen to slits. From the tightness of her lips, all gathered and pressed small like a gum wrapper, he could tell that she would cause some trouble. This was his fate, after fifty-five years of trying to make a decent life: an insane woman holding him hostage. She greeted the judge with practiced words, eyes humble, all manners and borrowed modesty. Strands of her newly blonde hair peeked out through her headscarf, either a mistake, since hijabs were checked at the women's entrance, or a typical domination of Sanaz's good sense by her vanity. Why was she here? Only days ago she had accepted their separation; only yesterday she had promised that if he would only spend one night in a hotel, she would gather her things and go. She was a naturally fiery woman, so this calculated sort of crying, the prettiness of it, alarmed him more than all the wild rants of the last months.

"*Agha*, thank you for hearing me," said Sanaz through some impressive wheezes and sobs. "I have to tell you that this man, my husband, he's lying to you. Whatever he says is a lie." Her sister stroked her shoulders. The pair looked so convincingly sad, exuding so much feminine helplessness and need that Bahman had to take inventory of his own many failings as a husband. What had he done?

"Your Honor, I swear," said Bahman, "I don't know what this is about. Sanaz *joon*, you know I will pay the marriage gift. You didn't have to wake the whole city."

The youngest of the men in dirty shoes scoffed. He was chewing sunflower seeds. Sanaz's brother-in-law slapped his hand as he brought a kernel to his teeth.

The judge, realizing that this silly girl was Bahman's latest wife, smirked wearily at the throng, maybe because he had respected Bahman a minute ago. "Young lady, he's agreeing to pay the money. He has letters proving the amount—"

Sanaz interrupted the judge, causing Bahman's stomach muscles to collapse on themselves like cheap shelves under the Sufi canon. Did she want to get herself tossed in jail? "I have these witnesses," said Sanaz. The sunflower seed man huffed again, readying himself to spew back whatever he had been fed earlier. Now Bahman remembered the familiar man, the one with the wooly beard, one of the witnesses for hire loitering outside the courthouse. In the minute or two of muteness after grasping the depths of his wife's malice and trickery, Bahman listened to her explain to the judge that these three men (these imposters whom the judge probably passed that very day as he entered the courtroom) had witnessed Bahman hosting rebels with green wristbands in his home, that he had welcomed them and fed them with food and alcohol and hours of Rumi worship.

Glancing sidelong at Bahman, she uttered the first truth she had spoken since arriving: that her husband believed what the Green Movement people believed (which, to be fair, wasn't a belief, but the embarrassing truth that the people had voted overwhelmingly for Mousavi. *Where is my vote?* The protesters took to the streets of Tehran when an Ahmadinejad victory was announced, and each night on their rooftops they shouted *Allah-o-akbar.* Did Sanaz claim that they plotted some part of these demonstrations and rebellions in Bahman's house?). "I have been seeing it myself, suffering it every week since before the election," Sanaz explained.

"All right, collect yourself, young lady," said the judge. "We will dig into this matter until our spoon hits the bottom."

Bahman tried to appear composed. He wanted to raise his voice above the din, as now people were shouting. His lawyer had started to question the merit of the witnesses and they, in turn, began speaking all at once, and Soleimani pretended to be insulted. What did she hope to gain? She had come within a fox hair of implicating herself, an excessive way to punish a negligent husband.

"Your Honor, you're an educated man," Bahman said, trying to seem unconcerned. "You've seen the lies people make up to get what they want. Arrest me if you want. Send me to prison. But please grant me a divorce first."

"*Agha*," said Sanaz, then promptly corrected herself—what a quick study she had always been—"*Your Honor* . . . if you divorce us, I'll lose my home. And this man is false and two-sided. I only wish for you to investigate."

A sourness spread through Bahman's stomach and traveled up to his mouth. What had she done, all night alone in his house? She had asked to collect her things and he had spent the night away. Had she changed the locks? Taken his furniture, planted evidence? The thought of the photo albums, souvenirs from Niloo and Kian's childhood—he wanted to run home right then and check. When Niloo was in first grade, she had a pencil case from London. It was pink plastic with three white butterflies near the zipper. He had saved it in a drawer along with her schoolwork. In second grade, she wrote him a poem. It was called "Babajoon" and it had rhyme and meter; the cadences had a touch of Mevlevi verse. The child was clearly gifted. One night when she was three, he whispered this discovery to Pari. Niloo must have overheard. After that, every evening she sat at his feet and propped open his medical books to demonstrate her cleverness. She showed him her drawings, even recited dozens of children's songs from memory. Bahman had her poem memorized and was convinced the paper still smelled like her sugary hands, always sticky from some jam jar or pastry. Once, near the end of his affections for Sanaz, he caught her reading it and he snatched it from her. She said, "I was careful," and walked away. Now, all he wanted was to go home and open all his drawers.

The judge put two fingers to his lips and pinched off a flake of dry skin, then rubbed one eye with his palm and looked at it, as if expecting blood. "Doctor, those are some grave accusations." His tired voice strengthened Bahman's resolve.

"One thing doesn't have to do with the other," said Bahman. He glanced around at their hungry faces, ready to pick his carcass. How had he not seen them circling? What does a pretty young woman want with an old man like him anyway? She had been plunging her fingers in his bowl for years, and now that his love for her was spent, her family wanted his last shreds for themselves. Who'd want the trouble of a divorce, when they could hang on to his house, his money? They preferred to keep him married and under suspicion—no more traveling or opium or freedom, the things that made Sanaz unhappy. Better to cut him off at the knees.

"So you're admitting to this?" said the judge, a bit too alert now for comfort.

"Of course not," said Bahman. "It's too absurd to dignify."

"Absurd he calls it," said Sanaz's brother-in-law, "with traitors on every rooftop and the country threatened." Then he nudged the wooly-bearded man forward. Bahman had to admit that the man was a better storyteller than himself. It was, after all, his profession. He described Bahman's sitting room, his pillows, his photographs, his samovar. He claimed to have been delivering food with his friend (he clasped the shoulder of the boy with sunflower seeds) and that neither of them was involved in the meeting. But a meeting was taking place; no question. And listen, here are all the damning words they heard, recalled (naturally) in list form . . .

Bahman wanted to leave—a slow awareness was blooming, not only of the desperation gripping his throat as the witness spoke, but of a quieter longing simply to walk away. From this room, yes, but also the city, this country. He wanted to gather his albums and papers, pack a suitcase, and go. Maybe to an apartment in Cyprus, or to a village in Shomal. He imagined himself living out his days in white drawstring trousers made of light cotton and rolled up to the knees. In the mornings, he would drink his coffee as he walked on a beach or in a garden. And then in the afternoon, he would smoke, eat a plate of fruit, and drink cardamom tea as he read his favorite poets, reciting to himself, testing his memory. He didn't dare dream of joining Niloo and Kian in America (or was Niloo living in Europe still? It had been so long since they'd talked). Anyway, how would he survive there, and meet his various needs? But maybe his daughter would help—she was a rescuer. When Niloo was small, she took a baby chicken from the farm in Ardestoon, to save it from being slaughtered. She wrapped it in a cloth and sat with it in the back of the car, cradling it in her little fingers all the way home to Isfahan. She named it Chicken Mansoori, after Ali Mansoori, the boy down the street whom she loved. Every day she fed it in the backyard. Its pen was still in the garden and Bahman planned to take that to Cyprus too. One day when Chicken Mansoori had grown into a rooster, and Bahman was exhausted from work, a little delirious from opium, and frustrated with its crowing, he had it killed. Not wanting to waste meat in wartime, Pari cooked it for dinner. When Niloo asked after her bird, Bahman didn't answer. He told her to eat her food, never meeting her gaze. There was a moment, though, when she knew. He was certain he saw the realization leak from behind her small face. She looked at her plate, then at her Baba. He could see that she was about to wail, but seeing his regret and discomfort, she stopped. She wiped her eyes and took a tearful bite. She ate her chicken friend. That's how stubborn she was, resolute to unknowable levels.

Now, out of bewilderment and despair, Bahman whispered, "Your Honor, you just granted a divorce to a dead woman."

And who bothers to remember all the other things that were said—the escalating accusations, the documents fetched, the other courts consulted—between insulting a weary, embittered judge and finding oneself in a jail cell?

When would he be allowed to call someone? Maybe to obtain some money for bribes? He would suffer opium withdrawal soon . . . and worse, sitting in that muggy room alone, he was still married and no closer to freedom. Except for this one growing hope: Niloo would help.

She was loyal. She chased the people she loved like a tiny pit bull, rescuing them, forcing conviction and hope into their hearts despite the pangs in her own.

It was time for him to leave this hellscape of a country.

"One long, slow madness," Bahman muttered to his lawyer, when he was finally allowed to see him, and the boy simply replied, "Yes, Agha Doctor."

Erotic Republic

AUGUST 2009

Amsterdam, Netherlands

After an hour on the closet floor, Niloo's promised draft emerges. She titles it RULES. Her opening words: *I tried to be exhaustive . . .* (the first rule of Niloo's life as a prolific Western woman, and of the many lists that have guided it). She presses send.

From: Dr. Niloofar Hamidi

To: Guillaume Leblanc

Subject: RULES

I tried to be exhaustive, given stuff we keep getting wrong. But add anything I may have missed.

(1) Each person does two nice things per day. Before bed, the other person has to guess those items and writes them down. We keep the list for purposes of knowing what we did for each other.

(2) 1 yell = 1 chore, 1 condescension = 1 chore

(3) On birthday or sick day, the person has final say, within reason. If a sick person yells or curses, they only get a warning, not a chore. The other person has to take care of them. They have to ask them what they need.

(4) 15 minutes of phone time from 9 am to 6 pm. Full concentration; no working while talking, but be considerate of each other's work. Must hear the other person say "bye" before hanging up. Try to end with "I love you."

(5) We eat dinners together, not at separate tables (if we're both home).

(6) Show interest in each other's work: if someone wants to discuss a topic or show something they wrote (like when I edited your briefs), you have to listen. Also, find an activity we both like (novels? tennis? *The Economist*?).

(7) After 10 minutes of fighting, if nothing is resolved, either party can call a time-out. Talk begins again after 20 minutes of time-out.

(8) Avoid little hurts. No casual mentions of divorce. No ignoring the other person when they're mad. No belittling their worries. No asking if supplemental work activities are worth the time or pay (actually, no valuing work in dollars or euros in the first place, because work is work).

(9) Have more sex? On weekends, if you wake up before the other one, maybe stay in bed till they're awake too?

(10) If another fight occurs, add more rules.

Her fingers dangle idly over her mouth as she rereads what she's sent—*That covers everything*, she thinks; *I should write a marriage book*. She gets up from her corner of the closet, stretches her legs, and tidies the Perimeter. She takes her laptop to the kitchen, where she starts to make herself a cup of tea.

She refreshes her inbox. Baba's name peeks out from among store ads and University of Amsterdam Listserv messages. He writes in Finglish (Farsi words in Latin letters—he throws in strange punctuations and misspelled English words just to make things extra headachy in that special Bahman Hamidi way). The subject line is in all capitals, as if Baba is screaming through her computer, a bizarre image since he never raises his voice. He calls himself "dad."

Subject: I AM READY

See you soon in doubai shayad bezoodi? {very nice pelace in doubai} Kian ham hast? man keh hastam. dad

(See you soon in Dubai maybe soon? {very nice place in Dubai} Kian is there too? I am there anyway. dad)

An email from Baba is rare and who knows if any reply would reach him—he has a new wife, a hotheaded young thing, possibly younger than Niloo (she doesn't want to ask). The last time Niloo wrote to him, the curt "*doctor Hamidi mashghooleh*" (Dr. Hamidi is busy) that landed in her inbox was surely this woman's work. So she refuses to reply now, though in the past month Baba has contacted her three times. He wants to organize another visit—their fifth since she left Iran in 1987. Niloo is finished with the visits—they are draining and painful and she's bad at them. She keeps offending him or hurting him and sometimes he looks at her all dead lips and jutting eyebrows as if she's a manuscript in a language he studied for a month back in fifth grade. These disconnects rouse her at night. The memory of them traps her breath so that it fails halfway up her chest, because she knows that it's the sign of an unnatural shift—something she once had has died.

In past visits, Baba has hinted once or twice that she might get him a visa. But the notion of helping her father become a desperate exile, given all his dangerous habits—the opium and the *aragh* that he claims "salt" his life in Isfahan—makes her shiver. All she can see are the ways her father exposes her, the many risks. He doesn't speak English. When he met Gui in Istanbul, he didn't stop spewing nonsensical Persian idioms. Instead of *I need to figure out my situation*, or even the stiffer, but still intelligible translation *I want to illuminate my fate*, he said, *I want to light up my homework*, because the word *illuminate* in Farsi is highly literal, as in turning on a lightbulb, and because the word for *fate* is the same as for *homework*. How can she inflict this man on the Western world?

She moves the email to a to-do folder and goes to fetch the screaming kettle.

When she returns, she finds a message from Gui.

From: Guillaume

To: Crazy Chicken

Subject: Re: RULES

I'll add the same thing I always say: you have to trade a few hours of work (or "supplemental work activities" . . . wtf is that?) for something useless. Not exercise or book club or *The Economist* or anything that helps your sweet little plots for world domination.

Wanna show you love me? Waste some time. Meet some low-key people. Cheese making, falconry, folk dance. How about that Iranian poetry group in the Jordaan? Have some pointless fun with all that crazy energy.

Why does he talk to her this way? She hates that he seems to have read traces of irony in a message she wrote with every sincere intention. Now she wants to fire back something sincere: *But I want YOU to show you love me!* Or something ironic: *1 condescension = 1 chore*. Instead she writes something long and clumsy: *My world domination isn't sweet or little. Also, Iranian poetry doesn't attract "low-key people." And it's extremely useful for collecting loyal armies of minions, soooo . . .*

Too upset to work, she makes herself a Shirazi salad: cucumber, tomato, and red onion drenched in lime and olive oil. She eats the vegetables with a soup spoon, then brings the bowl to her lips. She replays the conversation with Gui, stirring up her anger with each retelling. *Waste time?* Why does he expect her to behave as if she too grew up grinning drowsily through the sedative fog of her own privilege? Then, conceding that she didn't, as if she should drop every hardwired habit and fixation by virtue of being connected to him now? She drinks the lime and olive oil to the last drop—she isn't ashamed of this habit. It's just instinct left over from another life; olive oil is expensive, and so are limes. But the first time Gui saw her do this, he stared, mouth agape. "You're from another planet," he whispered. Niloo grinned and wiped her mouth. Gui knows very well that she can't waste time. She can't even waste used lime juice.

In the late afternoon, she walks to the Jordaan, to the narrow stone street on a canal so meager a fit person could jump over it. She doesn't admit she's come looking for Zakhmeh, the Persian squat and arts space that she stumbled onto a few Sundays ago while walking with Gui. "I can't believe this is here," she said as she cupped her hands around her eyes and peeked into the foggy window. She explained a little breathlessly that the name is derived from *zakhm*, the word for *wound*. But a man who had been smoking a few paces away—curious Iranians were always watching and listening when she took Gui anywhere—explained that a *zakhmeh* is a plectrum for Eastern string instruments, like the *setar*. He pulled one from his pocket.

She thanked the man in Farsi. He cast his heavy eyes on Gui and said without looking at her, "You're losing your fine accent, *khanom*. You should come and read some poetry with us." He nodded to a flyer taped to the window.

The event was called "Erotic Republic." "Nice," said Gui, reading no further. "Yeah, let's check it out." She wrote the details on an old business card.

Erotic Republic: a night of sensual poetry, memory, and imagination:

English–Farsi poetry night. All readers appreciated, applauded, worshipped! Gather here and share your most lurid stories, fables and myths, poetry, poetry, poetry. Come, listen, and share homemade soup. Doors open at 19.00. Entrance is free, but donations pay the rent (okay, we're a squat. Donations pay for coriander and tomatoes . . . and a healthy supply of herbal libations).

Now she thinks, maybe she does want to meet some newly arrived Iranians, people whose accents are still fine and whose memories of home are clear and unwarped. Besides, she loves stories and poetry. And Iranian food too.

She lingers in the neighborhood until the light wanes and people begin drifting into brown cafés and beer bars in the adjoining streets. In case she needs to duck out and work in a café, she has brought along her backpack, an accessory that has grown up with her, filling with more and more things as her shoulders have strengthened, keeping pace, so that it always feels as heavy as the first time.

Waiting for the right moment to enter, she grows impatient. She wants to watch these people who have familiar names and might be distant cousins, to study them as she has studied people and objects her entire life: from the men in her father's photos, to petrified mulberries in Ardestoon orchards, to Russian men in an Italian refugee camp, to packs of teenagers in an Oklahoma McDonald's. Now Zakhmeh has made her curious, and curiosity is one instinct Niloo rarely ignores.

Past the industrial metal doors of the former factory, inside the heavily draped gathering space that smells like incense and lentil soup, unwashed pillows marinating in the sweat of strangers and a bounty of weed, she seems strangely American—the room is filled with a mix of dreadlocked Dutch and Middle Eastern hippies, artsy Persians, some *hijabi* women, and men in all kinds of dress. The artsy ones with long hair and Green Movement wristbands thrill her most—she left Iran too young to experience the underground creative scenes, the parties, the clubs and shows. Not that she partook in any of those things in America. If it had been illegal, though, she might have made a point of developing an interest from a safe distance.

She walks unnoticed into the room, tosses ten euros into the donation jar, and plops down on a big sage pillow, swinging her backpack to her front and wrapping her legs around it to avoid taking up too much space.

An older Iranian man with bushy white sideburns offers her a bowl of lentil soup. His spoon is still in the soup and he has taken a few mouthfuls. She smiles, remembering that offering a child food from one's own bowl is a familiar, uninhibited gesture that her grandfather and every Ardestooni man used to make. She takes it and eats. "*Merci*, *agha*," she says. Thank you, sir.

"Please . . . call me Mam'mad," says the man, and she greets him again by his first name, a lovely rural version of Mohammad that she knows intimately; two of her childhood friends, sons of village caretakers, opted for the same gentler form.

"Will you be reading tonight?" he asks in Farsi. His accent is educated, but he has a lisp. The *sh* in "tonight" slipping out like a soft, bruised hiss. He is wearing a faded brown jacket, the plastic temples of his glasses lost in the white fluff cascading down his cheek. He looks older than Baba, by a little, and smaller built, by a lot.

"No, *agha* . . . Mam'mad *agha*," she says, flushing. She didn't expect to be nervous here. She pulls one leg behind her haunches. "I'm not one of the readers."

He clicks his tongue. "No, dear, there are no readers," he says, spitting now and then. "People go as the poetry moves them. See there?" He points to a stack of papers and a glass of water atop a low stool beside the microphone. "They have poems you can read to us, or you can tell your own private story, or read something you wrote. It's all unregulated. No rules, no Dutch people. Do you require a smoke?"

"I see some Dutch people." She points to two men with blond dreadlocks.

Mam'mad is already shaking his head. "Swedes. Less ice in the veins." Then he leans toward her and adds in English, "I hate the Dutch. Fuck Wilders." In his thick Iranian accent it comes out *Fack Vilders*.

Though Niloo has never stumbled onto this scene before—the refugees, activists, artists—she has attended a Green Movement protest or two, hovering in the periphery. She has watched the news from Iran every day since June. She wonders if people like Gui and his colleagues are aware of what the Iranian exiles suffer here in the Netherlands, without homes, always under threat of deportation, some living in squats, others on the streets. Often when news of Iran pounds too loudly in her head, she diverts her attention to Geert Wilders, the deeply racist (and anti-Islam, anti-immigration) conservative party leader who wants her people out of Holland. He is to be tried soon for hate speech against Muslims, having called the Koran a fascist book and Mohammad the devil. "Islam is the Trojan Horse in Europe," he once said. Sometimes his rants sound like her Baba, except Baba hates all religions, not just one. It baffles her that a country so progressive on health care, elder care, and education can allow this man anything but a clown's platform. And yet . . . his Party for Freedom (PVV) is growing, and he could become prime minister.

"Fuck Wilders," she says and finishes her soup.

Later she accepts a smoke from Mam'mad, whose wry humor reminds her of Baba when he's in a dark mood. Halfway through the third reading, she notices a younger Iranian man standing in the back, near the door, smoking with a dark, sharp-chinned woman around forty who keeps touching his chest with one finger. She has thick black curls like coiled twine. The man glances at Niloo and nods. Even in the dim light, she can see that his face bears scars.

A shy young woman with a girlish voice reads a poem about love and sex. A homeless man wanders in, but no one notices. The couple in the back lean against each other, their flaws covered by smoke and dark, each unknowingly giving the reader the same amused and encouraging but baffled look as the other.

"There was sleep, there was wakefulness / There was desire, there was repulsion / In conflict and union, like a hand grasping a collar."

When the reader finishes, the crowd is generous with applause, whistles, and shouts, and she lingers at the microphone for an instant, then rushes off, keeping careful watch on her shoes. The host, a thin man with a soft middle and a European nose, dressed in sandals and high-waist jeans, approaches the microphone slowly, as if the air has turned to pudding. Niloo tries to shake it off, but a foggy stiffness is taking hold. Touching her head feels like waving a hand through paint. Mam'mad's joint must have been full of hashish. Turning to him, she catches a few words of complaint: "Too easy a choice, that poem . . . for a night called 'Erotic Republic' . . ."

Someone responds, "You want erotic, turn on Dutch television at midnight."

Mam'mad clicks his tongue and brandishes the back of his hand. "Inane comparison. You obviously haven't read a word of modern Iranian poetry." The back and forth delights her, these adults exchanging jabs she doesn't understand while sharing a pillow, eating from the same cauldron of soup. The intimacy is familiar and intoxicating, something she hasn't experienced for herself, because in Ardestoon she was only a child watching from a corner of the *sofreh*.

As the night unfurls, the women tell stories. Most of the men are too high or drunk and prefer to listen. The stories range in detail and in tone, from the tragic to the hilarious, but they are connected. Everyone wants to unburden about their days away from Iran, trying to create a life, failing, succeeding, fumbling, finding unlikely allies. As the women speak, voices from the floor rise up to interject, asking questions, bantering with the storyteller, mocking a character or an event.

"This is the story," says a large, throaty woman, a saucy auntie type with heavy breasts squeezed into a bright red wrap shirt, "of the famous spotted banana."

The crowd hoots and Niloo is certain a lewd story is coming. But the woman talks of shortages in Iran, of trade restrictions and scuffles in the streets, of vendors who sell the rare fruit for ten times its value. Sometimes in the whole of Isfahan or Tehran, she says, finding even a single small banana is impossible. Then she talks of her cousin, the shady entrepreneur who, when they were children, marched up to his unsmiling father and demanded that they sell the rainwater in their yard for profit. When he grew up, this cousin found that by the time he smuggled in his bananas from Istanbul or Dubai, they were always rotten, black spots covering their outer skin. To get them fresher would have been too expensive, so instead he informed the South Tehrani public that he was the only vendor in town with extra-rare, extra-delicious Thai spotted bananas, which he would graciously sell at thrice the price of an ordinary, plain-skinned banana. "That part of the story is hardly worth telling," she says. "He was a good salesman and he made his money. The interesting part comes when I moved to London last year. So I arrive. I poke around for some Iranians, thinking I'll need friends. I find some. I go to their house. We eat. We talk. This family has lived in London for a decade and the wife is fancy and always dressed up and speaks English like a *bolbol*. She takes me to the market, and she marches (in her fancy shoes) right up to the boy in the fruit aisle and she says, 'Where are your spotted bananas? I only see the ordinary kind.'"

The crowd erupts. The woman laughs into her plump, delicate hands. Her nails are painted crimson. She goes on a bit longer about Iranians who land in Heathrow and go looking for spotted bananas first thing, buying up the garbage at every produce stand and pretending to love the mush inside the rotten peel. "Dirt on all our heads, we're so stupid." The crowd hushes, someone tosses a napkin at her, but mostly they nod. The timbre of her laugh changes. She whispers, almost moans, into the microphone. "Oh humans, humans, we are *all* so stupid."

Niloo thinks, *Maman will love this story. Kian will hate it. And Baba probably knows the cousin, or someone exactly like him.* What would Gui think, if she were to include him in the telling? He would laugh, kiss her, and feel bad for a minute or two.

During a lull, Mam'mad nudges her. "I'd like to hear you tell one," he says, as if they've known each other for years. "Go on. Get up now, *khanom*."

"I can't," she says, but her feet are itching to move. She feels bold and craves to participate. She wonders what story they would like. Should she tell them about Maman at Food for Less? About trying to learn sixth-grade slang? About the tic in her neck? No, she decides, she should describe the day at the dry cleaners two months ago. On that day, as after the incident at Marqt, she didn't try to explain herself to a baffled Guillaume. She didn't know how. But here no storyteller is doing any explaining; it seems unnecessary. The stories unfold detail by detail, and the heads in the crowd nod and bow, their understanding palpable in their expressions, in the quiet way they bring their cigarettes to their lips, the way they rest their chins on their knees and let their soup congeal beside their bare feet.

At the microphone, she clears her throat twice and launches in, trying to mimic the tone of the seasoned performers. The crowd is welcoming and warm, and they don't interrupt her as much as they do the regulars (they are *real* Iranians, she tells herself, and are taking it easy on the American). "A few months ago, the dry cleaner, a Chinese man around fifty, rips my favorite jacket." Mr. Sun had ripped her jacket and Niloo had flipped out. She had owned that jacket for six years, the only clothing she kept in her corner with her treasures, the only purely aesthetic, nonfunctional item to earn a spot in the Perimeter. How was a person to feel safe if a thing that important could just be thrown around and torn up by a professional hired specifically to protect it? What kind of order was that? If Mr. Sun could tear her jacket, then the embassy could confiscate her passport, and the bank manager could leave her credit card number on a scrap of paper on his desk, and what's to keep the whole world from falling into chaos? She doesn't go to much trouble to explain the Perimeter. "The square meter of space I take with me from country to country," she says and nudges her backpack, which she's tucked under the stool, with her foot. Everyone in the room chuckles or nods—each has his own movable bounty.

That afternoon, Gui was working late and she had gone to the dry cleaner in his place. She didn't know Mr. Sun or his meticulous ways. And so she yelled. He yelled back. She accused him of shoddy work. He accused her of lying about the rip. They kept upping the ante, until Mr. Sun muttered something about a spoiled American not knowing anything about his life, his children's lives. An inexplicable ball formed in her throat and she ran out with her torn coat. She sat in a café for twenty minutes, trying to decide what to do. But eventually she went back, stopping first at the Middle Eastern grocery store nearby. She apologized. She told Mr. Sun that she wasn't American and if her character had spoiled, it wasn't in the way he thought. She gave him *baghlava*. Mr. Sun's eyes clouded over. He said only, "Your clothes are my clothes." A sentiment made powerful by its gentleness, it would be familiar to Eastern ears, but the Dutch would struggle with it and quickly forget.

The crowd laughs gently, they send warm encouragements to the front, and she sits. She leaves out her teary bike ride home, her torn jacket draped over her handlebars. She had hoped Gui would hear the story and know why the ball grew in her throat, why it was vital that Mr. Sun accept her as one of his own, another person far from home, and not classify her as one of the comfortable locals who have never suffered. But Gui said, "Oh, Niloo, he's just an old man." Then he sent a large tip and made everything worse, because the *baghlava* and Mr. Sun's comment had made them like family, and Gui's gesture returned him to his role as their help.

A few hours later, the charged crowd whirrs and buzzes out of the squat, back to their private spaces—maybe some of them in that very building—and she lets their current carry her into the cool, watery Amsterdam night. The couple, the man with the scar and the woman with black curls, pass by Niloo and disappear into a brown café a few doors down, her arm wrapped around his waist as he smokes. Niloo notices in the streetlight that his scar is white, a creamy blotch traveling down his forehead past his brow, like milk dripping onto his face.

Agha Mam'mad stumbles out in broken sandals. "Are you okay, *khanom*?" The streetlights reflect off the canals and the starch of crafted beers hangs in the air. "This city," he says in Farsi, lighting a smoke and shaking his head as if seeing it for the first time, "it feels like the first page of a children's book . . . after the cookie house is found and everything is lit up and smelling like sugar" (he speaks with his hands), "before the black wind comes and the branches start clawing at your face."

He tells her that he arrived four years ago from Tehran, where he left his wife and two daughters. He was a professor there, but here, he is only a refugee. He hopes to find a job, to send for his family. Sometimes he cooks pomegranate stew in the communal kitchen of the squat. But mostly he likes to sit on the cushions and listen to stories from the other refugees, and to talk to activists who come to have fiery conversations late into the night. He tells her about a young man named Karim, who after ten years of illegal residence in Holland and several petitions for asylum, is homeless on most nights and wanders into Zakhmeh for the occasional meal. "And did you see Siavash? The arrogant boy with scars? He's spoiled, all his life American freedom. He's not trapped here. But he stays as a part of a human rights group. Right now, all their talk is the election."

"The election in Iran?" she says, still a little hazy from the joint.

"Where else?" Then he seems to remember the dangerous mood here in Holland, the fact that even in Europe he hasn't escaped hostility. He mutters into his hand, "Oh yes, well . . . fuck Wilders," as he breathes onto his icy fingers.

She giggles despite her best efforts. Thoughts tumble around in sequence, disappearing and reappearing and making her dizzy. Mam'mad takes her hand and pats it like he's shaping cutlet batter. He examines her face and says, "Don't worry, *khanom*. Trying to hold on to a thought after two puffs of hashish is like drifting away on a boat while trying to grab for one specific twig onshore. Impossible."

Later she will find that Mam'mad, when high, is all about the similes. But he's right about the boat and the twig—what was she about to say? Out of nowhere she blurts, "You have nice teeth." She is remembering her own Baba, who is this man's age and for whom a person's teeth contain every clue. "I see you don't grind."

He releases a phlegmy coughing chuckle, his eyes and mouth bracketed by three distinct sets of parentheses. Soon she will learn that when Mam'mad fakes a smile, the eye brackets go missing while the mouth ones remain, unnerving since she will come to watch for them. "Odd little lady in a big jetpack," he hums. "You must visit me tomorrow. I'll make you a good lunch with *torshi*." Persian pickles.

She breaks into unexpected laughter again. "Group three," she croons to herself. Mam'mad stares, the brackets around his eyes deepening as he awaits an explanation. She thinks, why not let him into this wonderland she inhabits all alone, inside her imagination, this ordered universe of charts and categories and comforting rules? If she could color-code the world, she would. It's how she discovered anthropology—at seventeen, she found herself always lingering in fast-food restaurants and cafés, her stillness trance-like, watching people come together and disband for hours. Their rituals enthralled her even then. Now, putting them in neat boxes is her favorite pastime and her casual taxonomies are flawless.

"I've figured out," she says to Mam'mad, "that Iranian exiles in the West can be divided into four *mutually-exclusive-collectively-exhaustive* groups." She counts on her fingers as she explains the concept of MECE. "You ready?"

"Go on, strange lady," says Mam'mad, sleepy eyes dancing. Somewhere in her notes, she still has her classification of exiled Persians. She lectures from memory, leaving out the more insulting details. But in her notebook, she's written it like this:

Group One: Money Persians. These took their money out before the fall of the shah. They settled mostly in California, mostly in real estate. They built Tehrangeles and seem unashamed of that, as they are unashamed of their blue velvet furniture and hefty indoor columns. Draped in gold and bathed in perfume, they do cleanses and flash about in packs, spilling out of their red Mercedeses, designer labels blazing off their bodies two or three at a time. When Money Persians have Western guests, they serve beluga caviar or honey pastries, fresh pistachios, champagne.

"The worst ones," says Mam'mad. "These idiots give us all a bad name!"

Of group two—the best one—she allows her new friend to know every detail.

Group Two: Academic Persians. Scattered in small colleges and univer-

sity towns, they read fat, dusty books. If they didn't get out before the revolution, they don't have much money and seem fine with that. Money Persians embarrass them. They've fled westward because they value their freedom to think and create, to study what they like. They shiver with political fury and listen to music from chic sixties Tehran and read The Blind Owl *and pressure their children to attend Harvard. Every young Persian thinks his parents fall in group two, even if their house has Corinthian columns or smells like fried cilantro. To American guests, they serve Baked Lays with cucumber-yogurt dip.*

"I'm in this one, no?" says Mam'mad. "Or is group three for the serious scholars?"

She edits group three as much as possible through the mist and fog in her brain, but becomes distracted by the struggle to remember the exact wording.

Group Three: Fresh-off-the-boat Persians. They may have been here for twenty years but the musk of the village follows them. They read the Koran. Their houses smell like ghormeh sabzi, *or at least fried cilantro. Often their teeth need work—this isn't an issue of class, but of habit. Even rich villagers are villagers. They hang* ghilim *rugs bearing Nastaliq script on the walls. If they come into unexpected money, they sink it into fake watches or visit the Grand Canyon. They hope their children will try for good universities, but secretly wish them to stay close to home. They know what Harvard is, but not Yale. They don't burn with need for it, as do groups one and two. They pickle and store things (garlic, shallots, onions) in big jars in the garage next to the derelict car and try to serve it to Western guests wearing tight smiles, who sample one item.*

"*Ei vai*, you're putting me in with these bastards because of one mention of pickle?" Mam'mad teases. "Which group is for tiny, stonehearted backpack ladies?"

To which group does she belong? she wonders. Maybe she's just American now. She hurries through group four because Mam'mad has spent all night surrounded by its members and she doesn't want to bore him. He seems to her now like an amalgam of Baba, Uncle Ali, and all the Ardestooni men she has known.

Group Four: Artists and Activist Persians. Fiery, wandering, no ambition beyond tipping the world off its axis. They drink a lot, smoke a lot, rant against religion, have imaginative sex with strangers. Sometimes they wander to California or New York and play the Arab character on a cheap daytime soap or telenovela while they finish their book of stories or their album. They write letters to poets currently in residence at Evin prison. They grow old in white ponytails and floral skirts that hint at Northern Iran, but are actually purchased from farmer's markets in Fort Greene or Camden Town or the Jordaan. They read the news and can really dance. To guests, they serve beers, mixed nuts, and whatever hasn't gone off in the fridge, as local natives would.

"Ahh, and our squatting friends," says Mam'mad, nodding at a spot beyond her head, as if he can see her list floating there. "Khanom Scientist, I think people aren't so straightforward . . . but I still want to offer you lunch and pickles."

"Okay," she says, momentarily forgetting her Persian manners. Then, unable to hide her alarm in her hazy state, "Oh, God, should I have refused three times?"

"We're living by Dutch rules now," he says. Every time Mam'mad mentions the Dutch, he seems to be struggling not to tell someone to go fuck himself. "My daughters are far away. We'll eat and you'll tell me stories of your family."

"That sounds nice," she says and starts the long walk home.

What stories of the Hamidis can she tell Mam'mad? They are like all the other families, separated by miles and years and changing habits. When Niloo was growing up in Oklahoma, her mother served her classmates chips with creamy yogurt dip, but also mixed nuts, leftover banana bread, Persian pickles with delicious bites of stewed lamb—there's no classifying Pari Hamidi. Maybe Niloo will tell Mam'mad about Ardestoon, or about her marriage and career, the things she has accomplished in the West. Maybe she'll talk of that night at Jesus House, the hiccup between two lives. Maybe her stories will discourage him from bringing his own daughters here, because, if he does, they might morph into Western women and begin to baffle him.

She might tell him secrets from her night walks. That nothing feels finished enough, ever. That she left something crucial back in Isfahan and can't remember what it is. That sometimes she envies her mother's religious fervor, the freedom to relinquish control. She wants to say that she's exhausted. That, despite her father's most sacred belief, she isn't brilliant or worldly or elegant. She's just a village girl, a twiggy refugee kid under a boulder of a pack, finally turned American. Hearty and iron-legged, she doesn't rely on fragile genetic adornments like talent or brains. The thing she has is stamina; and if she calmed down, as everyone advises her to do, she would be nothing. But don't mistake Niloo for another frantic exile, because she begins healing before she's hit the ground and she knows the rules now. Mostly she wants to say that she tries so hard. She tries harder than anyone. She tries when she should be sleeping and loving and making memories and mistakes and friends, when she should be learning how to turn the gears without so much straining.

Or maybe she'll talk about work instead, her research on early primate families, the procuring and sharing of food. Safe topics, millennia in the past. Sometimes she daydreams of showing her published papers to her cousins in Ardestoon, climbing the nearby mountain together, digging for artifacts.

Shuffling quickly along the canal, head weighed down with thoughts of Mam'mad and the squat, she tries to plan her morning, but her mind wanders. Baba would have relished tonight's poetry reading. But if he were to relocate to Europe, as he's hinted wishing to do, he'd fall squarely into group three. He would drive a taxi and lose his medical credentials. He would wither and every ounce of his childish joy would drain out of him, leaving his cheeks slack. He would die cracking sunflower seeds in a parked cab, atop a fading Nain seat cover, coarsely woven in reds and blues, rolling his prayer beads under his thumb and remembering.

The absolute value of the universe would plummet, leaving every seaside and orchard and city center, every morsel and melody, inexplicably blander.

Someone behind her rings a bike bell, but Niloo doesn't turn. She thinks, *I'll tell Mam'mad about the time Baba came to Oklahoma.* The bike bell rings again. For the past twenty years, whether in New Haven or New York or Amsterdam, anyone who passes Niloofar Hamidi on her long night walks slows to look, having seen, for a moment, only a backpack with legs.

Twenty minutes later, as Prinsengracht curves eastward and her head clears, she begins to wonder about Mam'mad's legal situation. How did he come to live here? She knows that the EU rules require refugees to seek asylum from the first member country on whose soil they land. In the case of fleeing refugees, or ones without connections, that country is almost never the Netherlands, since it requires flying over water, an exit visa, an entry visa. The most desperate flee to Turkey and make their way into the EU by land. Or they try their luck in Greece or Cyprus. And yet many Iranian immigrants have settled here: some are knowledge workers; more have family to sponsor them. Money, a foreign degree, or a European partner doesn't hurt (Niloo, an American scholar, might figure in their numbers, but that seems like a lie). A man like Mam'mad, a professor, would have come to Amsterdam for a conference or a research trip or at the behest of a university. Then he would have blown through his visa limit, found a community, and requested asylum.

He wouldn't have bribed anyone, as Baba would if he were to come here. He wouldn't phone up nefarious friends in the drug trade to grease his path.

Turning her key in the door, she hears Gui move in the kitchen. He sits in the dark, eating muesli in his pajamas. Bent over his cereal bowl, legs extending far under the table, he looks exposed. At six-two, a foot above Niloo, he seems all the more vulnerable, like a collapsible hiking pole she might take on a dig and fold in half after each use. "Did you wait up?" she asks. He nods and extends an arm. She drops her backpack and curls into a ball on his lap. Sometimes she forgets how much bigger her husband is until she's wrapped up in his limbs like a nugget. The hashish fog is wearing off. "That fight was awful," she says. "I'm sorry for my part."

He watches as she stirs his muesli, picking out a walnut and a raisin. "You don't have to try so hard," he says. She looks up at him, puzzled, and searches his bowl for another walnut. He pulls her closer, kissing her head. "Some things can be easy. The grocery store, for instance."

The way he says it, it sounds very much like the truth. This is how he wins cases, she marvels.

But she doesn't tell him that she's proud. Instead, she talks about her lunch with Mam'mad. See? She has found a hobby, like he wanted—refugees.

"Did you go to that guitar-pick . . . poetry place?"

"Zakhmeh," she says into his neck. "Yep."

"Don't take on their problems, okay?" he says, all worried eyebrows and chewed-up lips. "Isn't there something more low stress? It was just poetry, right?"

"It's not work related," she says. "I've made a friend. Isn't that exactly what you were getting at?" He brushes sandy brown hair out of his eyes with a cupped palm, as if pulling a floppy strand through an invisible cylinder, a gesture whose origins Niloo has often wondered about—did he, as a child, watch his beloved mother pull out curlers? He stares at her with sad eyes. She puts on what she hopes is a playful tone. "And, by the way, I don't need adopting," she says. "You didn't find me on the side of a road selling peaches. We met at Yale."

He loosens his arms around her shoulders. "This is exactly what I'm talking about," he says. "You say shit like that and freak out over bank cards and you think you're fooling everyone with that glare, but, Chicken, you come off like the girl at the party acting cool while her skirt is tucked into her panties."

She laughs, open mouth full of walnuts, and wipes milk off her lips. Then, catching Gui's craving for something true, "I feel like our fights are getting so much worse. The things we say." He nods, resting his chin atop her head. He doesn't speak, so she whispers to his neck, "Can we not fight anymore?"

"Okay, no fighting," he says. A corner of the Zakhmeh flyer peeks out of Niloo's pocket. He pulls it out. "I was thinking, let's make a space where we put *our* important things. We could tape this to the fridge and go together next time."

She glances at the fridge, where Gui has taped her list of rules. "You want to listen to Persian poetry?" she asks, moved though she hopes he'll say no.

"Of course," he says. "If it's your thing, it's my thing."

She smiles, thinking of Mr. Sun, but she doesn't remind him. She shrugs and takes the flyer from him, crumples it in her fist. Later she will tuck it into one of the folders in her own private corner of the closet, where it will be safely hers. "This one is just for tonight though, and tonight's over. Next time."

She gets up and starts toward the bedroom. The temptation to tell Mam'mad about Baba's Oklahoma visit has passed. But having recalled the memory, she wants to sit with it for a while, to turn it over alone. In another life, Mam'mad might have been Baba's friend. She can imagine them matching wits, smoking hookah and cracking seeds, discussing literature and politics.

Gui takes her hand and pulls her back. "Okay, next time," he says. He kisses her face, chewing the fleshiest parts, a habit since their first date when he asked, *Can I bite your cheek?* He rubs her chin with one finger. "I'm glad you have a new friend."

The First Visit

Oklahoma City, 1993

No single event can awaken within us
a stranger totally unknown to us. To live
is to be slowly born.

—Antoine de Saint-Exupéry

Our first visit was in 1993. I believed Baba was coming to Oklahoma to stay. We drove to the airport around noon on a blistering Oklahoma Sunday. Maman allowed us to miss church for it and we took pleasure in putting on casual clothes, packing bottles of ice water. Kian brought an old Game Boy. The sun blazed through the windows and within five minutes we were sweat-stained and nauseated. Kian and I wore thrift store shorts and T-shirts with faded brand names; Maman wore jeans and a nice blouse from Iran. She was trying to strike a balance. Iranian women fret constantly over their looks, but she didn't want Baba to think she missed him.

She fired questions at us, oblivious to the answers. "Are you excited to see your Baba?" "Kian, do you have your poem?" "Niloo, I told you, no shorts. Do you want your Baba to think you've become some kind of American *dokhtare kharab*?"

Maman's biggest fear for me since the day I turned thirteen (a year earlier) was that I would become a *dokhtare kharab*, a "broken girl," which is the Iranian way of describing a sexually free person who happens to be female—she thought I was more prone to it than average, because of my shared DNA with Baba. The male version of the word, as in most cultures, is something along the lines of *playful*.

Kian nudged me in the ribs and started singing an annoying song he had made up that made Maman giggle. Sometimes she would tease him by humming his toddler revolution song. "The caged bird is heartsick of walls," she would croon in a baby lisp. Kian would sing the rest and they carried on their mother-son infatuation. I hated it. I didn't know to miss Baba in those moments.

Maybe because I was a daughter, or because I was *Baba's* daughter, Maman reserved all her austerity for me. She forbade me from wearing a drop of makeup and gave in to my demand to shave my legs only when she saw that my hairiness defied modesty and she could neither let me out looking like that nor force me to wear long pants in the stifling Oklahoma heat. Always crammed in tiny rooms with Maman and Kian, I craved the smallest privacy.

Sometime during our years as asylum seekers, I stopped playing children's games. I forgot books I had loved and lyrics to Farsi songs, and started to dream about having my own apartment in a big city. In Oklahoma, I made secret plans, borrowing college admissions guides from the public library, readying myself for my second escape—this sleepy flatland was no home to me, and it would be worth any hard work and indignity now if I could just find my own. The other children had never met someone from the Middle East, never considered dreams or demons other than their own, and they didn't invite me into their narrow universe. They didn't explain their song lyrics, the rules for dodgeball, or how to pronounce the many words I mangled. Left to entertain myself, I lived inside my imagination. Soon I decided that to find safety here and to re-create the sense of home, I needed two things: money and the air of being a *real* American (an elusive formula that brought me daily shame). In order to prepare for my excellent future in a big city, I lived off pita bread and egg whites, swam a thousand meters daily, and never stopped moisturizing my legs. I studied twelfth-grade calculus seven hours a day.

"He won't think I'm *kharab*," I said to Maman. "He's seen my grades."

"Grades have nothing to do with it," said Maman.

I scoffed. "Are you new to Baba? With enough As, I could go to school naked."

"Niloo!" She slammed her hands on the wheel. "Don't start." She took two breaths. "Please remember that, to your Baba, you will seem so changed. He might have a hard time. Just try to be the sweet Niloo and Kian I know are still in there."

I started having nightmares around the time we arrived in the first refugee hostel. The dreams changed over the years, but never disappeared, and I came to think that missing limbs and phantom stranglers and dying parents were simply the price of sleep. At fourteen, most of my nightmares involved my classmates exposing me for this or that. I was afraid they would find out that I had missed an entire decade of American music, that I was from that country that forces women into drabness, that I knew only about a quarter of their slang. I was afraid they'd find out I was afraid. My only antidote to the fear was math and science, concrete pursuits Baba had taught me to trust (a purer love of study didn't kick in till years later).

Some nights I dreamed about Baba kidnapping me and, in those dreams, his eyes were dead and I knew it was the other Baba, the opium Baba, the tooth-hunting Baba, and that I had to get away.

"Where will he sleep?" I asked, though we had been through this.

Our apartment was nothing remarkable as immigrant situations go, but to me it was a nightmare. Some time spent in typical pass-through countries, Italy and the United Arab Emirates, had depleted the funds. We had Maman's small income and a dark, two-bedroom apartment on the first floor of a two-story complex. At first, Maman and I shared a room. Then Kian and I. And soon, we would probably switch back. It depended on who she thought needed more privacy at the time, herself or Kian. Never me, because privacy was the sole missing ingredient between me and *dokhtare kharab*. She kept it from me like the accidental drop of egg yolk that might turn a bowl of fluffy meringue peaks into a flat, sloppy sugar soup.

We agreed that Baba would sleep in one bedroom with Kian, and I would share with Maman again. We also agreed that Maman's "friend," Nader, who had come from Kermanshah before the revolution, would not stop by during Baba's stay. On most nights, Nader would appear around six or seven and cook various delicious meats for us. He always had pungent things marinating and sloshing in clear bowls in the fridge—goopy red and yellow mixtures full of fleshy raw chunks that became exquisite after a quick bake or sauté or barbecue. Nader could stand shirtless in headphones, cigarette dangling from his lips, holding a skillet of broccoli and looking like a doofus, then flick his wrist and somehow land every single piece on its other side, not a spear burned. Sometimes he'd ask me to add a pinch of turmeric and when I did, he would wince. "A pinch, kiddo, a pinch!" As if *a pinch* means anything.

"Don't call me kiddo," I said, "and pinches aren't really a scientific measure."

I wished Nader would go away. I vaguely knew that Maman and Baba had divorced—Baba had been unwilling to leave his village, his respectable job, his roots, and his opium. After Maman fell into great danger in Iran, they had no choice but to go their separate ways. Besides, Baba had helped her escape, and if they had stayed married, how could he deny involvement during the hours of questioning that followed? I understood the situation, however begrudgingly. It wasn't loyalty to Baba that made me dislike this new man—Nader was just annoying.

On the phone, as I grew up, Baba always asked for stories and photos, especially photos. "Send a stack of the doubles. Anything you've taken, not just the special ones." And when we were too distracted, he would find excuses: a document he needed or a magazine he wished to read or a bottle of special American moisturizer. Maman made time to send these items, and so he would say as he gave her his lists, "Please include a stack of the kids' photos. Don't forget."

Eventually, when Maman became busier with two jobs and church and night school, when I started high school and swimming and more college prep, the only thing that would get us to the post office was requests for therapeutic socks, because we knew Baba wasn't lying about the dangerous varicose veins on his legs. We imagined him aging in that difficult country where these things aren't so freely available and people learn simply to suffer. So, every few weeks Baba would call. "Please send more of the special tight socks," he would say, then add, "Maybe throw in a stack of your doubles. Where was the last roll you shot? Is it a good story?"

It would be unfair to say that by fourteen, I had forgotten my Baba.

I thought of him often. But I stopped missing him and, before this trip was announced, I had stopped actively hoping that he would join us. It began to feel likely that he never would, and that my parents' promises of those first months out of Iran were mostly lies. I became a teenager. I worried about my future constantly. I was desperate to fall in love, and I was desperate to keep from falling in love, because I knew that I had to flee Oklahoma, as my mother had fled Iran.

Now, by some miracle Baba had secured a tourist visa to visit us, and I cradled the secret hope that he was joining us for good—Baba and I would have to scheme, of course, as in the old days when we snuck cream puffs into the house; Maman had said nothing of it. We arrived at Will Rogers World Airport a few minutes early, feeling awkward in our skins, in our haircuts and clothes. We waited at the terminal for him to disembark the plane from JFK Airport. As the passengers filed out, some of them fresh from a short trip, others ragged after long international flights, I felt a shiver in my leg. I wanted so much for every next passenger to be him. Each time I saw the shadow of a grown man turn the corner, or a familiar gait, or a person laden with bags, I was certain it was him and my right hand flew to my right ear. If there's a gesture more soothing than pulling on one's own earlobe, I have yet to find it, and in those first immigrant years this habit became a second tic for me—I had rid myself of the one in my neck shortly after our arrival. Maman took my hand and held it to her chest, and we continued to wait.

In the end, he surprised us, walking out last, with the flight attendants, smiling his big, hairy Cheshire grin as they handed him his four cigarette lighters and book of matches. "He's shorter," I whispered to Maman. She didn't hush me or tell me to watch my manners. She looked at Baba in a daze and said, "You're *taller.*"

When he saw us, he burst into an exhausted guffaw, laughing as he spread out his arms and tried to scoop up all three of us at once. It was an awkward motion, and passersby kept glancing at us, but there was no stopping it. Baba's joy was like a piece of luggage tumbling down a steep escalator. You don't try to stop a thing with that much mass and momentum. You get out of the way. He was laughing and crying, swiping at his eyes with a big hairy hand, making such a show. I don't remember my Baba having ever been so loud, so graceless. Red tufts burst from his shirt, which was unbuttoned to his chest. His hair was a mess, and now that I was taller, I could see the spot of bald in the back, among the baby-soft wisps that were still cut in a long, youthful style.

"Is this my Niloo?" he whispered, putting a sweaty palm to my cheek. Somehow my words flew away and I stood there dumbly, not saying hello, not saying *it's good to see you, Babajoon*, as I had practiced. When he touched my cheek, I wanted to jump back, not because of the wetness of his hand but out of some forgotten instinct, an old fear. But I smiled. He said, "Niloo *khanom*, you're so tall." He looked at me for a long time and when I tried to cut the silence by saying hello, he burst out again, "Oh, you have your incisors back! Let me see." He was about to put a finger in my mouth but I recoiled. My expression must have revealed my horror because his eyes darted to his shoes, he pulled back his hand, and he said, "You're very grown-up, Niloo *joon*." He sounded hurt, but I told myself that I had my boundaries, and I had no interest in overhearing nighttime whispers about how I need orthodontics or how I should have my wisdom teeth extracted early. No. I was fourteen. I wanted both of them to leave my body to me.

Baba turned to Maman. "*Salam*, Pari *joon*," he said, his voice kind and low, as if greeting a fellow mourner at a funeral. They hugged silently as Kian and I shifted our weight, fiddled with our backpacks, pulled strings from our fraying shorts. Baba shook Kian's hand, a proud half smile frozen on his face, and we walked to the car.

Without thinking, Baba went to the driver's seat, and then there was an awkward moment when they switched. "My turn to sit in front," said Kian.

"Your Baba is sitting in front," said Maman, her voice flat and stripped of all emotion so expertly you'd think she were corralling children onto a bus.

"I'll sit with Niloo in the back," said Baba. At first I was uneasy. So, to cut the tension, I asked about Uncle Ali—how was he? Did he have a girlfriend? Did he ask about me? Did he know that I have front teeth now? Baba laughed. "He misses you very much," he said. "And he's seen all your photos. I made sure he saw."

The rest of the way home, he asked me questions. About school, about my teeth, my favorite subjects, how much science I had learned. I was happy to drone on about science, since it was safe and concrete. "Pari." Baba looked up at Maman in the middle of my summary of igneous rocks. "Why does Niloo have an accent?"

"I don't have an accent!" I shot back, because again they were discussing details of me as if I were a defective blender.

"Do you speak Farsi with them?" he asked her.

"Yes, we speak Farsi," she said, "but they speak English all day at school."

He grunted and looked at me, his childlike grin breaking out again like a fast-moving rash. "Do you read poetry?" he asked. I shrugged. He began talking about the importance of poetry, about all the hidden meanings of his favorite poems. As he spoke, he sometimes touched my arm or my shoulder or my cheek, as if I were a piece of silk he was sure he was going to buy. Once, he pulled me to him and gave me a hug that lasted almost a minute, patting my back until I had to push on his chest and free myself. He didn't seem to mind. He blathered on and on, and I thought, did he always talk this much?

Halfway through his speech, which was animated and fiery, he rested a hand on my knee. I swept it away with a swift motion, like batting away a spider. He gasped, but he didn't say anything. I'm sure he took it as some kind of weak and misguided fear of men that I must be developing, which he would discuss with Maman later. "Why are you making her this way?" he would say. "Is it your church?"

Despite my fading memories, I remembered that Baba was a hugger, a kisser, a patter of backs and squeezer of cheeks. But no man had hugged or kissed me in more than five years. The most affection I got from Nader was an occasional high five. Now, Baba squirmed on the sweaty plastic seat beside me, tucking his hands in his lap, projecting his distress—something invisible seemed to be slipping from his grasp in dramatic fashion, and my only clues to his private struggle during that forty-minute car ride were his clenched jaw and his pale knuckles pressing into the seat cushion. He looked straight ahead, hungrily chewing his mustache, as if trying to calculate his real daughter's coordinates. He looked like a man who, given a modicum of magic, would travel through time and take back those six years apart, and the careless tooth extraction before that, and whatever else may have caused his daughter to swipe away his hand. I was old enough to see the pain in Baba's eyes, and if the moment hadn't passed so quickly, I would have said that it wasn't him, that I just needed air-conditioning and some water and a quiet moment alone.

But I didn't say anything to assuage his sadness. There are creatures a person can see at thirty to which she has no access at fourteen. In youth, she can see only the end of the creature's tail or the line of its back as it passes in the dark. I know now that Baba wanted to pick me up and wave me around like he used to do, to squeeze my face and check my teeth. I barely said hello, arms crossed over my T-shirt. All I wanted at that age was to disappear, but this stocky red-mustachioed man had showed up ready to experience America loudly. Over those weeks, he ate ice cream twice a day and counted the price of everything by the number of root canals it took to earn it, and his addictions endangered us more than once. We took him for Mexican food; he took one bite of guacamole and said, "Is taste like Nivea cream." He asked me if I had learned to hold a cigarette like a lady, and he offered pistachios to the plumber.

At home, Baba looked around and nodded at the couch, grunting under his breath. "I'll sleep here," he said. "No need to trouble yourselves." The apartment contained no notable signs of Nader, but it was tiny, with a half kitchen jutting into the living room and no dining room or foyer. The shared space consisted simply of a couch pushed up against a small window, a round Turkish coffee table, a television on a chipped cabinet with the glass missing, and two metal chairs with thin green cushions. All of this sat atop a horrid blue carpet that came with the apartment. The kitchen, though, was fully stocked with knives and woks and pots of many sizes because of stupid Nader and his obsession with frying and sautéing and marinating everything, always wearing his stupid headphones. A part of me wished he would show up here all shirtless and chain-smoking and blasting U2, so Baba could tell him he was a doofus and throw him out. Imagining that scene made me giggle and when Baba whipped around at the smallest happy sound, I fixed my face into a frown again.

He placed his suitcase beside the couch and did a quarter turn, first one way, then the next. Then he turned back to Maman, and said in a voice that didn't sound casual even to me, "Pari *joon*, can I use your phone?"

Maman stood behind the counter in the open kitchen, piling homemade cream puffs on a plate. "Why?" she said. A look of alarm passed over her face as she spoke. "Do you want to call Iran? It's late there."

"No," he said, rummaging through his pocket. He stared at a scrap of paper for a moment and plunged his hand back into his pocket.

"Oh no, no, no, Bahman," said Maman, dropping a teaspoon and bursting into the living area. She spoke in a loud whisper, pushing the words out as if through a gap in her front teeth. "You won't call any friends here. No friends, do you hear me? How did you even find someone?" He started to speak, but Maman interrupted. "That's the end of it. No socializing." She stormed back into the kitchen and started rewrapping the cream puffs as if she were punishing him with no dessert. Her fingers shook as she worked, cream splattering, her pretty blouse staining. "We just got our green cards," she muttered. "How can you be so foolish?"

Everything seemed weary and intense with Baba in the room. Even the harsh light through our single window drained me, though I had felt it and sat in it and used it to warm my legs every day for years. Sometimes in our earliest days, I used to sneak out of bed when Kian and Maman were asleep and stick my bare stomach against the glass. The heat was such a luxury. I pretended I was on a tropical island.

"Calm down, Pari *joon*. Everything is fine," said Baba. "No need to put those away." He smiled wide at her, and at her pastries, with boyish contentment.

Maman stopped, her shoulders dropping, a small breath escaping. She looked at her hands, only now realizing that she was putting away the sweets she had spent all week baking. She unwrapped them again and placed them on the coffee table.

I didn't know what had happened between them, of course. I was young and had no idea whom he wanted to call and why. Now I know many Iranians flung far from home, strangers turned friends by virtue of a single common trait. In their adopted cities, exiled Iranians have no more caretakers or errand boys to deliver their illegal indulgences. They learn how to make friends fast.

Late that night, after Kian and Maman had gone to bed, I found Baba on the phone. He sat cross-legged in his undershirt and pajama bottoms atop a bright orange sleeping bag on a row of couch cushions that Maman had set up on the floor. Holding his glass of hot cardamom tea, his knees pulled in tight, he looked like a person sitting on a life raft, crouching low, trying to keep all his limbs in. He whispered in Farsi, and so my first thought was that he was making an expensive call to Iran against Maman's wishes.

But after some nodding and a few approving grunts, he said, his accent thickening to the village drawl, "It's an honor, *agha* . . . What luck to have friends in faraway places . . . No, don't speak of it. I'm your servant. Until tomorrow." With that he hung up. When he saw me watching, he called me to him. "Come here, *khanom* who looks like my daughter. Do you have any pictures to show your Baba? New ones?"

I shook my head. I didn't move toward him, a comfortable old fear returning.

He said, "How is that possible?" and he threw up his hand in that single dismissive gesture that our people share with Italians and Spanish and all fiery people—not the Dutch. "In Iran, girls your age are addicted to photos. Your cousins, do you remember them? Your cousins sit around your grandmother's living room and play with their Polaroid all afternoon. I brought some. Do you want to see?"

"I hate photos," I said. Recently my Iranian nose had started to bloom, and my skin was oily and dark. Worse, my front teeth had come in crooked. The idea of Baba suggesting orthodontics terrified me. So, I added, "It's vain and un-Christ-like."

"*Khak too saram*," he said, dirt on my head. His eyes bulged like the science class hamster after a long squeeze. "What the hell are you talking about, Niloo *joon*?"

I shrugged. He hauled himself off his haunches and turned on the television. Sitting beside the monitor, he changed the channels manually until he came to a trashy soap opera. He craned his neck toward Maman's bedroom and, hearing no sign of wakefulness, he said, "See that woman there?" He pointed to a heavily made up, coiffed, and sprayed woman in a halter top having an animated argument with a similarly adorned rival. I blushed at the sight of so much exposed American breast in Baba's presence. But he didn't seem to notice. He said, "I'd rather you grow up to be this useless to the universe than to become a religion pusher. If this disaster"—he pointed to the lady, his fleshy finger in her face—"is absolute zero in value, then Jesus and Allah pushers are deep in the negatives. All this god business will mess you up, Niloo *joon*, and then it will kill you. And you won't go anywhere after. Understand?"

I nodded, unaware of a profound confusion taking root. To Maman, Jesus was our family's only remaining identity. He was our way out of Iran and the reason Kian and I would go to top American universities. Little else had mattered in Iran, but she was even more fervent here. Having lost her profession, her volunteer work, and her community, exiled in remotest Oklahoma, she lived only for Him. Her every decision had to be seen to serve her God—even the choice to partner with Nader, who was peripherally tied to the church, and, if you ask me, mostly in it for the community outings and sanctioned access to multicultural divorcées.

"If you want to find God," said Baba as he turned off the TV, "study the natural sciences. Earth, the human body, anything you can touch, or see traces of, or watch through a microscope. Then, if your spirit is still hungry, memorize poetry. That's the only immortality available, Niloo *joon*, those voices from another time." I didn't argue since his instructions didn't seem to interfere with Maman's faith. I could easily satisfy them both, so why bother trying to figure out who was right? "Did you know that in the old days, every Persian scholar was expected to write in verse? Half of Avicenna's medical writings are in verse. There's so much mystery and beauty in the physical world without resorting to fantasy and god worship."

Rearranging himself on his raft, Baba said, "Go find some photos." He picked up the receiver again and dialed from a number in his cupped palm. I hadn't noticed the paper scrap nestled there. I asked whom he was calling, but he waved me away, muttering something about having to ask a hundred times for photos. I counted the number of digits he dialed—only seven. He wasn't calling Iran. He wasn't even calling Oklahoma City. Whoever his friend was, he was right here in our tiny suburb.

I went in search of my eighth-grade album. Maman had helped me cut photos of my friends and activities into fun shapes and paste them into a book along with colorful images from magazine ads (fruits and candies and things; no cosmetic or alcohol ads, even though they had the best graphics. I begged her to let me include a gorgeous lime wedge hanging off a dewy, crystalline vodka bottle. She scowled, horrified). My search must have taken a while, because when I returned to the living room, the strangest scene was unfolding. Baba was answering the front door in his pajamas, shaking hands with Nader.

I lingered in the hall, waiting for something to happen. Maman was in the deepest sleep. With two jobs and church, she slept every minute that didn't lead directly to someone's physical or spiritual feeding. Even if she had known that Nader and Baba were meeting now, she wouldn't have wanted to be woken. The poor don't get the luxury of fussing over awkwardness. They deal. So I stood in my turquoise socks, one foot on my thigh like an ostrich, my album tucked under my arm, waiting for someone to punch someone like in the movies.

"Hey, kiddo," Nader greeted me, slapping Baba's back as he entered. I held my breath. Surely Baba would explode at this rude gesture from a man a hundred years younger than him. "Been practicing?" He was looking at the foot on my thigh. Sometimes while at the stove, Nader taught me yoga moves from his travels. We would raise our arms and sun salute as we sautéed. Spatulas in our teeth, we would downward dog. I had good balance and flexibility and I liked practicing the poses on my own. But now, I dropped my foot and said, "Don't call me kiddo." I added, glaring, "Baba, this is Maman's friend, Nader."

Nader wasn't bothered. "Finally," he said, "I meet the famous Dr. Hamidi. It's an honor. Do you want a smoke, Doctor?"

"I don't smoke tobacco," said Baba coldly. Though he did; of course, he did.

"Neither do I," said Nader. Though he did too. The man smoked for breakfast; what was he talking about?

"Oh yes?" said Baba. "Fine then. Much obliged, Nader *joon*." He reached for his shirt. Why was he *joon*-ing Nader? They were out the door in three minutes, Nader's lanky body in a graying T-shirt gliding out after Baba's lumpier, buttoned-up one.

Hours later, the men returned, all backslaps and darting eyeballs and dancing fingers. They didn't come in, but circled the apartment and stood on the shared terrace out back, talking quietly. I watched them through the glass and once in a while caught a word here or there, nothing meaningful. What could they have to say to each other? I retrieved my picture album from the cushionless couch where I had left it, and I slipped out to the back. They didn't notice me, and so I lingered, thinking that if I was caught I could use the album as an excuse—*Oh this? I'm not spying. Just wanting some father-daughter time.*

An aside: Over the years in Amsterdam, I've studied Iranian fathers and daughters. Persian men belittle and abuse their wives, demanding total subservience. They insist on delectable suppers, sparkling floors, and clothes that smell of jasmine, all without fuss or complaint. Their mothers served them, after all, and they need it to survive, but they suffer an unconscious guilt over it. So, when chance gives them daughters, a fear sets in. What if someone treats their hatchling the way they've treated their wives? So, they sacrifice themselves to this precious creature. They become her practice field. They offer themselves as the ground holding her up, the shifting plates of their backs the terrain for her small feet. They teach their girls to be aggressive and cunning and to rule over them, to trick their fathers into buying presents, to bat their eyelashes and stomp on hearts, never to tell their own husbands "I love you" because that's giving up too much power. Forced to witness this spectacle, frustrated wives (having once been someone's muse and Machiavelli) spoil their sons, lavishing them with all the attention they lack from their husbands, teaching the next generation that a woman's love is delivered never in words, only through service. The result of all this is generation after generation of entitled boy-men and brick-fisted, manipulative women, a dynamic that may offend the civilized, but is sustainable and self-propagating.

My Baba didn't spoil me as other Babas did, but even he couldn't escape this twisted kind of father-daughter love that garroted our social world. We saw it everywhere and it snared us too—a little. So, I waited by the door, eavesdropping for ten minutes before announcing myself. They were talking about Maman, the story about Baba's last days in Tehran University when he would bring her berries and almonds from Ardestoon and hide them in her apartment with clues of their whereabouts, written entirely in verse. I knew this story.

"You were in love," said Nader. "It's a blessing."

Baba scoffed. "Blessing," he said. "A pretentious word. I was just lucky, like you. And I was open to it. In my gut, I was open to the thing." Nader nodded; he never looked uncomfortable. Baba shrugged. "You're a churchgoing man. You can call things blessings if you want. But I think everything is random, and I'm right."

"You should come to church with us," said Nader, taking three short drags of his cigarette. "I'll make ribs after. We can have it with real rice, no sticky garbage."

"Thank you," said Baba. Nothing more. They puffed in silence for a long while. Then Baba peered into the dark. "I imagine things aren't so lonesome here," he said, his back bent, his gaze on his shoe, "when you're in a church."

Nader nodded. "That's true," he said, "for the kids too."

Baba scoffed, his voice straining. "But they've forgotten their home. I tried to talk about Ardestoon. No interest. And Niloo's becoming a damn ascetic. She says she's given up ice cream; did you know this?" I could see the annoyance in Baba's eyes. As a child, I had seen him become violent, but the monster was so deeply buried now—what would cause it to emerge? Not Nader. Nader wasn't enough.

"Is the wedding soon?" asked Nader, leaning over the fence that separated the shared terrace from a small grassy area. A wave crested in my stomach. What *wedding soon*? Whose wedding? One of Baba's sisters? My beloved Uncle Ali?

Baba shrugged. His voice was now gravelly and low; I struggled to hear. "It's just talk," he said. "She's a simple woman, a villager; I'd almost rather hire her to do some light work. I don't know what I'm saying. I'm sorry. I don't want to upset Pari."

"Pari is fine, Agha Doctor," said Nader. "She's complicated. An iron cage around that heart. A fortress. She's impossible to hurt."

"Impossible?" Baba smirked and shook his head at Nader, as if to say, *and you know Pari, do you?* He put out his cigarette. Seeing that he was about to turn toward the apartment, I jumped out, afraid of being caught spying.

"Baba, I brought pictures," I said, holding the album on top of my head.

"Oh, Niloo, my Niloo," he sang as he followed me inside. "What good instincts you have. I want to see every picture you've taken. Where are those cream puffs?" He turned and waved goodbye to Nader, who took a last puff, licked his teeth, and made his way around the apartment and back to his car.

The next night Baba disappeared. He didn't say where he was going and he didn't take much, just his leather satchel with his cash, IDs, and green prayer beads. ("For secular counting only," he often said. "Is tranquilizing, to count.") He left before Maman returned from her second job at the pharmacy. When she found him missing, she muttered to herself and ransacked his belongings. She opened his suitcase without the slightest hesitation or guilt. She simply unzipped it, tossed aside shirts, rummaged through underwear and socks. When her hand grazed an inexplicable lump, she took out one of Nader's steak knives and she punctured the lining of his expensive suitcase as if it were the plastic around an English cucumber. In those days, there were no airport scans of suitcases and manual searches were random and never took into account the fact that a crafty bon vivant with money and connections might have false linings sewn in. "Shameless, lying dog," she whispered as she pulled out the cotton-wrapped cans of Caspian caviar, the boxes of homemade sesame brittle, the used pipes with that dangerous pungent smell.

For hours she raged. When Baba returned at six in the morning, she was still awake, waiting in a kitchen chair, breaking off split ends with her fingernails, her precious sleep sacrificed to the promise of releasing her fury on his gingery gray head the instant his wandering foot touched her property.

She knew where he had gone. And he didn't try to deny it—he had found an Iranian exile with a *manghal* and a willingness to trade hits for cash. He had gone to this new friend's home, sat at his *sofreh* and reclined on his floor pillows, smoked and eaten and drunk with him, and offered his family a "gift" of pistachios or fruit leather or caviar from home. The family had demurred, practicing the Iranian art of *tarof*, refusing the gift until it was offered thrice. Finally they had accepted it, knowing all along how many fifty-dollar bills would be tucked inside.

It seemed they had even given him a place to sleep it off, because Baba looked unchanged to me—only tired. My parents fought for hours. There's hardly any point in recounting the details. Maman felt used. He had taken advantage of her kindness again, and he had endangered his own children's future—what about our green cards? What about the impression he was making on his daughter, who was already showing signs of wantonness?

By the time the hot Oklahoma sun had peaked, Baba was tossed out of our home. He moved into the Red Carpet Motel, a dingy, musty place with dark rooms arranged in a horseshoe pattern around a cratered parking lot. I insisted on accompanying Maman to drop him off. I never admitted my fear that he would leave and return to Iran, maybe stopping to wave goodbye to us through a window. Kian came too, but he stayed in the car with Maman while I helped Baba carry his bags into the room. The bed was on wheels, a thin white sheet covering the mattress and a single pillow. The sight of a Cheetos bag and tissues left in the trashcan by the last resident (or a careless maid) saddened me and I turned to go, afraid my feelings would spill out. Baba exhaled loudly and kissed me goodbye. "Go, Niloo *joon*, we don't want to make her madder."

And so began two weeks of Baba trying to atone for his bad behavior by taking us on exciting American outings. Eight of those days were at a Western-themed water park called White Water Bay, a strange amalgam of hackneyed Americana, exploitative Cherokee kitsch, waterslides, surf motifs, and overpriced Tex-Mex. It was unclear whether the schizophrenic park thought it was in Oklahoma, Montana, California, or (to my bafflement even back then) someplace near a rain forest.

Baba discovered the park while watching television in his motel room that first night. I knew the commercial, a frenzy of water splashing at the camera lens, hard-bodied twenty-year-olds chugging diet sodas and tackling each other, and a neurostimulant of a song by the Surfaris that was basically some cackling and the word *wipeout* howled over and over in an echo chamber.

The first time Maman dropped us off in front of the ticket station, I just wanted the day to be done. Many of my middle school classmates hung out at this water park. And here I was, after years of trying to seem American, arriving with my mustachioed father, his great cask of a belly blanketed in ginger fur, his neon Persian script trunks, a cigarette barely hanging on to his lips. He was a spectacle just stepping out of the car, even before he bellowed in the ticket line, in broken English, "This! Oh watery paradise! Let us find proper verse for this day!"

"Let's not," I said in a threatening whisper. "Baba, stop it! I'm serious."

"Stop what?" he said in loud Farsi, exhaling a long tendril of smoke.

"No more Farsi," I said. "And do you have to talk so loud?"

Kian didn't seem to care. "Can we go on the big slide first?"

"See, Niloo *joon*? Kian has it right," said Baba, taking the longest drag and flicking his cigarette right into the next line. He had switched back to Farsi. "We live for us. Not for the watchers. Be free now that you're in a free country." He paid for our tickets with a wad of cash roughly the girth of two *Rubaiyat*s, and ignored the glare of the ticket taker as he lit another cigarette. On the way in, I'm pretty sure he gave one to a loitering teenager.

A few hours into the day, Baba, who is light-skinned and ginger, started to burn. He stood by our lounge chairs for ten minutes, rubbing lotion into his arms and legs with great care, leaving a white residue all over his body "for added protection." Before I could rush off, he begged me to do his back. I wanted so much to run away, but his skin was flushed, even his knees a few shades redder. I hurried to lotion his back, looking around for classmates, but the sunscreen wouldn't absorb. The thick layer of hair on Baba's back was making it foam. "I'm done," I said, and ran away to join Kian in the rapids, leaving Baba to fill his time alone.

Once or twice throughout the day, I spotted him ambling through the park, full of wonder in his straw hat and tangerine trunks.

Sometime later, Kian and I wandered to the Acapulco Cliff Dive, a monstrosity of a slide shaped much like a stretching basilisk, with a short initial drop, then a long, steep free fall that flattened out again near the end. When we arrived at the bottom of the ride, an athletic college boy was coming off the bottom, shaking and in turns swearing and cackling to himself.

"Wanna go on?" Kian asked, glancing at me quickly, then away again. I could tell he hoped he wouldn't have to try this.

"I'm not getting in that line for a dumb slide," I said, to spare him.

So we stood there and watched people barrel down. Two swim-team types later, a familiar shape took form at the top of the slide, which was so high the figures atop it were reduced to specks, recognizable only by the color of their hats or T-shirts. But something about the gait of the person laboring to maneuver his bulbous body, basted in white, into starting position caught both of us unprepared. Kian looked at me, his brown eyes, already round as coins, widening. Then, before we could exchange two words, his body came thumping and slapping down, as he screamed in ecstasy and abandon and fear "Oh great god" again and again in Farsi.

He waved at us as he picked himself up from the landing pool. Then, striding past us as if we were ungrateful traitors and not his impressionable adolescent offspring, he said, "That slide is like a shot of liquor from a Rashti bathtub!" He pounded his gleaming lotion-white chest and strode off to get in line again.

The water park transported him, maybe in a way similar to his opium.

For weeks Baba enjoyed American life in deafening fashion, sliding down the Cliff Dive and eating too much ice cream, and going to visit his new "friends" somewhere we weren't allowed to know. I'm glad now that he enjoyed it, because he never got another American visa. He got kicked out of the park twice for smoking in restricted areas and for giving out cigarettes to his "staff" of wayward boys, teenagers who fetched his candy and stood in lines for him in return for the smokes. (I spent a lot of time hiding with a book in the changing rooms.) After each eviction, he got back in by bribing the management from his gargantuan bundle of cash.

And so it went, in the sticky heat, until the afternoon I walked from a church camp meeting to the Red Carpet Motel, thinking I would surprise him.

When I knocked, the door gave way. It had been closed hastily and hadn't clicked shut. So I went in, cheerfully calling, "Babajoon, I'm here." He had been with us for weeks, and I knew in the privacy of my heart that he would stay for good. Each time he joked with Maman, I grew more convinced. Being around him was becoming easier too, and I was forgetting to fear for my teeth.

The room was dark, though it was midday. The window was sealed shut and sodden towels covered all the cracks. The room smelled so awful, I had to breathe into my hand. The bed and the floor beside it were covered in photographs—his childhood with his mother in old village garb, his first days at Tehran University, black-and-whites of relatives from decades ago, a picnic in an orchard, then with Maman in Ardestoon in their early marriage, the family at the dinner table in our house in Isfahan, me and Kian as babies, and even some Oklahoma photos he had obviously stolen from my album. I ran a hand through them, looking for recent photos of Uncle Ali, but found none of Baba's current life. I didn't hear any noises from the bathroom and, though to an adult the scene would have been transparent, I just thought he had gone out to get some ice cream. He was obsessed with the astonishing array of American ice cream flavors—butter (butter!) pecan and rum (rum!) raisin and cappuccino chunky chocolate.

I unlatched the window, gathered the wet towels, and went to the bathroom, thinking I would discard them in the tub. I pushed open the bathroom door, and he was there, on the closed toilet lid. He wasn't sitting exactly, but slumped, his familiar white undershirt and pajama pants soaked in sweat. His knees were far apart, his hands hanging over them, twitching now and then, his head between his legs so that his silky youthful hair clung to his forearms, like moss against a rock.

He must have sensed me there, because he tried to raise his head. But it lay heavily by his thigh. I heard several deep breaths, efforts at breath. I said, "Baba," and he finally managed it. He lifted his gaze and studied me, as one might study a stranger. I waited for him to smile, to say *hello, Niloo*, but his stare was so long, so dark and terrible, so empty of reason and memory, but somehow not devoid of feeling. Though he didn't believe in heaven or hell or god or demons, wherever Baba was, it was otherworldly. Behind his glare was something raw and unprocessed, animal. Not hate exactly, though people who hate often have that look. It was terror.

After a swallow, he whispered something, in slow croaking syllables. But a gale of other sounds overpowered his words. The trickle of water in the tub, this sweaty stranger's pained breath, the screaming construction outside; these sounds rushed my ears instead. He reached for a box of tissues but his hand trembled around it, near it, over it. Then he looked at me and asked for it, "Niloo *joon* . . . tissues." But I couldn't. He tried to hold on to a towel rod, his hand slipping twice, but I didn't rush to help him. This was the man who, not so long ago, had carried me on his shoulders, whose fleshy back had been the ground.

All I could think to do was to run away, leaving him there to recover or not.

The next day, as he gathered his bags for the airport and explained to Kian and me that his return flight had always been arranged for today (hadn't he told us before? he was sure he had), I didn't argue. He said, "Sweet Niloo, you know I can't stay forever." I hated him, not just for this, but because he had forgotten the previous night, my presence in the motel room. And though this was the first time he confessed breaking his promise to me ("I can't stay forever"), I already knew. It was obvious in that motel bathroom that he had chosen to live away from me, that there was something he loved more: not poetry or medicine or family, but oblivion.

I often wondered how pleasurable it could be, and growing up, I asked Maman to describe his delerium to me. She said a few words about the bliss of it, the feeling of complete cohesion with the universe, but mostly she talked about the agony of withdrawal, the sweating, vomiting, and chattering teeth. She talked about her two attempts to cure him, locking him in the house for weeks, feeding and bathing him, bringing him music and books. The first time, he snuck out. The second time, he was so desperate for a *manghal*, so consumed by this creature need to be released, to chew off his ties and go hunt for it, that he chased her to the shallow end of our empty pool and beat her with a garden hose until she gave him the keys.

Though I've seen Baba three more times since Oklahoma, I can't imagine how he lives now. Do his days look like mine, reading trade journals at his desk, stopping at the bakery and cobbler on the way home? Or does he spend his days under a leafy canopy in Ardestoon? Does he lie to his new wife? Does she watch for that moment when her clever husband might transform into something beastly? Nowadays in Amsterdam, a first puff of weed or hashish carries me to that motel with him, but I don't dare try opium. My work offers me oblivion. Often I wonder, what is this urge to set off alone toward some imagined home? Have I inherited it? It must be the way the wanderer endures, a survival instinct from our earliest days. I try to picture it in aggregate—every day across the world, how many wretched travelers crouch in grimy bathrooms, searching for a way to explain that they can't stay?

Every person has a dozen hidden faces. My memories tell me that Baba's Oklahoma visit was a hedonist's manic dash through a permissive, bountiful country, a brief pleasure hunt. I was too young then to see the sadness in his eyes when I crossed my arms and looked away, when I didn't help him off that bathroom floor, and on our final day, when I hardly said goodbye. I see it now in photos, his arm perched awkwardly on my shoulder as I shifted my weight the other way.

House Arrest

JUNE 2009

Isfahan, Iran

In his jail cell, Bahman worried his counting beads and recited verse aloud, trying to regulate his breathing. *Live where you fear to live*, says Rumi, *be notorious*. It seemed to Bahman that Rumi respected the pleasure seekers, the ones who hunted for the next tumbling of the heart in the cracks between minutes. Those wakeful ones, sucking joy from the bone-dry day. Well, Bahman had tried, hadn't he? All his life he had tried, chasing every bliss to its fading. He had loved his wives, but never lingered, sedated and eroding, in a comatose marriage. Though he could have taken four wives at once, he knew enough to love only one. And now look. His mouth was full of cotton and his socks wet, his feet itchy and cold. He shouldn't have removed his shoes to sleep; this was jail, not his bedroom. In a dry corner, he twisted, loosening his belt, desperate to get comfortable under the scratchy blanket.

He spent only one night there. The next morning, his young lawyer arrived with a minibus full of character witnesses, holy men, and small-town dealmakers, Bahman's friends and patients and frequent guests. The boy strode in as if he might actually know what he was doing, and he brought a cream puff box full of cash too. Bahman's cash, but nonetheless, the boy did it. *What a good feeling,* he thought, *to be so well loved in one's community—or if not loved, needed in more than a peripheral way.* Each of these men was afraid of what a jailed Bahman might say of them, or where they would find a host as malleable or with pockets as deep.

Back in the judge's chambers, Bahman had the great honor of staging a public apology to the man who had sent a poor girl to jail for two days then back to a marriage she had suffered such fevers to escape, wailing and fibbing and throwing her body about. All night, lying awake, Bahman thought of that girl, imagining her wiping her eyes on her chador in a cell nearby. Were her socks wet too? He kept returning to the question of whether she had a lover. If she didn't, how irredeemable her life would seem. Any poet worth his ink would recommend suicide or the quick procurement of her life's great passion. But given the impossibility of summoning such passions when they're needed, then the blade, or bullet, or to be extra poetic, the cobra's venom. No, he decided, it's more natural for the man to kill himself.

Bahman reminded himself to ask his lawyer, after these proceedings, if he had found the girl's name. He would invite her to a meal and he would offer money. But first, he would write and mail a letter he had composed in his dreams, a plea to Niloo to figure out a way to get him out of this wretched place.

Last night, as he had drifted into a rare islet of unconsciousness, Bahman dreamed of the trip to see his children in 1993. Everything he had done had shamed his daughter, and her face was forever turned away. She seemed to have forgotten all their schemes, the two of them sneaking ice cream with spatulas aloft, her baby chicken, the way she shrieked and laughed her way through childhood.

He often wondered if Niloo had loved Nader like a father. What tragedy the life of that man; how early a story, a good story, can end. In all these years, Bahman hadn't found courage to ask if Pari had loved her companion in exile, if his death had shaken her heart from its proper place. He did ask Nader once what he felt for Pari, but Nader was a practical sort, not prone to fits of romance as the Hamidis were.

The courtroom was emptier than yesterday. His lawyer had secured an early time for him, before the throng. The judge said, "The accusation is very serious."

The lawyer pleaded with the judge to make things clear, as Bahman was needed in the community. "We must illuminate the doctor's fate."

Bahman had assumed that once the judge received his gift and his apology, all would be forgiven. He was about to opine on this, when a sharp sting in his forearm told him that his lawyer wanted him to choke on it, as they say. How did the boy acquire a *chogan* stick and balls in one night? Regardless, good for him. For the first time, Bahman thought to call him by his name, instead of "the boy." He whispered, "Yes, yes, I know, Agha Kamali. No need to get physical."

"This Green Movement business is outside the purview of this court," the judge was blathering on, "and I'll tell you, I thought it was only misguided young people indulging in nonsense. But you're fifty-five, my friend. And who knows, maybe a grandfather, from how much you know of your own adult children."

Even couched in politeness, it was an obvious tactic. The judge was goading him, making the apology sting. Well, Bahman was too old and tired to care about the bile that spewed from an old mullah's mouth. He would swallow his tongue and go home to a hot meal and a bath and a long smoke from his *manghal*.

"What we will do," said the cleric, touching the edge of his turban, "is pray and reflect on this. First the divorce and then the Green nonsense." The door of the judge's office was closed now, but the window let in a cool morning breeze. Someone tapped gently on the door. At first no one answered it, because the judge was speaking. "I do believe that this woman, your wife, has financial motives, as do all women, but this one seems exceptionally cunning. I feel sorry for you. But at the same time, we must be reasonable and unbiased." The door clicked open, a tentative hand on the other side unable to decide. The person listened, Bahman could sense a shifting weight behind the door, and after a moment he recognized the scent—fried onions and cleaning vinegar and crushed hyacinth.

"Please quickly. In, in," said the judge to the creeping door. Fatimeh, his second wife, popped her head in, smiling, eyes downcast, as she greeted them. She was wrapped in a dark headscarf, its polyester gloss obscuring the dull wheat-stalk print stamped all over the fabric. After she had announced herself, Shirin bounded in, grabbing Bahman by the waist so that there was no question about the identity of these two. "Aaah," said the judge. "The second Khanom Hamidi?"

She said, "Yes sir," like an obedient kitchen maid. She always spoke this way, deferential, though she saw everything, a dozen narratives and motivations and possibilities at once plain to her.

Bahman squeezed Shirin's chin. She had grown since he last saw her.

"Agha Kamali asked us here," said Fatimeh, nodding to Bahman's lawyer, her voice almost a whisper, though she was wise enough to include Shirin in her introduction. Bahman had forgotten how tiny Fatimeh was. Smaller than Sanaz, who was waif-thin and soft from avoiding food and sports, both of which might smudge her garish lipstick. Sanaz was from a flashy middle-class family, the kind who displayed their every drop of gold. His first wife, Pari, had been athletic and shapely, a university girl who could swing a tennis racket. But Fatimeh was a poor village woman, overfed but undernourished. Her teeth needed much work, but she had never let him repair them, her fear of physical pain eclipsing her reverence for truer sufferings, the ones in the heart and mind. This cost her much of Bahman's respect.

Bahman held Shirin's cold, wet hand. The child was plump, and her girlish, imploring behavior seemed much younger than her eight years. How he had missed chubby, delicious Shirin, though she shared none of his blood. It had been a year since he'd seen her, but Shirin was indeed Bahman's own daughter, sweet as her name, a child who loved music and dancing and food. They were each other's second choice, a beggar's version of Niloo and the toothy wandering poet, but they were a team, bonded by their heartbreak, their lack of physical graces, and their desperation for sugar. Also their need for an instant cure for every ache and desire.

Shirin drank up life the way Niloo had stopped doing.

"As I was saying," said the judge, smiling at Shirin, then clearing his throat hard. "For however long it takes to sort through the matter, the divorce and then this . . . accusation, Agha Bahman, you will remain in your home." Bahman blinked twice at *Agha Bahman*, forcing his body to keep the protests in; only yesterday, he had been *Dr. Hamidi*, his proper, hard-earned name. It was a lucky thing Sanaz wasn't here to enjoy this, as she was at home protecting her territory and feigning distress. Her brother-in-law and her lawyer, a squirrelly man barely taller than Fatimeh, would carry the verdict to her. The judge continued on, "We will place you under house arrest for a time. Your wife will remain in residence there also, for your comfort, to manage life as usual. No visitors except close family, since your friendships are much in question now. I'm thinking of your protection, because if the wrong sort are seen there . . ."

Bahman turned to Kamali, his lawyer, who was nodding, as if to say, *Yes, you don't have to point out the absurdity.* Bahman spoke anyway. "Your Honor," he said, "that woman's entire goal is to drive me to suicide. Surely there's an alternative—"

"*Agha*, I don't see one. Do you see one?" said the cleric.

Though Bahman saw several, it was obvious that the only acceptable answer was no. He said instead, "House arrest is such an expensive proposition."

"Yes, thank you for thinking of it," said the cleric. "We will have two cars in front, one in back," said the judge, "and we will settle the salary of the men with you later on." Then he dismissed everyone from his office, gathered his robes around his thighs, and headed to the samovar and the cream puffs.

But before he had taken two steps from his desk, Fatimeh's tiny voice pinged like a coin falling to the floor. "Your Honor, what about Bahman's illness?"

Was she crazy? A hammer in Bahman's chest pounded its way upward. Kamali too seemed unsure, though he shot a glance at the cream puffs as if to say, *We've paid the man. It makes sense to mention it . . . you're not the only addict in Iran.*

"*Agha*," Fatimeh went on, "Allah knows if there's anyone to take care of him in that house. I've studied nursing. His daughter near him would be a cure in itself."

In that moment, chubby Shirin took a loud breath and said, in her honey-glazed voice, "Are we going to live with Babajoon again?" The judge's cheek muscles seemed to collapse; Bahman imagined that this man too had a child-shaped wound.

And yet, the entire business was a mess—what a notion. He glared at his lawyer. Why had he invited her? Did Fatimeh need a place to stay? Had she used her entire marriage gift? She was a hard worker. Why hadn't she come to him in private?

"This illness," said the judge, standing between his desk and the tea table. "This is the sort of illness that becomes worse . . . with time . . . in the house?"

No one spoke. *Everyone in this room knows*, he thought, *and yet no one can say the words*. If they did, the game would end, and the outcome would have to be different. One must always protect the lie.

"Yes," said Bahman, "that sort of disease." He chafed to remind the judge of the basket of cash he now enjoyed, or better yet, the cream puffs. What kind of person takes a man's pastries and then makes him display all his dirty business?

"Agha Bahman," said the judge, shaking his head, again robbing him of his title, "would you like your former wife to be your caretaker during this time?"

Bahman didn't know how or why, but his lips uttered, "Yes," before he had completed a thought. Without Fatimeh, he realized, he wouldn't survive the withdrawal—or Sanaz's rule. Maybe she could even fill his *manghal* once in a while.

"Then we will need to grant a temporary marriage so she can live with you in the house," said the judge. "Is that a solution you would both accept?"

What diseased minds, these clerics, thought Bahman. This one clearly wanted to keep him bent over the ottoman for a few more minutes. He had come to court to escape one marriage and now he was shackled by both arms. Two wives; who could fathom such a nightmare?

"I'll draw up the agreements," said Kamali, rushing to accept. Sensible, because who knew if the judge would get a sudden itch and throw on a few more punishments? "The marriage can be set to dissolve in three months. We can renew if Your Honor needs more time to decide the two questions at hand, though we trust your speedy wisdom." He turned to Bahman. "No divorces or big payments at the end of it. Temporary marriage is very easy, Doctor, don't worry."

"Well, that's settled," said the judge, ambling to the tea table and stuffing the first pastry into his mouth. "Bring me whatever you draw up this afternoon." Then he waved to Shirin. "Goodbye, little *khanom*. Try not to end up in this place again."

That night Bahman slept at home, in a child's bedroom, the only room that didn't lock from the inside. Shirin had once lived in the room and it still smelled like her. Strangely, he didn't like this. Why should that be? he wondered. What callous instinct to love only the smell of your own natural child. He tried to sleep, but Sanaz had been ranting all night long, pitching the household on her head, as they say. Since finding out about Fatimeh's temporary marriage, she hadn't stopped crashing around the house like a shot mule. And she was brazen enough to call up all kinds of half-stewed ideas about feminism and marital justice (important topics he would've welcomed if her interest were genuine) that had seeped into her brain with zero critical filters or adjustments, via the satellite dish Bahman had bought for her. He tried to be kind. Her generation, born after 1979, had a jumbled, trivial access to the West, just enough to make themselves ridiculous. She didn't have what Niloo had.

The next morning, he kept himself shut up for as long as his body would allow, and when it became clear that no one would spare him the humiliation of appearing at a meal with his bizarre new family, he decided to go downstairs. With stiff muscles he pulled himself out of bed and tried to swallow, but his throat was sore. Everything seemed to be watering—his nose, his eyes. The dark days were coming. He had lived through them twice before. Right then Bahman promised that he would not fail this time. Maybe this was an opportunity, a chance to try to detox without making these poor women suffer the ravings of an ailing addict, as he had done in his youth. Silently he apologized to Pari, wherever she might be.

His mobile had been taken away, but the authorities had not bothered with the spotty Internet and television that he had installed in the house. Seeing this, Fatimeh had brought an old computer to his room and even set it up for him. God bless that woman, she was as dependable as his father's guard dog. Before going downstairs, he called his mother in Ardestoon from his computer, assuring her of his safety and asking for her to prepare a package for Niloo. Maybe spices. Yes, she had a delicious hand, didn't she? She would prefer spices to fabric or *ghilims* or tea.

In the sitting room, a deathly silence had filled the space between Fatimeh and Sanaz, who sat at opposite corners of the *sofreh*, each atop pillows they had brought to his house as young brides. Shirin sat on a cushion beside her mother, who kept her gaze down and made morsels of white cheese and *lavash* bread for the girl, allowing her to place the slices of cucumber. Fatimeh sweetened Shirin's tea just enough to satisfy her, one spoon only, despite her objections. Now and then Sanaz cleared her throat or muttered things like "troublesome people" while fixing her eyes on the pair. Bahman wished she could be more welcoming; Fatimeh and Shirin had been his family once. In his pajamas, he felt exposed. Then, as if to make it worse, one of the *pasdars* stepped in. Sanaz jumped up, holding a cup she had just finished pouring. Apparently, she had decided to befriend the guards. "Here's one for you, *agha*," she said. The man removed his shoes and tossed them on the pile in the foyer. He thanked her and took a sip. Sanaz poured two more glasses. "I can take them out. Don't trouble yourself. Sit. Sit." The man sat. Now Bahman's sacred space, his dinner *sofreh*, was occupied by two unwanted wives, a child he hadn't fathered, and a man whom he was paying to keep him captive. "Excellent," he bellowed as he plopped himself in his usual spot by the wall facing the front door. "A full *sofreh*."

The guard shifted on his haunches. "How are you feeling, Agha Doctor?" It seemed everyone knew now of Bahman's condition. Funny that they should judge, when so many of the men and women in this country were in the same position.

Bahman glared at him. "Have some cheese, son," he said. "Young people need protein and calcium." He had meant to be menacing, but as soon as he opened his mouth his body released a long yawn. Then another. It was starting; he knew these symptoms well, wasn't afraid of them, but now he had lost all authority in the room.

They sat for a while, the women pulling their hijabs tighter. Shirin questioned the young guard, delighting Bahman. She asked him where he had grown up, how he decided to be a guard of people's houses, if he played soccer, and if he wanted to play with her outside. The boy fidgeted and gulped his tea. At eight, Shirin already wore the gray school scarf. He couldn't play games with her in public as one would play with a child. "No," he said, avoiding her gaze. "Thank you."

"She's a child," said Bahman, not bothering to hide his disgust. "You have my permission if you want to play soccer. Shirin, take that scarf off now. We're inside the house, and you're six, for Allah's sake." The *Allah* he threw in for effect.

Shirin was about to object and demand credit for all her eight years, but Fatimeh, seeing that this lie would spare her child all kinds of discomforts around the house, put an arm around her daughter's body and tickled her until she cried and forgot about it. The guard looked distressed by this spectacle. He got up, refilled his cup from the samovar, and disappeared outside. Sanaz, who had been watching aghast, said, "What is wrong with you people? This is serious business."

"Oh, now you want to be serious," said Fatimeh, the bird-soft voice that had often sounded shrill in their days together now singsong and droll. "What are these silly games? Making crazy charges against your husband and putting us all in danger? This isn't a game, Sanaz *khanom*. There are bad things happening in this country. Who taught you to treat your family this way?"

"With respect," said Sanaz, her arm cradling her stomach, "you're not my family." Sanaz had this strange habit; her arm was always wrapped around her stomach, as if she thought her organs would spill out.

Two bites into breakfast and already the nausea was setting in; usually that came later for him. Bahman shot his wife a glance. She looked past him, busying herself with an obscene blonde strand. "I'm going back to bed," he said. He hadn't smoked for over fifty hours.

"I'll start dinner," said Fatimeh, watching intently as he pulled himself off his haunches and started toward the stairs. "Something nourishing to ease the transition." Ease the transition? Did she mean that she would lace it? *Oh please, cruel gods*, he prayed, *let the woman have a spice jar like the Ardestooni grandmothers*.

"I'm cooking dinner. This is my house," said Sanaz. In three years together, the woman had never made so much as a yogurt for Bahman.

They had standing orders at Hotel Koorosh and at Shole and the local *kabobi*. Or they ate frozen dishes that his mother and other Ardestooni women provided on weekend trips.

"Sanaz!" he snapped. But before he could chastise her further, the three bites of bread and the tea came rushing up his body. He doubled over and vomited on the stairs, slipping and catching himself on the railing, then collapsing to his knees.

The two women rushed to him, neither bothering to speak. Fatimeh, who despite her smallness was much stronger, put his arm around her neck and helped him upstairs, crooning, "It's fine. It will be easy; very easy." For three years he had taken great care to seem strong in front of Sanaz, and now she was stunned into silence. She cleaned up the mess ineptly but quietly. From the top of the staircase, he smelled the jasmine cleansing oil that she was flinging liberally all over the floor.

All afternoon he listened to the BBC and watched foreign news stations on the bedroom television. Fatimeh adjusted the box to face him when he lay on his side, the only position that didn't invite more nausea. He was grateful now for Sanaz's satellite dish, since the Green Movement news was so different on Iranian television than everywhere else. Every few hours, he heard Sanaz take the guards their meal, a chore that seemed to please her, though it was the family's obligation.

Given all his recent troubles, Bahman had fallen behind on the election unrest. There had been protests; he knew this already—friends and family were calling from everywhere to see if he was safe. Every night people gathered on roofs and chanted *Allah-o-akbar.* Every day they flooded the streets, setting bonfires and overturning vehicles, bins, any standing thing, screaming, "Where is my vote?" In universities and other bustling places, green wristbands adorned every young, Westernized wrist—those educated, secular young people who wanted freedom from

Islamic rule. Every news source was watching. Al Jazeera called it "the biggest unrest since the 1979 revolution."

Bahman remembered those early days, when the revolution was a movement of the people and not corrupted by religion and greed. All uprisings begin with hope. Many lose their way. Despite that, 1979 was a good year. It was the year Niloo arrived. This recent turmoil seemed very different to him, though he wasn't involved in either. Back then he was in the throes of love and first-time fatherhood; this time he was stuck in a bizarre purgatory of his own making.

The protests had been going on for some days now, and last week, before he closed his office for the night, three men had broken in. In Tehran, protestors had attacked shops and offices, banks and private vehicles. They had set things on fire. They seemed to have no purpose other than to express their rage. "Down with the dictator," they yelled in the afternoons, so that the din of their voices overpowered his own dental drill and he had to pull down the shades as he performed routine extractions for fear of a shaking hand. This revolution, it seemed, was a roaring fire with little kindling, much like a love affair that you know won't last and so you burn through it all the more feverishly. These young people weren't prepared to die for freedom and a new government as his generation had been. They had their satellite dishes and nose jobs and fancy labels. They had access to ski resorts and Western music. They had education and some semblance of the Internet. What was there to die for? A principle? Maybe the poor were suffering, but it's not the poor who make things happen. And the conscientious rich were only about their online-*bazi*.

The day the men had broken in, Bahman tried the usual pleasantries. But they were too hot and stimulated and wanted nothing to do with reason. So he offered money. This gave great offense; one of them turned over his receptionist's desk. He said firmly, "Friend, I'm with you about Mousavi, but this is a medical office, do you understand? You have nothing to gain by spoiling tooth-fixing stations." Then he pulled out a wad of cash, making them realize that he was offering much more than they had imagined—maybe this amount wasn't so insulting. In the end, expelling the three boys from his office cost less than a thousand American dollars.

Now the news seemed to say that things had gotten worse. People had died in protests all over the country. Journalists had been arrested and expelled. The Western media had been blamed. European exiles were gathering in front of embassies, universities, and in squares across the world, the possibility of change, of homecoming, drawing them together and igniting their sleeping passions for Iran.

He rolled over to spit into a trashcan beside his bed and changed the channel to an Iranian news station. Here was something new he had missed: a few days ago, a young woman, only four years younger than Niloo, had died in the streets in front of her pleading, weeping father and a crowd of others. Someone had shot amateur video of her death, and so the Iranian media had no choice but to address it; Neda Agha-Soltan's passing was already being watched the world over. According to the Iranian news, she was a protester. And her death was the responsibility of a novelist, Dr. Arash Hejazi, a literary man who Bahman knew had won awards and translated great books to Farsi. Were they saying he pulled the trigger?

He turned to the BBC, then CNN and Al Jazeera, trying to cobble together the real story. As he waited for new reports to begin, he called up Neda's video on his computer, leaving the still image on the screen while he searched for articles. Many of the websites were blocked. Some people had taken text from various reports and posted it on social media. The world was mourning Neda. For this moment in history, she was young Iran. Would anyone ever think of 2009 without remembering this poor child? Though he had no stomach for the violent and the gruesome (his poetic disposition taking over the minute he removed his scrubs), Bahman decided to watch the footage.

She wore jeans and a scarf. Blood was rushing over her face. He thought he saw her choke once or twice. Someone's hand was pressed over her chest wound, and her father was wailing, begging her to open her eyes. Bahman had to pause halfway because a strange panic was rising up in his own chest. Where was Niloo now? Where was Kian? He hadn't spoken to either of them for over a year.

Soon a new program began on the BBC. Once again, Iran's stolen election was the main topic. And now Neda too. The reporter said that, a few days earlier, during the massive Saturday protests, a Basiji had shot her in the chest, though she was only a bystander, not protesting. She was declared dead at Shariatie Hospital, but the state refused to allow mourning or a funeral for her. Any gathering would result in the arrest of her family. And yet, she had become an icon—the video of her death now a sick relic of this second revolution. The novelist Arash Hejazi was mentioned: he had tried to revive her; maybe that was his hand in the video, holding her chest.

Something hard rolled in Bahman's stomach. It was as though the oncoming withdrawal had been a toxic vapor, and now it was solidifying inside his body, strengthening and morphing into a hand poised to torture him. As it tickled his throat and scraped its long nails across his stomach lining, he watched the video again and again. He watched it four times, turning his computer this way and that, trying for a smoother picture. He vomited twice, ate some rock candy, then the nausea dug in again and an unsettling fog dulled his senses. He drank tea but didn't call on Fatimeh or Sanaz. For hours he thought of Neda. Her jeans. The blood rushing over her face. He thought of his own daughter who had escaped this madness and recalled a young woman who hadn't. Sometimes fate summons you to act—when would this poor trapped girl ever cross paths with another person who might help? He emailed his lawyer. "What was the name of that girl in the court?"

Two hours later, Agha Kamali replied. "Hello, my friend. How is your health? The name of the girl is Donya Norouzi. What a name, yes?"

Naming is an act of poetry—that names can be prophetic was one of the few mystical beliefs Bahman held. Neda, for instance, means *voice*, the voice of an uprising, perhaps. How grand and fanciful he had been in naming Niloo and Kian. Shirin simply meant *sweet*. Donya Norouzi, though, was the best Bahman had heard in years, its bearer worthy of rescue. He uttered it to himself over and over as he copied her phone number into his notebook and drifted back to sleep.

Donya Norouzi. *A new-year world.*

The fog grew thicker, but somehow pleasant. In this soupy, feverish delirium, he could pretend to be stoned, or in a dream state, and his body felt light, free-floating. Once he rolled off the bed and it felt fine to hit the ground, like his body was covered in soft padding. Twice Fatimeh came in with food, the healing aromas of eggplant and sour pickles and saffron rice preceding her. Later Sanaz slipped in while he was drifting in and out of sleep, and she played on his computer for a while.

In the early evening he switched on BBC news. This time, he watched footage of protests across Europe, usually in front of Iranian embassies. Exiles had staged demonstrations in Paris, London, Vienna, Berlin, The

Hague, Rome, Dubai, and even in American cities like New York and Los Angeles. Over the images of black-haired masses spilling into streets, drenched in green, mouths gaping in anger, a voice talked of an awakening among the comfortable Iranian diaspora; here was a new fervor that roused their native longings. Was Niloo or Kian among them? He watched extra carefully when the camera spanned the protests in The Hague and New York, unsure how far they were from his children's homes.

Fatimeh's eggplant was unchanged. The onion sautéed in hot olive oil to the point of maximum sweetness, the garlic fried last so it was never bitter, never burned, each slice of eggplant skinned, salted, and sweated individually, so that every morsel contained only the best of the vegetable. Fatimeh's eggplant was an exercise in excellence and care, much like her barley soup, her lamb shanks, and her *ab-goosht*, which contained hardly any filler, any gristle or shards, only the tenderest chunks of meat and a single bone stuffed with marrow. He suspected that she took from smaller bones to make the one on his plate overflow with the decadent matter. Fatimeh was a nurturer devoted to service, not a scholar activist like Pari, or a fainter and seducer like Sanaz. Years ago, on the first night of their marriage, he noticed that Fatimeh made separate salads for them. For him she used only the heart of the lettuce, and she served the outer leaves to herself. Her roughness and simplicity pleased him. Though it was a shame that their physical relationship had always been lukewarm and uncomfortable. Hence her affair with the poet, he supposed. He didn't blame her. How could he?

"Why are you here?" he asked when she popped in with tea. "I didn't ask for help. Why did you come to court?" He was groggy and must have sounded accusing.

"Agha Kamali asked me," she said. "What should I have done? Said no when your lawyer says you're in big trouble? . . . Go to sleep."

He flitted in and out of sleep for another long while. As the hours passed, they slowed. The morning had gone by as normal, but the early evening felt like a day, the shivering growing in intensity, the skin of his arms and legs itching, the vomiting hitting violent new peaks. How quickly the disease set in. After three vomits, Fatimeh's eggplant was long gone and he was sure four or five hours had passed. But the clock showed fifteen minutes. He decided to distract himself with photos.

Bahman's albums were his treasure. He had never allowed Sanaz to touch them, as they were locked in three drawers below his desk. He had brought them into this child-sized room with his other things after arriving home from jail. Now, looking at Kian playing with his toy truck, staring at the camera indignantly, and Niloo eating sour green plums with salt, her hair in pigtails, devastated him. He wished he had photos of Niloo's wedding. He tried to blame his emotions on the weakness of his body. He began to shake, his shoulders shivering at first until his entire torso was heaving and tumbling and heaving again.

No, he couldn't do this. Why should he do this? He was a man with a name, connections, and money. Dirt on their heads; let them all die with their religions and their laws and their masochistic philosophies. He had his own gods, his own prayers and sacraments. He had Rumi; Rumi understood need. Man is only flesh, he mused, and he ambled out of the room renewed, determined to save his own from pain.

He found Fatimeh in the kitchen, chopping celery into spears. "Fatimeh *joon*," he said, trying to regulate the volume and quaver of his voice. Still, it trembled and he had to take a quick breath after every three words. He sounded like a man who had spent a week in a meat locker. "Fatimeh *joon*, you put nothing in the eggplant?"

She blinked a few times, trying to work it out. "Did I put something where?" Then she got it, and her thick eyebrows shot up. "*Ei vai*," she said, laughing silently.

"I'm going to call Ali," said Bahman, scanning the kitchen, suddenly aware that his head was moving far too much. He tried to hold still and lost his thread for a moment. "I'm going to call Ali. He can come over for dinner. He's family."

Fatimeh didn't chastise him. She said, "The guards will smell a *manghal*. And they come into the kitchen sometimes. He has to cook you something at his house."

"Yes, yes," he said. He noticed Fatimeh's bare feet, her long red toenails. When was the last time she clipped them? Why would a person bother to polish her nails and not clip them to an appropriate length?

Standing by the living room phone, he dialed his brother's number. He waited, gently panting. But before Ali could pick up, Sanaz sauntered in and started in on him. "Who are you speaking to?" she said, crinkling her nose. He realized that he hadn't showered in over a day and had sweated through his clothes many times over. *To hell with it.* "You have to put your calls in the log." Sanaz nodded toward a yellow page taped to the paisley olive tablecloth that draped the tea table. Years ago, Pari had found the coin-shaped table in a bazaar near the Thirty-Three Arches.

He ignored her. Ali would cook him a fatty *beryooni*, and he would fill it with opium. He would do this every day, and he would deliver it in a medical kit, and the guards would have no idea of the scheme. They were children. What did they know?

Sanaz approached. He hadn't hung up or made a gesture to write in the log. She said, "Bahman, you're going to get us into trouble." What nerve she had, speaking of trouble as if she wasn't the source of every bitter morsel he swallowed. She reached across him and clicked on the cradle, disconnecting his call.

Now all the unspent anger of the previous days, all the blame-taking and rationalizing and the demurring, swallowing every response, quickened and boiled over so that all Bahman felt over his nausea and stomach pain and desperately itchy limbs was raw animal rage. The receiver still in hand, he roared at her, "You vile thing, I want you gone," and he smacked her hard across the face. And though he hadn't wanted to do it, and would never have chosen such barbaric ways in a rational state of mind, he felt no guilt, only a sweet, gushing release.

After a silent beat, Sanaz began to shout. She cradled her stomach and flung curses at him, and though her voice rose with each word, she was never shrill. She sounded ardent, like a martyr. She rushed to grab the phone from him. In a frenzy of dialing (who was she calling? her sister?), she knocked a pen and Niloo's nativity statuette off the table. Fatimeh and Shirin appeared from the kitchen. The front guards too had heard. Two men entered without bothering to remove their shoes.

A single day had passed under house arrest—one single day. He took a breath, trying to slow the chattering of his teeth. He would die here, he was sure of it, in this slow-burning netherworld that was shaped like the home he'd once built.

"What's the trouble?" said the young guard who had come to breakfast that morning—was it only this morning? What hellish protraction. The guard held a fresh cup of tea, which Sanaz must have brought to his car. Bahman looked at his wife, now whispering and sniffling, her hand covering the receiver.

"It's nothing," said Fatimeh. "I got into a fight with her. I'm sorry."

The guard stared bewildered at Fatimeh, because what is one to do about the domestic squabbles of women? His wives were in their own home; and they weren't the ones under arrest. The guards muttered to each other until Sanaz hung up her call. Bahman assumed that she would now end this miserable charade, maybe have him thrown back into jail, though, as a husband in an Islamic state, he did have the loathsome right to hit his wife. Still, the world was populated by jealous, scheming humans and these particular humans liked Sanaz better than they liked him.

And yet, Sanaz said nothing. She crossed her arms and shook her head and sniffled again. Fatimeh offered the guards some dinner, if they would be good enough to come to the kitchen table, since the *sofreh* was in the laundry. She led them away, with Shirin trailing happily behind, distracted by the unexpected meal.

"All your talk of education and feminism and America," whispered Sanaz, clutching the nativity statuette to her chest. "All your talk. You're an animal."

He wanted to ask her why she had spared him with the guards when she could have used the incident to turn the divorce far in her favor. He said, instead, "Why do you hate me? What did I do that you have to cause all this commotion?"

She glared at him, her eyes desperately sad. "Why do you think you can throw people away? If a person didn't study exactly what Niloo or Pari studied, they can't be smart? Or chic or interesting or . . . enough? You're pompous and cruel."

Sanaz liked to exact her own creative punishments, and that night her reason for keeping silent in front of the guards revealed itself. As he lay shivering under three blankets, the minutes creeping onward through a riot of clattering pots and high-pitched spats and crashing plates from downstairs, someone knocked on his bedroom door and entered without waiting for a reply. It was the wooly-bearded man, the witness from the courtroom, along with Soleimani, Sanaz's brother-in-law. Neither had taken off their shoes. They stood by the door, watching him, and in his fever Bahman thought that he had been right earlier—Sanaz *was* calling her sister. Bahman's first instinct was to greet them, but as soon as he opened his mouth, he was overcome by nausea. His body hinged forward and he vomited again in the bucket Fatimeh had placed beside his bed for that purpose.

The Hospitality of the Dutch

AUGUST 2009

Amsterdam, Netherlands

Gui asks every few days about Zakhmeh, hinting that he'd like to come along. But Niloo's responses are always ungenerous. Instead, she calls her mother in New York but doesn't say much. After four years of marriage, Niloo still refuses to throw a wedding—it feels like tempting fate to let Gui get involved with so many Iranians. God forbid they should demand a garish Persian spectacle. Sometimes on the phone, her mother whines in English, "I need photo for when I get old."

"It's a hassle, Maman *joon*," Niloo says. "And Gui doesn't care."

"Okay, so Gay is not care. What about *your* people? We need photo."

Niloo long ago stopped battling her mother on the "Gay" issue. Maman has her familiar syllables and no idea of the difference and that's that. Gui thinks it's funny.

Now, when Maman raises the topic, using as her excuse Baba's constant desperation for keepsakes, Niloo says, "Baba has his own wedding photos. Plenty."

"Niloofar, stop that snarking," Maman says. She has recently taken to peppering her English speech, already salted with Farsi words, with garbled adolescent slang from the Internet. "You stop that nasty-*bazi*. I am *so* over it."

Niloo changes the subject. She decides against telling Maman about lunch with Mam'mad or the refugees at the squat. Instead she talks of her research on the jaws and teeth of early big game hunters. She's talking to Pari Hamidi, after all, once-esteemed Iranian doctor and academic, social renegade, a woman who respects all scholarship. But her mother just spews a bunch of emotional nonsense. "Primate . . . why is important?" she says. "Study what happens in Iran! They steal election over there! Crazy bastards. Iran is all over in the shits. I never understand why you study anthropology. These garbages they dig up from earth, they're too long dead. No longer useful to thinking; to modern thinking."

"Okay, Maman," says Niloo with a sigh. "You're cutting out. I have to go."

"I cut out?" Her mother's voice recedes and Niloo hears her tapping on her screen with a long fingernail. "I got no wave," she mutters at her cell, then, the phone back on her ear, adds, "Send photo to your Baba. He thinks about you all the times. And say hello to Gay." She hangs up without pausing for a reply.

Niloo knows Bahman misses her and that he wants to schedule a fifth visit. In his email he suggested Dubai. It feels strange to allow him to get too close. She's afraid she will bungle things, ruin his fantasies of her—and don't we all need our fantasies to survive? Sometimes, she still gives in to visions of herself as a senator or Nobel laureate. Why muddy up Baba's dreams? Besides, he's not Baba anymore. He's just another sad Iranian addict, a population in the tens of thousands.

At lunch, Niloo meets a decade-long Iranian refugee, a quiet man named Karim whom Mam'mad mentioned before. Though Mam'mad treats Karim like a son, Mam'mad moves and dresses like an educated man and Karim does not.

"Hello, Khanom Cosmonaut," says Mam'mad as he opens the door. He straightens his glasses and looks her over in a fatherly way, as if he's admiring that she dressed herself today. He reaches for her backpack. "Give me that thing before your spine crumbles and you have to abort your moon mission."

Though she's looked forward to speaking Farsi and eating Iranian pickles and sharing stories of home, she has an excuse prepared in case she needs to leave fast. What can these refugees, men alone in a new city, want from a friendship with her? She hopes they realize that she has no connections at any immigration office.

He offers her a treat from home, sour cherry *sharbat*, the sweaty glass blurring three shades of crimson that she mixes together with a long spoon. As she enters, the younger man, Karim, gets up from atop a pillow and extends his hand. Mam'mad points out that Karim and Niloo are close in age, a fact that seems to embarrass Karim. His handshake is weak, as if he's afraid of hurting her, and she realizes that, as a rural Iranian, he has only recently learned to shake hands with women. Lunch is already set up on the floor, a green herb frittata and garlic pickle that he has made on a hot plate. Mam'mad lives in one room overlooking a narrow canal, one of the darker, gaunter ones in a nice district thanks to the egalitarian Dutch practice of placing public housing in every neighborhood. His is likely a student room, a temporary space. He sleeps in one corner, on bedding arranged neatly on the floor, and eats in another, on a set of pillows and a *sofreh* cloth that matches the ones at the squat. To be here and not in some refugee camp in the middle of nowhere meant that some Dutch foundation, maybe Hivos, must have taken interest in him.

The three perch on cushions, on their haunches, eating off the *sofreh* as if they are back in Iran. It thrills Niloo, like a childhood game of pretend. They play Iranian songs; she remembers the prettiest one, "Age Ye Rooz" (If One Day), a song for traveling lovers. They talk of their lives, though Niloo mostly listens. Mam'mad is a scholar. He's lived a quiet life of discipline and study. He is accomplished in both mathematics and literature, has taught both at university level, a rare thing. After some talk, she suspects that he pays for this room in part with his own money. He has reached his fifties without despairing of reality (only people), or seeking solace in oblivion. Niloo has never met an older Iranian man like him, one who isn't addicted to something, and his presence comforts her. Karim, though, has many dependencies—his wife, Iran, maybe opium. His rough hands hint at farm work.

She asks why they are here without their families. "Did Hivos bring you?"

"I escaped with a smuggler." Karim speaks so quietly that she has to strain to understand him. His eyes remain on his plate as he chews his bread slowly.

Mam'mad dips his bread into a puddle of oil beside the herb frittata. "I came with Scholars at Risk. They invite you to give a few lectures, and if it's too dangerous to go home, they help with asylum petitions. But I did the classes years ago and no one's lifted a finger. I'm stuck," he adds. "Karim is even worse off. Unskilled, illegal."

"If not for my family," says Karim, the misery in his voice settling over the *sofreh*, paling the food like a gauzy sheet thrown over it, "I'd go home today, right into Evin prison." A flash of yellow, a rotting tooth, peeks out as he speaks.

"Maybe Niloo *khanom* can help you," says Mam'mad, keeping his tone casual and his hands busy tearing sprigs of parsley. *Ah*, she thinks, *the request*. She shifts on her pillow and puts down her bread, just in case. "It might be a perfect match," he says. "Karim needs an English translator with the right accent and Siavash is overextended as it is. Just a few hours of your time to go to some immigration offices, Niloo *khanom*. Karim will do whatever work you need in return."

Karim nods. "I'll do the work regardless." He hardly whispers. Pale and worn down in a faded striped shirt and old khakis, Karim sits with his back straight and his gaze down, unable to get comfortable. The nervous expression tightening his gaunt face makes Niloo think he's younger than he looks, twenty-seven or -eight. Neither man shows any skill at veiling the fact that Karim has been invited expressly because they think Niloo can help him.

"What accent?" she asks, imagining Gui's reaction. "And who's Siavash?"

"The young man with the scars. He's American too," Mam'mad sighs, as if he hates telling her this. "The embassies and the agencies are run by poorly educated Western bureaucrats. If your translator has an American or Dutch accent, like yours or Siavash's, your story gets believed. If not, then not." She has an urge to protest. How could a process so important, a process that brought her to America and gave her this life, be so haphazard and subjective and ugly? Mam'mad adds, "And not just that. The well-connected liars with the dramatic stories get the best treatment because they're happy to rub every detail in the officer's face.

Meanwhile, these office fools, they completely ignore the quiet torture victims who are too traumatized to relive anything, and don't know any good translators anyway." She watches Karim, who betrays no emotion, his eyes on his meal. Isn't it shameful for him to be discussed this way? But the men seem used to this talk, and Mam'mad carries on. "Karim has told his story ten different times. Every time they ask for details, he flinches and says something vague, and they think he's making it up."

A heaviness bears down on her chest but she strains to hide her emotions. It would embarrass Karim if she cried, so she doesn't. "It can't be like that," she says. Mam'mad shrugs, turns both hands, showing his palms as if to say, *Why would I lie?*

She imagines herself as an adult refugee, trying to navigate the maze of embassies and procedures and unspoken rules. The idea chills her—if only she had left a few years later, her accent, her education, and her life would be different. Niloo can still conjure the tedium of standing in sweaty, smelly embassy lines in Rome, waiting for her mother to explain their situation. She recalls Maman's shaking hands, her nervous voice, her lilting English. Was it the wrong accent? Did the officer pity her because she was young and pretty and a mother? Or was it her story that compelled? Years later Maman told her that the reason they were believed was that the officer interviewed Niloo and Kian alone and saw that the children were, in fact, raised as Christians. Niloo remembers that afternoon at the embassy. She had been bored, working on a math worksheet while Kian colored a picture of a cowboy. When the lady asked about Jonah, she hardly looked up. She rambled about whales and how big one would have to be to swallow a person and how when she grew up she wanted to travel and dig up the bones of that whale, and find the spot on Ararat where Noah docked. When the lady asked her to identify Saint Peter, she said, "He's not a saint. That's what Catholics think and they've been wrong since Luther and Calvin. He's the one who denied Jesus three times."

"Did Mohammad ever deny Jesus?" said the officer, hoping to catch her out—maybe the Hamidis were Muslims in Protestant clothing, maybe they had some leftover allegiance toward Mohammad and Hassan and Hossein.

Niloo looked up at the officer. She was already shedding the bouncing Ardestooni girl, her voice dulling. "No," she said, "but neither does Satan."

And that's why the United States granted asylum to the Hamidis—one stupid answer to a stupid question between a shallow-thinking bureaucrat and a child desperate for black-and-white. That's why she slept for a night at Jesus House and went to Yale and met Gui and studied the ways of the human race and became an atheist. It makes her laugh to remember herself then. "I'll translate for you, Karim *agha*," she says, as she helps herself to her discarded morsel and to more pickles. "No need to do any work."

Mam'mad claps and hoots and shakes Karim by the back of the neck—there is a small smile hiding under that downturned face. Then Mam'mad talks of Karim's family in Iran, his life in Holland, and his crimes. Karim only listens and nods. Back home, he was accused of smuggling opium. "Since when does the Islamic Republic crack down on opium?" she asks, suddenly afraid. She thinks of Baba and his vices. (With alcohol Baba is careful, a merry, sheltered drunk, his glass kept full by a constant stream of friends who gravitate to him for a good time. Opium though . . . it unleashes a reckless, slobbering, angry fiend.)

"Only for their political enemies," Mam'mad reassures her as he refills Karim's glass. Everyone has an addict back home, some beloved person who can never stray too far from the poppy fields. "Don't worry, Niloo *joon*." It pleases Niloo that he's already calling her by the most familiar version of her name. She senses Karim relaxing; when he shares a few words about his wife—featherlight hair down to the middle of her back, the way she skins almonds all day and burns the skins to make kohl for her eyes—Niloo feels finally at home at Mam'mad's *sofreh*.

Over the next few weeks, Niloo visits Zakhmeh regularly. She eats several meals with the two men (always humble egg dishes) and they become an unlikely trio walking Amsterdam's most obscure canals by night. Each time, Mam'mad tells stories. He explains how Iranians end up in Holland. "Scholars come here, they languish, they never find work. They are sent home," he says. Always he adds something about himself. "I should be a knowledge worker, not a refugee," he often mutters. "Siavash keeps stalling on the papers." Siavash, who has learned passable Dutch and by now knows his way around all kinds of immigration forms, has been volunteering to sort out asylum applications for Mam'mad and his family.

Usually the older man bemoans his lost credentials for a while before recalling some other complaint. One evening in his apartment, he says, "Tell me, Niloo *khanom*, why do the Dutch greet travelers this way? I don't mean immigration. I mean . . . nobody has even welcomed me to the neighborhood. Did you know that?"

Compared with hypersocial Iranian ways, Dutch culture is lonely. No casual conversation from strangers, no grand shows of generosity. Mam'mad tells her that, despite years sharing their street, he still has no invitations, not even for a tea, even after he used his limited earnings to take *baghlava* to every one of his neighbors. The Dutch love their dogs more than the stranger down the road. And the worst part, no respect for the learned class. "Did I offend them?" he says, his voice tensing. She wants to assure him that this is just their way, but he rambles on, "In Iran I was harassed, arrested, my daughters stopped in the streets. My work was torn apart by people without even a first degree. And then I arrive here, and the same shit followed me. This Siavash, he says he'll help but who knows his motive, where he came from. Maybe he wants my petition to fail. Who knows? Ahmadinejad's people, they have their hands in everything, even abroad."

This sudden paranoia is familiar. She heard words like this in Italy and Dubai, in the refugee camps. It spins out of the waiting and idleness, combined with the smallest fearful memory. She wants to make him laugh, to reject gloomy thoughts of unwelcoming natives, so she tells him about the Dutch. Maybe she can make him understand that there are no plots, that the people of Holland are bred cold.

"You're not missing anything," she says. "When the Dutch invite you to lunch, they serve one slice of bread, ham *or* cheese, not both. Sour milk and then, to top off the insults, *one* cookie next to your coffee."

"One cookie?" he says, bushy gray eyebrow rising. "I don't understand."

"I mean they don't bring out the whole tin," she says with a nervous laugh. "They put one cookie beside your coffee like in a restaurant. It's Dutch stinginess."

"*Ei vai.*" He slaps one hand with the other. "I've never seen that."

"That's because all your Dutch friends are squatters and hippies," she says. "The poor, progressive ones . . . they like sharing."

Karim nods and dips a toe into the conversation. "I've heard people say that if the Dutch invite five people for dinner, they make exactly five potatoes."

Mam'mad shakes his head. "Generosity is a poor man's gift," he says. "What happens if you're at a Dutch house and want a second cookie or another potato?"

"You suffer silently," she says, her tone grave as she flashes a big smile at Karim, who adds, "Or go home."

"Shameful!" Mam'mad says, distracted from his troubles. He pushes a plate of radishes toward her. She takes one and wraps it in a mint leaf and eats. She notices, when Mam'mad is sober, his lisp disappears. He sounds like the university professor he was in Iran. This amplifies the charms of his lisp, a sign that he makes a practice of refining his speech, that he seeks rigor in the day-to-day. If Baba were here, he'd consider it a falsity and pour the man drink after drink until the lisp returned. Then he would examine his palate to see if he could fix it. He would see no hypocrisy in this. Mam'mad probes for more and Karim too seems interested. "What else?"

"Let's see," she says. "Oh, the restaurant bill is literally called *the reckoning*."

He slaps the floor. "You lie!" He shifts to his right leg, hugging one knee and adjusting the pillow under him. He nudges Karim. "Are you still listening? Cold-blooded bastards. I suspect hell is run by a Dutch demographer with a clipboard that hangs around his neck on orange rope."

"Exactly." She tucks her legs neatly beneath her haunches, the bottoms of her feet facing the wall. Two years in an Isfahani girls' school has taught her to sit this way. She searches her mind for other Dutch oddities; she enjoys Mam'mad's surprise.

"These Dutch," Karim mutters with a long breath. "Our hell is probably different from their hell." Mam'mad catches Niloo's eyes from over his glasses, and they abandon the subject. He gets up from the island of cushions to fetch a tin of cookies, because Iranians, Niloo has noted, take hints where there are none.

A few days later, during her lunch hour, Niloo accompanies Karim to visit his caseworker, an elfin man who seems annoyed by her presence at first. When he realizes that her English is better than his own and that she isn't intimidated by his position—she hopes he sees in the way she runs her nail on the cheap wood of his desk, the way she eyes his name that slides in and out of a plastic plaque, that she wouldn't accept his job if offered it—he addresses all his questions and responses directly to her, bypassing Karim, who shrinks into his body a little more.

Afterward, she whisks a sweaty Karim to the nearest brown café, a typical Dutch watering hole. "That was good!" she says. "Everything will work out soon."

For the first time, he looks directly in her eyes. "Do you really believe that, Niloo *khanom*?" Then he drops his gaze again.

The despair in his voice saps her of the will even to keep walking, as if someone stuck a tube in her arm and syphoned off all the wonder and resolve. She has never lived with such absolute lack of hope. "Don't say things like that," she says, feigning cheer. Karim pulls open the heavy wooden door of the bar. "Everything will look better with a drink in our hands. I think I'll have a glass of smoky red. What will you have? Should I order us a bottle?"

"One day, Niloo *khanom*, when things are looking happier," he says, "you'll have to tell me how you managed to become American. Because as far as I see it, every immigration office is the same. They're all like the *dehati* fiancé who takes you ring shopping again and again and never buys you one."

He waits for her reaction with a crooked half smile, unveiling a missing canine tooth now that he trusts her. The enormity of the gesture, and its smallness, moves her and she promises herself that she will do more for him, that she will deserve his trust. But for now, he wants her to laugh. So she does.

The night of the next storytelling event, she's unlocking her bike outside the apartment when Gui drives up on his scooter. "Going to the guitar-pick place?"

"Zakhmeh," she says, and leans in so he can kiss her cheek. "It's not hard."

"Hop on," he says, nodding over his shoulder. "Let's go together."

She stands there with her bike lock in hand, trying to think of an excuse to say no.

"Is this a Perimeter thing?" He gives her a wounded look. She wants to say, *It's a personal space thing. Can't any person need that? Does it have to be part of some Niloo strangeness for you to mock?* Niloo has developed a number of tactics for leaving the house unseen on storytelling nights. She calls Gui at work, asking what time he'll be home so she can leave half an hour before. She bikes on the canal side, not the street side, of the apartment, since Gui can't ride his scooter there. Now and then she goes straight from work, picking up a bite to eat at the corner shop along the way. Now she searches for a loving way to say no, but catches Gui's eager smile, and she finds herself unable. "Okay," she says. "But I have to stop for a snack. Tonight's yellow split pea." When he shrugs, she adds, "It's bad. Trust me."

She slides off the scooter as Gui slows in front of a bodega. Four years in Amsterdam have trained her in jumping on and off the back of moving bikes and scooters. "Are you sure you don't want to pick up a pizza or something?" Gui asks.

"No!" says Niloo. "We can't be extravagant about our food. The people in there are dirt poor." Gui puts up two hands. Looking him over, she cringes. He's wearing a tailored suit and summer riding gloves (who wears riding gloves on a scooter?) when she's purposely chosen a T-shirt with a rip at the hem and her oldest jeans, the ones with the unidentifiable bluish stain just below the knee and a small hole in the crotch—when they can afford it, Iranians value the chic and the flashy, and so it satisfies them to see an American Iranian, someone who has had everything they wish for, in tattered clothes. It gives them something to tease her about and it allows her to tell them about Yale while still joining them in complaining about rents or the price of the euro. It feels fair, balancing their circumstances a little. Inside the bodega, she picks out two *broodjes*, unenviable young cheese and butter on stale bread wrapped in plastic, and two cans of peas.

"Canned peas? Again?" Gui says, horrified—he has caught her eating them before, in the middle of the night with soy sauce, and each time he gags. "*Why?*"

"Canned peas are amazing," she says, which is true. She's loved them since she first tasted them at the refugee hostel outside Rome, where she ate them warmed and salted, or smashed into a piece of bread from lunch, every Saturday afternoon in the courtyard while reading her first English storybooks. Canned peas taste like Europe and no amount of prosperity will change that for her. "Don't worry," she says, lifting her backpack, "I brought a can opener." Gui pretends to bang his forehead on the handlebars but says nothing. She peers into her grocery bag, then nods at the briefcase tucked between his legs. "Do you have salt in there?"

He pulls up the kickstand with the top of his foot. "You know, I usually do take a salt shaker to work," he says, "but no, not today, sorry . . ."

"I meant from lunch," she says. "It's fine. I'll find some there."

"I really should pack for a people's revolution every time I leave the house," he says. "I mean, here I am routinely without my passports, my desktop speakers . . ."

"Yeah yeah." She climbs on and wraps an arm around his waist.

"Birth certificate, a security blanket," he rattles on as he pulls onto the street.

"You're just jealous of my super prepared ways," she mutters into his neck.

". . . iodine water . . . gorp!"

At Zakhmeh, Gui's clothing becomes impossible to ignore and Niloo starts to worry. What if Karim and Mam'mad think she's showing off her European husband? She knows it would shame Karim to meet Guillaume, and she hopes he isn't here.

At the donation plate, Gui takes a twenty from his pocket. Niloo grabs his wrist, drops in two euros, and pulls him inside. She chooses a lumpy sage pillow from the pile and places it in a far corner, and they sit. Gui looks around the room taking in the aging rugs, the dreadlocks, the cauldron of stew. "I like this," he says.

She pulls out her grocery bag and the can opener but Gui opts for the yellow split peas. By the time he returns from the soup line (where three nosy mothers accost him about who he is and where he lives and why he's here), Mam'mad is situating himself beside her. He jumps up for Gui, an eager gesture that saddens her; she wants Gui to respect this man she has come to admire.

"Niloo *joon*, you finally brought your husband. We're honored," he says, thrusting his open hand at Gui. His cheeks and eyebrows have lifted, making his face young, cheerful. Watching Mam'mad take Gui's hand in both of his, she recalls his longing for an invitation from a Dutch neighbor, and for a moment she's glad Gui came. "But I warn you, here you must sing for your soup," says Mam'mad. "What do you think, Khanom Cosmonaut?" He turns to Niloo, rubbing his hands. "Shall we make your husband tell a story?" He gives her a preview of the story he's planning. Finally, he was invited to the home of a Dutch neighbor for tea, and she brought out a single mini chocolate balanced on each saucer. "I thought, *Fuck Wilders, Niloo was right about the cookie situation.*" He takes her hand, patting it like dough, making her giggle. She catches a look of sudden pleasure (*was that an inside joke?*), then an encouraging grin, on Gui's face, as if he's nudging along an awkward child.

As the crowd settles into clusters, towers of empty bowls rising alongside them, Siavash, the other American, takes the microphone, his foot resting on the lower rung of the stool. He leads a discussion about the Green Movement and about the treatment of refugees in Holland. Now and then, people interject with stories or arguments. Siavash speaks elegant university English, sharing what he knows about displaced scholars, artists, doctors, activists. A stout-legged Dutch woman with shoulder-length hair and loose jeans hanging far too low interrupts. "Holland is very good to immigrants," she says. "Yes, it's our duty to help, but it can be frightening. You hear about protests, riots. And some of these runaways who come here . . ."

The crowd murmurs. Niloo wonders about the woman, recalling that this space is open to Dutch artists too. A sneer blooms on Siavash's lips. "The frightening ones don't run, *mevrouw*." His tone is sharp, but he drops his volume in an affected way that Gui will surely notice. "They stay. They're the ones we're running from."

"*We?*" On cue, Gui whispers in her ear. "Isn't he American born?" That he finds Siavash grating is no surprise. Gui is an accomplished lawyer; he can smell a politician and he despises hipsters, overeducated bums with their meticulous squalor. At least he's honest about his upbringing and the price of his clothes.

Siavash has a young face. Everything else about him is gritty and worn, from the long hair often in a loose topknot, to his graying T-shirt with constellations of tiny holes around the neck, to the shadows under his eyes and that vicious splash of white, a scar like a smear of cream, which he once explained as a chemical burn that happened on a trip to Iran. ("I don't believe he's ever been to Iran," says Gui during a break.) An angry knife scar protrudes like a caterpillar perched on his neck and a spatter of pockmarks, like chunks gnawed out by an animal mouth, ominously appear on one cheek only. His girlfriend, Mala, a watchful, angular former dancer from a wealthy part of Tehran, lingers nearby. She's in her forties and it is known that she pays Siavash's expenses. She wears flowing skirts over her bone-hard body, all knees and elbows, keeps her sloping tanned shoulders bare, and speaks awful English. Her arms are always crossed over her chest, in display of her naked distaste for sharing Siavash, especially with other Iranians.

When Siavash starts describing a protest in Tehran where he saw a woman beaten and dragged to Evin, Gui leans in again and whispers, "Jesus, this guy! And his story couldn't be more generic . . . 'saw a woman get beaten.' You don't say."

"Hush!" she says. "We're guests here."

Now and then, as Siavash takes questions, Gui leans in to point out the insufficiency or poor logic in his responses. But Niloo likes Sy. He has big white teeth, gleaming and uniform like marble tiles. Like her father, Niloo venerates village life while quietly judging people on the perfection of their smile. ("He couldn't loosen his fist for some veneers?" Baba would say. "Better to walk around with holes in your shoes than lowly teeth.") How recklessly can Siavash have lived when he has artful teeth like these? Besides, he is selfless. Karim told her that, since Ahmadinejad's people stole the election earlier in the summer, Siavash spends his days organizing protests and writing letters and op-eds.

"We have to organize demonstrations here," says Siavash. "And we need to get European citizens involved. Friends, you owe your fellow man your voice in this." He nods to the Dutch faces around the room, says their names, then turns to Niloo and Gui. "And even more than our Dutch friends, Iranians who've enjoyed the privilege of Western lives, like Niloo, like me. We need to be out there every day."

Now a soft voice rises up from a cluster of men in the back. She recognizes Karim immediately. He clears his throat twice and even so, he's barely audible. He speaks in Farsi and a man beside him translates to English. "Do you really believe anything will change?" Karim says, almost moaning. "Every time I go to a protest, I think, what if a newspaper snaps my picture and I never see my wife again? And then when a long time passes and nothing happens, or another asylum petition gets rejected, I think, I'll be roaming these streets without her forever. I've been here for ten years, *agha*. Not like your friend Mala's ten years. Most of that time I've been illegal. Room to room, or on the streets. I have children I barely know."

Karim seems always ashamed, like a beaten person, exhausted in mind and body, as if at any moment he might throw his hands up and announce he's finished, then immediately disintegrate into ashes. Niloo senses that no Westerner has ever wanted to be involved in Karim's life.

The state provided shelter for a time, bureaucrats gave legal advice, charities gave clothes, but the hands that delivered these institutional offerings kept a cold distance. Maybe they know that, once invited in, refugees need a lot of favors.

Mala exchanges a meaningful look with Siavash. How many uncomfortable glances has Karim pretended not to see? He shrinks back down and gulps a beer, and a man beside him touches his shoulder. Niloo remembers a time when she too thought she'd never have a home. In those early days without Baba, she thought she'd never have another happy day. Every morning she asked Maman when he'd join them. When did she accept that he never would?

"What if we do win," says Mam'mad, in a half-drunk mix of Farsi and English, "and Mousavi is made president and there are a few human rights improvements and a point made, et cetera? But our daughters are still under hijab. Our oil is still lubricating mullah pockets. Our sons are still addicted. Then won't you wish the hard-liners had won and provoked some foreign power to oust them?"

"That's why we organize," says Sy, "to get our European friends involved."

Mam'mad gesticulates toward the front of the room. "You talk about change, Agha Siavash," he almost shouts, the respectful *Agha* laced with sarcasm, "but you came here to help us with immigration papers. I ask you, what is the status of that? Has there been progress? Would a trip to The Hague be more useful than protests?"

"This isn't the place for that discussion." Sy's voice takes on a warning tone. "Another time in private, I'm happy to answer your questions."

"It's been years," says Mam'mad, eyes roaming as if to incite a rebellion. "Is enough being done? What's the trouble that it's become so complicated?" Niloo can sense Mam'mad's paranoia about to spill out. She wills him to drop it, and it seems he might. "None of it matters anyway," he mutters softly, but with such bitterness that people whisper and gasp. "I'm not a refugee. I should be a knowledge worker."

The room is silent; the very air seems to change, as if someone opened a door and let out all the warmth. Niloo's breath catches like a fish bone at the top of her chest. Now Mam'mad and Siavash are speaking as if they've forgotten the crowd. "Knowledge worker?" Sy snaps at the older man. "Mam'mad *agha*, do you know what that takes? You need to find someone to hire you, a real organization. And not just hire you for a month, but pay you more than fifty thousand a year. Do you have that? Do you have enough Dutch or English even to hope for that? What, you don't believe me?" He pulls out his smartphone and begins searching for proof.

"Fuck you and your informations," says a scarlet Mam'mad in failing English. He starts to walk away and stumbles on Niloo's pillow. Gui puts out a hand in front of her and Mam'mad excuses himself, then continues, "With your terrible American manners and your stupid phone. Have some respect for people who've earned it."

Niloo reaches for Mam'mad's arm, but he yanks it away. People are staring and murmuring, some crying. "Fuck *me*?" shouts Siavash. "Do you know how many hours I've spent on your papers? Do you think this is Iran where every younger person is your hired servant? We all have to deal with the same insane bureaucracy in this country. You're no more special than every other miserable fuck here. And if you haven't had every local agency up your ass for documents, it's because of me."

In the back, Karim is resting his head in his hands. Siavash's neck flushes and his breath seems to slow, as if he's waiting to catch the leaked words on his tongue and swallow them up again. He looks embarrassed before the hushed crowd. Now and then someone whispers, a spoon thumps against a plastic bowl.

"Damn, is this normal?" asks Gui, gripping her hand, pulling her to her feet, "Like you fighting with your mom? Or are they about to kill each other for real?"

Though Niloo's fingers have gone numb and her chest and throat are burning, a parched sensation like trying to ingest a woolen skein, she stops on the way out to speak with Karim. She feels dirty, sticky-shoed, coated in hoppy sweat and weed smoke. "I'm sorry the night's ruined," she says, unable to think of anything else.

Karim nods at Gui. He extends an uncertain hand. Instead of hello, he says, "Much obliged," as if Gui has done him a favor. He smiles wide but keeps his mouth closed, straining to hide his yellow and missing teeth. Though she expected this, though she knew that Iranian manners would cause Karim to treat Gui with a kind of cloying respect reserved for whiter men, she blames her husband for making him squirm. If Gui were pulling at a rope around Karim's feet, she wouldn't be much angrier. Now Karim thanks Gui in bad English for allowing his wife to help him. Probably whatever kinship she had begun with him is finished; they will never again talk of Iran over an easy drink.

Gui's face looks drawn. "I can try to get you someone from my firm," he offers Karim, as if he can simply lift Niloo out of this circumstance and insert someone else. "Niloo doesn't know the law." Karim nods at his shoes, at yet another Westerner who wants to help but is afraid to get too close.

"Don't listen to him, Karim *joon*," Niloo breaks in, in angry Farsi. "I'm the one who will help you. I'll do it myself. Nothing's changed. Don't worry."

. . .

At home, they dress for bed in silence. Niloo has another email from Baba.

Subject: DOUBAI? YES? PACKAGE?

Niloojoon, yek package barat ferestadam, gerefti? What about Doubai? dad

(Niloojoon, I sent you a package, did you get it? What about Dubai? dad)

She moves the message out of sight. Because if tonight has taught her one lesson, it is this: Baba's matchless spirit wouldn't survive the refugee life, and she doesn't want to tempt or confuse him by relenting to another visit. Would she send an innocent like Gui (however arrogant) into the bowels of Green Movement Tehran to be singled out and arrested? In the same way, Baba doesn't belong here, his bare feet, cradled for decades by warm grasses, soft Ardestooni riverbanks, and silky rugs, landing suddenly on this chilly, inhospitable soil. In exile, Baba's feral laugh would die in his throat. His sour cherry pockets would dry up. He would forget the boyish clapping of his heart, as Mam'mad and Karim have done. As Niloo did, long ago.

The Second Visit

London, 2001

Find the antidote in the venom.
Come to the root of the root of yourself.

—Jalal ad-Din Rumi

Our second visit with Baba happened in London in late August 2001. I was twenty-two and fresh out of Yale and a little afraid of stepping off American soil. But it was fortunate that I went, since Baba would be denied every subsequent request for a British or American visa.

Kian and I arrived at Heathrow airport in a daze of exhaustion. Jet-lagged and nauseated, I was at my crankiest, but Kian had reached new heights of bad temper. Having just finished his first year of classist, racist American undergraduate work-study, he was so fundamentally sleep-deprived that his every word was a bark. And now he was being forced to use his summer holiday and meager wages to see his crazy, overindulged Iranian father in the most expensive city in Europe.

All through the flight he brooded, headphones glued on, arms over his face, hugging himself against the aisle. "I smell cigarettes," he muttered. "That shit kills the taste buds." Kian isn't an easy excavation. I've found that the way to enjoy his company is to accept that we'll have one spectacular talk or sidesplitting hour for every six or seven of his mood swings, ill-timed political rants, and cruel asides. This goes for the entire family—yes, he judges us when we fumble and disgrace ourselves, but that's mitigated by the fact that he also judges us when we're witty.

Over the years, Maman and I have come across three situations in which he's not judging: when we keep our (always unwanted) emails short, when we're kind to service people, and when we cook something truly original. He also likes it when we nod vigorously at art, poems, cuisine, and other crafted works, because the artist may be watching—an oddly specific situation, but it happens to us often. "Nod for the sauce, Niloo!" he commanded in Farsi the last time we ate in New York. "That's the man's art you're shoving in your face, and he's behind that glass pane wondering what he's doing with his life. Nod like you're affected by the sauce, at least."

Add to this one large side order of Christian right-wing nuttery, and you have Kian Hamidi, future respected chef, son of Dr. Bahman Hamidi, bon vivant and opium-slash-waterslide enthusiast who has never nodded at anything unless he felt like nodding at it, doesn't take well to being judged, analyzed, or told what to do, and thinks every Christian and Muslim should find a deep well of shit and jump into it.

At least they both had a temper.

Baba rented a hotel room near Leicester Square for Kian and me. He would stay with relatives just outside town. Had I been older, I might have asked where he was going and with whom. But the memory of that night when I had found him slumped in the Red Carpet Motel was so raw and seething that I didn't linger on it. I didn't ask if he was staying outside town to feed his habit, or maybe he couldn't afford two hotel rooms on his black market sterling, a wad of cash that looked decidedly more modest than the one he had carried in Oklahoma.

Kian and I fell asleep the moment we settled into the hotel room, a little past noon. We weren't meeting Baba till the next day, and we thought we had earned a short nap. Later, we ordered cheeseburgers and fries to the room and stayed up watching BBC Two dramas and trying to fall asleep at the correct hour. When we failed to summon sleep, we fought. Because it was a long time ago and because of our fatigue and anxiety, we said much that I don't recall. I remember the worst things:

Two a.m. Kian, on my vocational choices: "You don't get art. You have no respect for what I do. You only respect data and grants and your name in soulless journals."

Three a.m. Me, on Kian's religious leanings: "Want to know something? There's no truth or beauty like holding a Neanderthal jaw in your hand, and knowing with absolute certainty that your Bible and Koran, and every serotonin-high nut lost in nirvana or ecstasy or Pentecost or whatever are all fucking confused."

At around dawn, Kian, voice hoarse with exhaustion, ended the fight on the sourest note: "You're dating a vanilla white boy who will politely drive you to misery and then in five years he'll leave you . . . quietly though. *So* quietly; don't worry."

We didn't say another kind word to each other for four days.

We met Baba for breakfast in a café in Covent Garden. From far away it was easy to spot him, sitting at an outdoor table, arms folded on his lap as if listening to a Sufi prayer, a cane resting against the wall beside him, sipping a very tall, very dark beer at eleven a.m., the foam in his mustache visible from across the square. He was older. I felt it in the space between my rib cage and my heart, the way it was closing up with each step. Kian whispered, mostly to himself, "God, I don't want to see him."

And because I hated Kian just then, I didn't reassure him, though the same fear and doubt afflicted me. Was Baba smaller? I wanted to turn back and run all the way to Connecticut and get into my senior year dormitory bed, where Gui's arms had cradled my head for so many nights that it had started to become home. Instead I said, "I'm excited to see my Baba." I wanted to remind Kian that I had been the favorite, that I was the beloved older child, that Baba and I had three precious years alone together, a luxury Kian couldn't fathom, years when I dripped ice cream on his neck and he howled from below my feet, when he kissed my face and said I was the sweetest creature, the tickle of his mustache on my cheek a lingering reminder of the constancy and firmness of the earth beneath my toes. Silently I thanked whatever gods exist for Gui, who had taken this fading, withering man's place.

Kian's shoulders collapsed a little as we approached the table. Baba didn't recognize us until we had almost reached him. He stumbled out of his chair, knocking it back and grinning and maybe crying beneath his outdated sunglasses. His hair was still red, salted now, and his mustache was thinner and fully gray. His back arched dramatically; he looked older than forty-seven. His body was smaller, softer, more splayed out. Then again, Kian and I were taller, fitter. At twenty-two and nineteen, we judged our Baba with the eyes we had. I gaped at his cane.

"Niloo *joon*," he said, his voice breaking. "Oh, Kian. Oh my boy, you're so tall." He dabbed his eyes, a little foggier and grayer than I remembered, and reached for his cane, then decided against it. He hobbled toward us and threw himself with absolute familiarity into Kian's arms. Kian looked at me over Baba's shoulder, his eyes flinching. But Baba kept squeezing him, gripping his own forearms around Kian's body, his green beads hanging off his fingers, as if Kian might run away, and something beyond our untouchable young souls leaked through Kian's skin and a change like gentleness came over him, brightening his eyes. He stood still for a long time, letting Baba hug him and weep onto his shoulder, to run his arms up his back as if to recognize this adult body his son now occupied, so much like his own, from a time.

We sat down and Baba ordered two more beers, tipping the waitress twenty pounds to overlook the breakfast rules. Immediately he started calculating. "Last time I saw you, Kian *joon*, it was eight years ago. How old were you? Ten? Eleven?"

"Eleven," said Kian, and turned to the waitress who was gathering our menus. "Can you make mine a coffee? Lots of milk and sugar?" He flashed the waitress a charming smile as if they were allied in some battle against the inconsiderate restaurant patrons of the world. "Whatever you have brewing. Thank you."

I ordered a cappuccino and took a breakfast menu from the stack under her arm. Kian glared at me and apologized to the waitress for my rudeness. She looked curiously at us, her weak chin dimpling as she repeated our drink order and walked away. "Don't apologize for me," I said. "You're not my PR rep."

"Shut up, Niloo," said Kian. "She's a human being."

Baba slapped the back of one hand with the other, an Iranian gesture of shock and discomfort. "*Ei vai*, what is this?" he said in a horrified half whisper. "What am I hearing? Kian, that's your sister. Save the venom for your wife."

I snorted, recalling this old Persian joke. Women in Ardestoon teased their sons with it and the joke had dulled, losing meaning. It simply meant *Be nice*. But Kian, unaware of this, muttered in English, "If I get married, I plan not to suck at it."

Baba turned to me. "What did he just say?" He pointed his cane at Kian, anger darkening his eyes. I know he understood some of it, but he demanded a translation. I offered something close to Kian's comment, sparing Baba the exact words. Kian shifted in his chair. Baba's face was reddening, his reaction so out of proportion with what had been said that Kian and I forgot our fight and exchanged a confused glance. "What do you know about marriage?" Baba said, spit flying out of his mouth. "What do you know about anything? You have no judgment for what is truly insulting."

I said in Farsi, "Can we just eat? No Hamidi should be allowed to utter a word on anything less than a full stomach. We're like animals."

"That is the truest thing I've heard today," said Baba, and ordered a full English breakfast with two extra roasted tomatoes and one extra egg and a side of sliced cucumber. For the bread he wanted *barbari*, which, of course, they didn't have, so he turned to me and asked what's the closest Western thing. I ordered him a toasted English muffin, a crumpet, and half a baguette—one of those should satisfy. Kian ordered a mushroom omelet and another pot of coffee. I asked for my next cappuccino with an extra shot and two hard-boiled eggs with butter. I had recently adopted Gui's breakfast habits. On Sunday mornings, he took great pleasure in choosing a seat directly in the sunlight, cracking eggs with a tiny spoon, mixing the insides with salt and butter, and remembering his childhood in Provence.

I looked at the cane again. Baba gave a wet, coughing chuckle. He said, "Don't worry, my girl. It's only the varicosis. I had a vein removed." He lifted his trouser leg and showed us the layers of white bandage from his ankle to his calf. Somehow this made me feel better—maybe because it was an ailment for any age, for former athletes, and in fact, Baba had suffered from it since he was in his thirties.

When the food arrived, Baba declared the baguette a sin against humanity. The crumpet delighted him though, and he called back the waitress. He shouted over the heads of three tables of baffled English customers. "Miss, please come with the quickness." He spoke in a kind of schizophrenic English whose shameful memory we must have repressed but was returning now, with *all* the quickness. "What this is, dear? This hard bread?" he said, waving the baguette. "Is rock. I break molar. But is no worry. Is no worry, miss, we fix. You must bring this England muffin"—he was pointing to the crumpet—"three England muffin, toasted browner. Is possible?"

"Three toasted crumpets," she repeated, unamused. "Yes, sir."

Kian, mortified at this ingratitude toward a service worker, said, "Everything was very good. The omelet was excellent. Cooked evenly throughout, onions seared just right." The waitress gave him a strange look—we were a sideshow act.

"And another darkest, darkest barley water," Baba said. "With the quickness, because I suffer these children." He leaned in on the second "darkest" as if to say that the previous beer hadn't been dark enough. As he spoke, he mashed bites of bread into the butter and floated them near Kian's mouth, then mine, then Kian's again, until Kian patted his hand away and flashed his sternest *this isn't Iran* look.

"Yes, sir," she said, "Guinness coming up." Baba nodded briskly at the word, his feline smile, that long pleasure grin, unchanged after decades, resurfacing.

When the beer came, Baba took one sip from his foaming glass and summoned the waitress again, this time motioning her over with his finger as he wiped his mouth. Kian slapped his face, burying himself up to his ears in his summer jacket. Baba said, "Is not Extra Stout, the Guinness." He wasn't asking.

"Right. Sorry, sir," she said. "We only have Guinness draft on tap."

"Yes, yes," said Baba, frustrated with his children and desperate for his morning beer. "Is not taps, the Extra Stout. Is bottle. Is too dark for general tastes." And he waved his hand outward as if at the legion of swill guzzlers all around.

Was there any question that the staff was talking about us in the back? Maybe spitting in our coffees? Who was this foreign clod and why was he so fluent in Irish beer? My head and neck ached and I wished this trip would end—it was a feeling so much like those days in Oklahoma that for a moment I was ashamed of myself. I was no teenager, after all. I was a worldly twenty-two. Shouldn't I be able to handle a man from another culture, a culture that I too had somewhere in my blood? I opened my *Michelin Green Guide* to a list of museums. "Where to first then?" I said. "I think Baba would like the Tate Modern, and the Portrait Gallery, there's a painting of Jane Grey's beheading and the light on her dress looks just—"

A smile crept across Kian's face. Clearly he thought I was feigning interest in art because of our fight earlier. So I said, to spite him, "We discussed it in my art history class at Yale." Kian hated it when I mentioned Yale. He thought I was becoming an elitist snob. So I added, "Oh, and Gui gave us a list of restaurants to try."

"I have a list of restaurants," said Kian with complete authority.

I decided to make a stab at peace. "Babajoon, Kian is going to become a chef. Everyone loves his food."

Kian didn't respond—he looked away from Baba as if expecting a reproach, and when he turned back, they exchanged an uncomfortable smile. Maybe Kian would have preferred that I keep quiet on the issue. Baba said, "Oh yes? I assumed you were studying real estate or medicine like all the other Iranians in America."

"Babajoon, real estate isn't something you study," I said. "It's something you do after you realize you're forty and you've spent the last ten years partying. Or if you're a failed novelist or dropped out of med school or something. It's the savvy mediocrity's quick backup plan."

Kian cackled at this, which gratified me.

Baba seemed puzzled. "Is this true? But there are all those Iranians . . . ?" I shrugged. Baba shook his head, and, of course, I saw his disappointment. At that age, Kian and I were the worst humans ever to roam this earth, and our loathsomeness had crystallized in universities filled with equally vile classmates. He said, in English now, "Is wrong, talking this way. Judging in this way. Is too much pride, both of you."

"He's right," said Kian. He must have been having Jesus thoughts again. "I'm sorry." I didn't respond because I wasn't sorry. I believed that the real estate business was useless, designed for garish people who planned to have zero impact on the world. These were the same people who filled wall cracks with toothpaste and pumped in fake apple pie smell just so they could squeeze a few extra dollars from young couples like Gui and me. Fuck them. "Sorry to disappoint on the med school hopes," Kian added, "but I like to cook. And it's creative. So that's what I'll do."

"Disappoint?" said Baba in the slow, easy English of the buzzed foreigner. He was half finished with his crazy dark beer. When he saw me looking, he pushed it toward me and I tasted it. It was crude oil. He said to Kian, "My son, cooking is art. And it is art from our own village and family. Is proudable, this choice."

We decided on the Portrait Gallery. Baba bought two packs of chocolate Maltesers "for the way." His cane clicked on the hard floors of the gallery in slow twos and threes, like code from a dying ship. He walked from room to room, arching his back and adjusting his weight to his good leg. "Why are these paintings uncovered?" he said. "Are they real? They just leave them here for people to touch?"

"People know not to touch them," said Kian.

Baba nodded and said, eyes and tone fully sincere, "So there are no Iranians?"

Kian burst out laughing. "There's a floor sign somewhere," he said.

Baba scoffed, shuffling along on his cane like a much older man, leaning back to examine each portrait from top to bottom. "I won't touch, in any case," he muttered, approaching a Holbein that pleased him so much that for five minutes he stood nose to nose with the unhappy subject, a minor courtier or statesman of the sixteenth century. "But I must tell you that I'm deeply tempted. Deeply."

Later he took my hand and tapped some Maltesers into it, his round cheeks moving behind his mustache, like a machine whose many pieces come to life at once. "Baba, put those away," I said, tucking the candy into his jacket. "It's not allowed."

"It doesn't say," he said, glancing around. "There's no sign."

Kian, his fatigue returning and desperate for an espresso stop, said, "It also doesn't say 'Don't take a piss on the floor.' People know."

"My son is very rude," Baba grumbled to himself, falling in step behind Kian, shaking his head to no one. "It's a lucky thing he can cook."

At a coffee shop outside the museum, Baba spun his green counting beads and asked questions about our lives. We spoke about Gui. "Is this the man you want to marry?" he asked. I said that he was, needlessly adding that we might marry by the time I began my dissertation. He asked about Kian's work and my grad school plans. After a long pause, he asked about Maman. We told him she had gone to Bangkok for some mysterious reason. She wouldn't tell us why, and we didn't press the issue. "I don't understand," said Baba. "What business could she have there?"

Between sips of his latte, which he kept sugaring and tasting, he took a folded photo out of his brown leather wallet and laid both items on the table. He had owned the wallet since I was born and it still smelled faintly of hashish. The photo was an image of some grayscale ancestor, an Ardestooni in a black suit, staring directly at the camera. I lifted it and stared in the light. It was the same man (or maybe that man's father) who had appeared in a picture he had given me years before, on our last visit to Ardestoon, when Baba gave me two photos to guard. I still had them in a box of treasures in my closet. He started to tell us a story as he sucked foam from the top of his latte and added another scoop of sugar.

He told us about our great-great-grandfather Hamidi, a doctor so skilled, people called him from all over the country to heal their sick. One day, some sultan or shah or vizier from India or Pakistan or Bangladesh (in Baba's stories, the most verifiable details are always the vaguest) sent for this doctor because his daughter was on her deathbed and in a constant state of agony. No one could fix her mysterious disease. By the time Dr. Hamidi arrived, the sultan (or shah or vizier) had lost all hope for his child. But Dr. Hamidi got right to work, mixing his herbs and the chemical combinations he had invented himself (doubtful), and within weeks, the doctor had cured the girl. Elated, her father threw a massive feast. He stuffed the doctor full of Indian (or Pakistani or Bangladeshi) delicacies for three nights, and when he was very fat, his servants put the doctor on a scale. He thought, *Well, they're going to butcher me now, the savages.* But they gave him his weight in gold and a caravan back home. And that is how most of Ardestoon was purchased.

"I tell you that story because your very existence is owed to the excellence of someone's work," he said. I had heard the excellence speech only about a thousand times and so I busied myself with my coffee. He was speaking mostly to Kian anyway. "When you make food for strangers," he said. "It must be the best. You can't dig in your freezer for leftovers or fill your stew with potatoes. You can't serve yesterday's hard bread. You must take pride! Food is joy. Joy is everything."

Kian's expression opened and he shifted forward in his chair. He didn't smile, only nodded, as if conferring on the gravest topic. Then, as Baba reached for more sugar, he took Baba's spoon from him, and sunk the grains to the bottom of the cup, sweetening the espresso instead of the foam. He discarded three scoops of sugary foam onto a plate and drenched the rest with two spoonsful of espresso, making Baba's latte softer and smoother, a delicious hazelnut brown. Baba shook his head, letting his beads dangle from his finger. He tasted his drink and smiled with his eyes.

For the next ten or twelve days, we explored London on foot and by Tube, Baba hobbling behind, asking us if we were certain of our interpretation of the Tube map and whether we needed some Maltesers. When he was tired, which was more and more often, he recited poetry that came to him from nowhere and was directed at no one. We chatted with English cab drivers and we sampled bangers and mash. Kian wanted to visit restaurants from his list, and we tried those, though Baba couldn't forgive the bland food—he ate a lot of Caesar salads with extra chicken breast and extra dressing. He loved Caesar dressing; it was a marvel to him. He called it "mayonnaise sauce"—Baba never deluded himself about the garbage he ate. We visited an Iranian restaurant, and it was the only night Baba was entirely comfortable, ordering the waitstaff to give us "the good meat" and "the newest vegetables."

Kian didn't object since the Iranian staff seemed to find this behavior normal, even welcome. No harm in a little run-of-the-mill Persian puffery, especially when it promises to end in a big tip. Somehow Baba implied the promise gracefully, raising the Iranian art of suggestion to new heights. We Persians *tarof* and pretend and make false offers. We enter contracts based solely on backslaps and shoulder squeezes. In the restaurant Baba would say to the waiter, between every insane request, every order of extra-aged garlic pickle, "The universe will reward your kindness" or "This is a higher-order of service, sir. We must find a way to thank you."

Every night Baba took a train to the home of whatever relative was hosting him. Each morning he arrived more exhausted, and so I assumed the relative lived far away, maybe not just in a suburb, but in another city. As days passed, he seemed increasingly burdened by some unsaid thing, as if he had come to London with this single goal and he was failing to accomplish it. He would start speaking over a beer, lose his thread, and by his third beer he was asking about Maman again.

One morning as our weak-chinned Covent Garden waitress, whom we now knew was called Molly, came to take our breakfast order, Baba put up his hand and said, "Miss Molly, is okay you come back in some minutes?" She said of course, poured our coffees (I think she saw the look of alarm on Kian's face), and left. Baba didn't touch his drink. He played with a loose button on his cuff. He said, "Children, I've been meaning to tell you about some changes in my life. I would like it if you carried the news to your mother in whatever way you think is best." I reached for my coffee. A foul taste was filling my mouth; maybe I knew what was coming. He said, "For some years, I had been meaning to marry again. It kept coming up and I kept putting it off. But finally, I have. I'm sure that's not a surprise to you and it won't affect your life.

But I need someone to take care of me. And this lady has been doing that for a while." He stopped, scanning our faces for reactions. I don't think my memory is distorted when I say that we were encouraging, waiting quietly for him to continue. He said, "There is another detail." He stopped, and it seemed he was trying to choose a version of a story, to decide if his adult children were strangers or allies. His gaze searched for something that we were failing to give him as he stirred his coffee without interest. He said, "There is a child."

Kian exhaled and pushed his cup away. In that second Baba seemed to decide. He waved a hand at Kian, as if to stop him from lashing out or making unkind assumptions. "She's adopted," Baba said. "We've adopted a baby girl, from Fatimeh's sister who's ill. She was born a few months ago. Very healthy." He exhaled deeply and rubbed his mouth and chin with his palm. For a moment, none of us spoke.

"Fatimeh is the name of your new wife, then?" I said, leaning in, though the whole situation sickened me. Once or twice Baba had asked me about immigrating to the West. With a child, that option would mean so much more misery; at the same time, he'd crave it all the more. I remembered Maman, when we first set off from Isfahan. The tangible, often staggering differences between a settled, educated mother, even one stuck in the Islamic Republic, and a desperate refugee parent were a daily punch in the belly. And look at Baba with his cane, already too old.

Baba smiled and nodded, relief and satisfaction coloring the slopes of his cheeks. "Fatimeh and Shirin," he said. "Those are their names."

Sometimes in the afternoon, Kian made excuses and left us alone for an hour or two. Baba and I wandered the city. We ate street nuts and tried to have conversations. "Do you want to see their picture?" he asked one day in Hyde Park. I didn't, but he was already pulling out his worn leather wallet. Staring out from a photo with uneven edges, as if cropped with small scissors, was a village woman sitting cross-legged atop one of my grandmother's best carpets, chipped toenails peeking out from under a long skirt, crooked teeth, a baby swaddled in three colors tucked under one arm. The sight of her shamed me—was this my stepmother?

Before I could think, I had blurted, "She's not from the city." Baba didn't respond. Embarrassed, I added, "That's a really cute baby. When she's older, you should enroll her in an English class. Just in case."

Baba's gaze dropped. He slipped the photo back into his wallet, careful not to catch the jagged edges on the lining. "And what if I want to teach my daughter to savor and enjoy her one brief life? What would you advise for that?"

I glared. "An easy life isn't everything, Babajoon," I said. "It's tough out there. No one hands you anything and they expect so much."

"Who expects so much?" said Baba, as if expecting an easy answer. I released a long-suffering sigh. "Okay, okay, Niloo *joon*. Let's not fight. Let's go for a tea."

A few days later, as we passed the American embassy, Baba slowed. "Niloo *joon*," he said, almost embarrassed by the request. "Do you think we could go in and ask a few questions? Maybe it won't be so hard to make a family request."

Standing on that leafy London street, I felt trapped, as if wedged into a brick lane, the close walls squeezing my rib cage with every breath. "Babajoon, without an appointment it'll take hours. And Guillaume and I might not stay in the States for long." He nodded too many times. Then he dropped the subject. In any case, in twenty-four hours, the timbre of the world would change, stifling Baba's wishes.

The next day, the planes hit the towers. Kian, Baba, and I were having afternoon drinks in a pub near Hyde Park. We had grown accustomed to one another, and to our daily routines, and our pace had slowed—we spent a lot of time in pubs and cafés. Baba was distraught. He was on his feet as soon as the bartender turned on the news. A crowd gathered around barstools below the television but no one sat, and I mumbled translations in Baba's ear. "*Ei vai*," he whispered. "It is a madness."

The people around us cradled their forearms and wiped their cheeks and rubbed their necks, their mouths. They worried their bodies as if checking for wounds. "They'll bomb us," Baba said like it was a finished thing.

"Don't jump to that thought," said Kian. "There isn't even a—"

"You think Hezbollah had no hand in this?" said Baba, his eyes glassy and hollow. Despite our truncated relationship, I'd seen Baba in the worst states, in drug-induced stupors, and in sadness and in loss. But I'd so rarely seen him scraped of hope. The man has hope stored up in his bones. "Well, think again. They're all helping each other over there. It's all the same religious insanity."

"Oh god, we have to call Maman," Kian said suddenly. He slid off his barstool, his voice jumping with alarm. "What if she gets stuck in Bangkok or something?"

Every five minutes for half an hour, Kian stepped outside and tried to dial Maman's mobile, her hotel, and her voice mail in New York. Baba and I sat and talked, nodding to Kian each time he excused himself. We couldn't order any more drinks because the bartender was distracted, and, for once, Baba had become conscious of himself as an Iranian, his usual fire dwindled to a few directionless sparks. He said,

"Niloo *joon*, do you remember when you were a girl and I came to your school to talk to your teacher?" I did remember, of course. It had been the best day. He had stormed into the school and scolded a teacher who had been cruel to me. Now I realize she was only a scared twenty-five-year-old and I had caused her to be berated by an admittedly frightening man who paid for many of the school's amenities. He continued, "I saw you doing the morning exercises. All those girls lined up, draped in gray, their little voices shrieking, *Death to America*, *death to Israel*. It was like a knife to the gut and it was the last time I visited. And now look. They've done it. Whichever group it was, does it matter? This is the result of god worship. Your mother's god as much as everyone's."

"Babajoon, stop being dramatic," I said, nibbling mindlessly on table peanuts. "The church does a lot of good in the world." I don't know why I felt the need to defend God or the church. I was an academic now.

"Yes," he said. He reached for his empty glass for the sixth or seventh time, brought it to his lips, and put it down again, gazing at it as if it had failed him. "The human heart is capable of great good." I went to flag down the bartender.

When I returned with three more bottles, including one Guinness Extra Stout, Baba was staring zombie-like at the television. I said something I had meant to say before. "Babajoon," I said, "I'm glad you have someone to take care of you."

He focused again as if he were woken from some dream. He said, "Thank you, *azizam*." He paused. "I think it's nicer having someone that I can care for. I was young and selfish when you and your brother arrived." He started nodding again, as if to some inner voice, his eyes a little sad. "Do you have someone to care for you?"

"Gui loves me," I said. "He checks on me when I'm sick and makes breakfast on weekends and talks about us to everyone. He's the nicest man."

"The nicest man," he repeated, smirking into his untouched beer. "Maybe I'm too old and Iranian to understand you, Niloo *joon*, but that answer alarms me."

"He's right for me," I said. "Stop reading into things."

"Okay," he said in English, "we toast your nice man." He clinked his beer to mine and said, an afterthought, "I tell you one rule of love. Don't trap. Don't be trapped." After that, he switched abruptly back to Farsi. "Is your mother happy? Is that man Nader still in her life?" He gulped down half his beer.

I didn't answer. The situation with Nader was complicated. He had disappeared dozens of times in the last decade. It seemed the man couldn't manage to age beyond twenty-five, forever a wandering boy. Maman stopped speaking about him years ago. But I knew she accepted his phone calls. I wondered where he was on this black day. Was he traveling somewhere in the world? Would he make it home? His passport, like all of ours, read "born in Tehran."

"I saw some recent photos of her," said Baba just as Kian was coming back from the latest phone call. "How is the atmosphere of her heart?"

What a thing to ask. I didn't want my response to seem hollow, so I said, "I think it's a little cloudy."

Kian's eyes bulged out of his head. "The fuck, Niloo," he said. He spoke fast English so Baba couldn't follow. "Don't talk about Maman to him. He abandoned us."

Baba's gaze flitted from Kian to me and back again. He shrugged his massive shoulders, sucked some beer from his upper lip. "What did your mother say?" he asked Kian. "Were you able to reach her?"

Kian said yes, but he wouldn't say more in front of Baba. Later he told me (and I told Baba) that Maman had traveled to Thailand to care for Nader, who had fallen sick in Bangkok a few months before. His doctors there had diagnosed him with stomach cancer. Having lived as a nomad most of his life, his relationships were quick and superficial and, afraid of indignity, he had hidden his condition. Maman found out accidentally, when one of his medical bills was sent to her address, which he often used when he traveled—here was a clue that had floated to her, as if by the power of his hopes. So, she bought a ticket to Bangkok the next day, packing two changes of clothes and a burlap sack of basmati rice. Maman and Nader were always a mystery, but over the years, her love for him revealed her fuller person to me, casting the faintest light in certain corners of her heart, and I learned that no matter how you betray her, no matter how often you run away, if Pari Hamidi loves you, you don't suffer alone.

That night we walked aimlessly through Leicester Square and Covent Garden, buying English treats and takeout curry that we ate on the floor of the hotel room, on a makeshift *sofreh*, while Baba inundated us with stories of home, asking if we recalled his favorite details, trying to persuade us that we're not from a bad place despite all that we would soon hear. At the end of the night, he reached for his cane, leaning beside him against one of the beds, stretched out his back, and said he would go to the station now. "Where do you go every night?" I asked. The answer couldn't be too troubling, given all that we'd already learned today about the world.

"I have a friend," he said. He put on his rain jacket.

That he didn't offer more made me angry. "How far away?" I said. "What train?" I made my tone purposely accusing.

He breathed out. "Please don't start," he said. "This isn't like last time. This is just because I prefer to sleep in a home, with a family, to eat our own food."

"I knew it," said Kian, gathering the takeout bags and the containers from which only Kian and I had eaten a meal's worth. "You can't live on Caesar salads."

"Please don't take offense," said Baba. He looked at his watch and sat down in the desk chair. "My friend Soleimani has family here. This man, he recently married into a family that I know. They like to cook for me. Hotel beds hurt. And we have some things to discuss." He paused. "When I travel to Cyprus or Istanbul or Dubai, Soleimani helps me." Even though he didn't say it, Kian and I had retained enough Iranian manners to know that he was telling us that he didn't have enough money, after that embassy-hopping trip through Eastern Europe and Asia, to pay for a second hotel room. Baba added, after a pause, "Now with this mess in New York, I think any new travel plans are finished."

Kian crumpled the paper bags into the garbage bin and placed it outside the door. He said, "If things are so hard, why'd you drag us here?"

"Drag you?" said Baba, his eyes watery and unfocused. I should have told Kian to stop, but I agreed with him—I was eager to go home. Though we were American citizens now, I wallowed in the nightmare of being rejected at the border. For a moment, Baba was silent, staring mystified at his foreign son. Kian's bluntness seemed to diminish him until finally, he said, "I blame myself for your arrogance."

"Let's not fight," I said, shooting Kian a pleading look. "I'll walk Baba to the station." I could see from Kian's face he wished he hadn't called Baba out.

But Baba was undeterred. "Do you know what Soleimani said to me the other night? He poured our whiskeys and he said, 'You have so much pride in being a doctor. All the esteem and opportunity you push into the light like decorations on your shoulder. It would just take a broken hand to take that away, Agha Doctor.' And then, to cover up his outburst, he said, 'I guess the smallest thing could ruin all of us.'" We waited for Baba to reach his point, but he already had—we had inherited his extreme pride, a canker, and we were too young to see it in ourselves. He quoted Rumi, shifting his gaze between us. "Sell your cleverness; buy some bewilderment."

I opened the door for Baba. I asked Kian to go to Marks & Spencer and fix us dessert. He nodded, his forehead relaxing. On the street, Baba said, "In pub, Kian say I 'abandon' you." He wanted to show he had understood, but then he changed back to Farsi. "That day at your school, when I heard those little girls chanting, I thought: *I will give up my children so they can leave this place*. I was afraid I'd never survive elsewhere, so maybe what Kian says is true." I didn't respond. Was this confession supposed to absolve him? I wasn't ready for that. I think he heard me in the silence. He put my arm in the crook of his and said, "This trip was a windfall. Even if this was my last visa, I tore something precious from the clenched fist of the universe."

"The clenched fist of the universe," I repeated, a delightful phrase. I saw him to his train. He shuffled to a window seat and waved to me through the glass, his smile playful, as if waving goodbye to a child. It reminded me of that other goodbye, years before. On my way out of the station, I looked at the schedule. His destination was two hours away. Four hours a day he rode on that train to be with us.

That night over strawberry and mango with lemon cake that Kian drizzled with caramel, I told my brother the things Baba had said. He ate quietly, his head resting in his hand. The next day, Baba didn't come to London. Kian called the number Baba had left and a Mr. Soleimani told us that Baba's varicose stitches had burst. Kian scribbled an address on the hotel notepad, and that night, we rode the train to a remote suburb of London. Kian asked if he might have free rein of the kitchen, and he cooked a feast for us, the kind with such meticulous attention to detail that it would put any Iranian grandmother to shame. He toasted walnuts, sweated eggplants, hand-crushed garlic, and picked fresh pistachios out of their double shells. Lounging against a wall of pillows with his tea, his hand resting on the bottom of his cane, Baba was the happiest I had seen him. He told stories all night, and the Soleimani family (six men, five women, and two children) listened raptly. Kian refused help in the kitchen, but we heard him chop and sauté as Baba recited verses and tales, the music of their talents mingling, these two intense, artistic souls, strangers to each other, making everyone forget that we were Iranians in the first days of an altered world. After dinner, Kian showed Baba a line in a poetry book and Baba smiled. "Yes, this is true. This is very true," he said, drinking in the words and his son's attention. "I will remember the wisdom and beauty of these lines. Thank you." And when I asked Kian what the poem was, he said, "Doesn't matter."

A New-Year World

JUNE 2009

Isfahan, Iran

When two thuggish ill-wishers who have much to gain financially from one's death enter one's bedroom unannounced, it's natural to indulge in a little deathbed hysteria. But Bahman didn't. He had seen such plays at aggression, the chest-thumping puffery and swagger of certain Iranian men (usually anxious ones with a little money and not much education, the kind from South Tehran), and he knew the limits of Sanaz's hurt and resentment. So not death, but they would hurt him.

The queasy paralysis of the withdrawal helped. He had been slipping in and out of a long stupor, and the painful spasms racking his body seemed wholly unrelated to any physical impetus. The entire event might have been a dream. Oh, how the universe turns on itself! How nimbly some infections spread, unseen until their work is done. Soleimani had once been his friend—had he harbored hatred for him in those days? Before Bahman married Sanaz, Soleimani's family had hosted him and his children in London. Now the same man shoved a pillow over his face, putting on a show to intimidate him. He leaned on top of him and spoke into his ear, promising to kill him if he touched Sanaz again. Bahman choked into the cottony mound, fabric filling his mouth and crushing his nose. He felt the man's cold spit in his ear but didn't struggle. Though his heart was pounding out a fitful rhythm, the weary organ threatening to explode out of his chest, he knew how much to expect. Mostly he thought, *How did my life come to this? I was the cleverest student in medical school.* And then, an unbidden thought, out of the ether: *Why did I become a dental surgeon instead of trying for more? Why did teeth seem to matter so much more than the heart or the brain? Was I lazy? Did I not trust myself?* Even as a young man, he had a special reverence for the human mouth. He had always been attracted to a flawless smile, and teeth fascinated him, these instruments of tearing that tie us to our primal ancestors, and yet are signals of modern refinement and grace. Now these thoughts came to him as he endured the pillow over his face, his body too weak and unwilling to engage in the drama of a few seconds without oxygen.

Soleimani lifted the pillow. He stared at Bahman with a cold gaze and said, "I would break your hand." Something writhed in Bahman's stomach. This was a credible threat—hadn't he once accused him of arrogance, claiming that all his pride would be gone with one fracture of the hand? "But your prospects are Sanaz's too." He punched Bahman in the gut. Bahman heaved clear acrid bile onto his pillow.

Then the two men left. On his way out, the bearded man cast an apologetic glance around the girlish room, eyeing the apricot wallpaper, the yellow plastic wastebasket. Bahman waited half an hour (or was it five minutes?). He sat up in his bed, panting, wiping his brow, and staring at the black television screen. He swallowed some water. He felt no pain in his stomach but his legs itched badly. And he sensed that the diarrhea phase was about to begin. He called to Fatimeh. She hadn't heard Sanaz let the men in. "That shit-eating snake!" Fatimeh said. "Please let me put some turmeric in the princess's face soap." Bahman chuckled. He had forgotten Fatimeh's rural humor. He gave her some cash and asked her to take it to the guards. "Tell them they could at least protect us from break-ins." Of course, Bahman knew that the intruders had also paid the guards. But what he was offering was undoubtedly more. How foolish he had been not to pay them from the start.

When she had carried out his errand, Fatimeh cleaned his sheets and helped him change his pajamas. A distinctive fresh scent, like lilac and tea leaves, filled the room as soon as the new sheets were on, and Bahman realized how much grime he had been living in, layers of sweat after a day of vomiting. The indignity of allowing Fatimeh to clean his soiled linens didn't bother him. This was his third detox attempt. And Sanaz had been the only woman from whom he had tried to hide the disgraces of being human, and of growing older.

Maybe Fatimeh, with her hardworking village sheen, was his only true friend. As she was leaving, he called to her, panting between words as a wave of nausea hit him in the throat, making his mouth water. These animal spasms repulsed him. "Fatimeh *joon* . . . when this is all over . . . let me repair your teeth."

Her brown and broken smile died and deep grooves settled on her cheeks, bracketing her face. Her marble blue eyes, a sign of northern blood like his ginger hair, clouded over, and she said, "Go to sleep," and closed the door gently behind.

For three days, he suffered. The diarrhea came and went. The shivers intensified and receded. The itching stopped. Waves of pain and wooziness and delirium crashed down on him, possessed his body, then released him. For an entire day, his face seemed to be melting, as every crevice began to stream, eyes and nose and mouth becoming loose spigots of mucus and water and blood.

Meanwhile, the women fought. Sometimes Bahman saw it, and tried to understand their individual grief. Had Sanaz never been confronted by a supposed rival who refuses to compete? Did Fatimeh hold out hope of returning to this house?

"What do you want here?" Sanaz would shriek when she couldn't think of any new cruelties to fling at Fatimeh, no more pots to salt or medicines to throw out. Once Sanaz threw out Fatimeh's spice jar from Ardestoon, and Fatimeh wept alone in her room, because each year the spice is different. That year's special taste had ended early for her, only three months after the New Year.

Fatimeh's tactic was often just stony silence. She only answered on every fourth outburst, and even then it was usually an under-the-breath "God help you" or an impish reedy-voiced reference to Sanaz's blood pressure.

Sometimes, when he was feeling well, Bahman entertained himself by goading them. "Why are you here?" Sanaz would ask Fatimeh again at lunchtime.

Bahman would grin wide, forgetting about the missing tooth in the back. "I like her food," he'd say. "It's full of butter."

"It's full of butter," Fatimeh would drone, hiding a smirk, keeping her eyes on her cross-stitch or on Shirin's coloring book. Shirin often sat in her lap as they ate.

"Come now! You like it too," Bahman would prod Sanaz. "Look how much we've both grown." And Sanaz's arm would circle her waist and she would glare.

"Who wants to do recitations?" Bahman would say. Then he would offer up an easy one for Sanaz, something from the *Rubaiyat* perhaps. "*Here with a loaf of bread beneath the bough*," he would murmur to himself, pretending to be stuck.

Sanaz would sit silently chewing, refusing the bait. But as soon as Fatimeh opened her mouth, Sanaz would say, as if she were doing him a favor, "*A flask of wine, a book of verse, and thou.*"

He would tap his chin and nod as if saying, *Oh yes, now I remember*, then with feigned difficulty, "*Beside me singing in the wilderness.*"

They always let Shirin do the last line. She would scream, "*And wilderness is paradise enow!*" At such times, Bahman always thought of the girl's natural father.

On the fourth morning, while the women and Shirin were food shopping, Bahman phoned Donya Norouzi. This woman's appearance in his life was a sign from whatever pitiless gods might exist. Regardless, he wasn't certain what hope he sought from her. He told himself he wanted to help.

A man answered on the second ring. Given Bahman's gruff, aged voice like smoky scotch, and his title, and his presence, he had no trouble getting her on the phone. A quick, "I'm Dr. Hamidi, DDS, please put Ms. Norouzi on" was enough. The trick of getting these rural men to put their women on the phone with another man was the cloak of the professional: no apologies, no explanations, and, most important, the ability to endure the silence that followed with a kind of ease that carries through the phone. He chuckled, thinking if only he had known this trick when he was twenty, a ginger university student with a footballer physique and a married lover he could never get on the phone. That was before he met Pari in a waiting room and fell instantly in love.

Donya seemed cautious, her voice breathless and low, her mouth obviously pressed to the receiver. Someone must have been listening, because instead of asking, "Who is this?" she pretended to know him. "Doctor?" she said.

He realized now that he had no sane reason for calling, and, yes, surely some man (or his nosy mother) was listening. He couldn't speak openly this way. He said, "Khanom Norouzi, I need to change your gum graft to four p.m. tomorrow. Can you come to my office then?" In his office, he could find out her situation, maybe try to help.

"Your office?" she repeated.

He gave her the address, making sure to specify thrice that it was a dental office. As he spoke, he strained to make his voice older, more jolly and foolish. With the listener handled, he added, to convince her, "I'm sorry I didn't say hello at the courthouse. I saw you, and I thought, who wants to be reminded of their receding gums in the middle of their legal matter. I hope whatever papers you were signing weren't too tiresome, and that there's not too much pain in your mouth."

"No, Doctor," she mumbled. Somewhere far off, he heard a click. It seemed the listener found Donya's gums too boring to wait for the pleasantries to end.

He was sure she would come. He hung up and congratulated himself. He hadn't been involved in a good scheme in years. When he was young, he created fun out of thin air. He used to play pranks on Pari every day. Why did he stop?

He thought, *Maybe I'll play a joke on Fatimeh*. But he couldn't think of any.

He wandered out to the front door and waved a guard to him. He was still ill, his hair stuck to his head from the constant sweating. "*Agha*," he said, holding out a handful of bills. "I need to visit my dental office tomorrow at four. Can you call the judge and get permission?"

"Call him yourself," said the guard, annoyed at having been made to stand and walk. "If he agrees, we'll take you." He took the money and returned to the car.

Ali secured the judge's permission. Again, it required money, but Ali's charm was unparalleled and he got some extra information too: the court was finding very little evidence of Bahman's guilt, and the judge would illuminate his fate soon. Not that a lack of evidence ever stalled a guilty verdict in this country: the judge must have hobbled to the realization that Bahman was harmless, not a plausible criminal to be made an example of, and useful to the economy and to the judge personally.

The next day, Ali came to the house and the two brothers accompanied one of the guards to Bahman's office building. Ali waited with the guard downstairs (this would buy more time), while Bahman, his pocket full of aspirins, went upstairs. For the first time since his latest varicose flare-up the previous year, he walked with a cane. Halfway up the stairs, he stopped and tossed two more aspirins into his mouth. His office was on the third floor of a modest complex, and a steady stream of banking and jewelry repair customers entered the front doors every hour. When he was settled in his leather desk chair, he looked out the window at the guard's olive car. At four o'clock, he spotted Donya entering the main door unbothered.

He wasn't sure what he wanted to say. He sat at his desk and stared at a locked drawer. Inside were cash and documents. Behind those, in an invisible compartment installed by the city's craftiest furniture designer, he stored extra opium and a pipe. His itchy arms and exhausted stomach, his ruined throat, begged him to open it. Just to smell it for one boundless moment. He resisted, retrieving only some cash and an envelope, on which he printed Donya's name.

He tidied his desk a bit—though Ali had already gone through the inbox, the outbox, last month's receipts, and the calendar. She entered without ringing the bell, perhaps thinking that this was a clinic and not a private office. "*Akh*, excuse me," she said when she found him sitting alone at the desk beneath a giant photo of a four-year-old nurse (Niloo, 1983), mouthing "Shhhh." The best thing about that photo, the thing that most people noticed, was that Niloo wasn't making the universal quiet gesture. She was touching her nose with the pad of her finger, and looking at something in the same palm. The only indication of her intention was the menacing pursed lips and gathered eyebrows.

"Khanom Norouzi?" said Bahman, getting up. "Come in. I made tea." He was aware that he sounded like a teenage suitor, and indeed he was nervous.

"Look, *agha*," she said, loosening her scarf, "I know what you want. You heard my situation and you decided I need money, right? You think we could arrange a temporary marriage for a few hours?" Bahman flushed. Mortified, he tried to speak, but wasn't his purpose indeed to offer her money? Wasn't he, in fact, holding an envelope with her name on it? And yet, why did simple kind acts always go this way? Maybe it was punishment for giving so little to Pari and the children when they left. Donya looked around the empty office, then at his cane. "No patients today, *agha*?" When Bahman coughed into his hand, she softened. "Look, don't get upset. I can use the money, but I'm sorry to tell you that my divorce never went through."

"No, *khanom*, you misunderstand completely," he said. "Please just sit down. I don't want to marry you, or anything remotely like that."

She sat in a plastic chair across from him, adjusting her navy manteau around her haunches. She tossed her yellow sunglasses on his desk. "My teeth are fine."

He could see from across the desk that they were not. Her maxillary central incisors were crowding each other like riffraff outside a cheap butcher shop. He said, "I feel moved by your situation. I saw that you were forced to stay."

Her brow wrinkled and she stared at him confused. "And?"

"I only want to help. To share what luck I've found." He pushed the envelope toward her. "I have a daughter. I only want to see some good come to you."

She looked inside the envelope, her suspicious gaze back on him when she saw the amount. He had given her the equivalent of three thousand American dollars, a sum that might pay her rent for six months, if she wanted to live alone in the city. He searched in his pocket for the aspirin and took two more with water. She seemed unsure whether to refuse three times as was customary. This might be an amount too big for *tarof*. "What do you want?" she asked again, reaching for her glasses as if she might take the money and run out the door.

Suddenly he had no fatherly advice, no words to offer. The money, it seemed, was all he had to give. He shrugged. "I'm still stuck too," he said, wiping his brow. He felt so weak and he imagined that he could smell the sweet opium in his desk. Maybe he would smoke it once this lady had absconded with her windfall.

She sat silently for a moment, her shoulders relaxing; maybe she was talking herself into trusting him. "*Agha*, are you sick?" she asked. "Are you dying?"

He laughed. Yes; maybe he was looking and acting terminal. "I'm just tired," he said. "Take the money. I hope we both get unstuck soon. We made it out of jail, didn't we?" He tried to dust off his old Cheshire grin, a ghost of his youthful smile.

She tucked the envelope into her handbag and eyed the name plaque on his desk. "Look, Dr. Hamidi," she said, "I went through the same anger and regret at first, and then I realized something: What does it matter what the law says? If you're married or divorced, none of it matters outside the borders of this shit country."

"Which happens to be where we live," he said, reaching for his beads. Briefly he wondered why this woman's perspective mattered to him. Maybe she reminded him of Niloo, or maybe this was just his time to hear what was echoing all around.

"Not for me," she said. She picked her cuticles as if uncertain about trusting him. "Not for long. Look at what's happening in the streets; riots, killings, arrests. Neda. If you make it out of the country, you can throw yourself at some embassy's mercy, *agha joon*. There's Istanbul or Dubai. Just go and live your life."

He chuckled. "Just abandon it all," he said, "like some vagrant. I'll leave that to the young." He thought of a time when he could have left, when he could have joined Pari and their children. Instead, he had locked himself in this office, passing the hours in a miasma of opium smoke. He had waved goodbye through the window, unable to leave behind his practice, his reputation, his warm village, and his photos.

"What do you have here that's so important," she said, pulling a loose strand of hair out of the sunglasses, "especially if your path put you in that court?"

As she was leaving, he called after her, "*Khanom*, can I ask why you wanted a divorce? Was he an addict or a philanderer or what?"

She smiled. "Those are just reasons for courts."

"What then?" he pressed. "Did you fall in love? Why the hysterics?"

She shrugged. "It's a curse to be a bad fit. It's like spending every day trying to force a hundred mixed-up lids onto the wrong jars. People think that's not enough reason, but it's the one thing that's unfixable. It poisons everything."

Alone again, he sat at his desk, fondling the tiny key to the compartment. He was so close to freedom from this disease, closer than he had been the last two times. He tried to remember a time when he didn't need the wretched plant, when he could travel to the other side of the earth and simply wander, to have a coffee or a sandwich outside, speak to a stranger, not bothering or panicking about how to procure some. He thought of his first time around a *manghal*, when he tried opium with a group of young friends in a sour cherry orchard in Ardestoon just before he set off for university. They sat in a rustle of trees munching on sour plums and pistachios, and someone lit the *manghal* and filled it. Pari often said, when she tried to get him through those two detoxes by the power of desire alone, that those boys had turned him into an addict on purpose, so that he would be forever tied to Ardestoon, so that he wouldn't go off and live freely as a doctor in Tehran. Had they succeeded? He never stayed in Tehran. He made his home in the closest city to Ardestoon, returning every Friday to the village of his youth. Did he return for his mother and father, his warm community, the thick stews of his childhood sickbeds and the bowlfuls of mulberries from their orchards? Or did he return for the *manghal*? That first time he smoked, his body brimmed with love for the universe, for every woman in it, for every showy pirouette of nature. He wanted to be a part of it and to change it. He wanted to suck its marrow with enough recklessness to break the bone, break his jaw, break with the earth and float in the ether. That first time, it wasn't oblivion he wanted but to be a deity in his own orbit.

"How is the atmosphere of your heart?" his father asked once, after they had smoked together, their speech thickening, their words growing strange and poetic. His father wore a loose *shalwar* and skullcap. He farmed and didn't ask after hearts.

Bahman said, "As if it devoured every other heart and it's alone in the world."

His father nodded, and said, "The *manghal* is only for certain great moments."

Bahman stroked the mahogany desk his friend had built, its hidden panels and flawless curves. He recalled a 2006 visit to Madrid. Again he had wounded his children with his habit. It was enough. Fifty-five was no end. He dropped the key into his safe, pocketed a roll of bills, reached for his cane, and headed downstairs.

That night he suffered the depths of it. He tossed and turned, his nightmares melting into silhouettes of Fatimeh and Sanaz coming in and out with cold towels and sheets and hot food he never touched. Finally, the pain reached his deep tissue, an agony like marrow leaking out. Like bones stuffed so full that they might burst, staining his flesh. But he knew the end would come and he didn't beg for opium this time; he knew he wouldn't. He shivered through the night, his stomach cramping so often and so hard that in the early morning hours he soiled himself. He tried to hobble out of bed, to clean it quietly, but his arms were too weak. He made noises. He fell. Soon Fatimeh arrived with tea. She didn't comment on the mess. She simply started cleaning, humming a song she used to sing to Shirin.

The song brought on the urge to weep. He wanted to ask, "Why did you love that drifter instead? I gave you a comfortable life. I gave you so many possibilities." His mouth was dry, his voice raspy, but he managed to say some of it.

She wrapped the sheets in a tight bundle, tying them by the corners. She had never offered an explanation. Now too, she said, "I think we're all part beast."

The comment stung. Was she referring to his current state? Laid so low that he was soiling himself like a caged animal? He wanted to lash out, but he didn't have the strength or will. It seemed that his pride had seeped out along with whatever toxins his body was expelling. "I'm sorry," he said. "My body is failing." Humiliation weighed down his voice like a dense tumor in the throat.

Tucking the bundle under her arm, Fatimeh said, "Don't be crazy. I know everything about you. What do you have that I don't know?" He fell asleep on the chair as she was putting on new sheets. She woke him and rolled him onto the bed.

Five days later, Bahman would pass an entire day reading, drinking tea, and playing with Shirin. He would sink into his bed contentedly and exhaustedly, having lived his first day in three decades with neither opium in his blood nor any vomiting or shivers. A few days after that, he would return to work. He would spend his days waiting for Niloo to respond to his letter, and then, in August, he would give up. He would pack a bag and the next morning would leave Isfahan. Searching his office, the police would find no further evidence of his guilt, only medical supplies, office papers, and stacks of photos from his childhood and his children's in Ardestoon.

Maybe, in that final fitful and humiliating night, his body twisting under warm lilac sheets, as it tried to shake off this demon he had carried for decades, Bahman sensed the winds changing. Maybe he sensed that his arrest would soon end, and that it was time to rend some joy from the clenched fist of the universe. Lying in a haze, trying to ignore the sensation of a thousand insects crawling across him, he planned his last days. He would give up his house, signing it over to Fatimeh and Sanaz, begging them to get along. He would take the cash in his desk and one modest bag and ride to the airport with his brother Ali in the same car that carried his children away decades before. Then, with his purchased exit visa, on to Istanbul.

He would have to abandon many beloved things. Not just his house, but his name and place in the world, his community, his patchwork second family. It pained him especially to leave his sizeable collection of photos. But of all the musings and unwanted wisdom he had received in the past months, only two remained fresh in his ear. *What do you have here that's so important?* Donya had asked. The photos? The money? Money was for living, and photos were paper, images from a life he no longer lived. They were stray sparks from a fire too far away to offer warmth.

The second voice that tickled his ear was Fatimeh's, the claim to know him absolutely. How sad it is when someone who has left your orbit, whose memory has receded, holds such intimate knowledge. Meeting them again feels like renewed loss, and it's full of tremors and watery eyes and involuntary responses much like a bout of opium withdrawal, not only because every familiar detail—their blue eyes or their yellowing laugh or a charming turn of their hand—is like a coil of skin peeled from the heart, but because they took away that knowledge of you with them, that snapshot of you, out into the world. And as they changed, everything that they knew changed too. And so you are unwittingly altered.

In this world, there were a hundred variations of him, like dolls made in the same workshop, identical except maybe a narrower head, sleepier eyes, or bushier eyebrows—details that would attract only the briefest pause in anyone but a collector, someone with their heart deep in it. These versions circled the earth, in people's memories of him, in their stories, and each time he greeted a friend after a long absence, he would meet himself anew. Thinking of this and of his children, he tried to recall how he had seemed to them in Oklahoma, then in London and Madrid and Istanbul. Sometimes on the phone, he sensed their childish awe of him waning and had to excuse himself and hang up, their disappointment quietly flooding his lungs like an unseen current. Now he was on his way to them for a fifth time; maybe he would reach one of them this month or next. He conjured those many incarnations of himself, trying to imagine how time will have distorted them. He recalled a line that Kian had shown him in a poetry book in London years ago. *Beware o wanderer, the road is walking too.* And so he tried to shift his lens to match theirs, to see the moving road underfoot, and when he couldn't, he was afraid.

An Addict in Dam Square

SEPTEMBER—OCTOBER 2009

Amsterdam, Netherlands

In Farsi, there's an expression of longing, *my teeth itch for you*. It covers many animal urges. Lovers say it to each other. Parents say it to especially delicious toddlers. Kian used to get it constantly as a kid, his fleshy balloon cheeks always on the verge of being chomped by some adult's waiting maw. Siavash said it once to a leg of lamb he was barbecuing. Lately Niloo's teeth have begun to itch: for the new community she's found, its hearty stews and vintage songs, for work, for the apartment she is building with Gui, for Amsterdam, and for everything Iranian.

She has begun to spend all her free time at the squat; not just the storytelling nights but other events too: folk bands, *setar* players, a local violinist, a Q&A with a minor politician. She even shows up on off nights just to talk to the young Iranians who live there, the ones who came recently from Tehran or Isfahan or Shiraz, usually escaping charges of moral crimes: underground music, homosexuality, involvement with anti-Ahmadinejad intellectuals. The refugees share two small rooms in the back of the squat and cook Persian food every Thursday. Siavash joins them on those days. They play soccer in the early afternoon, then cook together, eat, smoke, and drink well into the morning hours. Niloo always stays till the end, and she has never again invited Gui to come along. When he asks where she's going, she tells the truth, but won't entertain any offers to intervene or discussions of the dangers her new friends pose. She knows he wishes she'd found a different type of Iranian friend (maybe some Group Two women for safe chitchat over lunch on some Amstel River terrace). Now that she has chosen her friends, though, Gui is constantly trying to manage her involvement, to offer his own services so she might step back. Once she overheard him sighing into his phone to Heldring, "She's befriended a refugee." He waited a long time as Heldring opined. Niloo ignores these efforts. She accompanies Karim to more offices, translating his stories to elegant English.

Often afterward she invites Karim for a beer and cheese fritters; usually he declines. One day she finds him sitting alone on the stone ledge of a canal, near the spot where they have arranged to meet. He is singing a song from before the revolution, late sixties or early seventies. She sits beside him, her legs dangling over the water. He tells her about his wife, his baby daughter, and the guitar he left at home.

She calls Mam'mad to discuss Karim's health. Is he depressed? Mam'mad doesn't return her call for several days and when he does, he's vague. He sounds older, his voice hoarse. When she hangs up, Gui suggests a weekend in Paris, but Niloo says she's too busy and goes to sit in the closet and think.

"So you don't think it's hypocritical." Gui starts up one night, even though she's already turning the doorknob, her jacket in hand.

"Oh Christ, why hypocritical?" she sighs.

"Look, do what you want," says Gui from the couch. He's reading a novel they've agreed to read together but Niloo hasn't yet begun. "I'm just saying instead of translating for this Karim, you could look into your own father's situation."

"What situation?" she snaps, and they're off. She spends the rest of the night fighting with her husband, a more frequent occurrence as the months pass.

On story nights, she devours poetry and Old Persian tales; they all do, the stories dissolve the grimness of the passing weeks for men like Mam'mad and Karim, their lives dripping away day after day in limbo. Soon, Karim finds a temporary job and Mam'mad takes to hermitage and she spends her evenings with Siavash and his tight-lipped girlfriend, Mala. She comes to think of herself as an Iranian immigrant again, a child refugee, not an American expat—the difference having to do with options, purpose, and personal control. Like many Middle Eastern immigrants, she watches the growing influence of Wilders with awe and trepidation. She reads up on his political career, his rants against Islam ("Take a walk down the street . . . before you know it, there will be more mosques than churches"), his casual racism ("Netherarabia will just be a matter of time!"), his proposals to tax women in hijab and place moratoria on "non-Western" immigrants, and worst of all, the way he appeals to poorly educated rural farmers with his openly hostile attitude to Holland's large Middle Eastern and North African populations. Wilders controls the PVV, a frighteningly popular party. In a message to refugees, he says outright, "You will not make the Netherlands home." After that broadcast, she fights with Gui, who claims that Wilders is just a politician appeasing his constituents. She leaves the apartment, slamming the door behind her. She texts Siavash and asks if he has eaten.

"That man is the Ahmadinejad of the Dutch," says Siavash, shaking his head. "The same cartoonish villainy, but worse, because he doesn't have to resort to fraud. He has serious followers." They are sitting in a Turkish restaurant where the owner plays a drum-like string instrument, maybe an *oud*, a few feet from them, and the waiter refills their eggplant as urgently as one would refill water. Sometimes Karim works here, busing tables for cash and sending the money to the poor suburb of Tehran where his wife and children still live. Tonight Karim is nowhere to be found, but they decide to stay anyway. "I wonder where he's hiding," says Sy.

"And Mam'mad," says Niloo, "where is he?" Siavash shrugs and heaps yogurt-cucumber onto her plate. She dips her bread in it. "It's not like him," she mutters.

"We should leave them alone for a while," says Sy. "They're in the same bad situation. They want to go to their secret corner and moan about wives and visas."

Weeks ago, in August, Ahmadinejad was inaugurated for a second term as president of Iran and, again, protests sprang up everywhere. "Death to the dictator," the people chanted, and demonstrations in and out of Iran continued. Since the election in June, the newly stoked fire among the Persians of the West has grown into a full roaring flame, maybe accomplishing nothing more than the sense of closeness it creates to their native country and its history. Regardless, Niloo and her friends have attended most of the events in Amsterdam and The Hague, often stopping for drinks afterward with fellow protestors, or going off by themselves to dark, dingy brown cafés, talking for hours over fries and cheap carafes of red wine.

All through September, Mousavi and fellow candidate Mehdi Karoubi encourage protests. A large demonstration is held in New York outside the U.N. General Assembly. In October, Karoubi is attacked by Basij militia at a press gathering, the most recent episode in a campaign of harassment against the two candidates. Furious, Siavash and two of his friends, students who have just arrived from Tehran and protested there as recently as July, barely escaping arrest, organize a demonstration at the Spinoza Monument, a statue near Waterlooplein on the Amstel River. They cut out masks of Mousavi and Karoubi and glue them onto sticks, captioned with Spinoza's famous quote, "The purpose of the state is freedom." Niloo dresses in green and joins the protestors, holding the sign over her face as a small array of local magazine writers photograph them and ask for quotes. A journalist from the BBC appears, takes a handful of photos, asks a single question, and leaves. Siavash does all of the talking.

At home she tries to respond to Baba's email. She says in Finglish, *Babajoon, can you talk on the phone? I don't know who's reading these.*

A reply arrives two minutes later—Baba couldn't type that fast if someone lit a match under his palms. And it's not in Finglish, but in Farsi letters, using a Farsi keyboard. *You have been the worst daughter. You write as if nothing is happening, just a casual hello. The country is going up in flames. Your Baba is suffering a hundred things. You ungrateful, selfish girl. It must be your mother's toxic blood.*

She writes back in a way only her Baba would understand, using children's books they once read together. *Babajoon, what shrill, girlish voice you have.*

Another swift reply: *You ignore his emails. He's always waiting. What's more urgent than your family suffering in this chaos? Maybe you don't get news over there.*

Niloo chuckles at the clumsy attempt to chastise her. She's heard stories of this woman from her mother and Kian. She doesn't love Baba; she loves drama. So, Niloo replies with the insult that's most effective on all four groups of exiled Iranians, and therefore, probably the ones in Iran as well: barefaced class shaming. *I didn't realize Baba hired a house girl. Please tell him to call his daughter.*

He won't call. Baba has always behaved strangely on the phone. Once, years ago, he called her after months of silence. She had the afternoon free, and briefly she craved to share her stories with him, to hear his. But he only asked about her health and whether her phone number was permanent and, three minutes later, said goodbye. "It was good to hear your voice," he said, his voice gruff and shaky but resolute—had she misstepped again? Then he was gone, leaving her many stories hanging off her tongue. Later Maman told her that calls from Iran are expensive. "That's all it is, baby *joon*. He called from a good heart. Don't make it negative."

Two seconds later, a final email from Baba's account, an almost lovable approximation of English: *Fock you.*

When Gui comes home, she is lying on the couch, her face buried in a decorative pillow. Lifting her head, she feels the embroidered pattern imprinted on her cheeks. Gui sits beside her, strokes her hair, and so she tells him about the protest and the emails. "Why did you engage with her?" he says. "You wrap your mouth around the exhaust pipe of humanity and then you ask, *Why do I feel bad*?"

"Who's the exhaust pipe of humanity?" she asks, defenses rising.

"I mean the collective garbage from everyone," he says. "The narcissism and drama and misery. You suck it in like it's a strawberry water pipe." She smiles—Gui learned to love fruit pipes last year in Istanbul, her fourth trip to see Baba.

That night, she sits cross-legged in the storytelling squat with her new community, these misfits with whom she shares noses and dark hair, restless fits and native tastes. They eat lemon-barley soup and watch themselves on BBC One. Everyone cheers when Siavash speaks, and his smile thaws his features and warms the room. If his gaze rests, even on a stranger, his eyes are generous.

Niloo cancels two beginning anthropology lectures in a month. She lies awake at night, fantasizing about being a newly arrived immigrant again, about how different it would be if she were an adult and not a child. She imagines being stronger than she was then, poor but independent, about having a young lover who speaks her native tongue, who eats the same dishes and understands Maman's jokes, a man to whom her parents will sound as educated as they are.

She starts going for drinks and coffees with Siavash, thinking a friendship with him is more realistic than one with Mam'mad, who is her father's age and has all but disappeared, or Karim, who has hit a lucky streak in his never-ending search for work. Sy feels closer to her age, not because he is (Karim is two years older, Sy five years younger), but because they both grew up in America, where aging happens at a different pace. Too tired to fight, she doesn't tell Gui.

She accompanies Siavash to three outdoor speeches, and the crackling tension among the students, the young immigrant families, often illegals and squatters, exhilarates her, fueling her passion for this new phase. She is part of an important movement; she has friends linked to her by blood, culture, and native words; she feels something like purpose. It seems that for years she has lived under a mild, teetering sedation, waiting for a spell to break, for something to puncture her skin, releasing the weariness and bringing her back to the waking world.

For a while, she stops making lists. Reading over the rules she made for Gui months before, she blushes. She doesn't mention them again, and stops interrupting him at work. One day, in a fit of nostalgia, she sends him a message. *I love you, Gui. I'm thankful for that frantic, naive Niloo who chose you*. His reply, touched and surprised and solicitous, saddens her. Has she been so neglectful of his heart?

Then, one night, a treasure arrives. The doorbell rings and Niloo unwraps herself from under a shawl, letting a pile of printouts and notes flutter to the ground as she stands. The wood-beamed flat is cold in late fall, and Niloo has grown eager to move into her new apartment. Outside, a sweaty teenager shaped like an oil drum holds a package out to her, keeping his foot on the top stair as if taking that last step might cost him his tram home. With each breath, his belly spills out of his red jeans like soufflé batter rising from a red ramekin, then recedes as if someone has opened the oven door. He grunts *dank je wel* for her five euros and leaves without goodbye.

The box is unlabeled and unsealed, the flaps folded in a crosshatch as if to flaunt the sender's trust in the carrier. A faded logo in Farsi contains a single familiar word. *Ardestoon*. It's enough to make Niloo recoil from the box. She wants to make tea first, to prepare herself for exposure to its contents, last revealed in Iranian light. But she doesn't. She sits in her chair, kicking away the papers, and tears through the brown cardboard. Her grandmother has tucked a photo of herself inside, atop a mason jar of *advieh*—mixed spices. The jar is wrapped first in a torn piece of blue fabric, then a plastic bag, then a page from an Iranian newspaper. Unwrapping it is archeology, and it thrills her to dig down to the jar. Through the murky glass, the spice shines a deep sunflower yellow, with flecks of browns and oranges scattered in. More blue fabric peeks out from under the sharp metal lid.

For a seventy-year-old Iranian villager to send a package of unlabeled herbs from her tiny riverside farm to Amsterdam is an unreliable and expensive feat, and so it makes sense that she skipped the post and enlisted some Europe-bound relative—like her granddaughter Niloo, Aziz *joon* is a logical, precise woman, weighing every option. That relative likely landed in London and sent the package to a cousin in Holland, and the cousin gave it to a neighbor or courier and so forth.

To Niloo the worth of the package is incalculable, the smell of it transporting her to her grandmother's kitchen. Then she spots the letter at the bottom of the package, its telltale handwriting, its dingy, smudged paper, a bureaucratic pastel blue, infecting the entire box. So it seems that the spice jar isn't a kind gesture, after all. And maybe it isn't such a treasure either, just a cheap trinket to disguise and transport the letter, which must have already failed to reach Niloo once or twice. The logic of grandmothers is practical and sharp. The hand-stamped postmark in the corner of the letter reads *airmail*, but then over the mangled attempt at *Nederland*, someone has written in Farsi *undeliverable*. The return address has been scratched out. But who could miss the signs? Everything that her Baba touches smells the same way, that earthy stench of hashish and opium that still lingers on Niloo's birth certificate and on an old copy of Rumi's poems that he once sent.

She stares at the envelope for a while, then stuffs it unopened into a kitchen drawer that Guillaume is unlikely to check, the one with can openers and carrot peelers. Why does he insist? Doesn't he know that there is no paradise to be found here? The smell of Baba's drugs on her fingers makes her sick, so she washes her hands and throws away the box. She wants to cook with the spices right away, to powder some chicken thighs with them, or mix the pretty yellow concoction with some bread crumbs and sauté some mushrooms in it. The idea of waiting suddenly seems impossible. She finds a pot and starts warming olive oil. She chops the ends off an onion and peels the skin with one practiced motion, anticipating that soothing sizzle.

Working with that jar, she forgets her meticulous habits—Gui often teases her for measuring everything with laboratory precision, scraping the excess sugar from tablespoons with a sharp knife, displacing water with a chunk of butter to know the butter's exact volume. But the jar makes magic of her fingers, and she sprinkles and pinches and tosses with Ardestooni abandon. The yellow turmeric stain on her fingers delights her. It conjures Nader, the young lover of her mother's haunted, heart-skinned first years as an immigrant. He is dead now. He used to stand around shirtless with giant earphones on, whipping eggs, and as a pitiless child, Niloo hated him. It also brings back memories of her grandmother, and the grandmothers of her school friends—every old woman in Iran has fingers stained by turmeric root.

Every night for a week, Niloo cooks with her grandmother's spices. She wonders, will Gui notice the change in his food? Every year Ardestooni women mix an enormous batch of *advieh*. They fill a hundred mason jars and give one to each family so that everyone's food tastes similar that year (except maybe the rebellious grandmothers who use the jar to hide their opium balls; their food is, of course, the best). Usually they grind over thirty spices in the mix, all from leaves and roots and nuts, nothing preserved or bought—turmeric root and cumin seeds, naturally, but also coriander, ground teas and flower petals, onion, garlic, maybe ginger, a fistful of fenugreek and pinches of peppers. Each year the quality and the ratios change, maybe even one or two key ingredients, so that over a decade the taste and smell transform, but year by year they only adjust, like a lover aging.

But Gui doesn't notice, and she begins packing up her creations in plastic tubs to take to Mam'mad, whose all-egg diet can't possibly be healthy.

Fueled by a constant hunger, she returns to the squat. She searches out protests and shouts slogans at cameras. She watches the BBC, hoping for more coverage. She listens to Siavash discuss racism and Zwarte Piets (November will bring this Dutch horror into full view again; children and adults in blackface, playing the Dutch Santa's gold-hooped "helpers"), immigration policy, the fate of amateur arts in Holland, and Wilders, whose subtlest rise in power threatens the lives so many have built here, on the cold, hard soil of this unwelcoming country.

In late fall, an Iranian illegal threatens to burn himself. They lose days trying to track his family, bringing him stews over basmati rice so he might feel at home, trying to find a trustworthy psychologist who might speak to him. He never eats a bite and his family can't be reached. The psychologist starts coming to the squat, but they never call any Dutch agency. The Dutch, Mam'mad reminds them wearily, wouldn't try to understand the man; their solution would be cold and swift.

Mam'mad, who has grown gaunt and pale and has stopped harassing Sy about his papers, visits the man one night, asking to speak with him alone. The man finally eats. Niloo stays awake wondering what was said between them.

A few days later, one of their Dutch friends, a painter named Wouter, goes missing. Siavash says, without even a moment's hesitation, "Call the police."

"You trust the Dutch police now?" Niloo says, eyebrow raised. Mala is already pulling out her phone. "You won't even call a hotline when a guy screams suicide."

"For a Guillaume or a Robbert or a Wouter?" he says. "I trust them implicitly."

He seems unmoved; it is simply a thing he's come to believe after years working with refugees in Holland. But with Siavash, it isn't just Guillaume or Wouter and their European privilege in this country of immigrant haters. Or Wilders and the doom he'll bring on artists and immigrants and squatters. Sy might be praising his dinner and he'll turn it political: *I'm loving this so much right now; I wonder if Ahmadinejad knows there's an Iranian out there left unfucked for a few minutes.* And he considers everything about the Western world dull and lifeless: *Don't you see how gray everything is compared to Iran? Have you forgotten the lemons like candy and the grasses that whistle and lamb kabobs and salty corn on the roadside on the way to the Caspian Sea? Have you forgotten the music? Oh, Niloo* joon, *the music . . .*

Often he speaks in many directions: his childhood in New York, Mousavi's moderate policies but lack of charisma, the World Cup, the shady way Iranian elections are run. At the microphone on story nights, he talks about falling in love in troubled times, from a jail cell, across class and religion. "Glorious," he says. He calls everything *glorious*, cheapening the word. It's like a deep breath for him. When he speaks, Mala devours his words. Late at night in bars, she pulls the rubber band out of his topknot, so that his greasy black hair falls onto his shoulders. She works her fingers through the tangles as if his body is on loan to her. Her hunger announces itself, interrupting casual talk. Mam'mad and Karim seem to dislike her.

What Niloo loves about Guillaume, she thinks, is that he doesn't need her, and she doesn't need him. Not the way Sy and Mala need each other, like two sides of a shameful transaction—their relationship feels like one long bank card refusal, petty amounts of cash the chief question and a line of people watching and waiting.

The next night after work, she calls Gui and tells him she won't be home for dinner. At the squat, she sits beside Mala, eating barley soup on faded floor pillows and talking about the Green Movement, about Mousavi and Karoubi and Neda Agha-Soltan. They discuss the upcoming trial of Geert Wilders; will he be held responsible for hate speech? Mam'mad grows animated in his anger and smokes an entire joint by himself, his lisp so pronounced he is barely intelligible. "He's a racist in charge of a major party. If he becomes prime minister, we have maybe two years of Erotic Republic and shitty music and waiting around for asylum. Then he'll kick most of us out. You wait and see. You find the smallest thing to love in purgatory and they take that too." Mam'mad meanders home, refusing company. He mutters, "It's hopeless," and disappears down the road in sweatpants and sandals, his head hung low.

Afterward, Sy walks his bike beside hers along Prinsengracht, the reflection of the moon and the street lamps lighting their path, the canal black and bottomless, turning endlessly away. They talk about Gui and Mala and the arc of love, and about Mam'mad and Karim and their lonely wives in Tehran waiting month after month, the many impossible expectations and the strange inevitability of goodbyes.

"Both those guys will find someone new," says Siavash, guiding his bike with one hand. With the other he lights three matches still attached to his matchbook so that the whole thing catches on fire. He tosses it into the canal and takes a drag. "New love is cocaine. It's exciting and it quickens your heart and makes you want to leap into a canal. Old love, established love, that's opium. It makes you warm and relaxed and content in your skin. The problem is, cocaine is so much harder to kick."

"No it's not," she says, one hand in her bike basket, trying to keep it from leaning and dropping her purse. "There's nothing more addictive than opium."

He shakes his head. "Highs are better."

"You've never seen an addict try to recover," she says, refusing to allow Baba to invade her thoughts again. Siavash gives her a look that says, *I've seen a hundred*.

Soon they approach the turn in the horseshoe and Siavash starts talking about the buildings and the architecture, the great hidden stories of Amsterdam. A damp chill hangs in the air, nighttime dew covering all the railings and lampposts so that their hands and jeans and bike seats are perpetually wet and she has to continually retrieve the towel she keeps in a compartment in her bike seat. Yellow light from the closed bookshops and chocolatiers and antiques shops paint the cobblestones and the bridges in soft faded hues, like a photo from a dusty stack. A few feet away, a young couple is kissing hungrily against the wall of a closed café.

"See? The cocaine," says Siavash, smiling and flicking his cigarette butt in their direction. "They don't even know the rest of the city exists. Try offering them warmth and peace and oneness with the universe right now and see what they say."

She laughs, though the truth of it pains her. "It's not like that for everyone. Mam'mad will go back to his wife. You're just angsty about Mala."

"Says the biggest cokehead of all of us," he says, pulling out his phone. His brow furrows as he reads a text message. He stops walking.

"Oh please," she says, "I've been married for years."

"I don't mean him," says Sy, waving a hand in her direction. He types as he speaks to her. "He's the opium. Now you're in love with you. The original you. Not this boring American lady who makes lists and—"

He stops talking and is silent for a long time. Another text pings and he mutters, "Holy shit," and lets his bike fall to the pavement, though in Amsterdam, you hold on to your bike like a child always threatening to leap into the water. "Oh fuck fuck fuck." He fumbles to pick up his bike, clanging and cursing as he jumps on. "Mam'mad is losing his shit in Dam Square."

Niloo's fingers are numb, but she pedals after him, dewy Amsterdam air condensing on her neck and hands. If old love is opium, then it must be more dangerous than new. Withdrawal from it drives the addict to the edge of a roof. It distorts his thinking, reducing life to the basest needs. It makes him moan and beg and collapse and rave for release. Nothing compares to knowing there is no more.

When they arrive in Dam Square, people are already hurtling toward him, trying to quench the flames with jackets and sweaters, with water from bottles. They beat him with fabric, and he falls to the pavement, still aflame. Some people gather and watch, hands clasped to mouths. They pull out phones, trying to decide what to do. They're like hens scattering. Has someone called the police? Siavash stumbles off his bike and joins the throng throwing their outer garments over Mam'mad. Off to the side, a man smothers his fiery jacket before returning to flog Mam'mad with its scorched remnants. Out of instinct, Niloo grabs the soaked towel in her bike seat. It's full of rainwater, but what can a hand towel do? The flames are too high to place it on his face and she's afraid. By the time the fire is out, only seconds before an ambulance arrives, Mam'mad is still, no more thrashing, his arms loose over the pavement. Niloo watches Siavash hover over him with trembling fingers, trying to decide what he can touch. He waves away the crowd, pours a little water carefully over Mam'mad's mouth.

Now she approaches and gives him the towel, which he places over his friend's disfigured forehead. Drawing closer, she lets out a guttural noise, like a mangled wail. She recoils from her friend, wiping the tears and mucus from her mouth. Mam'mad's face is a ruin of soot and blood and charred flesh, his eyebrows and eyelashes gone. She thinks of Siavash's burns, the violence of acquiring such scars, and she imagines that maybe Mam'mad too can survive. A tuft of scorched hair, still white, by his ear reminds her of the first night, when he gave her soup and called her Khanom Cosmonaut, when she told him her four categories of Iranians and he laughed, because people are more complicated than that.

Though he's clearly gone, his face unrecognizable, she wants to shake him awake, to say: Mam'mad *agha*, this is all wrong. You're not a reckless young man. You're a professor. You deserve to be a knowledge worker. Now her knees buckle and she crumbles to the pavement. She tries to trample the regret already blooming, but flashes of their days together return quickly, one after another: the many humble egg dishes, the longing for an invitation from his neighbors, the days when he disappeared with Karim, the two feeding off each other's misery—she should have known. She turns away. The police section off the area around the fallen man. Siavash and Niloo are pushed away with the crowd.

Afterward, they rush to the squat to check for news. What drove Mam'mad to set himself alight? Did he speak to anyone? Though the entire community is gathered in the tiny room, fogging up windows, emptying glasses and piling them in the sink as they release their grief with endless talk, a sickening truth goes unspoken. Mam'mad got the idea from another man they knew, a man who, like Mam'mad and Karim and many others here, was desperate for help and didn't get it.

Their usual story night moderator reads the news aloud from a laptop. The Dutch outlets sound so different from the Persian ones. He reads first from the BBC:

"*. . . According to reports in the Dutch media, the man had an argument with a group before setting himself alight. He soaked his clothes in a highly flammable liquid and is reported to have stood motionless and silent as bystanders and shopkeepers attempted to extinguish the flames using coats and buckets of water. Police said there was no immediate explanation for his act and that an investigation into the case was under way.*"

"*No explanation*," someone shouts. "*Argument with a group*. Lying bastards."

The moderator nods, wipes his forehead with a handkerchief—the bodies crammed into the squat have soured the air, making it humid and stifling despite open doors. Now he reads from *Payvand News*. After the first line, a loud groan rises. Some say prayers. Others mutter into each other's necks and shoulders:

"*An Iranian man who set himself on fire in Amsterdam has died of his injuries. The unidentified man was aflame for more than two minutes, and all efforts by passersby to douse the fire were unsuccessful. His reported motive for the self-immolation was the Dutch government's denial of his plea for asylum. According to Associated Press, the Dutch government has tightened restrictions on immigration over the past decade due to growth of anti-Muslim sentiments.*"

A woman in the back shouts at the moderator, "Read the first one again." No one has to explain the differences. Though over the next few days, many liberal Dutch sources too will highlight the problem. Radio Netherlands Worldwide will disperse damning truths to the

Dutch- and English-speaking public. They will say that Mam'mad talked of suicide in interviews and wasn't taken seriously, that the Dutch authorities offered no help, that they deport many doomed men and women without mercy. Dutch television programs like *Nieuwsuur* will interview some of the people in this very room. The moderator will be quoted: "He was fed up, like a lot of people here. Roaming the city at night. No status, no travel documents, no future. He smiled and pretended he was an invited professor, but that ran out long ago. His money too. Almost sixty with a lapsed visa? You can't even get dishwashing work with that. If he had returned to Iran, he probably faced the same fate. He was scared of being arrested and executed." Siavash's comments will be moving, powerful, expertly condemning. "There were all kinds of signs . . . The authorities may be right to reject a request and deport the asylum seeker, but if he's still here after years and you see him deteriorating, becoming mentally finished, there comes a time when you have to take responsibility. You cannot just show someone the door."

The Dutch immigration authorities will respond that all procedures were followed without error. They will offer up the word *tragic* and drop the matter.

After the evening's mourning, Niloo lifts her tingling legs off the cushions. "I'm going home," she says. Is it her home, this place she's headed? For decades she's tried to make homes for herself, but she is always a foreigner, always a guest—that forever refugee feeling, that constant need for a meter of space, the Perimeter she carries on her back. Over the years, she has learned to adapt, to start over in each new place and live as if she belongs there. It feels like lying, even more so now.

Pedaling eastward, she thinks of her spice jar, its heady scent and golden hue, and a years-ago conversation with Gui about tarragon and turmeric. Adding turmeric makes a thing Persian. That ripped-up root that bleeds when crushed, staining kitchen counters, oven mitts, even the soil, a dark yellow. The soft, papery fingers of grandmothers back home, jaundiced to the last—did Mam'mad once have an Aziz *joon* with henna hair and yellow thumbs? *Oh, Aziz* joon, *how I miss your hands.* The warped stem gets in the blood, leaking up from the loam. As a child, Niloo walked bare-toed on that warm soil, on the tired backs of those who loved her, and she sank down until her feet planted. Here the ice-hard ground doesn't yield to strangers' feet, and her friends wander, a scattered village of poets and pleasure-seekers, burning to be seen. "I am here!" Mam'mad cried out in his final act. *We* are all here, still waiting, addicts clustered together in a squat, broken from the earth like turmeric root, staining everything.

The Third Visit

MADRID, 2006

Sit, be still, and listen,
because you're drunk
and we're at the edge of the roof.

—JALAL AD-DIN RUMI

In late December 2006, I arrived in Madrid for our third visit, unhappy down to my toes. In the privacy of memory, it's easier to admit: nothing good could have come of that trip, and it started like a farce. After years spent apart, Kian and I sat beside our parents in a rented apartment in Plaza Major, watching footage of Saddam Hussein's hanging. Just below our living room window, costumed Spaniards in colorful wigs were buying churros and beer and sparklers in the sunny square. We fidgeted on a bright red couch, silent, hungry, a little musty and jet-lagged, but unable to look away. First we watched the official video released by Iraqi television, then the shaky cell phone footage, the men shouting, taunting him. "Go to hell," one said. Another begged, "Please, the man is facing execution." Then the dictator reciting some prayers and a sickening thump. Baba lit a cigarette and walked away, mumbling. "That wicked man is finally gone," said Maman. "Praise Jesus."

"Your Jesus did this then?" said Baba, turning in the doorway. Maman didn't respond, just closed her eyes and breathed. "Everything has turned so ugly. This filth was once the Persia of Rumi and Hafez and Avicenna. This muck is us now."

"Baba, take it outside," said Kian when Baba's cigarette started to fill the room with smoke. Kian followed him out, opening the cherry red latches on the windows. "I don't want to live in an ashtray for a week."

Maman had recently gone blonde—a bad decision for an Iranian no matter how old you are, but particularly gruesome for a darkly complexioned fifty-year-old who has studied and traveled and lived. You're supposed to be able to see yourself more clearly than the *nadid-badid*, the riffraff, I often told her, but on this trip I held my tongue. It had been a trial to get her to come to Madrid in the first place, on our third reunion with Baba since we left Iran. "Why do I want to see that man? He was the ruination and the torment of my life." Maman has never shied from the dramatic.

"You're not going to see Baba," I said. "You're going to see Madrid and get to know your son-in-law. You'll have your own room." A year before, Gui and I had married in private and moved to Amsterdam. Neither of us wanted a wedding.

We hadn't yet slept in our colorful Spanish apartment. We arrived on four separate flights that morning, said polite hellos, marveled at the reds and the blues, and dropped onto the couch. Now we were watching the news and taking out our exhaustion on one another. "I'm going out for groceries," said Maman. "Put my things where you like." She heaved herself up and threw her shawl around her shoulders.

She was punishing me because Gui hadn't come. Less than a year of marriage, and I was in Madrid with my parents and brother, about to celebrate the New Year without my husband. "This is a bad sign, Nil," said Kian. I told him to mind his own business. Baba turned away, hardly veiling his shock that we hadn't improved since London. Gui had canceled because he was assigned to a case that promised all-nighters through February. I missed his scratchy morning stubble, his smooth, warm shoulders, but I was relieved to delay introducing him to Baba. So, Kian had taken Guillaume's place and we were four again, for the first time in thirteen years.

"If only they had killed him before he murdered and pillaged thousands of people, and bombed our best cities, and decimated our economy, and basically took a shit on the whole region for decades," Maman said as she put on her coat.

Baba looked at her, his nose wrinkling. He shook his head. "Why do you say such things? The man just died in the ugliest way. Why do you say this?"

"And of course you're feeling sympathy," she said. "Nice."

"Guys, don't start," shouted Kian from the kitchen, where he was surveying the fridge, examining the cooking knives. I heard the hard *chop-chop* of a sharp knife cutting through a cucumber or a carrot he must have found.

"That's not the ugliest way," said Maman, spitting rage, hands flying. I wished she hadn't come. "If you watched the news instead of memorizing old Sufi garbage a hundred different ways, you would know. The worst way to die is after torture, or amputation, or with mustard gas like those poor Kurds. The worst is a mass grave. That man died in an instant, called himself a martyr, and is buried with his family."

"He was a monster and he paid," said Baba, rubbing his face in his hand and trying to walk away, but somehow failing, as if Maman's admonishing voice was a leash around his neck. "Stop dancing in the blood. Please, respect for death isn't the same as respect for the man."

"*That* man you feel sympathy for," she muttered as she slammed the door.

After Maman left, I assigned bedrooms, giving the one with big windows to Baba, since he's hairy and gets hot at night, and the one with the philosophy and cookbooks to Kian, since he's a moody insomniac with a taste for the unknowable and the delicious. I dragged the bags into the rooms and returned to find my brother and father eating slices of cucumber and salt, not talking to each other.

They were chewing in the same rhythm, like two cartoon mice. "You two look like the same person thirty years apart," I said. Baba beamed. Kian rolled his eyes. Baba got up and sliced a cucumber in half from top to bottom. He salted it lovingly, as if dusting an artifact, and he held it out to me, his dark, hashish-stained fingers cradling it on the sides like a splint.

I joined them at the table, the three of us crunching for a while. Baba mumbled, "I can't stop hearing that thud. That noise . . ." He rubbed his temple.

"All right, stop," said Kian. "Don't mention it again in front of Mom, okay?"

"Why you call him *Mom*?" Baba said in his crappy English, a little accusingly.

"You mean *her*," I said. "You should take a refresher course every few years."

Kian looked confused. "Where the hell have you been?" And he was right of course; we had long since become Americans. Kian jumped up from the table, dropping a cucumber spear onto a plate. "I don't even know why we're here."

He stalked off to his room to read cookbooks and brood.

"He grows up so . . . sour," said Baba, still in English. "He reads more poetry . . . or these Bibles like your mother? I prefer when he reads poetry . . ."

I shrugged. "It's not one or the other, Baba *joon*."

He changed back to Farsi. "It is if you don't want to make yourself crazy."

"Part of the Bible is poetry," I said. And because I knew he was about to start on Rumi's love of wine and the Bible's pointless teachings about self-deprivation, I added, "Jesus drank wine. It's an interesting historical document, at least."

"All right, *azizam*," he whispered, clearing his throat with difficulty. He had unbuttoned his shirt down to his navel and his white undershirt was spotted with sweat, thickets of gray chest hair sprouting from every side. "All religion is evil."

I noticed a bead of sweat on his brow. "Are you hot?" I asked. We had yet to figure out the heater, and the rest of us had kept on our sweaters and shawls.

"I'm fine, my sweet Niloo." On these trips, Baba tended to get uncomfortably nostalgic at the smallest kindness. It made me want to go watch TV.

Later, Maman returned with three bags of groceries, each one of which would have had me wheezing up the six flights of stairs to the apartment.

"The packaged things were in Spanish." She unpacked cherry tomatoes, pomegranates, lamb. She had picked up skim milk instead of full, and buttermilk instead of heavy cream. Baba joked that we could mix them and have something almost usable. When he sniffed the buttermilk, putting it to his ear as if it would identify itself, she laughed, but caught herself. She wanted to keep her anger.

The real reason for Maman's anger was that Nader had just died, and she had no one to whom to confess her grief, because, after all, if she confided in her children the world would turn on its head and we would all stumble around in white blind confusion before being sucked into a black hole. Still, we knew. Maman had cared for this man and now he was gone, disappearing first to adventures in Turkey and Greece, then vanishing from email and telephone, ashamed to reveal himself in such a state, then deteriorating into a skeletal version of himself and dying young and alone in a Thai hospital. The news of his death had reached us three weeks earlier.

Over a dinner of stewed eggplant and lamb shanks, Maman sighed and spoke vaguely of her travels to Asia. Baba looked around as if missing something. "What's the trouble?" he said. He wiped his brow again and blinked four or five times.

Kian gave him a puzzled look. Baba made an exaggerated clownish version of Kian's face back at him, and Kian tried not to laugh. He turned to Maman. "Did you add more cumin to this? After I browned the lamb?"

Maman looked up from her plate. "Of course," she said, as if she had been asked if she believed in democracy and God and the villainy of the Islamic Republic.

Kian took a weary bite. "I'll be happy to cook here, Maman *joon*. You relax." He ate carefully, as if the extra cumin might damage his taste buds. He was right, though. Kian scowled over his plate until Baba took one bite of my kale salad and said, "What this is? Is like lettuce fell in love with piece of fabric." Kian snorted into his hand. "Try it," Baba said, encouraged. He made a lump of kale with his fingers and thrust it at Kian's face, but Kian pushed away his hand.

Long after our plates were empty, Baba's quick chatter continued in many directions. Now and then he wiped a corner of the serving plate with an idle finger and licked the sauce or dabbed a grain of rice and placed it on his tongue. Halfway through a story about his mother's latest venture in Ardestoon, teaching teenage girls artistic carpet designs, he stuck a pinky in the bare lamb bone, already picked clean of its meat, and dug around for leftover marrow. He continued with his story as if his fingers belonged to another creature, as if he didn't even see them there. "She misses you kids," he said of our grandmother. "She's very old. Did you know that Ardestoon is on the Internet now? Would you like to see? They have a page about the aqueduct. It's just as I told you—an engineering marvel."

"Baba, stop that," I said, unable to watch his coarse fingers anymore.

He looked down at his greasy hands. "Oh, I'm sorry," he said, then seemed to think better of it. "Why does everything embarrass you? Who is here to impress?"

What Baba knew, and what I have come to know, is that I was embarrassed in front of myself—the new Niloo, the Niloo I was trying to build. He was tainting me with every flick of his yellowing fingers, as Maman was doing with her yellow hair. They were stained, the two of them, and I didn't want to get too close.

He wiped his hands and muttered, "Next time, what if I stop over in Dubai and have all traces of Iran professionally cleansed from my body? Like a car wash for the poor fools who aren't as refined as yourselves—would that satisfy you?"

True to form, he grumbled for exactly two minutes before forgetting his unhappiness in one unbroken lump, tossed away like the discarded lamb carcass. It happened the instant Kian brought out the games and the chocolate.

We sat beside the window watching the early revelers in Plaza Major and playing cards for candy pieces. Maman said, "Niloo, now that we're all settled, where are the photos of your big day? You must have something. One photo."

Baba sat up in the fuzzy armchair he had come to like (two minutes after arrival, Baba in English: "Why this chair is hairy?"), dropping the cards he had been sorting on the table. "Yes, where are the photos? Let's see them."

I sighed—*this again*. "We've discussed this," I said to Maman.

"How can there be no photos?" said Maman, running her fingers through her insanely blonde hair. "It makes no sense. Who gets married without photos?"

"Leave her alone, you guys," said Kian. "Niloo's not into artifacts like you two." He chuckled at his own wit. Lately Kian had stopped mocking my profession. I think he even respected it. Baba nodded vigorously, his nose back in his cards.

"We had no wedding to photograph," I said. Then, feeling vicious, I said to Baba, "I never saw photos of *your* wedding. Where are those?"

"Ouch," Kian whispered. Sensing the end of the game, he ate a poker chip.

"*Vai*, Niloo." Baba gave a weak gasp. "That is very unkind."

Maman put on her glasses, as if they would amplify her cold gaze. "You know those situations are different. First weddings matter in different ways."

Baba shifted in his fuzzy chair. He was chewing the inside of his cheek and looking generally uncomfortable, his cards now discarded faceup, telling us that the game was, in fact, over. "I should tell you all," he said. "I'm making a small change."

Maman got up from her chair. "I'll make tea," she said. Baba's hands folded, and he started nibbling on his mustache. After a moment's thought, he dropped the subject. Later, after Maman had gone to bed, Kian and I sat up drinking with Baba. He told us that his marriage was ending, that he felt drained of energy, stuck in a dying country and useless with age. He said he was in the process of marrying a third woman, someone much younger who was loosely related to the family we had visited outside London five years before. He hoped that in this marriage, he could be healthier, feel younger, live more openly to the demands of the universe. After two whiskeys, he talked about dyeing his mustache. "Your mother seems to have taken up the boxed dye. I think at our age, it can't be avoided, yes?"

I woke up at three in the morning to the smell of Turkish coffee and the trill of hushed laughter from the living room. My parents were talking politics and making fun of Spanish foods. They had eaten half a plate of boxed churros that Maman had bought and, instead of chocolate, they were dipping them in honeycomb Baba had smuggled from Ardestoon in his suitcase. Baba was animated, sitting forward in his chair, hands flailing as he spoke. Maman looked tired, her legs tucked under her on the couch as she let the steam from her coffee warm her face. She had tied a large black headband behind her neck and over her head, so that the blonde peeking through looked almost elegant. She hushed Baba now and then. "You'll wake the children," she said, her voice throaty and relaxed. It might have been 1985.

Baba was talking about Saddam Hussein again. "Well, Pari *joon*, he did win two elections with *over* a hundred percent of the vote. You can't argue with the will of the people. Especially not the will of *more than all* of them. That would be madness." Maman's laughter, a deep clear echo like a note from the belly of a violin, drifted into the hall where I stood.

"Ai, Pari *joon*, Ahmadinejad is the same kind of garbage," Baba continued, rocking back and forth. It was a subtle but unnatural movement of which Maman seemed unaware. "This year alone this simian has shamed us in a hundred ways. He tells the international community the holocaust was invented, he hangs teenage boys for what? A round of adolescent horseplay! He makes the most puffed-up statements on camera. Did you know there are claims floating around that Iranians cured AIDS? Tell me, is this not a wonderland of foolishness that we're living in?" His hands were flying over his head and even from the hallway I could see them shaking, the green beads coiled around his swollen fingers rattling. He reached for his cup again and as he sipped, he panted, his breath heavy and quick with energy, his tongue dipping into the coffee before he sipped, like a toe testing frigid lake water. Baba loved animated talks, stories, debates. He even loved being contradicted if it meant a chance to release. But this behavior seemed intense even for him.

"Well," said Maman, "he wants to deflect from the uranium efforts. Maybe he hopes to be underestimated." She looked into her cup and smacked her lips. "Enough of this for us both. It's so much stronger than coffee. Where did you find it?"

Baba shrugged. "Istanbul." He seemed bored by the question and left unsaid the *Where else?* He said something about a bazaar in Sultanahmet and scratched the back of his neck just above his undershirt.

The spot was fire red, as if he had been scratching it all night. "Did you read the news from Isfahan?" he said, his tone shifting suddenly. "They cloned a healthy sheep called Royana. I visited him with Ali. It was very nice." Then he added, his tone mischievous, "He looks very tasty."

Maman laughed. I poured myself a cup and plopped down beside Maman, who was holding her arm out to me. She stroked my hair and we talked about the cloned animal, about science in Iran and the universities there. After a while, we returned to Royana the sheep. Baba said, "I bet Kian could make a feast out of him."

"Do you remember," said Maman, "that time we ate Niloo's chicken?"

"Ah yes, the esteemed Chicken Mansoori," said Baba, letting out a big sigh. Then he looked at me, his eyes flashing with unreleased laughter, and he put his hands together in feigned contrition. "My darling, I'm so sorry we ate your chicken friend." Maman snorted and wrapped her arms around my waist, burying her vanilla-scented head in my chest. Baba added, "But it was your own fault for choosing such a delectable name. I mean, half the time I thought he was called Chicken Tandoori. What did you want? We're only poor carnivores, driven by our basest instincts."

"It's a good thing Gay didn't come," Maman said. "We are so embarrassing."

Our ruckus woke Kian a few minutes later and he joined us with his own cup of sludge. He had tried adding the evaporated milk to it. It wasn't bad. By then, Baba was glassy-eyed and flushed pink, sweat pooling under his arms, above his stomach, and on his lower back as he ranted about a local mullah who was stealing from his savings account using a cousin at the bank. During his explanation of the bank's slapdash system of identity verification, the mood of the evening changed.

Suddenly, Baba was alone on that side of things, and we three were exchanging worried glances. He went to the bathroom twice in the middle of that story.

When he was gone the second time, Kian asked, without ceremony, as ever, "Is he on something? He's definitely high, right?"

Maman shook her head as if to shake the thought off into the ether. "It's just the coffee. I know what opium looks like; he would be half asleep and babbling about the stars. Plus, I went through his suitcase; I got promises. This is coffee."

Baba opened the bathroom door and ambled toward us, his steps irregular but energetic. He wiped his forehead with a hand towel and said, "Ahhh, Madrid," as if completing some earlier reflection. Then he continued his story like he had never paused and we let him, though we were all a little afraid. Images from that night at the Red Carpet Motel crept back into my thoughts, and I returned to bed cradling my fears, but I was too fainthearted to question him.

I promised myself this: I would never introduce this man to Guillaume. And if I had kept any friend or acquaintance from Yale, I wouldn't introduce them either.

That night Baba's heart stopped. Luckily, he wasn't alone. He was still in the sitting room telling stories to Maman, who, with her eastbound jet lag, didn't expect sleep to come till sunrise. His breath grew short during one of his stories and he staggered into his favorite fuzzy chair. As soon as he sat down, he was overcome by nausea and itching, and a few minutes later, his heart began pounding so ferociously that he stood again, walked a few steps, then dropped onto the couch, clutching throw pillows, manic in his eyes, manic in the clumps of ever-young, sweaty hair fanned across the cushions, manic even in his teeth, grinding, wincing, terrified. Maman ran to the neighbors' and banged on their door, begging in English and Farsi and in simple sobs to call an ambulance. Since it was our first night in Madrid, she hadn't seen the emergency numbers tacked to the kitchen corkboard.

When Maman stormed back in with our sleepy neighbors—two Spanish sisters with a dozen earrings and half a shaved head between them—Baba was near fainting, his color drained, his eyes closed, his breathing erratic like the pained sputters of a dying engine. Kian helped him to the floor, wondering aloud if he should be laid on his stomach or back. He gave Baba water, most of which ended up on the pillow and on Baba's undershirt, and propped up his head until we could hear a breath. By the time the ambulance arrived, Baba's lips were blue.

In the morning, the doctor, a broad-shouldered Indian man with a severe Roman nose and night-shift shadows, told us that Baba had admitted to taking Adderall to mask the effect of opium, of which there was plenty in his blood. Being medically competent, Baba hadn't overdosed on either drug, but he had come close. He was old enough to make mistakes, and his drugs were from black markets. Plus, he was a habitual opium user and had almost no experience with uppers. The doctor assured us in his soothing accent, a gently rolling English-Spanish-Hindi hybrid, that Baba was stable. He seemed persuaded that Baba hadn't combined the drugs recreationally, but only to mask the presence of opium; maybe he wanted to shield us from it. The doctor seemed sorry for us, the corners of his eyes drooping every time he said Baba's name. He said, in that universal doctorly tone full of sterile compassion, that since Adderall wasn't illegal and since Baba's travel itinerary made it plausible that the opiates in his blood were consumed outside Spain, he wouldn't notify the police. This was a kindness. We all knew what had happened. Then he offered Baba medicine to hold off withdrawal until we left Madrid.

Baba stayed in the hospital for two days. He slept a lot. He ate a lot of unsalted soup and crackers. He didn't complain about the food.

On New Year's Eve, Kian and I ran out to the nearest square to buy churros (Maman had become addicted), party hats, and silly 2007 eyewear. We wanted a photo of the four of us celebrating, even if it was in a hospital room. Who knew when we would all be together again? The last time had been in 1993.

After his release, Maman wouldn't look at Baba and his regret and misery were palpable. He haunted the apartment with shoulders hunched, his once exuberant hands tentative. He stared at me pleadingly as if he wished he could crawl into the skin of another man. Mostly he slept and read his books as the rest of us visited the royal castle, parks, monuments, the Prado, and every baker and butcher we could find. Maman floated from place to place in her big shawl, sampling curious meats, looking up historical details, and asking vendors for recipes. It struck me that she and Baba were no longer in the same cultural category—Maman wasn't displaced each time she left her home. She seemed so much younger than Baba. She didn't struggle and suffer and hunt for *lavash* bread. She didn't look for an Iranian host or a welcoming *sofreh*. She ate Spanish food. She learned Spanish greetings.

At my insistence, we visited the National Archaeological Museum. At Kian's insistence, we went to Botín, the oldest restaurant in the world, a stony, cavernous space with stews and suckling pigs and soft candlelight. Each time Baba was mentioned, Maman changed the topic. Kian said, "Fuck that man." I didn't object.

When we came home from Botín, Maman went straight to bed. Kian said he was going for a long walk, and I stayed up with Baba, watching television from the opposite side of the room, not speaking. I wanted to leave, but we had agreed that someone should watch him every night.

He sat in a corner of the red couch, a little bent, a quilt over his legs. With half his body covered, he looked frail and weak. "Come and sit beside me," he said, patting the couch. "Turn off the television."

"Are you hungry?" I asked, coldly. He smelled like sweat and cigarettes and a long sleep. "We brought you some stew from that place."

He shook his head. "I wanted to speak to you," he said as I sat beside him on the couch. He pulled me closer, draping the quilt over my legs too. I didn't resist his fatherly gestures. What would be the point? Finally he said, his sodden eyes fixed on me, "I understand why you didn't want a wedding."

His sorrow moved me. He deserved to feel every bit of this guilt, but I wanted to spare him a deeper wound. "It's not you guys," I said. "Weddings take planning. It's not like Ardestoon, where a dozen grandmas pull it together in a week."

"We are barbarians." His voice trembled. Before I could react he waved his hand around as if to say, *I didn't mean that; let it go*. He moved on. "I want to tell you a story," he said, a brightness cutting through his dim watery gaze, like a flicker from the other side of a long fog. "This is about the four lavish weddings in your mother's family that are said to have attracted four big curses. As you know, in Iran, curses are more potent than in the West." Already I liked this story. I knew why he was offering it: absolution for not inviting the family into my romance. He straightened the quilt as if we needed it to protect us from djinns. The gesture seemed instinctive, and I wondered if he had a habit of telling stories to children, maybe to Shirin.

According to Baba, the idea has been tossed around that maybe the women in my mother's line, starting four generations ago in some saffron field in western Iran, live under a curse that is released by their extravagant weddings (the jealous eye, they say), each marrying for love and watching it fall to ruin in dramatic ways. So that's four ruinous endings of which I would have been number five—that is, if I hadn't been clever enough to avoid a wedding. "Niloo *joon*," said Baba, "you have always been ahead of the curses. Later, I will tell you about the seven times your life came into grave danger and you escaped by a hair." But now the wedding curse:

The first was in a saffron field. My great-great-grandmother, raven-haired and cunning-eyed, married a saffron heir who, soon after, vanished.

The second was in a white orchard house. The saffron heiress's daughter, who wasn't as beautiful but had money and charm, married a man who, ten years later, was murdered by his own villainous doctor.

The third, well, the third is not worth telling. Maman's mother ruined her own life with her silliness and bad choices. "She was religious and you can't blame everything on curses," he said. "Sometimes it's God's fault. We'll skip that one."

And finally, Maman, who fell in love with a horrible addict in medical school and whose hopes were the purest, the highest, the most splendid of them all. She tempted the fates at her wedding by announcing that she was the happiest wife in Isfahan and Tehran and Shiraz and Rasht.

Baba went on to say that I was lucky; I wasn't superstitious like the first two, who lived in an Iran that's gone to legend, or religious like the second two, who flung themselves at Christ with all the heartiness that they thought had long ago leaked out of their skin. "You're a logical woman," he said. "But you have to be careful still. The progression of these stories from merely unlucky to truly wretched is so linear that even I have to believe there is a stronger force at work." Well, I thought, maybe the notion of a curse was easier to unpack and sit with than the dozen drug binges, the hundred ugly lies, the thousand or so humiliating scuffles; all that our family had done to one another.

There is a curse; we are its worthy victims—this is a better story.

"Maybe you should leave Iran," I said, my tone icing over, even as his was softening into a croon. Not that I didn't love being given the fatherly treatment I had missed all these years. But I had looked forward to this trip, and Baba had sullied it. The least I could do on behalf of Maman and Kian was to keep any kind syllable from escaping my lips. At the same time, I wasn't about to offer to help him—not after this. So I added, "You always talk about settling in Cyprus or Istanbul. Just move."

He shook his head as if summoned back from a dream. "The house," he muttered, frowning like I was a confused little girl. "And my practice. That's my life."

I got up from the couch and pulled my cardigan tight across my chest. "I guess if I had built a home I wouldn't want to leave it either." I started to go. "Goodnight, Baba," I said. But then I remembered our talk in London, how he had questioned my instincts. I turned back. "Do you understand now why I chose Gui?"

"He's the nicest man," he said flatly. I waited, so he added, "I assume, Niloo *joon*, that you mean to imply that he has no vices. What can I say? That's enviable." I scoffed, which angered him. "I'll arrange for you two to come to Istanbul soon. I have to meet him. Whatever harm I've done, I regret. But your family is your family."

That night I finally saw Maman cry, though I'm not sure for whom or what. I hope she released a lot of things. On my way to bed, I passed her room. Her door was ajar, and she was weeping on her pillow. Some instinct told me to leave her. Her tears weren't urgent or bitter. She didn't need the crook of an arm to sob into. These were old, weary tears. She didn't heave or shudder. She just tipped over and spilled out, quietly, as if washing her eyes, or cleansing a wound before binding it for good.

In those days I gave all of my sympathy and loyalty and care to Maman, and I judged Baba harshly. I wonder if, after Madrid, Baba lived the healthy, youthful life he had hoped to find in his third marriage. Thinking back on that trip, on the last days of 2006 and of a dictator's life, and the first days of my life in Amsterdam, I shudder that Baba and I were peering over the edge of similar peaks, each beginning a marriage, storing our hopes in bonds that would grow so slack in just three years. In many ways, I think, we were each sinking into a heavy sleep then. And three years later, the rattle of a scattered nation finally waking would rouse us too. It wasn't such a coincidence, I think, that Baba and I fell into step in this way. Every Iranian was in the same coma back then, and we all stirred in the same moment.

Family Formations Among Early Primates

OCTOBER 2009

Amsterdam, Netherlands

In the weeks after her friend's death, Niloo runs from grief toward her old habits. Research. Her 2010 syllabus. Furniture lists for the new apartment. She cooks using measuring cups and tests her bank card daily, buying gummy worms at corner shops, just to see. Gui tries to make her laugh, brings home her favorite takeout dishes, checks in from his office every afternoon. One day he catches her arranging a mountain of papers into sixteen neat piles. He takes her hand, as if delivering bad news, exhales loudly, and says, "Niloo Face, I have a very important question." She lets him pull her away from her paper forest, thinking he wants to talk about Mam'mad again, to reassure her that the world will heal. "The last time you copied something . . ." He pauses, touches her cheek. "Did you remember to paste?"

She yanks her hand away and tosses a throw pillow at his head. He laughs, catches the pillow. "Okay, okay . . . I'm sorry . . . but . . . just one thing." He lays an earnest hand on his chest. "I'm pretty sure I saw a page from the first stack float over to that other stack there. It was a while ago, so you'll have to check them all now."

"Yeah, laugh it up," says Niloo, and returns to her work. "You won't be laughing when I get tenure." He leans over the couch and kisses her nose and, for a moment, everything feels as it did when they were twenty-three and living in a buttonhole room with a rented couch, where he tossed his sweaty shirt in the wrong corner, unearthed her frantic safe haven, and decided to love her anyway.

She craves a night of solitary cooking. It's been a while since she's used the spice jar and she misses its smell, the rough grains scratching the pads of her fingers. Her mind drifts to her grandmother in Ardestoon, the smell and taste of her hands, sensations she can conjure here in her Amsterdam kitchen. Besides, she wants to do something kind for Gui. She decides to make lamb shank, one of his favorites, but when she opens the pantry to fetch the mason jar, it is gone. She checks the pots and pans drawer, thinking maybe she left it there while retrieving a roasting pan last time. She looks in the fridge and oven too. But the jar has vanished. The blue cloth and the cheap plastic bag around it have disappeared. Even the white shelf has been wiped clean of its orange dusting of spice, as if the jar never existed.

She bats away the pestering thought that Gui has thrown it away, as he's tossed away so many of her old T-shirts and stripped paperbacks and torn tote bags. Impossible, she thinks, but who else would have touched it? Their domestic world contains only two. No one else's hands reach into their cabinets. Aside from Niloo's new friends, they lead a private, nomadic life. Even on holidays, they set colorful, artful tables for two. They exchange presents one at a time, slowly.

For hours she searches, craving that lamb shank like she hasn't eaten in days. She becomes desperate to cook it, to eat it with her hands, to gnaw at the gristle. The evening is lost to the search and soon it's too late to cook. She gives up. She takes a plate of fruit into the bedroom and eats while flipping through science magazines, stories of digs and inexplicable artifacts. When she emerges for a cup of tea, she finds that Gui hasn't eaten yet. He's reading case briefs, highlighter in hand.

A shapeless anger boils up to her throat—she had wanted so much to make the lamb for him and he's ruined it—and she yanks the highlighter from him. "You threw out my jar," she blurts. He looks up, brow gathering. "The mason jar in the plastic and blue cloth? How could you do that?"

"Did I?" he says. "I'll buy you another one." He turns back to his printouts.

"It was mine," she says. "This is why I don't want your hands in my stuff. Couldn't you let it just be mine?"

He winces, gray eyes hurt. She slumps into a dining chair, resting her head on the table for a few moments, listening to him shuffle papers. "You were at the guitar-pick place and I had some free time, so I cleaned the pantry. I only threw away a few expired, garbagy things. Or, I thought they were . . . I'm sorry."

"It's called Zakhmeh," she snaps, "*Zakh-MEH.* It's not hard to learn. And you didn't have to get revenge just because I had one thing of my own."

She knows the accusation is unfair—Gui isn't vengeful. She's known what happened since noticing the last vestiges of yellow dust wiped from the shelves. He saw the blue cloth wrapped in cheap plastic wrapped in newspaper, tucked all the way in the back, and he thought it was trash, so he tossed it. This is Guillaume's approach to life, to possessions. Unless a thing looks pricey, it's worthless. Niloo wants to tell him that the jar would cost a few hundred euros at the organic market on Albert Cuypstraat, but that seems like the wrong point; that batch will never exist again. Her grandmother's fingers have been in that jar. They tore the blue cloth, crushed the petals. And doesn't he know her well enough to realize that when he stumbles on a bundle tucked away in a secret corner, it might be precious?

Now some uncultivated part of her, some irrational instinct she hasn't scrubbed out, wants to goad him until he bursts out. She doesn't remember the last time either of them released anger, or pleasure, or joy. Even at the squat she's tame, always listening though she has so much to say. Her father used to joke that one cannot ignore the ravings of the flesh. Lately Niloo has become curious about the urges she routinely restrains, all that misspent will. "Sometimes I wonder," she says, "if I put on my shittiest T-shirt for long enough, would you throw *me* away?"

His eyes, hazel under closer light, grow cold. He gets up and disappears into the bedroom, emerging twenty minutes later in sky blue pajama pants, his face washed, his hair wet and combed back. He watches her; Gui's eyes are always so sad. "So you plan to ignore the letter in the drawer?" he says.

"I'll open it later," she mutters, her head still resting on the kitchen table.

"I think you've had a shock and you feel guilty and you need to deal with your own family. Don't you care what your father wants?" Gui sits one chair away with a corkscrew and bottle. A glass of Valpolicella comes sliding under her nose.

"Thanks," she says. She takes a sip. A strangely Iranian flavor, this wine, like cherries from her family's orchard. Baba would like it. "I know what he wants."

"Okay, so give him what he wants," says Gui, sniffing his wine a second time.

"You don't know this man." She softens. "He's an opium addict. He's devoted to whatever pleasure he's onto lately. And he lies. A lot. He would ruin us."

Gui swallows loudly. He smells fresh, like shampoo and menthol aftershave. His voice drops, reaching a sorrowful place. "You're not Karim or Mam'mad." He says, "Why are you still so scared of losing your spot?" That name sends a hot ache through her belly. Gui stares into his glass. "For ages I thought we were making a home, but you're still waiting with your backpack all packed and ready to go."

"That's not even—" She wants to ask, *What does one thing have to do with the other?* But before she can finish, he's back on the letter. "Family is family. Have you seen the news out of Iran? All that burning and looting. People getting killed in the streets. Moral police cracking down everywhere . . . Doesn't that worry you?"

"I know exactly what's going on," she says. "You're the one who doesn't get it. You think it's better for them here? You think they'll have any kind of a life? And what about his addiction? You just want the world to see you feeling bad about it, like every other happy European, but your life is nothing but safety nets. Please don't lecture me on the pros and cons of turning my father into a damn refugee."

He groans. "I won't respond to that since you just lost your friend," he says, "but wow." He sucks his lip and rises, anger swelling his eyes. "Goodnight."

Her head feels heavy and she drops it onto the table again, breathing stale red wine onto Gui's fresh pages. Maybe she'll sleep here. She hears some banging in the bedroom, and then a few minutes later, Guillaume reappears. He's dressed in pressed jeans and a thin wool sweater, his favorite light gray one.

"Where are you going?" she asks, cataloging the possibilities. He doesn't answer. He clatters around in the pantry, gives up the search, finds an apple in the fridge, and heads to the door. She can see that she's hurt him, likely on purpose. They say your loved ones know just where to find your buttons; maybe that's because they installed them there. "He could've come with us twenty years ago," she says, aware of her shrillness the way a drunk person becomes aware of their bad breath, disgusted but too exhausted to change it. "Who needs him now? Nobody."

"I don't care anymore," says Gui. "Have fun playing alone in your Perimeter." He starts to leave. She is about to apologize. Gui is right. She's been unforgivably cruel. She's always cruelest to the most vital people. But then he says, turning at the threshold, "Maybe if instead of hoarding your precious squat, you had let me get those guys some real, professional legal help . . ."

She doesn't recall what she says next; the room has gone white hot and her toes are burning and she feels ready to collapse. She has spent weeks beating back this thought, battling it each time it visits her in her sleep. Can she deny that she refused Gui's help because she wanted the group to be hers only, that she wanted Zakhmeh to be a part of her Perimeter? She was so preoccupied with her husband's motives that she didn't think of how much it would mean for her friends. Gui leaves, not slamming the door but closing it quietly behind him like a guest.

An hour passes. She sleeps. Later, clearing up Gui's papers from the kitchen table, she thinks of the squat. She misses the crackling talk with its random political and literary turns, the cauldrons of soup, the dim, unkempt canal-side room furnished with aging pillows, men with blond dreadlocks, women in hijab, White Widow joints, and paperback Korans discarded on the same rickety folding table. She delights in knowing that her new friends are the sort of immigrant congregation that makes Dutch neighbors nervous.

Then she thinks of Mam'mad, ravenous for the respect he once had, diminishing, forever expecting to change back into another self, like a child waiting to fit into an animal costume, puffing up and receding again so that the skin of the beast collapses on itself, its head hanging, inanimate. And Karim, hunched like a collared dog, roaming the waterlogged streets, alone in a city where the most hospitable native might offer him a single cookie and a suspicious glance.

She sits for a long time. Niloo has always found sensible solutions, needing only a long quiet think to drag herself out of the stickiest bogs. Now she just stares, her thoughts turning to Baba. As a child, she believed he was the kindest man she knew. But slowly over the years, Baba became a stranger and she feels nothing but a dull ache for the energetic, gleeful father she once knew. People change. Everyone. And all love ends. She knows this now. Only hardened exiles refuse to change; they dig their feet in and try to root everywhere they land, even if the soil poisons them. They hang on and on, afraid to move forward. They don't let go of dead things. They don't toss the lime juice. They hoard trinkets in ragged suitcases. They pile up photographs of long-ago days, begging their children for doubles. They build a fortress in the corner of a closet. Maybe Gui was right. *You're still waiting*, he said—it's true. She's so terrified of losing her every small advantage that now her own Baba poses a threat. If she had accepted Gui as her home, would she shield herself so zealously? Would she be a secure kind of woman with a dozen purses strewn everywhere, each containing an old ID or a document she once thought important—none of it vital enough to save, because her entitlement to her life isn't granted by these things, but intrinsic? No one can snatch it away. Maybe that's the difference between refugees and expats. The difference isn't Yale or naturalization papers, a fat bank account or invitations to native homes. In that way, she is the same as Mam'mad and Karim. When you learn to release that first great windfall after the long migration, when you trust that you'll still be you in a year or a decade, even without the treasures you've picked up along the way, always capable of more—when you stop carrying it all on your back—maybe that's when the refugee years end.

She calls Kian. "Did you get a letter from Dad?" Kian asks.

She tells him that she has and stops there. "Hey," she says, because her brother works in the chaos of a restaurant kitchen and never uses fewer than twenty ingredients in his signature sauces. "Think you could replicate the stuff in the jar?"

"What jar?" he says. Then, after a beat of silence, he gasps. "He sent you food? That's so unfair. Was it *torshi*? Saffron?" She tells him the jar was lost.

"How do you lose something like that?" asks Kian.

Niloo takes a tired breath. "Gui threw it away." Before hanging up, Kian promises to try to call Baba, to see if he can get through. She warns him that the new wife is answering his emails.

Now that she's calm, she realizes how many hours it's been. She can't leave Gui outside, whatever ugly things they might have said to each other. The Hamidi clan forgives ugly outbursts. What matters, Maman has always said, is if you're watching over your family, appreciating them behind their backs.

She puts on a light jacket, steps out into the drizzly evening haze, and unlocks her bicycle. Often Gui goes to the apartment at night to check on the progress of the construction work, to fret about paint colors or to see if the new kitchen island, designed after their current one, matches the cabinets.

She wipes the layer of rainwater off her bike seat with the towel in the compartment below, tightens her sweaty bun, snaps on her forehead light, and pedals into the fog, past the museum quarter and a public park, some student housing and a brewery, to the Pijp, where they're building their new home. There's a bar here she loves. On Fridays when they first arrived in Amsterdam, she and Gui dressed in worn jeans and drank three-euro whiskeys there. Now, she comes here alone to smoke with refugees and Dutch musicians on the terrace. The terrace leads out to a canal and some boats; she checks there first. But Gui isn't here—she can't recall the last time he was. The bar is hers now. The bartender, a wolfish old man who's always slicing limes and whose knuckle tattoos read from pinky to thumb *l-i-e-f-de* (love), knows her name. He's familiar now with the sound of Farsi.

Untying her bike from beside the Ganesha mural on the back wall of the bar, she considers giving up, avoiding the spectacle of the construction site altogether. But something about this act of retrieval feels like her job. For years they've fought like two gerbils in a grocery bag, but they've never left each other outside. She pedals the final two blocks, the wind spitting flecks of dust into her eyes. The street is eerily lit and nearly empty, only service workers and stoned tourists on their way home. The night air leaves a wet residue on her arms. She shivers and pedals faster. Now and then a waiter or bellhop passes with bags of restaurant leftovers hanging off their handlebars. She turns down the long road toward the new apartment.

She drops her bike on the cobblestones, noting the beauty of her new street at night. The slender streetlights bowing, potted plants blushing in windows, curtains thrown open to reveal colorful light fixtures hanging over big wooden tables. Around the corner, the canal burps and sloshes.

The downstairs corridor is dark and smells like basement dust and new brick. An enormous piece of opaque plastic from the delivery of their kitchen island is crumpled in a corner near the mailboxes. She climbs four floors and stops at the door, turning the key as quietly as possible. She recalls that the best part of her day used to be hearing a key turn in the door. She would wait behind the door and peek out at him as he came in. His slow smile would bloom, the wrinkles around his eyes would appear, and he would lift her up, kiss her mouth, and say, "You bring the joy."

Opening the door, she whispers. "Gui?" The apartment smells strongly of drying paint and industrial glue. A white powder dusts the edges of her black slippers as she enters. They haven't yet installed blinds and the streetlights infect the living room in patches. Even when it's covered in soot and concrete and dirt, she loves this place. It is a sparkling, peaceful nook cut through by wooden beams, hovering over a canal lit by moonlight and those reverent streetlamps. The lone piece of furniture is a cracked cherrywood dining table atop crisscross legs that the carpenters have built and are leaving until the end to gloss and finish. A pile of discarded mail waits on the dusty tabletop, junk from agencies, alumni organizations, and others to whom they've remembered to give their new address.

"Gui?" she says again. This time her voice echoes through the bare space.

She goes from room to room. The master bedroom is rubble. She moves through it quickly and heads to the kitchen, guest room, balcony, then down to the basement. Finally, she hears a cough from the far end of the apartment. She hasn't checked the bathroom because they have no plumbing. Why would he go there?

Guillaume is tucked inside the bathtub, his socks and shoes stowed neatly in a corner, his jeans folded on top. He has arranged two blankets under him and one on top. She recognizes the utility blankets they used to move the wood for the dining table. He looks exhausted, sitting in the tub, playing on his phone. He looks up at her like a caught bird. His eyes plead, *leave me alone*. After having strained all night to handle things sanely, Niloo is overcome by a rushing grief. "I'm so sorry," she says.

The air is full of dust, stinging the eyes, but he's made an attempt to clean up, to make the space nice. In the corner, he's flung some used paper towels covered with soot. The rims of the bathtub are wiped clean, though the sides are caked with dirt. He has a roll of toilet paper, three bottles of water, an open jar of Nutella with a plastic spoon sticking out, and a premade lentil salad from Marqt. The lentil salad makes Niloo's throat close—they fought instead of eating dinner.

He stares at her with bloodshot eyes, searching for words. Often he speaks around things. When they were twenty-two, instead of saying he loved her, Guillaume pulled her close and twisted the sentiment into a question instead, forcing her to confess it first. "If I lived under a bridge," he asked, "would you come see me?" She told him that she would fill a backpack with gummy bears and olive oil and woolen socks and move under the bridge with him. He said, "I promise if we have to live under a bridge, it'll be the Pont Alexandre III." Over a decade, Niloo and Guillaume have learned each other's signals, how to be kind to each other. Though it struck Niloo once, while reading an essay on early primates, that animals aren't gentle or generous with their mates; nature's way is selfish and cruel and hungry.

Now, watching Gui try to find his words in the bathtub, she expects more caveats and placeholders, more phrases that circle the issue but don't venture too close. Instead he says, every syllable swollen with such misery that her stomach clamps into a painful knot, "Why don't you know that I love you?"

When she hears "I can't do this anymore," it takes a second to realize that these dreaded words have tumbled from her own mouth. And all her many small muscles engage again, the four bites of pear she ate earlier rolling around inside her stomach. "It's not enough just to laugh at the same twisted jokes and to say we love each other enough to live under a bridge. We have no roots."

"So we build roots," he says.

"Do you know what songs I loved as a kid?" she says. "Or what poem my dad read to my mom? If you heard them, you wouldn't even understand the words. Same goes for me. Don't you care about that?"

"Go away." He turns to face the wall. "You're not the only one who needs personal space." She spies a stack of highlighted depositions in the tub at his feet.

Now, out of Gui's bitter request springs a possible solution. She taps him on the shoulder. "Gui? Please listen. What if I move in here and finish this house by myself . . . just for a few months?" When he winces, she adds, "So I'm a permanent part of it . . . the whole thing, not just a portable little corner. And then we can sell it or you can have it, I don't care . . . I'll do a good job." She waits, then realizes how silly she sounds, talking of houses in the final slow beats of a decade together.

She takes off her shoes, lifts the blanket, and says, "If you're not getting out, then I'm getting in." His body is still, like he's waiting for the roof to collapse on his head. She feels renewed sadness bubbling up but pushes it back to the pit of her stomach. She says, "Fine, I'll be the outer spoon. Get ready to have your Perimeter breached." His shoulders twitch; she wants so much for Gui to laugh. And he does.

An hour later, she leaves Gui in the bathtub, sleeping off the fraught night. She finds Siavash and Karim eating a bag of pistachios on the curb in front of the squat, breaking them open with their thumbnails. She has never met an Iranian who isn't a serious stress eater, and since Mam'mad's death none of her friends have stopped eating, as if trying to protect themselves against the ugly world with a layer of fat. She joins them on the low step. Siavash pulls out his earbuds and offers her a listen. *Wake up, wake up, little sparrow*, the grainy song implores.

When the song is finished, they sit quietly for a long time. Then Karim takes Sy's phone, a gesture very unlike him. "Can I show you something?" Sy nods. Karim searches the Internet, finds an Iranian song whose name she recognizes—"One Day When You're in Love." The three huddle around the earbuds, their heads touching, cradling the phone. Karim's version is sung by a two-year-old girl and her father. The man's familiar voice draws a little gasp from Niloo. "Oh god, is that you?"

Karim smiles sadly, nods. "I made this years ago, the last time I saw my daughter. I played it for Mam'mad *agha* and he said we should send it to Geert Wilders with a note that says, *fuck you, you bleached bastard.*"

For two minutes, Karim plays guitar and his daughter sings in a crackling reedy voice like sugar candy, flinging her joy at the microphone, mispronouncing all the words. It reminds Niloo of the tapes of herself and Kian, recorded when they were each two, singing and reciting poetry with their mother. The best part of the song (Karim taps his ear just then, to say *listen here*) is the single moment when the child seems to understand every word and says them with palpable emotion—*Great god, oh god, I want to* stay *in love.* Then she goes back to mispronouncing words and reciting from rote memory. Staying in love, this girl seems to know, is the true challenge. Is she born knowing this? Has she grown up expecting every love to end? Did she expect her Baba to disappear one day into Europe's gaping mouth, maybe never to return?

Niloo's fingers shake, her keys jiggling hard against her knee. Karim catches her frantic hand in his dry, calloused one, covering it entirely so the tips of her keys jut from their enclosed fists like the beak of a small bird they have caught. "Calm down, Niloo *khanom*," he says. "It's not so bad if we're all still here."

Generosity is the gift of the poor, Mam'mad once said, and she knows that now. She thinks of Baba's letter, her fear of it. How bad can it be?

Alone in her bedroom, she stalls, returning a call from Maman before retrieving the letter. "I got a fuzzy voice mail from Iran," Maman says in Farsi. "Terrible connection, but it sounded like Bahman. Have you heard from your Baba?" For a desperate second, she considers confiding in her mother about the letter, the emails, and all the frightening possibilities they hold. But a marble forms in her throat and she mutters a quick no.

She lifts the envelope to her nose. How did a letter that smells like this make it out of the country? Likely the spice jar masked the earthy hashish smell. Maybe he didn't even care. She turns the flimsy blue parcel in her hand and tears the seal. She plucks out the leaf-thin sheet inside. Niloo knows what Baba wants—she is supposed to belong to a larger organism. But her connection to it feels unnatural now, like foreign cells trying to attach and grow.

Iranian families, Niloo recalls, are constructed as clans, or packs. Every time one of them sneezes, fifty relatives come running with pots of basmati and plum chicken. They are many, a bonded unit, and they come running. That's how it was in Ardestoon, where a lonely lunch meant fifteen relatives under a canopy of trees tearing into *lavash* bread with cheese and cucumber, teasing one another with songs, stemming mulberries, and salting sour green plums. If something happened to one of them, their roots were strong. But Guillaume and Niloo are like the Dutch now—they have been only two for a long while. She reads the Farsi words one by one.

"I don't understand this." She sits up in her bed, kicking aside the covers. Is the man high or just lying? Bahman Hamidi has a habit of lying. He does it often and with great relish. Before they left Iran, he looked Niloo in the face and said he would join them. She reads the letter again—maybe her Farsi has slipped. But there is no mistake. It seems that since June, Dr. Hamidi has been jailed inside his own house.

Small Joys, Like Sour Cherries

AUGUST–OCTOBER 2009

Istanbul, Turkey

In Istanbul Bahman had friends, but he instructed the taxi to drive him to the Ayasofya Pansiyonlari, the whitewashed guesthouse on a flower-lined street beside that grand rosy basilica, its namesake. When the chimes announced him, the manager, dressed in so much crimson he could light up a brothel, greeted him with a two-handed shake, slaps on the back, and smiling eyes. "Dr. Hamidi!" he said in an accented mix of Farsi and English. "Welcome back! We have the blackest, hottest coffee for you!" He led Bahman to his favorite chair in the balcony café.

To get out of Iran, Bahman had managed to obtain a legal exit visa (he had purchased it with bribes, which is one way of doing it). He had gone about that business quietly, in Tehran, hoping that the court in Isfahan wouldn't notice an international trip so soon after his house arrest. In case of an office search, he had left all of his family photos on the walls, some cash in his desk, and his brothers in charge. The plan was this: for as long as they could keep it up, his brothers, Ali and Hossein, would open Bahman's office, do cleanings, cavities, and x-rays, and even schedule operations that they would cancel at the last minute. In honest moments, which occurred tediously often as he grew older, Bahman could admit that dental work wasn't all that hard—his unschooled brothers had learned it easily enough. But then, he had always been a touch lazy and self-indulgent. If you're going to study teeth, you should study their evolution, like Niloo, or how to make them itch for new tastes, like Kian. He shook with excitement at the thought of seeing the children.

In the café overlooking the Aya Sofya, Bahman drank dark coffees and he made plans. He would obtain a three-month European travel visa—he had done this before to visit the children. He would travel to Holland, where he was almost certain Niloo still lived. Then, on day ninety-one, when his visa expired and it became obvious that he was throwing himself at the mercy of whatever Dutch back channel dealt with illegal immigrants, his lawyer, Agha Kamali, would send his remaining money to his mother and would wash his hands of the matter.

Bahman spent a long, hot day standing in line at the Dutch embassy. Niloo had never responsed to his letter—would she be disappointed to see him? For hours he watched the anxious travelers in the waiting rooms. He listened to Farsi conversations, never revealing himself. How fortunate he was to have some money to ease his path. He tried to imagine the journey as a poor laborer smuggling a family. How would he get the exit visa? How would he pay the lawyers and translators? How would he convince them he wasn't going to stay too long?

And yet, if you looked beyond the goings-on inside, these European embassies displayed such riches, occupying such stunning streets. He was reminded of a day in London, in front of the American embassy, when he had asked Niloo if they might go in. The kindness in her eyes had retreated behind a wall of panic. It saddened him to think of his daughter's shortcomings in the face of these unequal gifts. Did Europeans realize how lucky they were, to be a part of so much order and care through an accident of birth? What would his life have been if he had been born the son of an English barrister instead of an Ardestooni farmer? He would spend his days in manicured gardens, wearing white billowy trousers, reading poetry and drinking tea. At that familiar image, he chuckled at himself—all his life, this had been his dream: the white trousers, the tea in a garden, the books. Maybe it had nothing to do with the English; maybe that was his own private paradise.

He didn't get an appointment at the Dutch embassy that day. The next day, he was given a stack of English printouts outlining the application procedures for a tourist visa. He left with the pages and called a lawyer Kamali had recommended.

The lawyer spoke in stilted, bookish Farsi. "Why do you want to leave?" he said, guessing that Bahman had no intention of returning.

Bahman didn't mention the opium (that he would've left long ago if his hands and feet hadn't been tied to that cursed plant). "Thirty years is enough," he said, his sadness leaking out in his voice. "Iran won't change back. You've seen the situation. These kids don't have the stomach for revolution, and our generation even less."

"Well, sir, everyone's trying to get out," he said. "Tourist visas aren't easy, even for gentlemen like you." He shook his head and rubbed the sweat off his endless forehead. Bahman left his office without another word.

One can't put their fate in the hands of a man without hope—especially one so unmoved by an entire life suddenly vanished. Was it so commonplace, this thing he had done, that this miserable man couldn't muster one encouraging word? Had he not torn himself from the home of his childhood, from all that he loved, and all that bound him? Opium, yes, but so much else. He had freed himself, and that should astonish. Well, at least it astonished Bahman . . . maybe that was enough.

In late September, Bahman met another lawyer who was young and kind and had a good London accent, a university accent—he cost twice as much as the other one though he was half that man's age. The boy served mostly as a translator, which suited Bahman. With every mild-mannered translation he changed Bahman's words into their best, most refined variation. Sometimes he omitted things or added things and Bahman saw the wisdom in his choices. The young lawyer accompanied Bahman to the Dutch embassy, securing an interview for two weeks' time.

Bahman spent the next morning in the glass greenhouse where breakfast was served. He read Hafez and thought of his last visit here. The memory saddened him. He went for a long walk and returned to the hotel tired and sweaty.

In his room, he turned out his suitcase onto the bed. Suddenly, his clothes seemed wrong, the clothes of a villager with troubles. They stank of his old life. The luggage too smelled of decades of misuse—all the contraband he had sewn into the linings. He threw all the clothes back into the suitcase, took it downstairs, and left it on the street with a note in English: *Take please. Cloths of old man. Good quality.*

He walked to Istiklal Caddesi, the busy shopping street with a tram, dozens of pastry shops, and the famous American café he liked, the one with ice cream masquerading as coffee. "Where is the Starbuck?" he asked five or six passersby.

How different this trip was from all the other times he had come to Istanbul for visas; in those days, he had been confident of returning home and that confidence announced itself. Iran wasn't in such chaos then, and Kamali had done all the paperwork. Each time, he had secured his visa in a few days and spent the rest of the time shopping for one wife or another. Now the world had grown weary of Iranians and he wore his secret plans like a soiled undershirt; he was sure they could smell him coming. What would he do if he were turned away? If they saw in his nervous eyes that he had changed, that he was no longer bound to home?

He walked around for a while, sampling Turkish delicacies until he found a men's clothing shop. He bought four pairs of white trousers (three respectable ones with zips, one with a drawstring for some future garden), undershirts, and several breezy button shirts in light, carefree colors. "I want to look like British men in Topkapi and mosques," he said to the salesman. "The good ones, not the riffraff."

He also bought a hat to protect from the sun, dark glasses, a new cane, and counting beads in a darker shade of green. Later he returned the beads because they didn't move easily under his thumb, and it was all too much change.

That night he sat up with the hotel manager, who offered him a *manghal*. "I've given that up, my friend," he said. "It's not healthy." Then, after a moment's thinking, "Do you know someone reliable who could put a little color back in my hair?"

"Dr. Hamidi," said the manager in his own special Finglish. "You're a friend, so I'll say this plainly. I forbid you from whatever craziness you're considering."

"I'm about to become a trespasser in a place that wants me to turn around and go home," Bahman sighed. "Shouldn't I fix myself up a little?"

"Stop worrying," said the manager. He poured Bahman another coffee. "Your children will be happy to see you."

"Oh, you've forgotten my Niloo," Bahman said with a little laugh. "Those hard, disappointed eyes." The manager nodded and lit his own cigarette.

Two weeks later, Bahman returned to the Dutch embassy. He sat humbly through the interviews. He spoke of his son and daughter, his wife in Iran, and his dental practice. Of course, he planned to go back home, he assured them. He showed his bank balances and proof that he had traveled to Europe before, always going home on time. He showed a return ticket, bought and paid for. He even pulled out a photo of Ardestoon—*See how beautiful? See how the river sparkles? I tell you, no one ever leaves this village.* In immigration offices, as in divorce courts, everyone lies.

Then he waited. He ate lunches with his clever lawyer and spoke to Kamali on the phone. September came to an end and he grew restless. In October, he tried to call his children. He left a voice mail in Niloo's office but never heard back. Some days later, he was granted a short-term tourist visa to the Netherlands.

That night he sat up on the balcony with the hotel manager. The crisp autumn air fluttered the tablecloth and, for the first time in weeks, he craved the *manghal*. "This damn itch," muttered Bahman. "I've had the same bad habits all my life."

He thought of his last trip to Istanbul; he had drunk a hundred extra-hot Turkish coffees trying to avoid the mistakes of Madrid. On that first day, before the children arrived, one of the waiters here had sold him four mild opium cookies at a high price. He had eaten three bites a day to stave off withdrawal.

The manager nodded. "Maybe replace one old habit with another."

"Yes," said Bahman, and laughed to himself. He no longer needed to go scavenging for dirty cookies; but, he reminded himself, there exist in this world small joys that don't move you to abandon reason. "You wouldn't have any sour cherry lying around?" His friend smiled, took a drag of his cigarette, and shook his head. "Never mind. Pour us another coffee, will you? It's a very nice night. Very nice."

THE FOURTH VISIT

ISTANBUL, 2008

There are a hundred ways to kneel

and kiss the ground.

—JALAL AD-DIN RUMI

In Istanbul, I reckoned with the inevitable: introducing Baba to Guillaume. The notion of melding my two worlds had given me nightmares for nearly a decade, and after the disaster in Madrid a year and a half before, I promised myself that I wouldn't. But Baba had insisted on meeting my husband, and, when Gui found out, he gleefully insisted too. I agreed to go only because Kian wanted to do a summer fish tasting tour, learn some new kabob recipes, and shop for bulk spices at the Grand Bazaar. I figured at least Gui and I wouldn't be alone with Baba.

Lately Gui was spending much more time at work. I didn't mind; I had my own work and we had long agreed to prioritize our careers. Besides, Gui's job made our lives comfortable in ways I had never experienced before. What else could I want? A part of me delighted in showing Baba all that I now had. See? I've made a good life. Who would imagine that I was once a refugee kid in Oklahoma? That I had ever stood in a breakfast line in a hostel outside Rome, or worn ill-fitting clothes from the Salvation Army, or spent a night in Jesus House? This is happiness.

Our flight from Amsterdam Schiphol landed in the afternoon. Kian's and Baba's flights had arrived in the morning, so Gui and I went straight to the Ayasofya Pansiyonlari, where we had reserved three rooms, hoping to find them settled. At the front desk, a Turkish host, a peacock of a man with tense eyebrows, gold buttons on his royal blue jacket, and a shiny, disconcerting mustache trimmed too far in, greeted us. He had an affected manner, the flourish of his fingers, the lilt of his voice, like he had learned the art of luxury hosting from an old cartoon.

Sometimes I like to imagine our Istanbul trip from the perspective of the hotel staff. After several visits with Baba, we didn't see our own strangeness, the way we had transformed a little each year, drifting into disparity and becoming so foreign to one another that together we made no sense, like the mismatched elements of a face after too much plastic surgery. In our three years as Amsterdamers, Gui had begun to dress like the upper-class urban Dutch, and, for the trip, I made an effort too. We arrived in our thin gray jeans and linen jackets in shades of cream, our longish hair hanging over aviator glasses. We asked if our party had arrived—my father and brother, we specified, enunciating their names. The host glanced at Gui, his European face and floppy haircut, then back at his roster and said, "No, there's no one here for you. We'll let you know." He added that we could wait in the balcony café, or rest in our room, and someone would call us when our party arrived. Maybe, he said, they had gone for a walk around Sultanahmet or their planes were delayed.

"I checked the flights," said Gui, mostly to himself. "They arrived."

We dropped our bags in the room, a bright airy space decorated almost entirely in white. A four-poster bed framed in gold and the gauzy, fluttering curtains opening to a view of the Aya Sofya conjured an old Istanbul from books and movies. An hour later, we visited reception again. "I'm sorry," the host said, without looking up. "Only a small handful have arrived today. No one for you."

We decided to go for a walk. The street was whitewashed and pristine, the sidewalks streaked with tiny blood-orange flowers. They reminded me of our street in Isfahan, the way the high outer walls of houses were covered with spray roses, and the streets sloped downward from the best house at the top to the impasse where children played soccer. Every few steps, I would scan clusters of passersby or peer inside cafés for Baba and Kian. Most of the houses on this walkway were *pansiyonlari* rental suites. Near the end, the hotel café jutted out onto the road from a second-story balcony. A couple was having tea on one side, and an old man sat three seats from them, rapping his fingers on the head of his cane as he leaned against the railing, staring into the street, transfixed by foreign children and cheerful families.

"I wonder if they went to the wrong hotel," I said.

Reaching for my hand, Gui said, "I'm excited to meet your dad. And nervous."

"Me too," I said, and we meandered back and forth past that café, maybe thrice, looking up at the couple as they sampled a flaky pastry and at the old man with his cup of Turkish tea, staring out at the road, lost in his thoughts; he was in another world, but when he saw me, he smiled like a five-year-old.

At first nothing registered. Because I had seen Baba only eighteen months before and had a fresh image of him in my mind, I hadn't looked twice at the old man in the balcony; I hadn't needed to. But now the man got up, reaching for his cane, and hobbled toward the steps with a familiar gait. He pushed a hand into his arched back as he negotiated that first step, that boyish grin never leaving his face.

Except his smile was no longer ginger and toothy, but marred by two missing teeth and lost in a cloud of gray—gray skin, a gray mustache, hair that had gone entirely white. I stood dumbfounded. In just a year and a half, Baba had aged a decade—my Baba who had once had fire-red hair, who had played soccer and plummeted down an enormous waterslide. Had he spent the last few months obliterating his memories with the kinds of cocktails he had devised in Madrid? My heart throbbed and I wished for just a few more seconds to adjust. But Baba was almost at the bottom of the steps, and Gui was pulling me toward him. "Dr. Hamidi?" he said, extending his hand. And I had yet to decide if this *was* indeed Dr. Hamidi.

Baba approached me tentatively. I guess my behavior wasn't very welcoming. I recalled how he kept touching my face in Oklahoma, how he threw himself into Kian's arms in London, how the smallest kindness moved him in Madrid. And now, the drift had led us here, lingering two feet apart, unable to say hello. "Hi, Babajoon," I said, and the words caught in my throat. I hugged him carefully, because maybe he would break. Where were his back teeth? I wanted to ask this—where did they go?

Gui was thrilled by Baba's Iranian village look, as if he had assumed that I had oversold this aspect of my father. The green counting beads, the giant gold ring, the cane with a gaudy lion head, the yellowing pads of his fingers. As an old man, Baba was a spectacle, though after we finished our greetings, I realized that the only tangible changes were his missing teeth and whitened hair. He looked tired.

"Is pleasure," said Baba in his special English, which, after just two words, I knew had eroded. He openly stared at Gui, nodding and chewing his mustache. His admiration of my husband embarrassed me for hours after I should've forgotten it.

"Have you checked in?" I asked Baba in Farsi.

"Of course I did," said Baba. He returned to gawking at Gui, who stood six inches taller, examining him like an art installation, or a fancy suitcase he might want to buy, but only after much more research. Each time Baba's gaze became uncomfortable, Gui fired off one of the simple questions he had memorized. How was your flight? How is your dental practice? What do you want to do today? Baba just nodded and smiled wide. *"Il me comprend?"* Gui whispered to me.

As we strolled, I noticed the deeper, unnatural curve in Baba's back, and the tightly wrapped bandages peeking out from the space between his socks and his trousers, the sun glinting off his metal bandage clips. Was he shorter than he had been in Madrid? Was this possible? Confused and angry at the world, I stormed toward the *pansiyonlari* reception ready to release, but the manager had already seen everything. He watched puzzled as Guillaume and Baba attempted to converse just outside the glass door. Fondling his tiny mustache, he seemed to forget his affected ways. Before I could speak, he said, "We were waiting for an Iranian family for him, and maybe someone else for you."

"But he checked in hours ago," I said, flinging Western disdain.

He threw up his hands. "It didn't even occur to me, Miss. We get many European couples here. We're the number one choice for European couples. We don't get as many Iranian weekenders. Sometimes Tehranis, yes. The Iranian gentleman escaped my notice." He said *Iranian gentleman* with the clunky, showy arrogance of someone born just a little farther west.

"Well, it's lucky that people have names, right?" I said. He explained that my father had spelled Guillaume's name wrong when he had checked in. Still, I felt no kindness toward this man who had made Baba sit and worry for hours, just because he didn't look the part. What was he supposed to look like?

"I apologize," he said. "We won't charge for your father's . . ." He pretended to glance sidelong at a bill. ". . . six 'extra-hot' coffees."

His tone was infuriating. Did this idiot think he could buy us with a few cups of Turkish sludge? "Fine, but let me ask again," I said, "has Kian Hamidi checked in?"

The host didn't look at his roster or at the ancient computer in the corner behind him. He considered the question, then, his gaze darting past me at the door, said, almost distractedly, "There's an American backpacker in room five."

We found Kian in room five.

When he opened the door to the three of us, he broke into a stunned smile—we were mismatched even to him. He greeted us, then turned to Baba and said in choppy, practiced Farsi, "I want to be clear that I don't forgive what happened in Madrid, and that if I smell so much as a waterpipe, I'm out of here."

Kian and I took turns as translator. At the Grand Bazaar, I ambled between Gui and Baba and passed their words back and forth while Kian loaded up on cumin and fenugreek, saffron and ground ginger, and fifteen kinds of tea. He lugged bags of spices, never accepting help, but borrowing an extra ace bandage from Baba to wrap his forearms so he could carry more. At lunch, I took a break while Kian translated, his spices arranged on the table so he could smell and taste them again. He sprinkled sumac from his own stash on Gui's burger. Sometimes, when

Kian and I were distracted, Baba tried to communicate with Gui with his own mangled translations, importing entire unsanitized idioms directly from some fourteenth-century Isfahani village. Kian and I never interrupted Baba's spasms of English, though I wanted to—badly. I had almost no time alone with Gui and I was desperate to know his genuine impressions. Each time Baba started up, I pretended not to hear, and Kian went silent, smirking as Gui tried to work out what he was hearing.

One day, at a kabob house overlooking the Bosporus, Baba tried a pistachio-lamb skewer and he muttered, "This is very good. Is wedding in my ass." Gui's jaw stopped moving mid-chew. Kian snorted into his palm for a full minute. Baba grinned, happy that his mischief had been noticed. "What? You never hear expression?" After that, when Baba was worn out or in pain, he would lean back in his chair and say things like, "Dirt on my head!" or "Ghosts of my stomach!" After a good joke, laughter bellowed from his gut, and he would say to whoever had delivered it, "May God kill you." I had to explain to Gui that this, in Farsi, simply means, "You're terrific," or something of the sort. Without fail, when a kitchen couldn't fill one of his requests (he always special ordered plain yogurt, white rice, grilled kabobs, stewed chicken, and Caesar salads, as he couldn't eat most other things), he said, "The bride can't dance, so she says the room is crooked."

Every time Baba lobbed a new idiom, Kian wrote it in his notepad. Baba delighted in this attention and began an aggressive campaign to make Kian laugh, maybe to atone for Madrid and win back his son's love and approval by supplying all the fun we had missed on that other trip. Once, after a day of touring mosques and catacombs in Sultanahmet, Baba said, "I'm dead with tiredness," then realizing that his choice had been workaday, he added, pointing his remark at Kian with expectant eyes and zero subtlety, "My life is draining from my ass." It seemed that Persian villagers have a lot of sayings relating to the condition of their asses.

After every meal, Baba said to the waitress, "Miss, it is time to light up our homework," at which point Gui or Kian, whichever was sitting next to him, leaned back behind Baba's head and made the universal pen-scratch gesture for the bill.

Soon we learned to communicate through these sayings, and Gui began to understand Baba in ways I hadn't expected. They seemed, in fact, to be enjoying each other's company. They even convinced Kian to go for waterpipes. ("I swear is only fruit water," said Baba, "no addictions." Later he joked that Gui got addicted to the strawberry one anyway.) Sometimes when I arrived late to breakfast, served buffet style in a glass greenhouse in the hotel gardens, I would find Baba and Gui sitting quietly across from each other cracking eggshells and reading newspapers, each in his own native tongue. Baba would grumble, "Bank crisis spreads."

Gui would respond, "The Dow is bouncing back though."

Baba would look up from his coffee and wrinkle his brow. "What you mean?"

"Back up," Gui would respond. "Bouncing back . . . up." He was unconsciously adopting Baba's big hand gestures.

"Yes," Baba would murmur and nod and return to his paper, "Dow." Then he would look up again. "Is big trouble coming, you think? What is problem?"

And Gui would shrug and say, "The mortgage lenders sold wet wood." And Baba would chuckle and nod and crack into another egg.

For two weeks, the staff of the *pansiyonlari*, including the peacock manager, watched us and whispered, especially at breakfast. Each morning, the European lawyer would arrive with the aging Iranian villager, both hungry at first light, devouring hard-boiled eggs with butter, drinking carafes of coffee, hoarding the French and the Farsi newspapers. They spoke reverently of particular villages in Provence and southern Iran, howling at common details: stone kitchens, hearty mothers, toothless farmers at their market stalls. Just before breakfast closed, the American backpacker, yawning and grumpy, would plop down beside them, usually within minutes of his nervous Continental sister with her pastel clothes and panicky ponytails. The backpacker and his sister usually complained about the eggs. The aging villager always asked for English crumpets. And the French lawyer wrote their itinerary in the margins of his city map and studied it, referencing two guidebooks before declaring that it was time to begin the day. Their drink orders were absurd:

One dark tea in glass with cardamom and, if you have, English crumpet.

Une noisette. Merci.

One black coffee, only if it's ground on-site—I can tell—otherwise water.

One something authentically Turkish, preferably rural and ancient.

I noticed that Baba wanted to spend hours at breakfast and dinner. He seemed more fragile now; always tired, always thinking. Sometimes he recited lines of poetry to himself and shared them with Gui, who would jot down a few key words and look up the English versions at night on the Internet. "Your father quoted from 'Saladin's Begging Bowl' today," he would say. Or, "Found it! He's reading Hafez!"

In restaurants Baba became irritated, his stomach always hurting. I started to carry bags of almonds and raisins in my purse, since he could eat them without upsetting his stomach. He chewed with his front teeth, and once, when I saw him struggle with an almond, I had to excuse myself so I could recover. The restaurants were the most difficult, but he liked the kabob place overlooking the Bosporus, because its simple cuisine was identical to a Persian *kabobi*. We ate there three or four nights before the rest of us grew antsy about missing so many celebrated Turkish restaurants. He ate many Caesar salads, rejecting every fish as smelly, every piece of meat as undercooked. "My dinner bleeds! What barbaric place is this?"

I stopped caring about missing restaurants. In Amsterdam I had grown thin, though the scientist in me compelled me to feed myself. When left alone, I drank broth soups and ate puréed apples, carrots, and parsnips. I boiled things, steamed things, or left them raw. I skinned vegetables halfheartedly, so that they looked blotchy and afflicted. In less than two years, I had become the sort of woman who earns a parsnip at day's end. On the other hand, when Gui ate at home, I made lamb with butternut squash and prunes in turmeric sauce, or eggplants roasted in olive oil and garlic with whey. I baked cream puffs and served them with cardamom tea. I melted saffron into a teacup of butter and poured it over beds of fluffy basmati. Being a good wife was a simple science, easily mastered—I had a list.

I don't know if Baba saw my indifference to food. He kept putting half his kabobs on my plate. For days at a time, he conversed with us only in poetry and cuisine. In the evenings, he tried to get Kian and Gui drunk, just so he might feel better understood. Baba and Gui drank whiskey together, but Kian and I never joined. We were glad to outsource the drinking duties. One night, after a few shots, Baba said, "You are good husband, Gilom. Better husband than I was any of times."

Before bed, Gui told me that Baba asked him strange questions over breakfast. He wanted to know when we would have children, if we had discussed where our final home would be, and if he knew all of my hobbies. He said, "Person like Niloo cannot be bored. Or is trouble." I told Gui that Baba was just projecting.

We walked a lot, the four of us. Walking helped with the long silences, when Baba was too tired to speak English and we were too tired to translate. Gui didn't mind. Baba gave us no scares on that trip, and I suspected he was suffering through a mini withdrawal, trying hard to behave. Gui bought bottles of Cabernet and Shiraz for us to drink at night, in our rooms, over cards or books or games. He whispered, when Kian and Baba were out of earshot, "Your dad has an endless stash of whiskey. We have to switch to wine or I'll die of liver malfunction."

I missed the best part of the trip, the day we went to the bathhouse and I went alone to the women's bath while Kian, Baba, and Gui sat in the steaming, foggy rotunda together and laughed about the peering hotel staff while getting their shoulders kneaded out by a Turkish attendant in a *lunghi* cloth. I was massaged by an enormous woman in a blue Speedo who kept putting her arm down her bathing suit to straighten god knows what. I worried that Baba would have a heart attack breathing the hot, saturated air of the hammam. For the rest of that day, I battled a nagging loneliness, not because I had been separated from my family in the bathhouse, but because something felt finished. This trip felt like a last return. As I sat in the steam, I knew that this was my final trip with Baba—maybe because he was so old, maybe because I was so tired, or maybe because of the constant fear that Gui would see my family for what we were.

During our walk back, I spotted some pencil sketches in a shop window. Baba said, "This is Mevlevi art. Whirling dervishes. We must go and see Rumi's grave." Baba wanted to go in and talk to the artist, who said he could do any variation of the dervishes for us. I wanted the one in mid whirl, the dancer's arms high in the air, his head falling back. In the ten minutes we spent browsing the store, the artist had sketched a flowing, elegant miniature on cream stock, placed it in a red wooden frame, and presented it to me. I thanked him and asked if the dervish was inspired by an older pictoral depiction of the dance, or if it was his own creation.

"What are you doing?" Kian interrupted in distressed Farsi. "He just painted that and he's waiting for your reaction. Nod, praise it, do something."

Looking at the middle-aged Turkish artist with his paisley shirt unbuttoned halfway and his unassuming smile, I saw that Kian was right. This man was waiting for something from me. I praised the sketch until everyone looked satisfied, but I left distressed. Was I always oblivious to these unspoken needs?

Later, I tried to watch Baba for signs of fatigue or discomfort—though I didn't admit this, I was still looking for evidence of opium or worse. But he was even-tempered throughout the trip. Baba suggested we go to a Mevlevi dervish show. "The dance is prayer," he explained to Gui. "It's . . . a transcendence. Very tranquilizing."

At the show Baba closed his eyes and turned his beads between thumb and forefinger, nodding to the rhythm of the chants, transported. Behind us, a trio of American women talked loudly, reading from guidebooks and asking questions about the costumes, wondering when the show would end. In a quiet moment, they chimed in and Baba winced. For some minutes, I debated whether to speak up—Baba had been uncomfortable for most of this trip, the food, the walks, the language, the lack of drugs; only now, watching these white-clad men twirling, was he at home. I could see from his expression that he was trying to reenter his trance.

It took me ten minutes to find the courage to speak up, that fourteen-year-old who used to hide in water park changing rooms still whispering in my ear that it was *my* family who was out of place, *my* father who was embarrassing. Finally, I turned to the women. "This is a religious ceremony," I said. "Please shut up or leave."

Baba looked at me aghast. He whispered, "Niloo *joon*, why you are this rude? Let everyone enjoy in own way. Americans enjoy by talking."

The women smiled kindly at my Baba. They apologized and retreated into silence. Baba returned to his trance, cross-legged, eyes shut, oblivious. Gui took my hand and whispered in my ear, "Relax, Chicken. This is supposed to be fun."

For days after that, I felt like I had destroyed something.

Later, in Baba's room, Baba and Gui talked over whiskeys while Kian and I played a game we invented. In each round an ingredient is chosen—pomegranate or butternut squash or pork shoulder—and each player writes down a recipe. Best one wins. The better recipe is easy to spot, since we have similar palates, but we also incorporate a kind of honor system: if both players declare their own recipe superior, they can't cook the other person's recipe for six months. So freedom to experiment cancels out pride and we become neutral judges. We play this game constantly on planes. Kian usually wins and I collect dozens of new recipes.

Once in a while, we heard snippets of the conversation between Baba and Gui. "We must visit Rumi's grave," Baba suggested again.

"I think that's a few hours away," said Gui.

"Then next time," Baba murmured. Then he pulled a book of poetry, a volume of Hafez, out of his suitcase and told Gui about an old Iranian drinking game. "Look here, my son, you take the Hafez in hand . . . you take shot. You ask a question about future. You open book to any page. Your answer is on that page. You see?"

Baba insisted that Kian join the game. But Kian only pretended to drink, tossing his shots into a plant while Gui and Baba got drunk together, threw their arms around each other, and predicted the future. It must have been easy for them given the one vital trait they shared: neither had ever had a Jesus House night. They had held on to the untroubled ways of the native child, beloved by many, feet planted. Not the life Kian and I had lived. The game didn't last too late since it required Baba to translate from old Farsi to modern Farsi, then convey the meaning in English—not easy past a certain point of drunkenness. He would balance the book in one hand, tap a passage, and say, "Is about death . . . no worry. Is mean change." Then, in the next round, he would gather his fingers into a bud and touch his lips as if drawing out a thought. "Is about new love. . . . Is also mean change."

Once when Baba was engrossed in a passage, stroking his mustache, trying to focus, Gui turned to me with a shy grin. He shuffled on long legs and bent to look over Baba's shoulder, and I felt grateful for this man who loved my broken family.

I decided that I had been foolish to be ashamed of Baba, to let my need for security conquer every other instinct. I had spent years nursing the wrong fears. Baba's Iranianness, his village ways, weren't the problem. Just the opposite: if Baba were to uproot, every special thing about him—the Ardestoon he carried in his easy gait and his yellow fingers and his lion cane—all of that would be lost. Home would be lost. Living in America or Europe would end him, his lofty, infectious personality, his wonderful sense of himself. Deep down, Baba must have known this.

After a few more drinks, eyes heavy, Baba leaned across Gui and took my hand. "How old are you now, *azizam*?" I told him that I was twenty-nine. He said, his tone nostalgic, "I was around thirty when you left." Thirty-three, I corrected him. He said to Gui, "Is not easy, to build village." I have no idea what he meant. Maybe he was lamenting our scattered family. Or he might have meant that Gui and I should be careful as we make our plans together. More likely, he was thinking of his own troubles. I had heard rumors that his third marriage was difficult. Far from bringing him the health and youth and vitality that he'd hoped for, it had wrung him out so that he looked sixty-five, his body bent and stooped like a timid question mark.

Over and over I wondered: Is he still an addict? I never gathered the courage to ask. We caught up on my work, and before long, we stumbled onto a familiar discussion of the primitive and the refined. From the time I was fourteen, I knew that Baba and I shared a passion for this topic. He spoke of the village air. "It is healing to the soul, which above all craves nature and simplicity." I talked about literature and scholarship. Before long, the conversation included only the two of us and we spoke in easy Farsi, Baba asking me about my papers and offering opinions on Gui. He said, "You know, Niloo *joon*, I think a better way to observe the world isn't by how far from our natural state we've traveled. I think it's by whether we can go back and forth. That is a better evolution."

"That may be true," I said. "It's good to be adaptable."

"Though," he said, and he paused briefly and he changed to English. Almost to himself, he muttered, "The road, it travels too." I asked him what he meant. He looked groggily at me and said, "I think you should find Iranian friends. Peek at your roots sometimes. Practice traveling back and forth. I sense an anxiety—are you happy? Are you enjoying this fine life you've built?" The comment stung, but he seemed far past the point of noticing my reactions. Out of nowhere he said, "We have an election coming. It will be a spectacle, I think."

For days I considered Baba's assessment of me—was I happy? I had my work. I had a full life in Amsterdam. No, I didn't have any friends, and, no, I knew no other Iranians. But if I was afraid of anything, it was the possibility of stagnating. I didn't want to wither as Baba had withered.

I saw then how much these trips had drained me. Did they bring me any closer to Baba? Did they restore my roots or the childhood I had missed? All they did was tarnish my memories. The Baba I had known was trapped in the past, forever thirty-three, as I would be forever eight years old to him. Having never grown together, all we could do was rehash, returning to old ground, changing each other back to a faded snapshot after every goodbye. We couldn't fathom each other as we were now. Our visits, far from renewing us, were hastening our decay.

And surely Baba too was disappointed in my unwillingness to succumb to life's small pleasures, my inability to sink into every momentary bliss as he did. Maybe that's why he was an addict and I was not.

There was too much we couldn't repair. It was enough.

We left on a quiet Tuesday, when no other guests were coming or going. The hotel staff idled by, watching us linger over our breakfast, tucking our suitcases out of sight as we ate, dragging out our goodbye. We checked out together, and everyone *tarof*ed about who would pay—Baba offered to pay for all the rooms, but Gui and Kian refused. In another lifetime, Baba would have won this battle with ferocity and pomp.

But each man paid for his own room and they shook hands and promised another visit. Here I had another suspicion I was too afraid to confirm: Was Baba having money trouble? I hated that he had relinquished this small honor, ashamed that I had fantasized about impressing him with my new life. I smiled uncomfortably as the trio returned from the desk. Baba cast me a quick, patient look, one that was simultaneously humbled and angry, like he didn't want to be watched or pitied anymore by his own foreign child who had no access to the details of his life.

We called three taxis, each an hour apart, to correspond with our flights. Kian left first. Baba hugged him for a long minute and when he let go, Baba's eyes were cloudy and his chin trembled. He nodded a lot, trying to keep his emotions from spilling over. He patted Kian's shoulder and said, "Next time you will cook for us. I'll eat whatever you cook." Kian looked at his feet and shifted his bags of spices.

Then his son was gone and Baba's head hung a bit lower. His childish smile vanished. A waiter arrived with three Turkish coffees that he served to us right on the street, on a tray, "from the manager," he said. He stood straight-backed, watching us take small sips. I glanced at the lobby door. A maid averted her gaze. It seemed our story had spread; the staff wanted to witness us as we dwindled. They wanted to see our bizarre gathering come to its natural end.

We sat in the café in silence. Now and then, Baba and Gui made gestures at goodbye. Gui asked logistical questions about Baba's flight, his transportation in Tehran and Isfahan, the weight of his suitcases, and customs procedures in Iran. When our car came, most of the life had gone out of Baba's gait, and he stood leaning on the lion head of his cane. He didn't make a move toward us. I hugged him goodbye and let him rub my back, then pulled away. He said, "Niloo *joon*," but his voice broke. He swallowed and continued in Farsi, "Remember the family wedding curse?" I nodded. He said, looking beyond me, "I sense some bad luck with this no-wedding business. Please make your life fuller. Maybe have some babies."

I laughed and made promises. He turned to Gui. "Agha Gilom," he said, his cheer returning. "I want to say you something . . . Niloo translate?" Then he said in Farsi, pausing for me every few words. "All good things end, and I no longer believe that reduces their worth. I'm glad to have spent these happy days with you."

In the car, I let Gui stroke my hair. I felt scooped out, numb. When we reached the end of the street, I turned to look at my father, expecting to see him standing alone in the road. I understood that this would be my last image of him. I prepared to store it with that other image I keep: Baba at his office window, waving goodbye.

But Baba had turned toward the hotel, leaning both hands on his cane. He looked small, mystified, older than I've ever seen him. He tucked his cane under his arm and wiped his face with both palms. Two waiters rushed to him, one carrying a drink that must have been prepared as soon as our car arrived. The peacock manager had appeared and was leading Baba to his favorite spot on the balcony, one hand on Baba's cane and another on his back. Our car turned the corner then, but I imagined that for the rest of the afternoon, Baba sat at his table on the balcony and regaled the hotel staff with stories of Isfahan and of its villages, the fruit stalls and the lively women, and the lamb shank that comes apart in your spoon. It was a more fitting final snapshot than the one I had hoped for.

Just like Your Baba

OCTOBER 2009

Amsterdam, Netherlands

That week she moves into the half-built apartment, declining Gui's offers to help. She suggests that they don't speak for a while, afraid that hearing his voice would pain her, that it would make her think of all the firsts and lasts they've shared. She asks the construction workers to suspend work for a few days so she can settle into a corner; then they can begin again together. The man on the phone releases an exhausted breath, probably thinking of all the extra work she'll create.

She buys a hot plate and coffeemaker like Mam'mad's, a small comfort, though she expected it to feel more like that black interlude night at Jesus House. It doesn't. Pulling sheets onto a temporary bed, a shallow mattress in a corner of the floor, she thinks of her father and how he must be living. He claims to be under house arrest, though, given his fondness for tall tales, she hesitates to believe him. She can't deny that something has to be done, but now she's afraid she's waited too long. Who can she call? Baba's email address has gone completely silent.

After dropping off her suitcases, she pedals to the squat for dinner. Someone has made lamb stew with fenugreek and coriander, her favorite Persian dish. She donates five euros at the door and takes a plastic bowl from a pile, a floral yellow one. She recalls the fancy restaurants she's sampled with Gui, how none of them can match the taste of a meal at her grandmother's table, the herbs picked from her garden, the lamb butchered outside her door, the spices ground by her friends.

The squat is busy and the sink soon fills up with unwashed dishes. Here everyone pitches in, so she gathers a stack of bowls and heads to the kitchen. Mala and Siavash are there, talking to Maman Georgiana, the squat cook, a Dutch woman with stark white hair, a tall, bovine body covered in loose cotton dresses, and a web of tiny lines around her eyes. Siavash mutters something sympathetic, a "we're here if you need anything," which he spits out like an unexpected olive pit. Niloo leaves the bowls on a tray by the door and steals back into the living room. She stays only for a short while. It feels dishonest to indulge in an evening out when her marriage is so recently over. She feels in the wrong place, like the time in kindergarten when she watched silently as two boys searched all the jackets for coins.

In the dark of her half-built apartment, she whispers to herself in Farsi, the emptiness of the room echoing her hushed words. It seems the correct language for her refuge. She sings herself children's songs, the one about peaches, the one about a rabbit, the filthy village one about big-breasted mothers. The childhood tune she recalls best is Kian's revolution song. *A caged bird is heartsick of walls*—her memory of it includes all his lisps. Siavash and Karim have brought her oil lamps, flashlights, jugs of water, an extra stove, and a few pots and pans. She lights three lamps and places them around the bedroom, casting long shadows across the room. Since the kitchen isn't usable and the living area is toxic with dust and debris, she decides to occupy mostly the bedroom. Her peculiar new home feels like a return to her village roots, like being back in the caverns of her grandmother's dusty brick house, where for a long time there was no electricity and after that, it might go out in the middle of dinner or when they turned on a rickety television set.

She sits for a while, and when the floor grows icy against her haunches, she gets into bed in her clothes. Lying in this wreck, something important feels finished. It is as if in her fingers and toes she knows that the life she has built is done and that the passing decades will find her gone from here, inside a different future. For several hours, she sleeps the sleep of the sated women she used to watch in Tehran and Oklahoma, the ones who never worried because their homes never changed.

But the flesh doesn't adapt in a day and, in the middle of the night, she wakes in a panic. The smell of paint and wooden slats, concrete and dust, wafts everywhere and she imagines herself, for a moment, stuck in some nightmarish version of her childhood house in Isfahan. Right now, if Baba's claims are true, that same old house holds him in a kind of limbo. A drop of sweat, like a punctuation, falls from her hair. It rolls off her collarbone and into the hollow of her neck. When she lifts herself onto her elbows, the air chills her back where she's sweated through the sheets, her long hair sticking to her skin, slick and black like the down of oil-spill birds in science magazines.

She stares into the dark, at the spot where Gui might sleep. She has often told him that he smells like the mountains, dewy and grassy and evergreen. Now her sheets, smelling so strongly of nothing, keep her awake.

She swings her legs to the side of the mattress, feet hitting the cold floor too soon. She makes coffee on the burner. That first night is endless and dark, as many first nights have been. The hours weigh down her shoulders like a wool garment soggy with rainwater. The apartment seems to have swollen to triple its size and the image of Mam'mad, her first friend in so long, engulfed in flame returns to torment her. It sticks like a lead morsel in her belly. She tells herself that she can digest it in a few days. She will make herself digest it in a few days.

The next night, Niloo stops by her office to gather some books and journals. She hasn't come in for days and her mail has piled up. She tears open the first envelope; a stern Dutch warning from her department chair. She has canceled too many classes. The red light on her phone blinks urgently. She dials her password: three voice mails from colleagues and one other. The last message begins with some grainy whirring and a click. The lead pellet rolls past her navel—only calls from Iran sound this way. Then, her father's raspy voice, still comforting, like warm coffee or an old afghan, breaks the humming in fits and starts. The connection is terrible and she hears only every other word. He sounds tired. Older. He says something about a flight, something about Istanbul (maybe referring to last year's trip?) and then he hangs up. She listens to the message half a dozen times, failing to decipher the words. She deletes the others, leaving Baba's message; she will try again later. She tucks her mail into her purse and waits in the chilly, damp night for a tram, counting along with the arrivals clock from nine minutes, to eight, to seven.

She sits alone in the rubble of her living room, turning her flashlight on and off, staring at the half-built kitchen island, the marble countertop that she so carefully chose, lying on its side. Outside, a hard rain starts. What constant breathlessness in uprooting; it's the unbearable stretching on of life. How relentlessly it endures for you—a comfort. She makes tea on the burner and searches through journals from her office. She reads a colleague's piece, and three others, and, even though she isn't hungry, she counts out four hundred calories of protein in the form of hard-boiled eggs and raw almonds, and she goes to bed.

Around lunchtime, early morning in New York, Maman calls, first on Niloo's mobile, then at her office. Niloo ignores the calls but they continue at ten-minute intervals. Finally she picks up, and her mother begins shouting even before saying hello. She has spoken to Kian, who, given his eighteen-hour workday, didn't think through the politics of sharing everything Niloo told him. "I ask you!" says Maman, her tone accusing, her English slipping even further in her fury, "I ask you if Baba calls, and you say, 'No, he doesn't make the calls.' And I ask if you hear informations from Iran, and you say no informations! But is lie! Your sweet grandmother sits in Ardestoon in dreams of you, all the time is hoping you get her package and what you do? You say, 'No informations.' Iran is all in shits and violences and you have urgent request from your Baba and what you do? Nothing. Why you do nothing? Why you have no heart? I am shame of you, Niloofar. Shame of you."

Niloo wants to remind her mother about Madrid—their last visit as a family—and about the fright they suffered there. She wants to say to Maman, What do I owe this man who has broken my heart, damaged it over and over, so many times that it no longer looks like a heart? I can forgive people who injure once and leave. This man arrives every few years, always older, kinder, pulling me back, mending my heart so he can break it again. He offers promises and explanations and fantasies of a life that's finished. "One day we'll picnic again under the cherry trees in Ardestoon," he says—a lie. He's never said a final, respectable goodbye.

When Maman has finished her rant, she waits, panting into the receiver. Niloo can't defend herself. That isn't the biggest truth she has omitted and now her heart thunders thinking of the other one—her mother will have a stroke when she finds out that she's moved out. She tries to think of something calming to say, something with proper measures of regret and explanation. But Maman starts up again. "I just call to say you . . ." She realizes she is still speaking English and switches to Farsi. "I'm coming to Amsterdam in two days. Your Baba called from Istanbul and he says he's clean and he's trying the Dutch embassy. I'll just stay in the guest room like last time. Say hi to Gay." And, before Niloo can point out the insanity of believing Baba's promises of being clean or of wanting to stay, before she can work out how she will explain a vanished Gui and a vanished apartment and her relocation to a strange bed in the middle of a dusty construction site lit by oil lamps, Maman hangs up with such rage that the phone clicks twice, once when it falls on Maman's glass table and the second time when she successfully slams it.

Niloo scrambles to make the new apartment livable, buying more blankets and pillows and some chairs. She sweeps up all the debris in the living room and transfers it to garbage bags. She mops the last of the bathroom dust. She sprays every corner with insecticide, lays down cheap rugs, wipes the blinds. She buys eight more lamps and a vase of tulips. By the morning of Maman's arrival at Schiphol Airport, Niloo hasn't summoned the courage to tell her.

Hours later, standing in the foyer with her mother, staring over her mother's shoulder at her broken kitchen, strewn in pieces all over a vast unfinished floor, Niloo sees the futility of her dusting and lamp buying.

The place is a wreck, not a suitable home for a daughter you've dragged by the teeth from a war-torn country, suffered to educate despite her willfulness and likelihood of becoming a hedonist, then sent off to the best universities, and waited nervously to see settled and married. Maman runs a hand through her thick, shoulder-length chestnut hair, a style that suits her. "I need coffee before I can hear this," she says, her voice shaking.

At the café at the end of the street, over hazelnut espressos dolloped with foam, she tells her mother the story of the past few months, the peace she's found at Zakhmeh, losing her worries in storytelling nights, and about Mam'mad.

"Oh, Niloo *joon*," says her mother, stroking her hair. They sit next to each other at a picnic-style table in the center of the café. Maman has not let go of Niloo's hand for almost an hour. "Listen to me, baby *joon*, Iran breaks my heart too, but leaving your home isn't the answer." Then she adds, miserable, "And we love Gay."

Maman doesn't say much for the next six or seven hours. At home, she takes a nap on Niloo's bed, then gets up, washes her face, picks up her purse, and goes out. She returns an hour later with cleaning supplies, bath mats, shower curtains, and groceries. She has at least eight plastic bags hanging in two rows off her absurdly strong arms. For hours, she scrubs and scours and dusts and soaks. She tinkers with the temporary oven the construction workers have been using to make cheese *broodjes* and she bakes cream puffs and *baghlava* and Dutch apple tarts. She lets slip that she learned to make the tarts in preparation for her trip (which Niloo realizes is not spontaneous, but has likely been planned for some time). Without a word to Niloo, she takes a plate of sweets to the neighbor, introduces herself, and borrows a vacuum—unlike Mam'mad, Maman knows how to approach the neighbors here like a confident American: she offers sweets not to beg for welcome but with entitlement: *I need your vacuum.* She reaches into the pores of the space, peeling off layers of dirt that Niloo's hands haven't even touched.

By the time Maman is finished, three days later, the construction portion of the apartment is sectioned off from the living space. She walks to a fabric shop across town and buys huge pieces of cheap pastel fabric, the gauzy kind that obscures shapes and colors but allows the light to pass through. She nails the fabric into the walls of the unfinished kitchen and the living room, cutting the pieces so they hang a foot from the floor, creating a breezy cotton hallway that leads from the front door, through the livable part of the hall, to the bedroom and bathroom.

Niloo shares her bed with Maman, who is happy to sleep next to her. She prays a lot. Soon, Maman begins a massive cooking project, and Niloo has no choice but to interrupt her domestic meltdown.

"So why exactly are you here?" she asks. "You said Baba was coming too."

Wrong lead. Maman looks up from the sauce she is bringing to a slow boil, and says, "Is your father's expatriation and exile not going fast enough for you?" Maman waves a dishrag in Niloo's direction. "You know what your problem is? You're just like your Baba. You think only of your own satisfaction. Your entire moral philosophy is based on what is most convenient and desirable to Niloo. Well, tell me, what kind of morality is that?"

"Who said anything about morality?" Niloo says. The comparison to Baba stings. Hasn't she done enough to stamp out every primitive desire to the point of bleakness? Hasn't she killed the wild Ardestooni girl and avoided drugs and lovers and all the weaknesses to which Baba has succumbed? Hasn't she devoted her life to study and hard work? "This is just life. A turn in the road."

Her mother paces the room, manhandling lamps and wiping surfaces she has only just cleaned. "What about that poor, sweet boy you leave alone while you turn road?" says Maman in English, then changes back. "You say you're not happy, but you've been socializing with refugees, watching disturbing things, listening to the words of desperate people. Niloo, they want so much from you. Don't you remember the misery of those years? You've worked for decades to escape their fate. And now what are you doing? Your life was like a silk dress that blinded a dozen seamstresses, and you're putting a match to it." Niloo drops onto her haunches on the floor, which her mother has covered with cheap pillows from the street market.

That night Maman discovers a late-night Iranian grocery store and kabob shop in the Jordaan district and takes a tram there. Niloo knows the owner; he comes often to storytelling nights. She doesn't accompany Maman for fear of having to introduce them. On her way to bed, as she pulls the blinds, Niloo spots a familiar shape lingering outside—Siavash, trying to decide whether to ring the doorbell. She slips on her house shoes and goes downstairs. By the time she opens the front door and calls his name, he's unlocking his bike. "Just checking on you," he says, turning the Green Movement ribbons and stack of hairbands he keeps around his wrist.

Over his shoulder, she sees her mother approaching, a burlap sack of basmati rice cradled in her arms. When Maman spots them, her gait changes. Though laden (as ever) with bags, she shuffles over faster, as if trying to swim to a drowning child.

When she reaches them, she just stands there, staring dumbfounded at Siavash, who tries to help with her burlap sack. "Are you Niloo's mother?" he asks. "You look so much alike." But Maman's lips gather so tightly you might think she is trying to swallow her own teeth. "My mother brings burlap sacks of rice everywhere too," he says, laughing a little. "Persian mothers are the best."

The more Siavash tries to charm Maman, the more suspicious she seems, unable even to release a rote greeting—it's as if she has appointed herself Gui's advocate against every other male in Niloo's orbit. Niloo wonders if her mother will ever accept another partner for her. Finally, as Niloo leads her away, Maman finds her sharp tongue. She turns and says in Farsi, "We all need a rest. Please don't come back here for a while."

Siavash winces, raises a hand in Niloo's direction, and turns to his bike.

The next day, Maman calls the embassy in The Hague and begins the process of inquiring after Baba. Apparently, a temporary visa has been issued, the paperwork completed, and Baba should be on his way. Has he not contacted them, the woman on the phone asks; where are the family listed on the application? She seems to be inserting new notes into the application, and Maman grows alarmed. For the rest of the afternoon, she frets about whether the call might have hurt Baba. While Niloo is out, she fills the apartment with the smell of eggplant purée, salad *olivieh*, and chicken with plums.

When she comes home, Niloo falls into bed beside a sleeping Maman, whose hair smells like fried onion and turmeric. Waking a little, Maman rolls over and murmurs, "Your Baba called." Maybe she's dreaming; her eyes are closed and she mutters about Baba's visa and Niloo's new address. She is clutching her mobile. Niloo kisses her mother's oniony hair and tries to fall asleep too.

All night long, the pinging of text messages from Karim and Siavash rouse her—they are talking about Mam'mad; neither can sleep. They type in Finglish. Siavash is drunk. He can't keep the guilt at bay. He battled so often with Mam'mad; why didn't he just let him win one? How did he not see the old man losing all his courage, growing hopeless? He changed so quickly. Karim is consoling, his texts abbreviated because of two broken buttons on his derelict phone. It was a sacrifice, he says. Maybe it was for us, for the Green Movement, for the younger generation. Maybe the old have passion too, instead of just expectations and sorrow. Niloo replies that it was a useless, empty loss and some Dutch bureaucrat should be fired and jailed. She's angry for missing every sign, for being blindsided—when people at the squat spoke of suicide, she recalls, most often they were whispering about Karim.

The next morning, she wakes to a muffled conversation drifting up from beneath her window. Staring down into the street, she considers the strong possibility that she is hallucinating. Siavash is there, looking bedraggled, like he might have spent the night walking the canals, or waiting out on that sidewalk, or smoking in a coffee shop. And, beside him, as if plucked out of an absurd daydream, or from the pages of an old storybook, or a fit of the imagination, stands Baba, holding a single bag, wearing a short-sleeved button-up shirt and a strange floppy hat like an English tourist. He grips Siavash's shoulder with a massive hand, greeting him in Farsi, as he reaches for the doorbell.

Village Building

OCTOBER 2009

Amsterdam, Netherlands

It seemed clear that Bahman had underestimated the difficulty of village construction and management. The trouble is that the best people, the vital ones, often chafe against the part they're assigned and the whole thing crumbles down. How many times had Bahman tried to erect a community like his forefathers had done? Bahman's famous ancestor had built a thriving village as if it was nothing. He had watched it flourish and his descendants had scattered around the world, taking the legend of Ardestoon with them. How? Once when he was a boy, Bahman's father told him that you only need a handful of people to make a village that bustles and endures: a farmer with strong sons and respect for the earth, an honest butcher, a savvy merchant with a truck and a storefront, a doctor from the city, a poet to teach the children, a grandmother with a delicious hand, a gossip, a beauty, and a rogue. "Why a gossip and a rogue?" Bahman had asked. His Baba had said, "Without stories the village has no life." He added, a moment later, "The rogue usually has a *manghal* too. Look at Homayoun's boy. At every gathering, people wait for him."

Now, outside his daughter's home, in this European hamlet she had chosen, a young man who might have once been handsome greeted him; and though Bahman was a stranger to this village, he had no doubt that here facing him, lingering outside his daughter's door, stood its rogue. The boy was war-scarred, a detail that lumbered in Bahman's heart—what crimes his country had committed against its young. Though Bahman wasn't certain he was entitled to or capable of fatherly instinct, something stirred. For this lost boy, yes, but more for Niloo, who, in trying to steady him, might become his tattered sails. He clasped the young man's shoulder, his gaze falling on a clumsy knife mark on his neck, and asked questions.

"So she's made some Persian friends," Bahman said. He made a point of surveying the boy's ragged jeans, his muddy shoes, his three scarves intertwined, the oldest covered in pills as if each time one of them wore out, he simply added another strand to the braid. "Are you a student?"

"I'm an activist, a journalist, sometimes a student." He spoke and moved in a limp-wristed, needlessly open manner that young men adopt when their charms have always fallen on congenial soil.

"Where are your people from?" said Bahman. "That accent isn't Tehrani."

The stranger laughed, showing a row of milky teeth so excellently maintained, so harmoniously arranged, that Bahman had an urge to take his chin between two fingers and examine them. "I'm American," said the boy. "The accent is a mash-up. My parents are from Tehran, though. They sound like you."

"I'm Isfahani," said Bahman drily. His arms and neck were growing heavy from the long train ride, the taxis bouncing over cobblestone, and the maddeningly circular maps of this horseshoe city. "As is my daughter," he added. He never thanked people when they claimed his accent was Tehrani, first, because it wasn't; and, second, because they considered the remark a compliment.

After a moment's pause, Bahman said, "You remind me of someone." Though Bahman was a stranger, the boy seemed pleased to occupy space in his thoughts, unable to fathom an unfavorable comparison. Bahman pretended to strain for details. He scratched a rough spot below his ear and looked up at a row of windows draped in light bluish fabric, maybe Niloo's. He said, "A poet, a wanderer who fell in love with a woman I knew . . ." He paused; which version would he offer to her daughter's rogue, this man-child waiting on her sidewalk with a miserable smirk, his knot of oily hair and bloodshot eyes confirming a night spent walking. Even before Bahman had decided, the words gathered themselves into a bundle and slipped out on their own. "This man was very different from you, of course, in his education and upbringing, but he had the same remarkable teeth. He made his living as a roving office clerk." He counted with fingers running down an imaginary list, as if trying to recall it from a letter, "and, let's see, occasional *setar* player, extra security at underground parties, driver, maybe a witness for hire. One day, he left his daughter, a poor child of reckless romance, sitting by the gate of a mosque with her birth certificate and a note pinned to her jacket. He disappeared into the ether like a character in a bad American film."

The boy shifted on his muddy sneakers. He pulled on one of the three scarves draped across his shoulders and smiled kindly at Bahman, as if he pitied his senility.

Bahman continued, his voice singsong, unconcerned. He enjoyed playing the storyteller. The storyteller is simple, innocent. He doesn't lecture or accuse. He doesn't trouble himself with morality or justice, and he doesn't weigh down the story with notions of the way things ought to go. He is devoted only to the creation of the most enticing tale, and so is granted leeway to hide every one of these unpalatable things in the nooks and folds of the narrative. "None of us blamed him, of course," he continued, lobbing the sort of pointed Iranian caginess against which it takes decades to inoculate. "It's so easy to fall in love with these women without family. Their sadness is intoxicating, and, what are you supposed to do? Deny them happiness when they're alone in the world? You tell yourself, the universe gives us beautiful solitary women so they can wrench open our calloused flesh, to sting, cauterize, then be discarded like matchsticks." He paused to observe the boy; half his lower lip was tucked into his mouth and his thick eyebrows were gathering. He seemed lost for a reply. This gave Bahman great pleasure and he decided to end his suffering. He clasped his thin, knobby shoulder again, giving a friendly squeeze as he rang Niloo's doorbell. "I'm rambling. I mean to say that you children are lucky . . . raised abroad where life is simpler, with friends from home."

"Very true, Agha Doctor," said the boy, aping a Persian familiarity he must have observed among his parents and their friends. "I hope Niloo is coping all right."

"Yes," said Bahman, bristling at this half-known thing, this unwelcome change in Niloo's circumstance whose very mention felt engorged and violent. He patted the boy on the back again, offering a fatherly smile, and when the buzzer sounded, he pushed open the door and entered, leaving him to punt stones on the sidewalk.

From a transom on the second-story landing, he watched the young man as he walked away. What quality caused Bahman to suspect him? He had trusted Gui within minutes. Perhaps because Gui was willing to appear clumsy, trying out his handful of Farsi words humbly and with great relish. But men like this young Iranian, the charming, political sort, have a habit of bargaining with their love. They don't suffer, though they like to wear the cloak of suffering everywhere they go. The truth shows itself in the teeth. Fatimeh's is the mouth of one brutalized by the decades. But men like this mend quickly and move on, refining their art, absorbing empathy and kindness like a clever child absorbs a new language.

Could his daughter be entangled with this man, as Fatimeh had been with that other? Poor Niloo. What frightening, unfamiliar sorrows a sensible woman, a scientist and a scholar, must have endured to fall into such resounding silliness.

At her door, he hesitated. Climbing three stories had been enough to drain him, but another sort of discomfort presented itself. A flogging sadness struck Bahman as he rang the inner bell. He had gathered morsels of the story from Pari—loyal, faithful Guillaume abandoned for a time. *Marriage is hard*, he had told himself, *challenges abound*. Why should his daughter be an exception? Each day spent trudging shared ground, new strife settles over memories of old strife like layers of fine dust on a wedding carpet, obscuring its brilliance. But that doesn't mean you throw away this delicate handwoven thing; because didn't skilled hands labor over it, and fingers crack and bleed? Wasn't it obtained at great expense?

The door swung open, his daughter in pajamas and a sweatshirt to her knees, her hair in two chaotic ponytails like when she was four. His own mother had taught her to tie her hair this way, on a trip to Ardestoon when she sprang out of bed, yanked out the elastic at her crown, and wailed that she couldn't sleep on her back.

"Babajoon," she said, and held out her arms. "I can't believe you're here." Since she left him, Bahman had seen his daughter four times, and each time, though she had grown taller, or fuller, or more somber-eyed, she greeted him with the breathy excitement of that vanished eight-year-old. Suddenly he was aware of his age, of the pain and fatigue souring in his muscles. The last time he saw Niloo, she was being driven away again, as she had been decades before, leaving him in a hotel café in Istanbul. The staff had been kind. Two men in hotel vests sat with him, smoking and talking about children. It had been a slow day for the crew, half the rooms empty, and the manager (whom he had known back then only as a fastidious homosexual with wit and a skillfully stitched jacket) had brought a plate of *baghlava* for them to share. It felt very much like a gathering of friends at a teahouse below Isfahan's Thirty-Three Arches, and the manager had become Bahman's good friend.

Now in the doorway, Niloo's face was pale and she kept repeating, "How did you get here?" as she led him inside. "Who were you talking to outside?" she asked.

What he wanted to tell his daughter first was that he was clean, that he hadn't smoked for four months—though that's too short a time to be making declarations. He wanted to tell her that he knew he looked withered and bent, and that he felt it too, but maybe she could pardon his ill-fitting shirt and silly hat, his old man gut, because he was tired, his skin thinning, his jowls and eyelids leadening. He wanted to tell her that he had seen his country fall apart again, that looters had burned cars, and a girl had bled out on the street, and that his home had been invaded by ill-wishers of so many varieties, but that turning back was useless, because the road is walking too. He wanted to say that the detox had hurt, really hurt, that he was no longer married, and had spent the last two months standing in lines outside embassies with a new lawyer, filling out impossible English and Dutch papers, sputtering through interviews, eating smelly fish and bloody meat, and that he missed her—why had she been so distant in Istanbul? Why did she vanish into her body even before they finished their goodbyes, even before the cars came?

But now was not the time to say these things, because he needed a pillow tucked behind his back, a hot cup of tea with honey, and maybe a little lunch made by someone's delicious hand. Because this wet city was disorienting and tangled, and because his mind was full to the brim with the rogue on the sidewalk, and Niloo's pigtails, and Pari's sudden appearance behind her, he didn't notice right away the state of his daughter's home. Pari said, "Come in, Bahman *joon*. Let me get you tea." She hugged him warmly and said welcome and disappeared somewhere beyond an undulating wall of fabric. He dropped his bag by the door and slipped off his shoes, discarding them beside Pari's and Niloo's—he chuckled at the shiny rose pumps (a single grass blade stuck to one garishly thin heel) and the black loafers, because it was easy to tell which belonged to whom: Niloo's were the sensible ones.

"Why is the hallway made of sheets?" said Bahman.

"It's still under construction," said Niloo. "Come in, Babajoon, we have floor pillows in the sitting room. It's still a little dirty."

From somewhere behind the cotton hallway, Pari's English voice, higher pitched, buttery and slack-cheeked like a child's, carried over to them. "We fix! Is no worry!" He could see that, like him, Pari had an easier time lying in English. She shouted, "Here is all over tulips!" Bahman wasn't sure what she meant by *here*; probably Holland, since he saw no tulips in the room.

Bahman preferred sitting by the open window of the dusty living area, this interrupted space that secreted dirt from its unpatched pores at a speed much higher than Niloo and Pari's feverish scrubbing. Sitting in the bedroom struck him as obscene; he had spent weeks—weeks that ambled on like decades—trapped in a detox bed, and then in Istanbul he had slept in a small windowless room. And anyway, he had been alone in those places and never took the time for a restful pot of tea. They set up a *sofreh* on the floor between two fabric walls opening onto the biggest window. The mouth of the cotton tunnel seemed to suck in the breeze and the whole length of it shuddered so that the fabric never stopped caressing their arms and backs. Bahman adjusted his body on a pillow and placed a sugar cube on his tongue. Sometimes out of instinct, he still aimed to place the sugar cubes near his back teeth, but those were gone now.

"So it seems we're refugees together," he said, reaching for a joke.

Pari and Niloo didn't laugh, but he could see Niloo preparing to explain things he had already begun to know, things that felt unimportant now. He knew she had been unhappy for years, decades. Maybe Pari knew too, though it would take her some time to look at it head-on and to articulate it. Their daughter had made some stunning errors—she had stared dumbly at her own open wound and let it seep, never calling for help as her every joy bled out. This had happened to him many times, and each time he had tried to explain that he wasn't wallowing; that sorrow isn't a devil's contract that you forge in the dark. Sometimes you trip and fall in.

"Niloo *joon*," he began, wanting to ask, *where is Guillaume?* Instead he said, "I was just remembering the day I met the love of your life."

Niloo shifted on her pillow, tucking her bare feet beneath her haunches, as if to hide them. "It was a nice trip," she said blandly. She picked at a toenail and turned to Pari. "There's a *kabobi* on the Bosporus that crushes pistachios into the meat."

Her sadness wounded him, but he sipped his tea and spoke cheerfully. "No, not that. I came to the school to pick you up and you didn't want to go because Ali Mansoori was still on the playground," said Bahman. "Remember that?"

Pari chuckled into her fist. A smile surfaced on Niloo's lips. "No," she said.

"It was a big day," said Bahman. The sugar crunched between his canines and tickled his back gums. "You had made it clear that he was our future son-in-law. I confess, I never thought he was very suitable. He seemed like the negligent sort."

"He was," said Niloo. "I always had to follow him around."

"Good thing we ate him in effigy," Pari tittered playfully into her tea.

"You two talk way too much about that damn chicken," said Niloo. "It was a chicken. We ate it over two decades ago. Stop savoring it."

Bahman considered the accusation. Maybe they revisited that incident because it was a rare moment when all their basest instincts aligned, overwhelming all their nobler sensibilities: a child's affection, a kinship with animals, the civilized necessity of a butcher as middleman. They reverted to the primitive and each of them condoned it in the end, without argument or outrage. Eating the chicken Niloo had raised bonded them as more than a family. They had nurtured something in their home, killed it, cooked it, felt guilt over it. Someone deceived; someone forgave. They made a story and repeated it for entertainment and nostalgia. Among the three of them, they filled every role.

They each drank another cup. Niloo refilled the kettle and opened a box of Dutch waffle cookies. They talked about Bahman's travels, about his office, his house, the steps he and Kamali had taken to protect some of his assets. When he had tired of sharing his stories, he paused and eyed the half-finished kitchen that came into view when the curtain beside him fluttered. "Tell me about this apartment."

Niloo jumped up, gathered some crumpled paper napkins, and announced that she was going to the bathroom. When she returned, even before she sat down, she was talking about work. "I'm writing about primate families," she said. When had she learned the Farsi word for *primate*? Her Farsi hadn't been advanced enough in Istanbul or Madrid. In fact, he recalled feeling embarrassed by her weak translations. At times Bahman had understood a remark from Gui, and had anticipated Niloo's translation, hoping to confirm that his experience of the reunion and first meeting had been full, no words lost. But her version was clumsy and sparse and he felt annoyed with his daughter, who, given her education, might have rendered the words more elegantly in her native tongue. She did a better job from Farsi to English, and had delivered a sweet version of his last sentiments to Gui—though he had meant to convey a hidden second meaning, as is customary among Iranians. But Niloo failed to hear it. He had wanted to tell Gui that he was a good man—exceptional, in fact—and that meeting him had given Bahman a deeper understanding of the world. But given that all things end, especially unnatural things, he considered it likely the two men's paths would never cross again. This saddened him and he hoped he was wrong.

Presently Niloo continued on about her paper. "I can have it translated if you want to take a look. Translation is cheap here. I know a lot of Iranian students." Out of nowhere she added, "It's so strange to have you both here."

"Niloo *joon*, tell me about this apartment," Bahman said again.

Niloo busied her hands in her hair, taking out the rubber bands and putting them back in again. "I'm just trying to fix it up by myself. I mean, I may not stay here, but I've never put any work into a place, so . . . I don't know. My friends here live the way we did after we left Iran, everything temporary like you're always one day from being booted out . . . Anyway, Maman already knows." She said the last thing not as a courtesy, but a challenge. She didn't think he deserved to be involved.

"You should leave here," said Bahman, not bothering with politeness or boundaries or what kind of rights he might have earned as a father.

"Yes, no question," said Pari. "You should pack and leave today. We can book a hotel if you need a holiday from your regular life."

Niloo scoffed. "Leave something half done? Shocking advice from you two."

"This gesture seems unnecessarily hurtful," said Pari. "You should be kinder to those you've loved. It's better for your health."

Bahman nodded; he had thought the same but found no elegant words. Niloo always misjudged what she needed. He wanted to tell her, you don't need all the things the world has pushed you to want. He recalled London, her tired, desperate voice: *No one hands you anything and they expect so much*. But no one needs a PhD or publications or titles. You don't need a big city. You don't need hundreds of friends, or adventures, or any substance to fill your bones with life. You need some good lamb stew with kidney beans and fenugreek, basmati rice, romance sometimes, community always. You need a deep well of kindness for old lovers. The atmosphere of the heart matters; you draw your border around that and keep it clean. If you dispose of a love too brutally, you scorch the surrounding heart flesh where they lived, and then that atmosphere is ashen. Having walked away from his home, his photos, souvenirs of his children, Bahman knew that you don't need much—most everything we claim to want is the empty shell of something more essential; we're afraid to face the hard road to obtaining the thing itself. So we build a fortress of objects we crave to keep near. What did the photos of his children matter when they were gone from his life? And marriages, houses, what were these but waiting containers for love? He wanted to say, everything ends. Everything. All love and truth. Family is all. It regenerates, like reptile skin. It endures. But he said instead, "You don't have to work this hard, Niloo *joon*. Go home. You'll be more comfortable."

They sat for several hours, talking, resting. On his way to the bathroom, Bahman passed a rough wooden dining table sectioned off by the curtains and holding stacks of mail. He picked up a letter from the top of the pile. It was from Guillaume. He replaced it, went to the bathroom, and returned to the *sofreh*, where Niloo and Pari were now reading.

"Should we warm up dinner?" said Pari.

"Are you going to open that letter?" said Bahman to his daughter.

Niloo stared at him, blinking a few times, folding a corner of her page. Pari shifted closer to her, took the shawl from her own shoulders, and draped it around her daughter's. Under the wrap, Niloo released her shoulders and sank a little, like a fading child loosening her sticky fist from around a pulverized sweet. Bahman retrieved the letter from the table and watched Niloo open it. It was handwritten on office letterhead, four or five lines at the center of the page. Pari read aloud and translated for Bahman, her accented voice making the casual American phrases absurd. From English to Farsi, Pari's translations were near flawless, preserving tone and mood, every word a marvel in its precision.

Hi, Niloo Face, it began. This is what he called his wife? Rumi would quake. Pari glanced up at him, one eyebrow slightly raised, then continued:

Today I dropped a shirt on the closet floor thinking there's no more Perimeter. Then I thought, if Niloo came back, I'd be a better husband. I'd let you put all my stuff into piles and talk all day about monkey jaws and the five types of cavemen in inland Spain (or whatever you're interested in lately). I'd never throw anything out again. Last night I made that Shirazi salad you like and I drank all the juice. Please call.

Niloo flinched, burying her head in a pillow on her mother's lap, pulling her legs into her body as if to protect her organs.

"Oh, Niloo *joon*," moaned Pari, wiping her face. Bahman kept his eyes on Pari's hands as she tucked the letter back in the envelope like it was made of rice paper.

They sat in silence. Twice Pari started to speak, but appeared to think better of it. Then she whispered to Bahman, "Why did he drink the salad juice?" A laugh escaped his lips—he had wondered the same thing—but Niloo shot them such a betrayed scowl that Pari swallowed the stub of the thing like she'd been caught smoking.

They drank tea. Finally Bahman said, "I didn't tell you about my arrest. Being trapped in my house. Leaving. It was an education."

Niloo opened her eyes. "That's nothing like this."

Bahman continued on his own track. "This isn't about building a home on your own or being strong. Something frightened you and now you're afraid to leave your pile of stone, just as we're all afraid of leaving our piles of stone. But sometimes the wind forces you a different way. You strap on your pack and you move, because if you hunker down you'll eat too much dirt." His disappointment in her surprised him; he had done so much worse. If her self-sabotage was a dark spot in her vision, his surely blocked out the sun. Though perhaps that was all the more reason to be furious with her. She was supposed to be better, a scientist, American-educated, and she was supposed to be Niloo: an incomparable person, he had always believed.

But perhaps Bahman wasn't disappointed so much as confused by the science of it—how could someone related to him be so out of touch with her nature? Bahman had never been blind to his own wilderness, all that was basic and beastly in his soul. And yet he spent his life covering worn fangs with porcelain, making the primitive artificial. But Niloo's job didn't involve such lies; she watched people at their truest. She studied coarse truths dug from the earth. Where did her instincts go? When did she develop an itch to struggle? And where were her stores of joy?

As a toddler, Niloo had been wild and unrefined. He recalled Kian and his revolution songs; maybe every adult choice is a rebellion against the juvenile self. The child revolutionary finding God. The pleasure-seeking girl retreating into scholarship. The dutiful son of a stoic farmer finding opium. Or maybe it was simpler than that: Niloo Hamidi had woken from a coma much like his own, much like every modern Iranian who has lived in compromised ways—the lies, the addictions. Now her every nerve was alert and screaming. How would she greet the work that comes after waking? The hurt was spreading inward. His daughter was in detox.

That night they brought out all of Pari's food, the eggplant fried with garlic, the yogurts, the saffron rice. Pari paraded out salad *olivieh* and *ghormeh sabzi* (that magic old lamb stew) and placed them on the floor atop the *sofreh*. They sat hemmed in between the two draped sheets and feasted in the semi-dark, the windows open to let in the breeze and the lamplight. As they were arranging the food, in a private moment when Niloo went to make a call, Bahman and Pari agreed that they would wait here, sitting with their daughter through whatever spell had struck her. They would wait until she was ready to leave the apartment on her own.

"Was it difficult getting out?" Pari made small talk, one ear on her daughter.

"What can you say? It's hard for everyone." He sighed and smashed eggplant into bread for her. "I worried they were watching the office, so I left an entire wall of the children's photos. Eight years of memories and no doubles or negatives."

"Shame," she said. "I would have liked to see those again."

"And their sketches and poems," he lamented. "I was so ungenerous with those I wouldn't even let Sanaz go near the drawers. We had such fights."

Niloo seemed in no hurry. She returned with a bottle of red wine. At first Pari refused, her tight chin and lips disapproving. But she drank half a glass, and soon they were talking about Niloo's work again, then about Isfahan, love, refugees, and then all these things at once. Pari said a word about Nader. "God rest his soul."

Niloo said, "What if I have a Nader out there?" She was on her second drink.

Bahman scoffed and topped up his daughter's glass. "Eat some rice. It'll soak up all that lazy nostalgia." They piled one another's plates with saffron rice smothered in pungent fenugreek sauce, dipping their bread into the yogurt and the eggplant.

"I think there's something evolutionary about finding your person among your own kind," said Niloo, the wine trilling her voice like a dusty old violin string. "Not just an Iranian in my case, but maybe another immigrant kid."

Bahman chuckled into his fist—his daughter was prone to some serious Iranian drama. "What cheap sentiment," said Pari, waving a hand before her nose.

"And a common one," said Bahman, stirring the stew for buried beans.

"It's narcissistic to think you can't be loved by anyone except a clone of yourself," said Pari. She seemed more shocked by Niloo's inexperience than her fickle ways. Briefly Bahman delighted in a realization: they were ordinary parents sitting with their child, eating native foods, discussing her mangled heart.

"It's not fair to Gui," said Niloo. "The person he loves is a stranger. She got adopted by the French, you know." She tried for playful, but her voice cracked.

"We're all strangers to ourselves," said Bahman. "More so as we age. So, it's good to remember what you loved as a child." From his pocket, he poured a fistful of sour cherry into Niloo's hand. She burst out in her special laugh, an elated gush that he hadn't seen in years.

They ate. Niloo devoured the *olivieh* and joked about her plans. "It's dumb, but I kept thinking, *I can do this with my own hands. I'm not some Iranian villager.*"

"If you were some Iranian villager, *khanom*," said Bahman, "you wouldn't be sitting in rubble. You'd respect suffering enough not to needlessly impose it on yourself . . . you'd plug your wounds long before this craziness." He mumbled, almost to himself, "What am I saying . . .

even villagers are blind to their wounds. You should see the bared fangs in divorce courts. Madness."

Niloo speared an eggplant with her fork, and Bahman said, "*Ei* Baba, you have to do it with the bread. It's more delicious." He brandished his greasy fingers and grinned. Niloo dropped her fork and tore into a piece of bread, scooping too much and spilling half onto her lap.

"You two always had the worst manners," said Pari, reaching for napkins as he packed another morsel with his thumb and held it to Niloo's mouth, surprised (though what had he expected?) when she ate unthinkingly from his fingers.

"Me?" said Niloo, her hands and lips covered in oil.

Later, when Pari went to look for another box of Dutch sweets, Bahman overheard Niloo on the landing. She was whispering to Guillaume on her mobile; it seemed the Hamidis' stay in this half-formed wonderland would continue a bit longer. Partway through his eavesdrop, Pari appeared behind him to listen along, chewing her lips, watching their daughter with sad eyes. Niloo said, "It's like camping. I just want to be here a while, hang out with my parents . . . help Baba figure out Amsterdam without losing his mind." She laughed. Gui's voice carried over in patches. Bahman hoped he was telling her to be gentler on herself.

"I thought maybe the pastry place on Spiegelstraat," said Niloo, her tone soft, relaxed. "How many pancakes do you think it'll take to keep his soul from floating off to join the ball of brown souls Wilders keeps in his basement?" Gui's crisp laugh carried over in muffled bursts. "I would've liked to introduce him to Mam'mad. They would've liked each other." Then, a long silence. Maybe Gui was talking. Finally, she said, a sad undertow surfacing, "It was so good being married to you for a while . . ."

Pari exhaled, wiped her face with the back of her hand. "She'll find her feet," she said. Then she whispered in English, "I think our daughter is a late bloom."

The image moved him and he repeated in English, "A late bloom . . . Very nice."

Bahman returned to the half kitchen. He thought of his daughter's work—the examination of the primate. He too had always gravitated toward the natural, toward the roots of things, and yet here was something inexplicable: the human capacity for good, baffling quantities of good. It was irrational. He had never been a religious man, and didn't want to be, but what science explains this poetic drive in every person, however humble; the awesome feats of the heart? What was the mysterious ingredient that mixed with flesh and instinct to spark love? Maybe he was entering a new era of life, an era of awe. He lived in awe of every new city, of the generous travelers he had met, and of his own deteriorating body, the way, even as it aged and shrank, it could summon the strength to shake off opium's dark hand. He gave thanks for the women he had married. Pari's passion for her beliefs, Fatimeh's quiet, nurturing soul, Sanaz's bravery. He marveled too at humble, steady Gui, who was now finding his footing. Falling in pace with the changing road, Gui would learn, doesn't alter your deep tissue, which is made of tougher stuff. He wished the boy great happiness, and for his feet always to fall on gentle ground.

Back in his sickbed in Isfahan, he had imagined his own Baba whispering, "How is the atmosphere of your heart?"

In his delirium, he had responded, "I'm a barbarian. An animal."

His Baba said nothing. He wouldn't have reacted to such vanity. He was busy with the work of his farm. Bahman was no scientist, but his understanding of his daughter's universe amounted to this: Early primates evolved through changing teeth, ankles, feet. Barbarians advanced when they built communities, fashioned tools, shared the fruits of each other's work. They cleaved together, rejecting the instinct to set off alone, to scatter. They huddled in caves, then ventured out and built hovels and huts and houses, some communities surviving and some dying. One village grew into another, again and again for millennia, until a young doctor went to India and cured a sick girl and bought land outside Isfahan. Now that doctor's children had taken a step backward; they had scattered, a failed village. After so much evolving, building, learning, they had fallen back into solitary living. Bahman wondered if he might be able to stay, to live here in this watery city. Tomorrow, they would explore the city and they might also stop and hire an asylum lawyer for him. Maybe they would find a bank and tour some dental offices so he might work again. But first he wanted to drop in on this Iranian community that Niloo had found, to eat some lentil stew, to recite old poetry with new friends, maybe to perform a story of his own, adding his usual fibs and flourishes. As they ate, Pari had asked Niloo about Zakhmeh; why had she sought it out? Bahman knew. When you've lost something, you return to the place you last saw it and you search, turning that room upside down. Where else would Niloo search for her lost joy, her wild, childish heart, when last she saw it in a refugee shelter?

Later Bahman secured more sheets to the windows as Pari prepared tea. When they sat down, Pari said, almost to herself, "Do you remember driving to Ardestoon through that long desert?" He folded leftover fabric over his forearms and set it aside. "I was always surprised at the way the orchards and the river and the trees didn't come gradually. They happened in one left turn. Everything different."

He smiled at his first wife. "Yes," he said. "I used to hold my breath for it. A lifetime driving back and forth and it struck me in the ribs every time."

One day, later on, he wanted to ask Niloo some things. What quenched the primitive soul before science and poetry? Why do animals so often stray, choosing solitude? Do you think that a strong village needs an anthropologist or a dental surgeon, a scholar of jaws and a straightener of teeth, both fiddling with calcified nothings in search of some elusive beauty? Shall we phone Kian? And do you think, from your scientific perspective, that the village, every village, is destined to die?

Maybe so. And yet, of that old Dr. Hamidi's dispersed lot, here sat three, far from all they had known, around a familiar *sofreh* as if drawn together by magnets in their shoes. They might one day lose one another again. Over the years, their numbers had dwindled and swollen and dwindled again, so who could predict? But now they were three. He trembled with gratitude, with the urge to kneel and kiss the ground. They were three and three was enough. They were a village.

Author's Note

Kambiz Roustayi set himself on fire in Dam Square on April 6, 2011, and died the next day. He was an Iranian asylum seeker who, after eleven years of uncertain living in Holland, was about to be deported. Though he talked openly about suicide, Dutch officials did nothing to help him. The news clippings in my story are adapted from the real ones about Mr. Roustayi, and the quotes to RNW include portions of actual quotes given by Parvis Noshirrani and Roustayi's lawyer, Frank Van Haren. I set my character's death in 2009 to suit my story, and his features and personality are entirely invented. Though Karim and Mam'mad are fictional, the collective situation of refugees waiting in the Netherlands and across Europe isn't far from what I've imagined. My own story is similar to Niloo's; the enormity of my good luck still frightens me. Kambiz's death came at a time when I was leaving the life I had built in Amsterdam. His story stuck with me and inspired me to try to show the desperation of the many refugees living in limbo across Europe.

The quotes attributed to Geert Wilders are all real, though one of them ("you will not make The Netherlands home") is from 2015.

I'm grateful to the following for their help and support in writing this book: Thank you to The MacDowell Colony and the Bogliasco Foundation, where I began and finished this novel in a cabin in the woods and a villa by the sea. Thank you to the National Endowment for the Arts for the funding and the confidence to continue. The same big thanks to Laura Furman and the O. Henry Prize Stories (your encouragement has meant so much). Thank you to those who provided research, read drafts, and saw me through the long days: my family, my mom for unfailing support and my dad for inspiration from afar, the Leader family, especially Anna Leader, Tara Lubonovich, Boris Fishman, Tori Egherman, Matthew Steinfeld, Casey Walker, Karen Thompson-Walker, Lisa Sun, Hanna Chang, Tekla Back, Titi Ruiz, Alice Dark, Charles Baxter, Marilynne Robinson, Samantha Chang, Michelle Huneven, Connie Brothers, Deborah West, Jan Zenisek, Jen Percy, Elizabeth Weiss, Mario Zambrano, Christa Fraser. To Nordmanns: Elliott Holt, Chris Castiliani, Basil Gitman, Amos Kamil, E. J. Koh, Vladimir de Fontenay, Lee Maida, Jessica Oreck, Matthew Northridge, Ted Thompson, Amity Gaige. To my Bogliasco family: Alessandra Natale, Cathy Davidson, Kia Corthron, Ramona Diaz, Helen Lochhead, Alberto Caruso, Renata Sheppard, Julia Jacquette, and Ken Wissoker. To Julia Fierro, who gave me work while I wrote. To Gerosha Nolte and Radha Ahlstrom-Vij for daily encouragement. Thank you to my teachers and friends at the Iowa Writers Workshop, whose help with my previous (deservedly abandoned) manuscript continues to bear fruit: thank you for reading all the worst versions of everything.

To my patient and wise editor, Sarah McGrath. You've made me a better writer and your advice has saved me from so many bad choices. Thank you for believing in me. To my other editor, Danya Kukafka, you're brilliant! Thank you to Sarah Stein, Jynne Dilling Martin, Glory Plata, Geoff Kloske, and every passionate soul at Riverhead Books, and to my tireless agent, Kathleen Anderson, and her team.

Lastly, to Samuel Leader and to my Elena Nushin, you make every place home. This book is for you.